Most Secret

by

Kathleen Buckley

Most Secret

Cover Art by *RJ Morris*

The Wild Rose Press, Inc.
PO Box 708
Adams Basin, NY 14410-0708
Visit us at www.thewildrosepress.com

Publishing History
First Tea Rose Edition, 2018
Print ISBN 978-1-5092-2078-6
Digital ISBN 978-1-5092-2079-3

Published in the United States of America

He took a quick look over his wall
toward the house. A faint glow escaped chinks in the shutters in several windows of the house. No lights shone from the buildings that were probably the stable, barn, and dairy. No servant would be doing chores in the dark.

Rising again to a crouch, he followed his wall toward the one ahead, rather than go back the way he'd come. He would get back to the road from the other side of the property. There was a hut near the meeting of his wall with the one that ran east-west. It would give him a little cover from anyone who might be looking out of the house when he went over.

At the end of the wall, he took a deep breath, unfolded himself, and hopped over—

"Umphf!"

—and came down on something that was remarkably uneven.

It gave way with a thud and an almost musical jingling. And that muffled "Umphf!" It wriggled. Trying to disentangle himself and scramble to his feet, Alex felt something chilly and tube-like under his hand: the barrel of a musket. Now he heard furtive noises around him. *Oh, damn.*

"Make a sound, and you are a dead man," whispered a husky voice behind him. "My bayonet's at your throat."

Dedication

For my mother,
Helen Dorothy Burgeson Buckley,
who read to me.
As she did not care for children's books,
she read me the novel *Lorna Doone*
(and many other books and stories
seldom encountered by five-year-olds).

Chapter 1

"I suppose you are off to visit your cross-grained old uncle again," Jane's stepmother remarked. "As often as you go to see him, he ought to make you an allowance, to defray the cost of your keep."

Jane concentrated on tying the ribbons of her *bergère* hat before the mirror in the narrow entrance hall. Did her mantua become her? The paneled walls were a pallid pea-soup green, which made her gown's light blue look peculiar. She did not intend to argue with Elvira about her uncle with the footman standing ready to open the door for her.

"Furthermore, you are his heir, although that would change if he took a wife. He might even get a child of his own. Mind, if you see any sign of his marrying, you must scotch it."

"He does not often go out in society." How humiliating that the conversation would be repeated in the servants' hall.

"It makes no difference, Jane. Mrs. Cosgrove tells me her brother has seen him often at Drury Lane, and you may imagine what that means."

"Yes, indeed. Plays," Jane agreed.

Elvira Stowe made a moue. "You are foolish to suppose that bachelors frequent the theater only for the plays." She nodded knowingly. "And besotted men of Roger Markham's age have been known to marry unsuitable women."

"Uncle is very fond of the theater, which is but a short distance from his house."

"Really, Jane! Unmarried men go to see the actresses. There is a chamber called the green room where men may meet the actresses when they are not on stage. We do not talk about the result of meetings with such females. Need I say you must not discuss such things? But I owe it to your papa to supply you with the worldly knowledge you lack. To return to important matters, it is not only actresses you must guard against. If his housekeeper designs to make herself a good marriage, you must prevent that, as well."

"If that is how good marriages are made, perhaps I should seek a position as housekeeper to some well-to-do elderly gentleman, by way of ensuring my future." She might otherwise have pointed out that the cost of a housekeeper should be considered as a credit against her food, clothing, and pin money. They had not employed one for several years, since the last one packed her trunk in disgust. Somehow Elvira Stowe never had the time to advertise the position or interview applicants. The prospect of such exertion quite overwhelmed her, though it never kept her from social events. Meanwhile, someone had to oversee the servants, make out menus for the cook's guidance, order supplies, and keep the household account book. The week after the last housekeeper's departure, before Jane had taken over her responsibilities, lingered in her memory as what it must be like to live in the American wilderness, or in the days before civilization. Late, ill-cooked meals, unwashed bed linens, dirt and disorder, no fires laid, the servants bickering.

Mrs. Stowe raised her pale eyebrows and attempted to look down her elegant nose; Jane was several inches taller than she.

"Really, Jane! I don't wonder that you are unwed—at your age, too!—when you say such things. Please try to govern your tongue, at least when you are in company. You put us all to the blush."

Foolish to have expected her stepmother to appreciate irony. And it was hard to imagine how Jane could cause her family embarrassment when she was all but invisible. When they visited or attended dinners or assemblies, Stepmama, beautifully gowned, lost her customary languor and scintillated, if by scintillation one meant a steady stream of inconsequential chatter, flutterings of her fan, and flashing smiles. Jane, clad in gowns chosen by Elvira as suitable for a lady almost past marriageable age, did not shine. She could not make up her mind. Was her stepmother's motive to prevent any diversion of attention from herself or was it simply economy? What with Elvira's mantua-maker's bills, one of the boys being at Eton and one at Oxford, besides Rupert's young man-about-town ways, there was not much money left over for a mere spinster stepdaughter's wardrobe. It was not as though she were in her first season, as Elvira pointed out, when she might be expected to attract a suitor. *Nor even in my fifth or sixth season.*

"Mind you make sure Cook has not forgotten anything. We should have a Frenchman, not a rude old countrywoman like Mrs. Merry."

A French chef would hardly tolerate Stepmama's ways or be willing to work for what Papa would pay, but all she said was, "Cook has everything well in hand,

and I promise to be home in plenty of time."

"I want everything to be perfect for the Pleasaunces."

"Certainly, ma'am. There is nothing to worry about." Her oldest half brother's betrothal to Mistress Claire Pleasaunce would not be broken off over a bad meal. The footman, hearing a coach rattle to a halt, opened the door for her, and she hurried out before her father's wife could say anything more or find some errand that Jane could do on her way.

As she stepped out the door, her eye paused as it always did at the clumsy obelisk at the center of Red Lyon Square. She had heard someone claim Oliver Cromwell was buried there, after his moldering body was disinterred and hanged in Red Lyon Fields at the Restoration of the monarchy over eighty years ago. It seemed an odd thing to do, and if it had been done, there was no need to commemorate it with an ugly monument. A statue of a king or queen, such as some squares possessed, would be preferable. How much it would help was open to debate, the space being a long rectangle, calling to some people's minds a burying ground rather than a square. In sunlight the effect was less grim, and the summer's frequent rain had at least cleared the air of the dust, soot, and smells. Even after a day or two of fair weather, the houses and streets looked washed and cheerful. She would have enjoyed walking, for the first half of August had been cool, and the day was only pleasantly warm. But though her uncle's house was not very far, a lady could not walk alone in London, particularly in some of the streets she would pass through. Cook could not spare the scullery maid and Elvira could not do without the upstairs maid.

Visiting Uncle Markham was always a pleasure to her, one she looked forward to every week. Jane found his dry wit amusing, though Elvira called him cross-grained or crochety or eccentric. He did not suffer fools gladly, which was the real source of Elvira's aversion to him. Jane rather wished she could emulate him, but that would not be helpful in family life. She did not enjoy raised voices and slammed doors.

She was ushered into his library and inhaled the incense of tobacco and leather bindings. "I like this house," she said after the exchange of greetings. "There's history here."

"Ay, near a hundred and fifty years of it. 'Tis not to the modern taste, though it's served me well. It was close to my office when I was still in the importing business, and the wharfingers and bargemen did not hesitate to seek me out after hours, as they might in one of the fine squares. I'm comfortable here. But it's not a fashionable neighborhood. It's not even genteel," he admitted. "When you inherit it, like as not, you'll sell it or let it." The footman came with lemonade for her and a bottle of claret for him. "Not that you'll be taking possession soon. I hope to live another fifteen or twenty years. But I've been remiss, Jane. Sometimes one fails to notice the passing of years. Why aren't you married, girl? You must be rising four-and-twenty."

"Five-and-twenty, sir."

"That woman, I suppose. Didn't make a push to introduce you into society, and your father would never notice. Humpf! Mark me, Jane, it's time you married, and the sooner the better."

"Eligible gentlemen do not wash up on my doorstep like jetsam on the shore," she replied lightly.

Loyalty to her father kept her from saying more.

"That is why one's parents should take the matter in hand. However, since obviously they will not, I must. You will not wish to continue to be dependent on your father or on your half brothers."

That thought had occurred to her in the past year or two. It was fatally easy to dwindle into the daughter or poor relation who stayed home to care for aging relatives, and she did not anticipate coming into her inheritance for many years. *Assuming Uncle does not marry an actress and beget children!*

"Only today I suggested to Stepmama that I should seek a post as a housekeeper to some older gentleman. I've seven years' experience and manage a household economically."

"I warrant you neither your father nor your stepmother would give you a reference—for how could they admit their daughter was doing a servant's work? Further, you should have a home of your own. You could come to live here."

"How would it look, to leave my father's house to live with my uncle? I don't wish to cause them embarrassment."

"I could suffer a sudden decline in health and need my niece to live with me rather than leave me to the mercy of my housekeeper."

"What, when you are still so vigorous my stepmother fears you will marry and have issue?"

Markham gave a shout of laughter. "Who? Mrs. Jennings? She is ten years older than I, and if she were ten years younger, she would still not be my choice for a bride. Your inheritance is secure. But as a reason for coming to live with me, my...er...failing health is a good one."

"Until they heard how often you spend your evenings at Drury Lane, or see you coming home at dawn from some card party...or whatever."

"A point to you." He grinned. He still had strong, white teeth of which he was rather vain. "Does that woman not take you to balls and the theater?"

"She does..." How could she explain without disloyalty to her father?

"But she treats you like a poor relation, and your papa does nothing. Come, is that not the truth?" He already knew the answer, of course. She could not imagine how, when he seldom attended the same entertainments. He was very well informed about a number of things she would not have expected to come to his ears. "You should not let her choose your gowns, my dear, for that pale blue is not your best color."

"That's a point to you, sir," she admitted.

Uncle Markham sat frowning for a few moments. "I chanced to see your half brother come off a ship lying at anchor two days ago, when I was visiting with an old business partner of mine."

"Really? Rupert?"

"I wondered if he had perhaps an interest in some cargo."

"I don't think Rupert has any business dealings at all, let alone any that would take him aboard a ship, Uncle."

"It occurred to me he might be interested in smuggled spirits or wine. He has always seemed to be a young man with expensive tastes. That's the trouble with being reared with greater expectations than the family income will support. Better to grow up in a household where it's understood the sons will have to engage in some profession or genteel trade, as I did."

"I misdoubt his purse would pay for more than a bottle or two."

Markham laughed. "You're a cynical miss. It must give your papa and Mistress Stowe fits."

"It would if I spoke as freely to them as I do to you, sir." *Not that I do not occasionally forget to mind my tongue.*

They talked of other things, but Jane thought he seemed pensive. And when she rose to take her leave of him, he said, "If something should happen which makes it impossible for you to continue to live in your father's house, you must come to me. Promise me that you will not hesitate to do so."

Jane agreed, wondering if he were thinking of Rupert's marriage. If he and his bride took up residence in the Stowe home as would be customary, it would certainly make a great deal more work for her and be uncomfortable for everyone, as the house was rather small, with only three stories, apart from the basement and attic. Rupert and Claire could each have a bedroom, though it would mean shifting Matthew to Adam's chamber, and Adam to a smaller one, but the couple would have to share a dressing room, and they would not have a separate parlor nor Claire a boudoir. But the Pleasaunces had offered to give them a suite of rooms in their own larger house, so that danger seemed remote.

****

After his niece left, Roger Markham sat frowning for some time, before taking quill in hand to begin a letter.

My dear Tony:

No doubt you recall as clearly as I that bad business thirty years ago with Captain O'Brien. You never did regain full use of your left thumb, did you? We were both younger then, and perhaps more forgiving than we ought to have been. A few days ago, I called on an old business partner east of the Bridge and saw a family connection of my niece leaving a ship called the Sea Mew. Rupert Stowe is a young gentleman of little judgement or character, and he is unlikely to be engaged in any legitimate business. You know I was against my poor sister marrying into that family. I asked my friend about the Sea Mew, and you may imagine my surprise when he mentioned that the captain was Daniel O'Brien. I am sure you are concerned about events in North Britain, given what I have heard of the Young Pretender's presence in the Highlands, so I pass along my admittedly vague suspicion. What may have brought the Sea Mew and her captain to England, I will not speculate. I should have been sorry to see O'Brien executed, but I would be more sorry still to have my dear niece's family involved with that man.

I trust you and your family are well.

R. Markham

From Anthony Lattimer to Roger Markham:

Dear Hodge,

I received your letter with both consternation and gratitude. I well remember O'Brien and those days. Odd to think that he is now as old as we, for I always think of him (when my thumb aches) as the laughing young scoundrel he was then. I heard that after Sheriffmuir he betook himself to the Caribbean but then

9

some years ago returned to this side of the water and the Isle of Man, and subsequently was to be found in Brittany. If he is now in London, with things again on the simmer in the north, he may well be here on the same business as formerly. There is no reason to suppose his character has changed, even if his hair is now grey. However, as it is barely possible that your Rupert Stowe went aboard merely in search of smuggled brandy or the like, and given that his family is well connected, I will investigate the matter unofficially first. I intend to send an idle but clever young rogue to look into it. He wanted to go into the Army, but his family felt that his keenness of mind and his sometimes unconventional approach to problems would not be appreciated there. Or even tolerated. He does, however, have a flair for ferreting out information, which made him vexatious when he was younger. He will give his name as Alex Gordon. It is a thousand pities that the stage is no career for a gentleman, for he would excel upon the boards.

I will write at greater length but for now, I remain
Your old friend,
Tony Lattimer

Chapter 2

Rupert sauntered into the morning room, where she sat over the household account book.

"Why so glum, Jane? Pining for the curate? He's an uncommonly well-set-up fellow, for a member of the clergy, and I noted how long he spoke with you after church last Sunday. Our papa will be mad as fire if you betroth yourself to him when you could have accepted Pleasaunce. If you gave him any encouragement, Charles might renew his offer. You hardly spoke to him last night."

" 'Tis the household accounts that occupy my mind, not suitors. My sums never come out the same twice, and we have been spending a good deal more than usual. And I was not uncivil to Mr. Pleasaunce." She was not going to discuss Charles Pleasaunce, or his suit, or suitors in general. She did not like to be reminded of Charles Pleasaunce's courtship. He had always been courteous and sometimes witty. He was tall, possessed regular features, and dressed elegantly. Many young ladies must hope to win his affection. Jane had not permitted herself to form a *tendre* for him, as he had evidenced no particular interest in her, and why would he? She was only Rupert's half sister, prim, quiet, and unremarkable. Then her uncle had informed her and her papa and stepmother that she was his heir. They had assumed she would inherit something from him as his only living relative, but it had been imagined to be no great amount.

"Who would have thought it would be so much, when he lives in such a poor neighborhood?" Stepmama had inquired, rhetorically. "He dresses well enough, to be sure, and I have heard he frequents the theaters and various places of amusement, but he might do as much on no more than £1,000 a year."

Or even on £500 a year, Jane thought. Elvira had an inflated notion of how much money was necessary for comfort.

"You will be sought after by fortune hunters," her father had warned. "It would be unwise to let it be widely known. When some gentleman shows an interest in you for yourself, it will come as a pleasant surprise to him that you are worth as much as £5,000 per annum, or more."

She believed it was not common knowledge. However, her stepmother might have told someone and had discussed the matter in Rupert's hearing, and her father had certainly mentioned it to his friend, Paul Pleasaunce, Charles's father. Why else would Charles suddenly begin to press his attentions upon her? His ardor had not been real: the tenderness of his tone did not match the cool, appraising expression in his eyes. She had come to dislike him, not because he wished to marry an heiress but because he pretended to be interested in her rather than her anticipated fortune. Papa had been quite angry that she had refused his proposal. Rupert continued to mention it: he was a devoted follower of Charles, who was two or three years older.

"Father will have to increase the kitchen budget.

As much entertaining as we have been doing, we've been spending a good deal more than usual." Their entertainments were not large ones, for the house did not possess a ballroom, or a dining room that could seat more than two dozen at dinner, but a succession even of rather small dinner parties, card parties, musical evenings, and impromptu dances did run into money, not only for food and drink, but for beeswax candles, flowers, and musicians.

"We could hardly insult Claire's family and our friends with inferior refreshments and drink."

"No, indeed. But it does mean more expense."

"You should ask your uncle for money."

"There is no reason Uncle Markham should be expected to pay for our dinners, Rupert."

"Father will be surly as a bear to hear you want more to spend on food, when he has so many other expenses just now. Markham can well afford it, and you are his heir, after all. He cannot have many calls upon his purse, living like a tradesman as he does."

She levelled a gaze at him where he slouched in a chair, his legs stretched out in front of him, turning his carnelian seal ring on his finger. Her half brother, blond and very handsome, took after his mother. At the moment, his expression was peevish, yet another resemblance.

"If I were willing to ask him for money, I'd use it for a new gown or two."

"You should. You looked like a country cousin at the Montforts' rout. I was ashamed my sister showed herself so ill dressed. I wonder he hasn't noticed what a figure of fun you look."

Rupert was hardly likely to have noticed it until his

betrothed pointed it out.

"Like most men, he probably doesn't pay any attention to female fashions. And he probably expects my father to support me. I won't ask him for money." Before Rupert could continue to argue, she said, "He mentioned seeing you leave a ship a few days ago. Whatever took you to the docks?"

He sat up straight and stared at her. When he stammered, "The docks? Whatever would I be doing on a ship?" Jane knew he had been in mischief of some sort.

"That is what I wanted to know," she said casually.

"He must have been mistaken. Did you think I was going to run away to sea? As a cabin boy, perhaps?" he demanded with an unconvincing laugh. "I hope you haven't repeated this ridiculous charge to anyone else!"

"Of course not. No doubt you are correct, and my uncle was mistaken. He has only seen you a few times."

Rupert soon excused himself, leaving Jane to speculate upon what peccadillo might take a young man of three-and-twenty to visit a merchant ship. A gambling debt, she concluded. She would not have expected a ship's officer to frequent the same gambling houses as her brother, but perhaps they met at some low entertainment or sporting event. No wonder Rupert was worried about Papa's probable response to a request for more money, if he had had to pay Rupert's debt.

****

Rupert was petulant for few days, and no wonder, she supposed. She should not have questioned him about his activities. Young men were so quick to take offense at a sister's questions. Then he recovered his normal temper, so he must not be in serious difficulties.

"You are wanted in the master's study, Mistress Jane," Wilson announced.

Given the butler's formality, she must be in disgrace, but though she ran through the day's events to deduce what had annoyed him, she could think of nothing. Unless Rupert had complained about her? No, if he had, he ran the risk of his visit to the docks coming out. A gambling debt was forgivable, even if Papa were furious at the amount, but Rupert would not want him to know his debt was to a merchantman's captain rather than a gentleman. Their father considered Uncle Markham had lost all claim to gentility by engaging in business, which even his sizable fortune could not make respectable. Importing the luxuries everyone wanted, like China silks, Persian and Turkish rugs, figs, coffee, chocolate, wines, and she knew not what else, did not seem shameful. Now, if her uncle had owned and managed a coal mine, or been an ironmonger, Papa's objection would have been more understandable. She herself would not have cared.

No, likely it was no more than a complaint about last night's soup. Admittedly, it had been made from the remains of the previous day's meat and vegetables, but what could Papa expect, given the amount of money she was allowed for the household?

Her father was not alone. A thin, graying man of unfashionable habits—his stockings were rolled over the bottom of his breeches, in the old way—obviously of the professional class, stood with her father. That was unexpected. So also was her father's expression. She had anticipated irritation. Instead, he was grave. They had not risen at her entrance; they had already been standing. That too seemed strange.

"This is my daughter, Jane," he said. "Jane, Mr. Harris is Mr. Markham's solicitor."

"Mistress Jane, I regret to inform you your uncle is dead." But he looked less regretful than stern.

She could only stare at him. The world seemed to have come to a stop around her, though she could still hear the ticking of the clock on the mantelpiece.

"I beg your pardon. I should not have told you so abruptly. Perhaps you should sit? Please permit me to offer my condolences."

"Yes, sit down, Jane."

She edged her way to the nearest chair, feeling as if her knees might fold before she reached it. But even once she was seated, they remained on their feet.

"How can he be dead? He was in robust health last week. If he was ill, why was I not sent for?"

"Some digestive upset came on very suddenly last night. It may have been the result of a gift of shrimps he received and the cook served for his supper." The attorney's eyes were sharp as gimlets. "If you have other questions for me, I will attempt to answer them."

"I suppose I must arrange the funeral, but I know very little about such matters. Can you advise me?"

"It will not be immediately necessary, Mistress Jane. There will be a coroner's inquest first."

Her father said nothing.

Jane stared at the solicitor. "Why?" She had never heard of any inquest in their circle of friends or acquaintances.

"Mr. Markham's doctor was not quite satisfied with the course of his illness. Given his patient's previous good health and sound digestion, he could not readily account for the death. No doubt the shrimps were tainted, but as your uncle was the only one to eat of them, and none were left to examine…"

"Digestive illnesses are not uncommon," her father said finally. "Even fatal ones."

"That is true. But as I said, the doctor was not easy in his mind, and so the matter must be sifted."

"When will the inquest be held?" Stowe asked. "I will attend it so I can inform my daughter of the findings. There can be no need of Jane's attendance. Such affairs are unsuitable for ladies."

"You will be notified of the time and place," the attorney replied. "If the coroner feels it necessary to have Mistress Jane's testimony, she will be summoned."

Tears sprang to Jane's eyes. She blotted them with her handkerchief and attempted to bid farewell to the departing Mr. Harris in a seemly manner, but the tears would keep breaking forth.

She could not believe he was dead. How could it be that she would never see or talk with her uncle again? When Mrs. Merry asked what sort of cake she wanted for the next day, Jane came near to saying she did not give a hang. But of course, she had to care about it. In compensation, the necessity of giving the cook instructions, making sure the maids had aired the bedding, and inspecting the pantry occupied her for much of the day.

Elvira debated at tedious length whether to furbish up the black gowns she had had made for the death of her mama several years ago or to order new ones in the current fashion, and what degree of mourning was appropriate for the merest connection—only her stepdaughter's uncle, after all. Unable to endure it any longer, Jane changed into a slate-blue casaquin jacket and skirt, the closest thing she had to mourning. She liked the style, but what an ugly color! Her stepmother had chosen it. Probably the material had been a bargain because of the dull hue.

Elvira, catching sight of her as she went out to purchase caraway seed for seed cake, called after her, "Jane! Tomorrow you must visit the seamstress to have a suitable gown made. It's only right to show respect for your uncle, as he has left you his money."

Which is to say, to show respect for his fortune, she thought. Her uncle would have said something of that sort, and they would both have laughed. The numbness was beginning to wear off, and she foresaw that she would miss Roger Markham bitterly. She tried not to think, *more than I would miss my father.* Shocking to admit even to herself that Uncle Markham seemed closer to her than Papa. Were all fathers stern and distant? Papa certainly took an interest in his sons, though he was strict with the two younger ones. Rupert...Rupert was allowed too much license, in spite of Papa's growls when he ran up debts. Rupert and she were not close, although she had been fond of him when he was a child. She had had less contact with the younger boys. Papa ignored her for the most part, and her stepmother could always find something to criticize in her appearance or behavior.

The exercise was welcome. She was out of hearing of the servants' well-meant but painful comments and of her stepmother. Alone with her thoughts, she could reflect on her loss and fortify herself against grief. At home, she could only escape by shutting herself in her bedchamber and then someone would come to ask instructions or see if she needed anything, or to demand, as Elvira would, why she was sulking in her room.

Uncle Markham had taken an interest in her, supplying the affection she missed in her immediate family. He was—*had been*—her friend as well. None of the daughters of her family's friends were more than acquaintances. The ones her age were married and settled into domesticity; the unmarried ones were younger than she and silly. She had nothing to contribute to earnest discussions of childhood ailments and their treatments or arch speculation about eligible bachelors, many of them younger than she, and as bland and inane as the young ladies just released from the schoolroom. And they all took themselves and their concerns so seriously! It was her uncle's sense of humor she would miss most.

Was everyone's grief only for their own loss? Uncle Markham must be in heaven—for she did not believe God kept account of petty sins, or if He did, surely there was a column of good deeds and kindnesses that might outweigh it.

A voice at her shoulder murmured, "Mistress Jane Stowe, I think?"

Taken by surprise, she stopped short and turned to face a man with a lean, humorous face, not handsome but very engaging. His clothing was good but not rich; he might be almost any sort, from prosperous tradesman to a nobleman of simple tastes. His voice was unquestionably that of a gentleman.

Chapter 3

"Forgive me for accosting you in the street, but there were reasons I could not call upon you at your home. Quite apart from the impropriety of a strange man visiting an unmarried lady," he added.

"Are you a strange man?" The question popped out before she could stop it; something about him made her want to smile.

"So I'm told. May I carry your basket so I appear to have a legitimate reason to walk with you?"

"You can't simply go up to a respectable female and…and…" Words failed her.

"Yes, I can. Besides, we were introduced by Lady Montfort."

"Were we? I don't recall it." She would have. This outrageous creature was quite unlike the punctilious men she was accustomed to meet.

He smiled. "Alex Gordon, at your service. I am not surprised you have forgotten my presence as well as my name, considering the crush of guests at that affair— and so ill assorted, too—"

"Were you one of them?" She failed to suppress a smile, for the Montforts' invitations tended to be rather indiscriminate, and Lady Montfort did have some very odd relatives.

"Let us agree I was, Mistress Jane. It will make things so much easier." He had somehow gained possession of her basket. "Shall we continue?"

"As you have my basket, Mr. Gordon, I think we must."

He nodded and became serious. "In the normal course of things, I would have been introduced to you at your next visit to Mr. Markham. Let me say I'm very sorry for your loss."

"Thank you. But what is—was—your connection to my uncle?"

"He wrote to an old friend of his who is...dear me, how complicated this is to explain...who is connected to certain government offices. Mr. Markham believed he would know to whom to refer the matter of your half brother going aboard a ship whose captain is believed to be at best a smuggler. He—"

"What would 'worst' be, sir?"

"A pirate?" he suggested flippantly.

"Then I suppose I can understand why Uncle Markham asked me if I knew why Rupert would be visiting the ship. A pirate would be a very undesirable acquaintance. But why would my brother's visiting the ship be of interest to my uncle's friend?"

"Captain O'Brien is believed to have been carrying on trade between France and the Isle of Man, with, no doubt, stops in Scotland and Ireland."

"So he is a smuggler as well as a pirate?" That seemed more respectable than being a pirate. "I have things to buy in this shop, Mr. Gordon. I won't be long. Will you wait for me here? I am very interested to know how this concerned my uncle."

"With the greatest pleasure, mistress."

Jane hurried through her purchases and returned to find the very odd Mr. Gordon chatting amiably with a pair of chairmen, Caledonians both. Jane noticed with some surprise that Gordon seemed to have a faint Scottish burr although she had noticed no sign of it earlier.

He tossed the men each a coin and turned to take Jane's basket, offering her his arm at the same time.

"There is a great deal of smuggling, I believe, Mr. Gordon. And while my uncle was a man of principle, I shouldn't think he would be greatly worried about brandy or tea that had paid no tax. Particularly as he was no longer in the importing business."

They were out of the chairmen's hearing before he said in unaccented English, "And neither would I. That is the duty of the excise officers. But we are at war with France. If Captain O'Brien is bringing in…oh, French spies or something which affects the security of the realm, Mr. Markham might well have been alarmed. And if that is the case, O'Brien is my…ah…superior's lawful prey."

"But now that my uncle is dead, what more can you do? Though I suppose you might make inquiries about the ship?"

"I have done so, without learning much. It has left port. But there is another question in addition to what brought the captain to England. Your uncle was curious about O'Brien's presence here, and now your uncle is dead. It seems an odd coincidence."

"You think they are related."

"I cannot be certain, but the death was unexpected and the doctor clearly finds it mysterious. And he is not even aware of the circumstances relating to the *Sea Mew*."

"Oh," Jane said, pondering. "But surely it is only

coincidence? Who would know Uncle Markham was taking an interest in the ship? And why would it be important enough to cause someone to murder him? Particularly now the ship has sailed?"

" 'Who' is certainly a question. 'Why' is more easily answered, is it not? If O'Brien's activities threatened our government?"

"If he were a traitor?"

"Any sensible fellow would prefer to avoid the penalty for treason."

"Which I believe is very severe," Jane remarked.

"To be drawn on a hurdle while the crowd pelts you with rocks and filth to the place of execution, there to be hanged and taken down yet alive, to have one's entrails cut out and burned, and then to be cut into four quarters—well, five, really, as the head is taken off and displayed over Temple Bar. Yes, one might well want to avoid such a fate." He paused. "Although, as Captain O'Brien is Irish, it might be unfair to consider anything he did treason, as no doubt he regards England as having invaded and occupied Ireland. Mind you, that's not the view the Crown would take, merely my own feeling."

He glanced at Jane's face. "I beg your pardon. I forgot I was speaking to a young lady. I should not have burdened you with the details."

"I have no aversion to facts, sir. A young woman must always guard her tongue in order to be thought maidenly and therefore is often subjected to trivialities. I prefer to hear the unvarnished truth, however unpleasant. May I ask, are you not accustomed to speaking to ladies?"

"I am, but as I admitted, I am a strange man. We do

try to protect ladies and children. It must sometimes be annoying. Indeed, as a former child, I know it is."

"Protect ladies and let women fend for themselves?" she inquired wryly, to conceal the effect of his words. Gordon's artless admission made her want to laugh at the same time his unexpected perception caused her to blink away tears. One could not weep in public. She had never met a man who understood that to be expected to converse only about safe, uncontroversial topics and ignore unpleasant facts, was infuriating. Except her uncle, of course, and Jane was not sure he objected to it for the same reason she did. He would have called the bland conversation considered suitable for ladies "intellectual pap." She wished Uncle Markham had been able to introduce them; it would have made all proper then. She hoped it would be possible to continue the acquaintance.

"Consider the fact that a gentleman must pay his gambling debts or ruin his own reputation but pays his tailor's bill late and grudgingly, if he pays at all, and no one thinks the worse of him."

"No one? I could not respect a man who failed to meet his obligations."

"But you may be exceptional. Nor could I, in fact. Only think how uncomfortable it would be to owe money to someone. Anyone. I don't, by the way." He beamed at her.

Her cheeks warmed at the compliment. The only response that occurred to her was, "You appear to be quite exceptional yourself," but she could hardly say so.

When she did not speak, he went on. "After speaking with your uncle, I wanted to ask if you'd found out why Mr. Rupert Stowe visited the *Sea Mew*."

"No. When I mentioned it to Rupert, he said Uncle must have been mistaken. He made a jest of it and asked if I thought he planned to run away to sea."

"But you think he was on that ship."

"I do. He was too emphatic. Like a little boy denying he'd eaten all the Portugal cakes, with the crumbs down his front."

They were at the steps to the Stowes' front door.

"I will leave you here. If anyone asks, remember where you met me. I feel sure I can trust you not to tell anyone what we talked about or that I interviewed Mr. Markham, not even if you are asked under oath. Not that it's at all likely. I cannot tell you why I ask it, yet. And Mistress Jane?" He paused.

"Yes?"

"Whatever happens, you have no reason to fear."

He executed a neat bow and walked away. There had been something a little alarming in his parting words; all the same, she was sorry to see him go.

****

Later that day, while she was sorting through the linen closet for worn sheets and pillow cases in need of repair or replacement, her father came in search of her. This was so unusual, when she heard his voice, she started and dropped the sheet she was inspecting. She was more accustomed to be ordered to come to his study.

His face was pale.

"Sir, are you unwell?"

"No! Not at all. I am surprised and vexed. I have been informed that the inquest is to be held tomorrow at Markham's house."

"I should like to attend, if you—"

"You must attend, whether you wish to or not, and whether I approve or not, as the coroner has summoned you to be present. I will escort you."

Chapter 4

Excerpts from testimony given at the inquest upon the death of Roger Markham, as taken down by a clerk employed by Sir Thomas de Veil, Magistrate, of Bow Street, for his own use:

Coroner: Doctor Adkins, you have described the symptoms displayed by your patient. In your opinion, what was the cause of death?

Witness: I believe it to have been arsenical poisoning.

Coroner: Will you explain your reasons for thinking so?

Witness: The extreme pain in the stomach, the vomiting and purging, the color of the vomitus, and the cramping and numbness that are typically found in poisonings by arsenic were all present.

Coroner: That is very interesting indeed.

Juror: I would like to ask what Mr. Markham ate and drank to his supper?"

Coroner: We will hear testimony on those questions from Markham's cook and butler.

Coroner: Please identify yourself, ma'am.

Witness: Jane Ellen Stowe. Roger Markham was my uncle.

Coroner: Were you on good terms with your uncle Markham?

Witness: Yes.

Coroner: How often did you see him?

Witness: I usually visited him once a week.

Coroner: Do you know Mr. Markham's testamentary dispositions? That is to say, who benefits under his will?

Witness: I believe I do. I am—was—his only remaining family. He told me several years ago I was his heir. I don't know what other bequests he may have made, but I would think at least he must have left sums to his valet, cook, housekeeper, and butler, all of whom had been with him many years. He also gave to various charities, so they may receive something also.

Coroner: Did you cause to be delivered to him a gift of shrimps on Tuesday last?

Witness: No.

Coroner: And yet we have heard testimony from Mr. Markham's cook that the messenger who delivered the shrimps said they were a gift from Jane Stowe to her uncle.

Witness: I cannot account for it.

Coroner: Having established the identity of the deceased, and time and place of death, I ask the jury to state whether they have determined the cause of decedent's death?

Jury Foreman: We think it happened by arsenic poison, sir, and should be investigated as a murder.

Coroner: I thank you all for your service and will present your verdict to the magistrate's court at Bow Street.

****

Her father's mood was thunderous. He retired to

his study immediately upon their return from the inquest, only pausing to respond to Elvira's question as to the findings with a snarled, "As bad as they could be!"

"Whatever does your papa mean?" she asked Jane.

"The jury ruled it murder, ma'am."

"Murder! Surely not?"

"The doctor thought otherwise. Apparently, there were signs by which he recognized it as poisoning."

"Who could have done such a thing? Unless his cook, perhaps. Who could have a better opportunity? Or the kitchen maid, I suppose."

Jane did not feel she cared to mention that Uncle Markham had received a delivery of shrimps said to be from her, and that they had composed his last meal. Her stepmother went on speculating and marveling while Jane darned a small rent in a pillowcase. She felt quite ill herself, as the testimony might lead anyone to suppose she had been guilty of poisoning Roger Markham. Mr. Gordon's peculiar remark returned to her mind. He had said not to fear, which should be comforting, but instead raised a number of questions in her mind.

"At least, sad as the occurrence is, you will be coming into an inheritance," Elvira observed.

"I would far rather it had been postponed. My uncle expected to live many more years."

"One must be practical, and no matter what he expected, a man of fifty-some years can hardly assume he has so long left to him. The cook or the kitchen maid must have done it, and you may be sure one or the other will be tried and hanged."

Unfortunately, her father entered the parlor in time

to hear this opinion.

"Unless they try and hang my daughter, madam! Has Jane not mentioned that the jury clearly suspected her?"

"Jane? Ridiculous. Why should they think she would kill Markham?"

Jane blushed, feeling unreasonably guilty.

"The fellow who delivered the shrimps claimed they were a gift from Jane," her father said, tight-lipped. "And there is the inheritance."

"That does not mean they were already poisoned, if it were poison, and not simply bad shrimp. What shop sold it, Jane? No doubt there were other buyers who suffered ill effects from his shrimps. Or else someone in his household put the fatal dose in."

"Jane denied sending them." He glared at her as if she should have admitted doing so.

"I did not send them, however."

"I suppose we must expect her to be taken into custody at any time. You had best not leave the house, Jane. You are sure to be an object of curiosity and even hostility."

"What will people say?" Elvira wailed. She groped blindly in the pocket concealed between her skirt and the petticoat beneath it, and brought out a handkerchief and a vial of sal volatile.

"I prefer not to speculate," her father retorted, ignoring Stepmama's signs of incipient hysterics in the hope of averting them, Jane knew. "Jane, we will make your excuses to the Angleseys this evening."

This reminder of a very desirable social engagement caused Elvira to take a steadying breath and put away the vial, though she did use the handkerchief to dab delicately at the corners of her eyes.

But as it fell out, none of the Stowes were to be seen at the Angleseys' dinner, as Sir Thomas de Veil paid a call upon them at the inconvenient hour of six in the evening.

Jane, called away from mediating a dispute between the cook and the butler, met her father and stepmother in the corridor outside the parlor. "Under the circumstances, he could not be refused," Stowe muttered before the footman opened the door.

"I apologize for calling at this hour, sir, but my court runs long," de Veil said. "And the situation is delicate."

"You may well say so, Sir Thomas. I suppose you will wish to speak with my daughter?"

"Thank you for coming here to do it," Elvira murmured. "I was in dread a magistrate's officer would come for her."

"It's all nonsense anyway," Stowe said. "Jane would never do such a wicked and ill-bred thing."

Jane closely observed Sir Thomas, who was studying her father and stepmother with equal interest.

"I have no questions for Mistress Jane at this time," he said with a slight smile. "I can assure you there is no immediate likelihood of her arrest. I have received information which strongly suggests her innocence."

"Thank God!"

"Not that the blemish on her reputation can ever be wiped out," Elvira said.

Sir Thomas waited a moment, as if expecting one of them to say something more. Jane was obliged to ask, when neither her father nor stepmother did so,

"Have you discovered a more likely suspect than I, Sir Thomas?"

"While I have not yet discovered him, a confidential informant has divulged several potentially exculpatory facts. No grocer has been found who sold potted shrimps to any young lady of your description. They might have been bought in a shop or from an inn. Your cook and kitchen staff swear they did not make the dish nor did Mistress Jane. Mr. Markham's cook did not make them, and she, the housekeeper, and butler refuse to believe you would harm your uncle. I find servants usually have a shrewd notion of the characters of their employers and their families. Also, there has been an indication someone else may have had a compelling reason to make away with your uncle."

"But why would the boy say Jane had sent the shrimps if she did not?" Elvira asked.

Thank you for your confidence in me, Stepmama.

"Madam, a murderer will hardly stick at throwing the blame on someone else. Often the obvious suspect is guilty, but sometimes the availability of an 'obvious' suspect prevents further investigation which might reveal an equally likely suspect. At present, I and my constables are investigating information received, about which I can say no more."

Jane was insensibly cheered by the magistrate's visit, but overall the household's mood was glum. At breakfast, Rupert attempted to lighten the atmosphere, but his jocular demand, "So you made away with the old fellow at last! When will you get your inheritance?" for once drew his father's wrath down on him.

Even Elvira reproached him with, "What would anyone think who heard you, my dear? They might not realize you were only teasing. And even if no one heard, it shows a lack of feeling and conduct."

Being accustomed to her family's ways, she was not deeply wounded. Was greater warmth and affection to be found in other families? Perhaps not, to judge by the Pleasaunces. Mr. Paul Pleasaunce, Charles and Claire's father, was austere. Mistress Pleasaunce was a complete cipher who never expressed an opinion or even a preference. Claire appeared to be a young lady of shallow feelings.

She wished Rupert and Charles Pleasaunce were not such good friends, but Rupert had always regarded Charles as a sort of elder brother. She did not suspect him of leading her half brother into excessive gambling or libertine ways. She hardly knew what she feared. But since Charles had offered for her hand, she had begun to find something rather chilling about his cool, supercilious manner. How fortunate her uncle had not announced his decision to make her his heir until her twenty-first birthday, when her father was no longer able to force her into a marriage. Although being of age was not necessarily a protection if a young woman had no relative like her uncle to support her decision.

"Should we not send Jane out of town for a time?" Rupert asked. The rebuke had not affected his appetite. He spread mustard lavishly on a slab of ham.

"We can hardly do so without creating more suspicion," her father said. "De Veil would have to be consulted, and I am sure he would forbid it."

"Besides, how could we do without her? I cannot cope with all the household's problems without her help," Stepmama said.

Jane found herself suddenly out of patience and

made up an errand to get out of the house. She hoped no one would stare at her or give her the cut direct, but it could not be worse than her father's irritability and her stepmother's worry over the family's reputation. And Rupert, for all his joking, was on edge again. Perhaps his friends were saying things. Or perhaps he really thought she was guilty.

That was an unpleasant thought, so she banished it from her mind as she tied a *bergère* hat over her round-eared cap and went out for a bracing walk.

Chapter 5

A young woman, her opportunities for marriage passing, impatient of life in her father's house, knowing herself to be an heiress, if only the testator were dead, was certainly the most likely suspect in such a poisoning as Markham's. Nine times in ten, Alex thought, the suspicion would be correct. If not for her uncle's letter, Mistress Jane would be lodged in prison, awaiting trial, verdict, and execution. He wished he could have been present at the inquest, but he could not risk being seen there. However, he had read the verbatim account of the inquest provided by de Veil.

The delivery of the potted shrimps should never have been mentioned. That officious fool of a coroner, swollen with his own importance, had permitted too much testimony, when all the law required was identification of the dead man, and time, place, and cause of death. But there had been no opportunity to make sure only the bare facts came out. Now Jane Stowe would be under suspicion until the real murderer was caught. With luck, his trial would be so much talked of, everyone who mattered would know she had been innocent. Unless, of course, his identity must be suppressed for reasons of state.

His double tap at the kitchen door brought a quick response.

"Would you need any little chore done or anything

mended, young miss? There's not much I can't do or repair. I'm new come to town, and I thought, in a neighborhood like this, there's bound to be more than enough for the servants to do. I work cheap, too, if the cook will give me a bit of whatever she can spare, and a mug of ale."

The kitchen maid stood gaping at him, while he noted that her eyes were reddened and puffy.

"Molly, who's at the door?" The cook herself came up behind the girl and peered over her shoulder, wiping her hands on her apron.

"He says he can make repairs, or—or do anything we need," the girl stammered.

"I wish he could," the woman said grimly. "The master's dead, and we're all on end here. Even if I could think of anything needful, I don't know as the housekeeper—or Mr. Jessup, the butler—could have it done. The master's attorney makes all the decisions until..."

"Ah! Until your master's will is proved, as I think they say, and his heir comes into the estate," Alex suggested.

"You sound as if you know something of the law, young man."

"I've turned my hand to a number of jobs. One of them was doing errands for an attorney. I can understand you wouldn't want to spend any household money, but I'll work for a meal. Chances are the executor—that's a fine word, isn't it?—won't question the food you cook for the staff."

"Molly, don't stand there like a stock. Ask Mr. Jessup to come here. Maybe he knows something as needs doing."

In the end, they put him to work doing a few trivial tasks, things the housekeeper and maid would have seen to, had the housekeeper not been laid down on her bed with a sick headache, and the upstairs maid already gone to another household.

"Her brother that's a footman to a baron not liking her to stay in a house where there's been—well! an unnatural death, as you might say—found her a place with one o' the neighbors of the baron," the kitchen maid explained, having been pressed into service to replace the upstairs maid.

Alex helped take the hangings down from the master's bed and take up the mattress to air it.

"Which maybe ought to be got rid of, as poor Mr. Markham's dying was messy," Molly confided.

He had even polished the larger pieces of silver, under the butler's supervision (the knives, forks, and spoons being small enough to be slipped into a pocket).

"Hardly need a wipe, do they, Mr. Jessup, as shiny as they are. Not that I'm complaining, mind."

"I polish them regular. But I'm behind in my work this week, because of the inquest." Jessup, thin and elderly, was the very pattern of a butler. He had served Markham for over twenty years. "I want all to be in good order for when the late master's heir comes into the property." Alex's ears caught the slight emphasis on the word "when."

By the time they'd finished and sat around the big kitchen table, he had been accepted. The servants, worried about the future and also about Mistress Jane, were ready for a sympathetic ear.

"I'd never have told about the lad saying the shrimps came from Mistress Jane if I'd known anyone might think she'd done away with the master."

"It must be they don't think it," Jessup said, "or they'd have arrested her. I'll be glad when it's all settled, and she's mistress here."

"I hope she will live here, even though it would look odd for her to leave her family's home. For I must say, I don't think much of her pa and that stepmother of hers." This was Mrs. Jennings, who had recovered from her headache in time to eat supper.

Markham's valet volunteered, "I won't ever believe a bad word of Mistress Jane. She asked me to remain—on pay, too!—while I look for another situation, saying she would want me to sort out Mr. Markham's clothing, anything I didn't care to take, so it might be given to the poor. As good and pleasant as she is, she deserves good fortune and a long life. To suspect her of harming her uncle, that's plain wicked. And her family! They're supposed to be well to do, but I never saw a young lady so badly turned out as her. It's not lack of taste; it's seldom a new gown, and nothing by any fashionable modiste."

Molly, who had kept silent while her betters were speaking, said when a lapse occurred in the talk, "I wish I'd see that fellow that come with the shrimps again."

"You think too much about young men, missy. Letting the greengrocer's boy court you is one thing. We know who he is and what his prospects are. But someone that hasn't a settled job is no use. I don't mean you," the cook, Mrs. Harrow, said to Alex. "If you could get steady work, as I'm sure you will, you'd be almost any girl's favorite spark."

"My pa often says I should apply myself to one line of work. But Molly, was he not from the neighborhood?"

"No, he must have come from the shop where Mistress Jane bought the potted shrimps. Wish I knew where she got them."

"No, he didn't," the cook stated. "Don't you recall he said he was just doing a favor for a friend? I could tell he wasn't in regular employment. All those lads are impudent, but there was something about him that was different."

"He was very well spoke and handsome, too."

Apart from eating a plain but excellent meal, he had harvested a fine crop of information. Gentle questioning produced a description of the man: hair as light as tow or flax, very blue eyes with lines at their corners, and the tanned face that comes with working outdoors. From certain things Molly reported, Alex wondered if he might be a sailor. Tomorrow would be a good day to lounge around the docks.

****

Jane's father had decided most of their engagements should be cancelled, and that Jane should certainly stay home, in mourning for Roger Markham. She suspected it actually had more to do with the family wishing to avoid the stares and whispers of those who might have heard of the testimony at the inquest.

"It's fortunate the newspaper reported so little about it," Stowe said. Jane, who had surreptitiously read the paragraph in the paper her father had brought home, thought it amazing. However, that and perhaps Sir Thomas's visit, seemed to have soothed her father's temper.

Her stepmother was clearly torn between the desire to avoid public humiliation and regret that she was missing the social life she loved. She sighed as she embroidered panels for a pair of pockets. Jane was mending, which would ordinarily have earned her a scolding from Elvira, who did not object to the activity but did disapprove of its being performed where a visitor might see her at so ungenteel a task. Perhaps with no visitors likely, it seemed unimportant, compared to the embarrassment of Uncle Markham's death.

She refused to think about the murder or that someone had tried to incriminate her. She dismissed the cheering memory of Mr. Gordon as potentially damaging to her contentment. Was she contented? It would be best not to pay too much attention to that question, for her own peace of mind. If she were going to ponder discontent, the drawing room gave cause enough. If the upholstery had needed to be replaced, it would be easy to justify redecorating and changing the color of the walls. Unfortunately, Elvira had exercised rare sense at its last decoration and purchased extra fabric, enough to reupholster the chairs when they needed it, and the draperies were holding up well. If there were ever any spare money, Elvira would want to buy new furniture to replace the delicately pretty pieces in the Queen Anne style, which had been new when Papa and Mama married. Would new chairs with upholstery in some other color lighten the room? She feared not.

When Paul Pleasaunce was announced, Jane had the presence of mind to stuff her sewing into her work basket. Rupert, who had been lounging in a chair, lost in thought, straightened up and rose. Her stepmama automatically gave a twitch to her fichu and set aside her embroidery frame. Her father tossed the latest copy of *The Gentleman's Magazine* onto the table and went forward to greet Pleasaunce.

Jane gave a quick glance around the drawing room, hoping that it had been adequately tidied today. The staff were unsettled by the recent events, and she had been less careful than usual about supervising their work. All seemed to be in order. She curtsied demurely.

"I have come to ask a favor of you," Pleasaunce said, after the formalities. "My wife is desirous of visiting her aunt near Plymouth, and I am unable to accompany her. She is worried about the old lady's health and, as she has some expectations from her, would not wish to be backward in any attention. Charles will escort her and Claire goes too, but I hoped you would permit Rupert to accompany them. The young men can bear each other company."

She expected Rupert's face to show surprise and delight. What she saw was anxiety.

But her father raised no objection, and the worry faded from Rupert's face when Stowe said, "I have no doubt my son will be delighted to go. At the moment, ours is not a cheerful household. It will also provide our young couple opportunities to spend time together."

"Depend on it, Mistress Jane will soon be cleared of any suspicion. Some disgruntled servant was responsible and had a relative or friend deliver the crock of shrimp. Now, Mrs. Pleasaunce wishes to set out as soon as may be, the day after tomorrow if possible. If that is convenient for you," Pleasaunce said to Rupert.

"I will be ready, sir. Thank you."

Rupert must be more taken with Claire's company

than she had realized, to be so pleased to undertake a long journey in her company and Mrs. Pleasaunce's, and to such an unentertaining destination. Or he might simply be glad to get away from the atmosphere of gloom and his friends' comments.

****

A blond, tanned seaman with very blue eyes ("blue like my ring," according to a Billingsgate tavern wench who served Alex, displaying a trumpery ring set with a glass "sapphire") had been seen on the docks for a few days. Then he was gone, which was the way with sailors. No one Gordon spoke with knew what ship he belonged to. True, the *Sea Mew* had left port on the first outgoing tide after the potted shrimps were delivered to Markham's kitchen, but the Pool of London was a busy place and the *Sea Mew* was not the only vessel to sail. Alex Gordon was ready to stake his soul the pleasant-spoken seaman was the friendly fellow who made the delivery and that he had sailed with the *Sea Mew*.

Yet while Markham's suspicions about O'Brien's activities might be damaging to the captain's reputation, suspicion was not proof. Was it worthwhile to murder Markham for that? If it were, O'Brien must be leaving a trail of corpses wherever he went.

Why would he use one of his own sailors to silence Markham? It seemed foolhardy if he could hire some cutthroat. They were not in short supply in London if you knew where to look, as surely a smuggler would. Afterward, the hireling would disappear back into the alleys and warrens that were as alien to law-abiding Englishmen as Peking or Timbuktoo—and far more dangerous. Even if someone in the Watch knew the area, a catchpoll's chances of finding the murderer were small, the chances of arresting him and getting out alive still less.

Gordon did not believe in coincidence, and he trusted devoutly in Occam's Razor, ever since his tutor had explained it to him at the age of twelve. The simplest explanation that covers all the known facts is usually the correct one. O'Brien must have given the order to kill Markham.

A few lines in Markham's letter now assumed a new significance:

"No doubt you recall that bad business thirty years ago with Captain O'Brien...We were both younger then, and perhaps more forgiving than we ought to have been...You know I was against my sister marrying into that family...I should have been sorry to see O'Brien executed, but I would be more sorry still to have my dear niece's family involved with that man..."

Thirty years ago, Alex's father had been courting his mother. The events of that year seemed as irrelevant as the doings of the ancient Greeks. In 1715, three years before his own birth, the Earl of Mar led a rebellion in Scotland, and Alex's father married a Scottish lady. Now Scotland was again seething, with the Young Pretender landed and trying to raise a Highland army. Had O'Brien been active in the last rebellion? He must have been, to judge by that letter. Markham might have suspected the captain would support the Jacobite cause again, and also that Rupert Stowe might be involved as well.

With the *Sea Mew* gone, there was no more to be done with that end of the puzzle. The other end, however, bore further investigation.

He would have to scrape acquaintance with Rupert

Stowe. It would be awkward to winkle out of the servants what clubs or places young Mr. Stowe might frequent, which meant he would have to approach Mistress Jane again. It would have been best to encounter her at some party or ball. Arranging to get a last-minute invitation would have posed no great difficulty. He was popular with hostesses, and even if he did not know the host or hostess, he had resources who would. But between Markham's death and the suspicion thrown on Mistress Jane, the family might not be accepting invitations. He could not very well call upon her. In spite of the acquaintance he had claimed, her stepmother would never let her receive a man unchaperoned.

The next morning found him loitering on the route she was most likely to take if she needed to visit the shops for some household need. He hoped it would not be many days before she ventured out again, as the weather was setting in gray and rainy. He was a little uneasy about his inquiry into Markham's matter. The official investigation centered on the *Sea Mew* and its captain, and he had no part in that. Besides, he was more concerned with why Mistress Jane's name had been dragged into the affair. If you were delivering poisoned food, you could as easily—more easily!—say, "The gentleman didn't give me 'is name, just said 'e was a friend o' Mr. Markham's and 'oped as 'e'd enjoy it." If you were Captain O'Brien or his henchman, would you even know of Mistress Jane's existence?

Chapter 6

It took two damp, dull days before he finally saw Jane Stowe trudging toward him. She looked dejected; her eyes were focused on the ground. She came abreast of him before she noticed him standing outside a baker's shop on High Holborn—and then only because he murmured, "Mistress Jane?"

She gave a little jump before recognizing him.

"Oh! Mr. Gordon." She swiftly gathered her wits, continuing, "I am glad to see you again because I wanted to thank you for what you said the last time we met. I would have been very frightened if you had not told me I was safe. Especially when I learned someone had used my name as the sender of the shrimps."

He wanted to ask if that were the only reason she was glad to see him, but that would have been presumptuous, and anyway, they were the merest acquaintances. "It's good you weren't afraid. Er...do you always go shopping without a maid?" Idiot! She was sure to take that as a criticism, but he hadn't meant it as such. He could think of nothing else to say.

"Yes, usually the maids are busy, and it's not as if I were a young girl."

"Too young to be unescorted, and so I will escort you."

"The escort of a strange young man is ordinarily thought not to be a protection," she remarked, smiling, and allowed him to take her arm and her basket.

"There's no question in my mind one of Captain O'Brien's men delivered the shrimps," he began.

"I see." Was her expression admiring?

"I have not yet found that your uncle pursued any inquiries on the docks about the *Sea Mew*, apart from asking his commercial friend about it. The latter is a wine merchant, has a good reputation, and says he did not mention the matter to anyone else. To his mind, there was no significance in the name of the ship or its captain."

Jane nodded encouragingly.

"The question then is, how did O'Brien know that Mr. Markham was a threat to him? It's unlikely they'd had any contact in decades, and...ah..." Gordon felt a sudden qualm as to whether he should say more.

"I am not given to idle gossip, sir. Whatever you tell me, I shall lock within my bosom."

"Truly? May I watch?"

"Not literally, Mr. Gordon. It's only a figure of speech." She colored up prettily, but her eyes sparkled.

"That is too bad. Well, as I was going to say, the last time the captain and your uncle met, Mr. Markham and a, hmmm, friend of his did O'Brien a favor. Rather a big one. So it's not likely he's cherished a desire for revenge all this time. It seems to me whatever caused Captain O'Brien to poison your uncle must belong to the present, not the past."

"What was the favor?" she asked.

"As I am already divulging more than I should, I'll tell you. Mr. Markham and his friend had enough proof to have had him executed at the time of the 1715 rebellion. They let him go."

"I see. He must feel very badly then, if he did indeed kill Uncle Markham."

"I suppose he must. Quite so. Which would mean whatever caused him to commit the murder was of the utmost importance."

"How could your Captain O'Brien hear that my uncle knew his ship was in port?"

He grinned. "Which is the question I began with. It may not have been O'Brien who heard. It may have been an accomplice who then passed on the word—'gave him the office' is the criminals' cant term—or who committed the crime himself, to guard his own neck. But we are still left with the question of how the murderer heard of it."

"Oh," Jane said slowly. "Could my uncle have spoken of it to anyone else—besides talking to his wine importer and writing to his friend?"

"I am told he would have been well aware of the delicacy of the matter and unlikely to speak of it. Did you mention it to anyone?"

"The only one I told was my brother, as I said at our first meeting. Perhaps he told someone else. As being a sort of jest, you know."

"I remember. Your half brother, Rupert."

"I have three half brothers. Rupert is the oldest, Matthew is at university, and Adam is still at Eton. Perhaps Rupert mentioned it to one of his friends or several of them. Young men get together and drink and...er...so on, and of course they talk. No doubt you know how it is."

"Except for the '...er...so on,' yes. You told no one else?"

"No."

"If he mentioned it in passing to some associate of O'Brien's, the associate must be someone in Rupert's circle," Alex said. "I would like to meet your brother and try to find out who he told." But if it were only an acquaintance, how did Jane's name come to be used? Do young men talk about their half sisters over a bottle of claret or brandy? Gordon thought not.

"Mr. Gordon, why would the messenger say I'd sent the shrimps?"

To find her mind running in the same channels was disconcerting. In his experience, most people tried to ignore troubling questions.

"Whoever had him deliver them told him to give that message? As you have undoubtedly realized, the intention was to implicate you."

"And implicated, I would almost certainly have been brought to trial and hanged, without your help."

He shrugged, a little embarrassed. He had done very little on his own. "The only help I supplied was in providing to Sir Thomas de Veil a letter from a higher authority. I did not receive it in time to show it to the coroner before the inquest. Which might have caused him to limit the testimony."

"You also assured me I was safe, which was a source of great comfort at the inquest and afterward." She frowned abstractedly. "Unfortunately, you cannot meet Rupert at present."

"No?"

"He has gone to Plymouth with friends."

"It seems an odd time to leave Town."

She bit her lip. "My uncle's murder has made everything very uncomfortable. My father is irascible and snaps at the servants. I think Rupert's friends either made sport of him about it or began avoiding him. My stepmother is certain everyone is talking, and I'm sure she's correct. It made Rupert sullen half the time and inclined to stupid jokes about it the other half, which annoyed my father still more. Rupert's friend, Charles Pleasaunce, had to escort his mother and sister, who is Rupert's fiancée, to visit a relative near Plymouth, and Mr. Pleasaunce asked if Rupert might accompany them. My father and Mr. Pleasaunce have been friends since they were boys, and Rupert and Charles fairly live in each other's pockets. Papa gave his permission."

"Did Mistress Pleasaunce's family come from Devonshire, then?" he asked, casually. There was said to be a good deal of smuggling in Devonshire. "It's said to have a pleasant climate."

"So I understand, though Mistress Pleasaunce's mother's family came from France originally. I suppose this lady—an aunt, I think—married a man with property in that part of the country. Or perhaps mercantile interests, for I believe Plymouth is quite a center for the shipping trade. I don't recall the Pleasaunces mentioning her before, though they used to visit their cousins in France. I was quite envious. Mr. Pleasaunce's family came of French stock, too. Before the current unpleasantness made travel to the Continent impossible, we thought they might take Rupert with them some time, or he and Charles could even make the Grand Tour together. But that has been impossible since Rupert was old enough. It would have been very convenient, as Charles is a little older than he and more level-headed. Now Rupert is pleased to visit Devon," she added wryly, "although I do think it's mostly because of our current social embarrassment."

Alex smiled inwardly. A lady who could describe a war involving much of Europe as "the current unpleasantness" would hardly be overset by any family crisis. "I see. It's a pity I can't meet your brother, but probably it's not important."

Jane was silent for several minutes. He glanced at her face and wondered whether to probe or let her come to a decision unprompted. Clearly, she was pondering something. At last she said, "Mr. Gordon...what is a nine-pounder? Or an eight-pounder?"

It took him a moment to reply to a question so unexpected. The one he had anticipated was, *Did Rupert kill my uncle?*

"A nine-pounder is a small cannon. An eight-pounder sounds as if it might be a cannon also—the weight refers to the size of the ball fired—but it's not one I've heard of before. What odd books young ladies must read these days, to be asking about cannon. I'm sure my mama never gave such things a thought."

That earned a laugh, although a nervous one. "It must seem quite peculiar of me, sir. Mmmm, is the name 'Charleville' familiar to you?"

Gordon stopped short. "Mistress Jane, where are we going?"

"I thought to go to the milliner in Middle Row to purchase some alamode silk to replace a lining and some black ribbon."

"Ah. Let us postpone our discussion of, hmmm, places in France until after your errand. There are quite a number of people on the street here."

Judging from her look, she understood he did not wish to be overheard.

Ahead, a wigmaker's apprentice stood on the

sidewalk, powdering a wig. Better to let the excess fall to the ground or blow away than to dust every surface inside. An elderly gentleman gave the young man a spiteful look, realizing that his sleeve now bore traces of flour. Alex and Jane traded glances and stopped to inspect the treats in a confectioner's gleaming bow window before proceeding. Ratafia biscuits, rock sugar, chocolate almonds flavored with musk, iced almond cakes, jellies, coriander seed biscuits, preserved fruit.

"Do you need anything here?"

"No," Jane said decidedly. "Our cook makes most of these very well. More cheaply, too, of course."

The apprentice, satisfied with his work, retreated into the shop with the wig. They proceeded on their way.

At Middle Row, Alex shied at the door of the milliner's shop, rather like a horse refusing a fence, he supposed. But the shop was small and as full as it could be of silk and lace and ribbons and the like.

Jane laughed. "I won't be long. I know exactly what I want. You might look in that shop with gentlemen's accessories." She was still smiling as she turned to go inside.

She emerged only a few minutes later with a parcel tucked into the basket.

"Do you have any other shopping to do?" he asked. He hoped not.

"No, Mr. Gordon. If I had not needed the black ribbon, I would have postponed this errand in favor of continuing our earlier discussion."

"Then perhaps we might walk in Lincoln's Inn Fields. Your questions pose a number of others, and I fear the matter may be urgent."

Jane assented. She seemed less surprised than might have been expected.

There were a good many people about Lincoln's Inn, most of them hurrying on a cool, gray day, and many of them, Alex assumed, with weighty legal questions on their minds. No one showed any interest in a young couple strolling.

"Where did you encounter those terms? Charleville, and the other things?"

"The invitation to travel with the Pleasaunces came at short notice. Rupert's valet packed hurriedly, and Rupert was busy, too, writing notes to excuse himself from various social obligations. They left very early this morning."

Gordon nodded.

"The chambermaid came to me with a scrap of paper she'd found under his pillow when she stripped the bed. She can't read, but she thought it might be important. The words conveyed nothing to me, and that is why I found it worrisome." She brought a small square of paper out of her pocket. "I wanted to think about it this morning and try to decide what I should do, if anything. If it had been something obvious, like a shopping list, or the stages of their journey, I would have thought little of it. But it's not Rupert's handwriting, and...and..." She gave a little shrug and handed it to him.

9-pounder/8-pounder? None. Charleville 1717 2500

Open pans
Handle cart
Tear cart
Prime

Shut pans
Load
Cart in
Draw ram
Ram down
Return ram

"It has a rather agricultural sound," Jane commented, "but I don't know what it can mean. Except it worries me."

"I should think it might."

"Do you know what it signifies then, Mr. Gordon?"

"Yes—at least, I know what it refers to, if not its precise significance. The last time I read the words in the list, they were in the French language. It's the orders for loading a musket. The writer has abbreviated some of the words: 'cart' for cartridge, 'ram' for ramrod. I used to take an interest in military matters when I was younger. I thought I would like the army as a career."

"But you decided against it, or—" She stopped in midsentence. "I'm sorry. It's no business of mine."

"Oh, my father could have bought me a commission, but he was convinced I was not well-suited to the profession of arms. I've come to believe he was correct."

"Oh?"

"I don't like following orders, unless I chance to agree with them," he confessed cheerfully.

"Yes, that would be a difficulty. I understand there are apt to be a great many orders in the army."

"So we have here the loading drill, and the name 'Charleville' which refers to a French arsenal. Charleville is also sometimes applied to the musket

French troops use, as our soldiers' weapon is the 'Brown Bess.' The numbers…the Charleville musket made its appearance in 1717 and was replaced by another model in 1728. It may be there are some of the older model for sale."

She gazed at him, waiting.

"You mentioned lists, Mistress Jane. I think this is a shopping list."

"If you are correct, it's a disturbing thought."

"You are a very remarkable young lady," he said. "Most would either utter a little scream or titter and demand, 'Whatever could anyone want with such things?'"

"Yes, I'm utterly lacking in sensibility. My stepmother says I will never marry." Then she blushed.

"Your stepmama is mistaken."

She was eying him covertly. "Why did my brother have such a thing?"

"Perhaps he picked it up somewhere, and, like you, wondered about it. May I keep it? There is someone who should see the original and not merely a copy."

"But what if he writes and asks about it?"

"Then I think you should tell him the maid gave it to you, and you threw it away, not seeing any sense in it. But I don't think he will mention it."

"It can't be Rupert's. It's not his hand, and where would he get enough money for things like this? If it is a shopping list. He has to apply to my father regularly to pay his tailor's bill. Besides, he has no interest in military affairs. Even when he was little, he never wanted to be a soldier."

"If it's not his, it may belong to someone he knows. If it were a bit of trash he'd picked up, I doubt it would be under his pillow. What did he play at?"

"He pretended he was a knight of the Round Table. Or one of William the Conqueror's men. He's outgrown such childishness now, naturally."

"I'm sure he has." Alex tucked the note into his pocket. "May I walk you home?"

She was silent as they went. In sight of her door he said, without knowing if it would help or hurt, "The French soldiers drill until the best of them can load and fire three times in a minute. Two a minute is commonplace. I believe some can do four."

"As much as that?" She sounded appalled.

"Not every ball kills or wounds enough to incapacitate or even hits its target. Misfires are not uncommon. And sometimes after the first volley, the opposing lines meet, and the bayonet is employed as the primary weapon." Not that that thought was likely to mitigate her horror. Yet she should realize the importance of what she had found. More to the point, that whoever meant to buy those guns and cannons, whoever knew about it and did nothing, was guilty of assisting in the deaths and maiming they might cause.

"Who could possibly want to buy so many guns?" she asked, pausing a little short of the door.

He shrugged uneasily. "Speculation would be idle at this point. How may I contact you, Mistress Jane? In case your half brother does write, or you discover something else?"

"I think I shall form the habit of walking out every morning at nine. Unless it rains, of course, for it is difficult to justify going out for exercise in a downpour. My stepmother is not an early riser, and my father reads and writes letters in his study until he goes out to his club or the coffeehouse."

"Good. If you need to speak to me more urgently, write under cover to Miss Eliza Fairford. Her address is…"

Afterward, he took the first hackney coach he saw to report his findings. He must certainly remember to visit his sisters' old governess and warn her she might receive a letter addressed to her but meant for him.

Chapter 7

"A very nice piece of work," Anthony Lattimer said. "For our purposes, you have proven Markham may have been murdered because he knew about O'Brien's work in '15 which might lead someone to wonder what he was doing now. And knowing what his cargo is likely to be…you haven't left much for official channels to do. I will pass this on to, er, someone who will no doubt put a man on the French end now. Damme, the thought of so many muskets in Jacobite hands makes my blood run cold. Yes, good work indeed.

"Have you given any thought to my suggestions for your career? If you won't reconsider the law, you certainly have the wits for banking or any sort of business. I could arrange to have you taken into a merchant house or shipping firm. Times are changing, and by all accounts—ha ha!—the import business can be quite exciting. Markham enjoyed it very much, poor fellow."

"I really don't think I'm any better suited to the law than to the army, sir. The other might not be so bad. But couldn't I go north and poke around a little? If Captain O'Brien has connections in the Isle of Man, I might be able to garner a little more information. Perhaps names of contacts he has in Scotland; that would be useful, surely."

"Someone will be looking into that, but it won't be you. It's time for the career men to take over; that's what they draw their pay for. With luck, the navy will intercept the *Sea Mew*."

"Or I could go to Scotland and look into matters there. I can sound like a Lowlander. You know I'm good at that."

"Inquisitive, like your mother, yes. I prefer you not to practice your talents where some Jacobite might cut your throat or knock you on the head and drop you in the Solway. Why not go out to the West Indies or New England? Your Grand Tour was cut short, but a visit to our American colonies might be interesting."

"I think I'll stay in Town for a while to pursue my acquaintance with Mistress Jane Stowe, sir."

"A pretty young woman's ability to cast a spell over a man is almost enough to make one believe in witchcraft," Lattimer observed, tolerantly. "However, I trust your intentions are not serious. There's bad blood on her father's side. Her mother died very young, so it's his attitudes that will have shaped her."

"May I point out that you married a Scottish lady, sir?"

"Your mother's family were not Jacobites. Not her immediate family, anyway." He scowled and blew out an exasperated breath. "The Stowes were, even if it never came out. Not that I think she supports the Young Pretender. If she did, she would not have given you that list. The murder is a different matter, Alex. Isn't it possible she connived with her brother to poison Markham? Young Stowe's motive would be to protect his cause, hers would be for the inheritance, either to repair the Stowes' fortunes, or because she would like to be rich? There's ample motive for murder."

"I've met her, sir. I don't believe it."

"Not even for a fortune which would get her a titled husband? She's an aging spinster, and it does not appear her family is able to make a marriage for her. She may be desperate. And from what you've told me, she shows signs of wanting to shield her wretched brother, whatever mischief he may be about."

"I think she wants to believe he is not involved, or only in the most tangential way, and especially that he would not try to have her hanged."

"She'll be disappointed, then, because as sure as the sun rises, he's up to his neck in some plot. But he can't have solicited the murder for the purpose of inheriting. This girl is the heir, but under the law, if she killed Markham, she couldn't inherit. She wouldn't necessarily realize that, of course, which is why she's a very credible suspect. I don't know enough law myself to know if her nearest relative, her father, would inherit when she was executed, though I shouldn't think so. Furthermore, poison is a woman's weapon."

"She's not an ordinary young lady. She might be aware of the slayer rule. Even I know about it."

His father snorted. "If she's an exceptional young lady, that makes her more likely to be a murderess than if she were a gentle, meek, uninformed miss."

Alex went on, "I wonder if Rupert Stowe knows a murderer can't profit from his victim? He may not be stupid—though I suspect he is—but from one thing and another, I would wager he doesn't think very far ahead."

Lattimer gazed at him thoughtfully. "It's a pity we can't find you work that would make use of your brains, Alex. Your perception is almost equal to your ability to dig out information. I will never forget your mother's face when you explained to her in your Aunt Geneva's presence, no less—at eight years of age!— why Geneva disliked her. Thank God you eventually learned not to air your observations so freely."

"She didn't dislike her, sir, she loathed her. I've never understood why you didn't realize it." How could his father have so little perception about women he knew well when he was so keen-witted about men's motivations?

"I thought they were quite friendly."

"Aunt Geneva meant that you should marry that friend of hers, I think, and so resented Mama ever after. Mama knew, of course, but luckily was amused rather than distressed."

"Well…well…women's minds are a mystery, though you think yourself able to fathom them. You ought to apply that skill to the Pomeroy girl. If you won't settle to a profession of some sort, you could at least marry some young lady with an excellent dowry. She's really a very pleasant girl, when you get to know her."

"She may be, sir, but one would have to put up with such a spate of chatter about parties and fripperies and other young ladies' beaux." Alex grinned. "Before I go, may I ask why you didn't give me a hint about the direction of Mr. Markham's and your suspicions? You must have had a fair notion of the truth, given what he told you. It took me some time, because 1715 is almost a whole lifetime in the past."

"Not quite a lifetime," his father said dryly. "I was younger than you are now, and it's still vivid in my mind. To answer your question, I wanted an independent opinion, not colored by memories of the last revolt. Sometimes the official mind finds plots and complications where none exist."

"May I also inquire why you let Captain O'Brien escape? I gather you did, from Mr. Markham's letter. It seems quite unlike you."

Lattimer smiled crookedly. "Trust you to pick up on an inconvenient fact!" He leaned back in his chair, his eyes focused somewhere beyond the walls of his library. "Markham and I met the man two or three times, without realizing what he was. He was a gentleman, or at least could pass as one, and a good fellow, daring and full of fun. Precisely what any young man would aspire to be. That day, though, we caught him dead to rights. We could hardly believe it. And we could not bring ourselves to deliver him to the authorities. So we let him go, though we had a little exchange of swordplay first. We delayed his rendezvous until the intended landing place was held by dragoons. It seemed enough. How he did curse! Then he bound up my thumb—I'd received a cut on it, bloody and painful but not very serious—and we all had a glass of whiskey before we set him at liberty. Markham and I failed to foresee the future. He must have changed a great deal, to have become willing to murder Markham. Of course, both Markham and I changed over the years, too…" He shrugged. "Now, off with you. I have important matters to see to."

"Thank you, sir. You'll want to fire off a letter to, er, someone, no doubt."

His father almost laughed at that but covered it with a growled, "Hmpf."

Alex would have liked to ask another question or two, but years of government service had made the elder Lattimer sparing with information. He knew how to find the answers himself, anyway.

****

The Stowe household sustained another visit from Thomas de Veil. He apologized for interrupting their evening, which Jane found amusing, as the family had not been accepting evening invitations, and Elvira had taken to her bed from boredom. She would be disappointed to miss the visit, Jane thought.

Sir Thomas accepted a glass of claret, saying jocularly that no one could regard that as a bribe or accuse him of being a "trading justice" for taking a glass during a visit. Many magistrates were regarded as corrupt, though de Veil bore a reputation for great energy and intelligence in the performance of his duty. Jane understood he actually investigated crimes himself rather than waiting for murderers and thieves to be brought before his court.

"I am pleased to be able to tell you that no legal action is contemplated against Mistress Jane," he said, with a slight bow in her direction.

"Thank God. Then you have found the murderer?" Stowe asked.

"No. Not yet. You are not to repeat this, as it is most secret. I have received another communication from a certain department of the government, assuring me that there is no suspicion against your daughter, and that no further investigation of Mistress Jane need be made. 'Tis very irregular, but as you may know, one of my duties at this time is to ferret out Jacobites and possible traitors. Given certain items of information which have been passed on to me, and others which I have discovered, the motive for Markham's murder was political rather than personal. I am glad of it. It may be uncomfortable for Mistress Jane for a time, as the true reason for her uncle's death cannot be revealed to the public, involving as it does matters of state, and the risk of the lower orders panicking, but it will all be forgotten eventually. If Markham's attorney, who is also his executor, should wish confirmation, refer him to me."

When the magistrate was gone, Jane's father gazed upon her with more approval than she could recall his showing in many years.

" 'Pon my soul, things have turned out well after all. Tomorrow, I will pay a call upon Mr. Harris to ask when you can expect the will to be proved. I suppose you will sell the house?"

It took her a moment to realize that she had a right to make the decision. "No, I don't think so. At the least, I should go through my uncle's things. After that...I may wish to keep the house. I've always liked it."

"Surely you do not think to live there? I can imagine few things less appropriate. The street is given over to upholsterers and used furniture."

His approval had been short-lived.

"Of course not, sir. But I might lease it out. That would bring in a little income. Leaving my father's house would have a very odd appearance." Though her stepmother might prefer to live with Rupert and his wife, if she were widowed, or if Elvira were also dead, the Stowe house would be Rupert's or might be sold. In any case, the possession of her own home, even in so ungenteel a location, would mean she would not have to be a poor relation in her stepmother's or half brother's home.

"What a sensible girl you are!"

She was ridiculously pleased by his praise.

Chapter 8

The Pleasaunces' butler had no odd jobs to be done and was altogether less hospitable than Markham's. An irritable master or mistress, Alex concluded.

"Nor your housekeeper, neither? I can turn mattresses and save the maids' backs, take down bed curtains and draperies, carry boxes to the attic or cellar..."

"If we had work to be done, one of the footmen would do it, or we would send for a man we'd used before. The master does not like strangers in the house." the butler pronounced.

A woman appeared at the butler's shoulder. By her age and plain dark gown, Alex took for to be the housekeeper. "My sister's boy come to deliver a package from her and stayed to talk for a minute, and master would have it he was a housebreaker's spy."

"You know as soon as he understood the lad was your own nephew, he realized there was no harm in it," the butler said curtly.

"And particular as to his study, too. Though what he studies there, I don't know. Bess has been cleaning it for two years and never a complaint from him, and then one day he claims she's stirred up the papers on his desk, and now the door's kept locked and she can only get in to clean while he or the young master is there. Bess was in tears over it, and it means cleaning it a different time every day, according to when one of them happens to be in. The master won't like it when the weather gets cold and there's no fire lit or even laid until he's ready to go into it in the morning," she went on. Clearly, the master's eccentricity regarding his study rankled.

The butler, who must have heard it all before, said repressively, "I'm sure if it was one of the other girls, instead of your niece, you wouldn't waste a moment thinking of it."

"I would, Mr. Thwaite, because if there's a thing I can't abide, it's unfairness. She swore she never touched the papers, and she can't ever have done before, or he'd have mentioned it. He's not slow to complain if all isn't just as he likes it."

"But if she didn't move them, why would he want to keep his study locked?" Alex asked. He wore the shabby yellow wig again today which altered his appearance substantially, and not for the better. "Unless he'd missed some money out of there, and the papers was only an excuse."

"It can't be that," the butler replied, "as the money is locked in one of his desk drawers, and him with the only key. If the drawer was forced, Bess would have noticed that, and he hasn't mentioned it or had a man in to fix anything, so what I believe is, Bess stirred up his letters, not meaning to, you understand. Maybe brushed against them and they fell on the floor, and she was frightened to admit it."

"She's always been a truthful girl, having been brought up careful even if her da is a Dissenter." The housekeeper's temper was rising now.

"Least said, soonest mended in service," the butler

said.

Then Alex was encouraged to leave, though the housekeeper gave him a slice of pound cake to eat as he went. All he had learned was that Pleasaunce occasionally vexed his staff and had begun locking his study. Oh, and the cook made excellent cake, with a little brandy for flavoring.

Had his father intentionally failed to mention that if Rupert Stowe was engaged in a treasonous conspiracy, it probably involved his good friend Charles Pleasaunce as well? It seemed a logical deduction: Pleasaunce had connections in France, and Stowe had had a list of French arms, with quantities and drill instructions. Surely Anthony Lattimer had reached the same conclusion. Confirmation by getting an independent opinion or merely his habit of keeping his own counsel? Alex wished he could get hold of a sample of Charles Pleasaunce's writing, but there seemed no way to do it. It would be proof of Pleasaunce's involvement, if it matched.

The matter of Paul Pleasaunce's locked study was curious. If Bess the maid had been truthful, one might speculate there was something in the study that the elder Pleasaunce wished to keep secret. Breaking into it in the middle of the night was not a job for an amateur. That was the sort of adventure a boy of eighteen or twenty—or a lunatic—would undertake. Rather like letting a Jacobite smuggler get away! He himself had more sense. He would send his father a message about it. And arrange to keep out of his way, too, so his progenitor could not order him to desist from his enquiries.

****

Roger Markham's funeral took place one week to the day after his death. Fortunately, the weather had continued cool and the oak coffin was well constructed; no odor was detectable. Only the coffin and the carriages of some of those present hinted that the deceased was of some importance. The obsequies for a man of his wealth might have been considerably more elaborate. Jane and Mr. Harris, the attorney, agreed that given the circumstances, and the fact that he had avoided ostentation in life, the arrangements should be simple. Mr. Harris had prepared a list of Uncle Markham's close friends, mostly professional men and merchants, and sent out the invitation cards. He had taken care of the other details, too, for which Jane was profoundly grateful. Her own black gown was completed in time, and was surprisingly becoming, as she had ordered it without assistance from Elvira. Her uncle's servants and Jane, her father, and Mr. Harris made up the mourners, except for one man of about her father's and uncle's age who was obviously a gentleman. He did not seem to be acquainted with anyone else present.

"Papa," Jane began as they were on their way home, "did you notice that gentleman in the tobacco-brown coat who appeared quite different from my uncle's other friends?"

"I marked him particularly for that reason; he had an air of fashion and leisure. Your uncle's associates for many years have been men of the middling sort or City men. They may have come of decent families, but taking part in trade or business coarsens one. Yet when there is not enough money, the younger sons at least must follow some career, unless they have the good fortune to marry well. That man was apparently lucky in his family and is able to live as a gentleman should. I wonder he did not introduce himself."

Her father was still in good temper. Her conscience pricked her for believing that its source was her inheritance and not Sir Thomas's assurance that she was freed from suspicion. Unfilial it might be, but she had known her father too long to be blind to his faults. Not that one should think about a parent's faults but really, if one were honest, one could not overlook their existence. "He reminded me of someone, though I can't think who it could be."

"I'm sure I've never met him. I hope Cook has made that apple florentine for supper. I meant to ask you to tell her to do so, but forgot."

"If she hasn't, I'll have her make it for tomorrow."

****

Attorney Harris had said she might begin sorting through her uncle's belongings, as the inventory had been completed, and he had taken charge of all the business documents. She was doing it in stages, as time allowed. She had given the valet Uncle Markham's good clothing. He could sell it and make a little extra money, in addition to what he had been left in the will. The older, shabbier garments had been bundled up and put aside to be given to the poor.

She was going through the desk, sorting the personal papers. Mr. Harris had obviously been through them, as the drawers were neater than she recalled. Markham had always been orderly in his handling of business correspondence and bills, but his personal letters were a jumble. There was no reason to keep them, but she did not quite like to throw them away, so she boxed them up to store. His memoranda to himself were not worth keeping—"wigmaker!" "Order more clar."—but she found herself glancing over them anyway. She could hear his voice in them.

At the bottom, she found his commonplace book, where he noted down more significant things, almost in diary fashion. She found the last page he had written: "Emeralds for J next birthday? Ask jeweler." She glanced through the previous several pages out of idle curiosity. A notation to see his tailor; another about buying "all vol. Harleian Misc. pamphlets." Then, "Unconvincing. The old trouble? Visit Cocoa Tree. Write A.L. again." A page before that, dated the day she had last visited her uncle: "Ask R.S. to explain. Adam & Eve Tav."

She wished the two entries were as obscure as some of the others, but "Ask R.S. to explain" seemed all too clear. Rupert's visit to the ship troubled him. He must have arranged to meet her half brother at the tavern, and whatever explanation Rupert had given for his presence on the docks had not satisfied her uncle. The rest of that second entry was mysterious enough. The Cocoa Tree was a chocolate house, she knew, but what had drinking chocolate to do with Rupert or anything else?

"Write A.L. again" on the other hand, must refer to the letter to Alex Gordon's superior. One thing was clear to her: Rupert could not have had an innocent reason to be aboard a ship. If Rupert had confided some peccadillo to him, the sort of thing no young man would divulge to a female relative, Uncle Markham would have understood and sent him off with some advice on how to avoid future trouble. Rupert might not have unburdened himself to their father, fearing a bear-garden scold. Her uncle's more sympathetic ear should have prompted Rupert to do what he usually did in difficulties—transfer them to someone else. Had it been only a matter of Rupert owing money, Uncle Markham would almost certainly have refused to lend him any (*ha! lend, indeed!*), but he would not have found her half brother's story unconvincing.

What debt could Rupert have incurred that he would hesitate to admit? A gaming debt, a tailor or bootmaker pressing for payment, a woman needing support for their illegitimate child? She discarded the last possibility as unlikely. Rupert would simply have ignored her. Could he have wanted money to invest in a cargo? Marginally more likely, perhaps. Her father would not have approved of his son involving himself in something so close to business. If Rupert had spoken to her uncle about it, and the latter found it "unconvincing," it most likely meant he thought it not a sound investment, which, given that he knew something of the captain and ship, was reasonable. But then, why visit the Cocoa Tree? Or write to A.L.?

Mr. Gordon had not mentioned a second letter. Had he not been informed of it? Had her uncle not written it? Or was it policy, not to tell her everything he knew? Men were always concealing things, important things, from women. So tiresome of them! As if by not mentioning anything indelicate or dangerous, they could protect one. Obviously, Alex Gordon believed Rupert was involved in smuggling arms. But Rupert must be an innocent dupe as he was not clever enough to manage such a thing on his own. He could not be guilty of any serious misdeed.

She sat for some minutes, trying to decide. She need not tell Alex about the notations, especially if he had not seen fit to tell her about a second letter. Assuming Uncle Markham had written one, and Alex Gordon knew of it. Her uncle had apparently intended to visit the chocolate house first. Whatever did men do at chocolate houses, apart from sipping chocolate? They were not places a lady could go, any more than she could enter a bagnio. She thought they read newspapers there and talked, probably about coarse subjects they would not mention in front of their female relatives and acquaintances. She wished she could snort "Hmmpf!" like her father. The expressions of irritation or disgust suitable to ladies were far too mild.

But 2500 muskets, able to be loaded and fired three times a minute, made the matter serious. Uncle Markham had taken the presence of the *Sea Mew* and its smuggler captain seriously, and she thought, for all his airy manner, Mr. Gordon viewed the prospect of smuggled muskets as a grave threat. She would like to see him again. She could ask him if there had been another letter and what significance there might be in her uncle's intention to visit the Cocoa Tree.

Jane took a sheet of paper, selected a quill, and dipped it in the inkwell. It would be far more discreet to write from her uncle's house and send it by one of his servants than to do so from her home. Her stepmother and father would be sure to hear of it from Wilson or a footman, and would ask who she was writing and why. Her late uncle's staff, on the other hand—her staff, now—would not betray her.

****

When Alex decided to continue looking into

Markham's murder, in spite of his father's order, he had taken a room in a cheap inn. If he came and went from their Bloomsbury Square home in the sort of disguises he might need, it would come to his papa's attention (and worry the servants). Besides, he didn't want to have to explain to his mother why he was dressing like a country bumpkin or a laborer or a costermonger. He feared his current activities would strain even her sense of humor to breaking. On the other hand, leaving the inn dressed as himself would also cause talk. It might even be dangerous, if it led someone to the correct conclusion. To make the transition, he donned an old plain suit, such as might be worn for everyday by a country gentleman with no aspiration to fashion, or perhaps by a middling successful tradesman.

The footman admitted him just as his mother was descending the stairs.

He greeted her a little nervously. She was, as his father had noted, inquisitive. *Like mother, like son.*

She stared at him in perplexity. "Why, Alex, you're wearing a wig! I thought you preferred your own hair. And it's not as if it were scanty or an unfortunate color."

It had been too much to hope she would not notice.

"Yes, but having my hair arranged and powdered for formal occasions is a nuisance, when with my hair cut short, I can simply clap on a wig. 'Tis a great saving of time."

"Oh, very sensible. And the one you're wearing almost perfectly matches your own hair—though it's much tidier, of course."

"That is a convenience also, Mama."

Before he could excuse himself, she asked,

"Whyever are you wearing that old suit, dear? It's really not suitable for town wear, except for some poor man who can afford no better."

"I had an errand in a part of town where I did not wish to be an obvious target for robbery, ma'am."

She was clearly on the brink of asking why he would go to such a place, but he added, "And now I must change into something more appropriate, if you will excuse me? Er…are you and my father dining at home tonight?"

"No, we are promised to the Beamishes. And yes, do change your clothes, before someone sees you and thinks your papa does not make you an adequate allowance."

He bowed and turned toward the stair.

"You have a letter here, Alex. The oddest thing: why would Miss Fairford be writing to you? It came by messenger, too, rather than by the post. I hope all is well with her."

Alex picked up the letter lying on the hall table and reminded himself to have her send any future letters to his inn. "I sent her an etui filled with needles and a little pair of scissors and a thimble and so forth."

"That was very thoughtful of you. Every woman needs sewing things," Mrs. Lattimer said, dubiously. "Though I would have thought a book would be more to her taste."

" 'Twas in the shape of a book, which is what made me think of her. Simon Banford was buying a gift for his sister, and so I thought of Miss Fairford."

"How well you've turned out," his fond mother remarked. "Some young lady will be very pleased with you. Is there anyone yet?"

"...Not yet. Besides, I'm convinced my father would say I must undertake some profession before I can think of marriage. I dare say he's right."

She sighed. "That's very true."

He broke the seal and unfolded the single sheet, which after the salutation and briefly worded hope that he and all the family were well, stated that the sender had a letter for him, for which he might call any afternoon. Either the writer or Mistress Jane had realized a thick packet might cause curiosity. Use of an intermediary was a well-known way of receiving a letter from some recipient of whom one's family did not approve. Which would be any young man, of course; unmarried young ladies did not write to men to whom they were not betrothed except for brothers and fathers or other close male relatives. One would not expect a governess to act as a go-between, but it was best to be cautious. Alex had absorbed some of his father's secretive habits. He wondered, as his valet helped him change, what the elder Lattimer had done earlier in his career.

****

Captain Simon Banford said, "Alex, you idiot. Did you never buy a pound of something when you visited France on your Grand Tour?"

"No, why would I? And my tour wasn't precisely grand. Good, yes, but the oddest things kept occurring, and then I had to cut it short. A pound of what?"

"Meat, cheese...I don't know. Come to think of it, I didn't either. But my valet did."

"What's that to the point, Sim?" Alex inquired, thoroughly lost for once.

"I'd forgotten it until just now. Your asking about

eight-pounders brought it all back. If you were an artilleryman, you'd know the French use a cannon they call an eight-pounder, but their pound weighs a little more than ours, so it's almost exactly what we would call a nine-pounder. Why this interest in artillery?"

"Oh, I came across a mention of it, and I wondered, that's all. My honored papa says I'm inquisitive." Rupert's "shopping list" had crossed off the entry, but he could not help but be curious.

Banford laughed and drained his tankard. "You are, indeed. That's probably why you had adventures on the Continent. But it's time for me to report. Will you be at Dolly's Chop House tonight?"

"If I can, I'll be there." He had chosen his time to meet Sim Banford, knowing he had to go on duty. Otherwise, it might have been difficult to get away from his convivial friend.

"I don't know what you find to fill your time. You're seldom found at your club, you don't gamble…ah, I know! You have a charmer tucked away somewhere. Well, that's an acceptable excuse. When she begins to pall, we'll see you oftener, no doubt."

Chapter 9

"I hope I am not assisting you in a clandestine relationship, Mr. Alex," Eliza Fairford said.

"No, really, ma'am. I am only helping the lady. She is a recent heiress, and there is some suspicion that her family covets her inheritance. In any case, she is not a girl, and her stepmother and father have made her their housekeeper for years," he added, his powers of invention flagging.

"Oh, dear. Families can be so unreasonable. One is always hearing of girls forced into unwelcome marriages, or else deprived of opportunities to wed." She gave him a speculative look. "If her inheritance is large, and she is a pleasant lady and not too old, some young man might be fortunate to secure her interest."

"Yes, indeed."

He read the very brief communication in the nearest coffee house.

Jane requested that he meet her at the same place they had talked before, meaning Lincoln's Inn Fields, no doubt. She would be there at nine o'clock each morning until she saw him. She might simply have passed on in the letter whatever information she had but on the whole, he applauded her discretion. Also it provided a reason to see her again. She had added only one line more, followed by her initials. "Was there a second letter to his old friend?"

The question nonplussed him. If there had been a second letter, why had his father not mentioned it? He could guess, having heard his father say, "The fewer people who know a secret, the better." If such a letter existed and contained some matter Anthony Lattimer considered sensitive, he would suppress it without a second thought.

The following morning, Alex wore one of his better suits to visit the park and was rewarded by the sight of Jane sitting primly on the bench. She looked up as he approached but confined herself to a cool nod of recognition before moving over to make more room for him.

She explained briefly what she had found in her uncle's notebook and gave him a copy of the lines.

"I don't think this would have meant anything to his attorney," she said.

"No," he agreed.

"Do you understand it, Mr. Gordon?"

"Parts of it are suggestive."

She gazed at him expectantly. He was very partial to young ladies with black hair. Her eyes were green. He thought he had once read a novel in which the heroine's eyes were described as being green as emeralds. Jane Stowe's eyes were the color of gooseberries. He liked tart, full-flavored gooseberries; they reminded him of blue skies and warm days. He did not need to remember his father's advice about secrets to know that he should not enlighten her.

"It would be best if you didn't know, Mistress Jane."

"But I know about the muskets, sir. My brother is somehow involved as an innocent victim. Surely I have a right to know?"

She hoped Rupert was innocent of all but foolishness, Alex thought. As he might be; but her half brother was not his concern. Not his primary concern, anyway. "I will have to find out, if I can, whether he did write another letter," he said.

"That would be a very good idea."

He would rather not ask his father, who would almost certainly order him—again—to cease prying into the affair, but there might be no way to avoid it. And he would as certainly carry on in spite of parental disapproval.

While he was pondering whether there might be another way of finding out, she went on, "I am curious about the Cocoa Tree. Why did Uncle Markham mention going there?"

"Well…it's a chocolate house…"

"So I have heard, Mr. Gordon. But what has it to do with French muskets?"

"It's popular with Jacobites and their sympathizers."

"Then, if my uncle went there, he might have attracted the attention of someone who was connected with Captain O'Brien? Who, I suppose, might be sympathetic to the Jacobites' views."

"It's possible." Or someone connected with Rupert Stowe. But of course she wouldn't want to be reminded of that.

"Then the 'old trouble' to which my uncle refers may be the Jacobite rebellion of 1715? It makes sense if the captain was involved with that one. There is danger of a new rebellion."

"…What makes you think so?" Ladies did not read

newspapers—gentlemen ordinarily went to chocolate houses and coffee houses or their clubs to do so. Had she heard something from her half brother, or perhaps her father? Even his own mother seemed unaware of how serious the situation in Scotland had become.

She colored. "I read *The Gentleman's Magazine*."

"Your papa permits you to—"

"No, I read it when he's not home. Some of the articles are very interesting."

He tried to recall how much indelicacy was to be found in that publication. Perhaps not a great deal, after all. Or it might be decently shrouded in Latin in the poetry section. It was certainly surprising to find a young lady reading it. Unless many ladies did the same and simply did not admit it? What a daunting thought!

"As there have been a number of articles which make it clear there is a good deal of unrest in Scotland, it seems obvious another rebellion is expected. There were rumors of one two years ago, after all, though that came to nothing."

"You are correct, mistress. You will therefore understand the matter of your uncle's death, and his suspicions, are being taken very seriously."

"Pray, cannot Captain O'Brien be arrested and questioned?"

"His ship has left port but is being sought, I hear." He should not have told her, but she was closely concerned in the affair and such an intelligent young lady, he had not the heart to disappoint her.

Jane sighed. "There is nothing more to be done here, I suppose."

Alex suppressed a sigh of his own. He would like to know about that second letter. There was a chance he could find out without asking his father. "I may be able to ask a few questions here and there. I might visit the Cocoa Tree."

Her alarm was rather gratifying. "That would be dangerous, surely, given what happened to my uncle."

"I can pass as a Scot. And I won't take unnecessary chances."

"What, pray," Jane inquired, "is a necessary chance?"

A chuckle escaped him. "I think it's going to the Cocoa Tree, and speaking like a Scotsman when I do speak, and listening. I won't try to lead the conversation around to rebellion, or treason, or…hmmmm, muskets."

"Oh! Well, that sounds safe enough. Can you pick up anything useful that way, do you think?"

"Did you never eavesdrop on your mama and her friends, or on your parents, when you were a child? I learned any number of fascinating things, listening to my older brother and his friends when they didn't know I was there."

"Not your mother and father?"

"My father can be…extremely sparing of speech. I only eavesdropped on my mother once, when she and two friends were chatting in her boudoir. Never again."

"Did she catch you and box your ears?"

"No."

"What, then?"

Alex felt the blood rush into his face. "They were discussing a…female…matter."

Jane was surprised into a laugh, which she quickly choked off. "I can see it might have been embarrassing for you."

"Oh, horrible. I was eight. When I went to school, I

knew more about the subject than anyone else—probably including the masters—but I never said a word. Better the other boys should have ridiculous ideas than they be burdened with the truth."

She kept her face grave, though her eyes twinkled. "Do you still feel the same way?"

He cocked his head. "No...I suppose I don't. But grown men do not discuss such things. Though the married men must be aware of the facts."

"I wouldn't be too sure of that," she said dryly.

"Do all ladies think men are so, so..."

"Ignorant? Yes, very likely many of them do. But one can't correct them; they would be horrified. Or outraged or think one very coarse and unladylike. I shouldn't be talking like this, but somehow, Mr. Gordon, you are very easy to talk to."

"Thank you, Mistress Jane. I might say the same of you."

She smiled acknowledgement.

"I'll leave you now. I may know something by tomorrow. Is it possible for you to meet me here again? Surely your family must wonder what takes you out every morning?"

"I give the staff their instructions after breakfast, and no one notices what I do afterward until much later in the day. Tomorrow, then."

At home, Alex sauntered down the corridor. He had learned from the butler his mother was out visiting. His father was...wherever he went two or three times a week when he didn't go elsewhere. He occasionally visited a government office in connection with his official position—whatever it might be. His father described it as "a sort of auditor of government efficiency." He made it sound like a minor post, almost a hobby, and rather boring, which kept people from asking more about it. In fact, Alex thought very few were aware Anthony Lattimer held any office. He had been used to call upon Sir Robert Walpole, First Lord of the Treasury, in Downing Street, until Walpole's resignation several years before. Alex had followed him once later out of curiosity only to find himself more curious yet. It appeared when his father was not at his club or a coffee house or any of the other places a well-to-do gentleman might amuse himself during the day, he vanished into Somerset House. Some court officials had rooms there, and some parts of it were used for storage. Some government offices were located there, too.

The staff had finished the morning's cleaning and were now about other business. His mother, even if she came home early, was unlikely to go near the library. With a last glance around, Alex opened the door and slipped inside, closing it quietly and locking it behind him. His father had shown him Markham's letter here. If there had been a second, it should be in his father's strongbox with the original letter.

His father said he was as curious as a cat. As a child, he had been unable to resist locked rooms and locked boxes. He had learned to open the locked desk drawers when he was ten. It had taken several weeks of cautious attempts whenever he could escape from his tutor. The concept was simple: a key has projections so he experimented first with every other key he could find, then with a bent wire. When he finally succeeded, the contents of the desk were boring. Then by the sheerest good fortune, he found a tiny drawer concealed under the desk, and only because he had crawled under the desk after dropping his picklock. The strongbox key was in it.

The key was still there.

When he was ten, the contents of the strongbox had been a bore, too: nothing but papers, not the pirate treasure he had expected. This time, he hoped for a letter. It would be positively disappointing to find jewels instead.

He sorted quickly through the box, looking for the same kind of seal and paper he recalled from the letter he had seen and taking care not to change the order. Most of the contents appeared to be government documents. It took only moments to find it.

Tony,

Today I dropped into the Cocoa Tree to see if I could gather any further Intelligence. Much of what I heard around me was the Usual seditious nonsense, all smoke and no Flame. I myself found it obnoxious that the late King spoke no English and so very obviously preferred the Principality of Hanover to his far more important English realm. It was unfortunate no Protestant heir more closely related to James I existed. But there is no use in raking up the past now. If 'twere only the Young Pretender and a handful of Highlanders up in Scotland, 'twould be no very great thing. However, some of our own Jacobites are in a Ferment, most particularly some frequenting the Cocoa Tree. They would bear close watching. I saw young Pleasaunce there, mighty serious with several other men I did not recognize. I recall that at the time of my Sister's wedding, the Pleasaunce family and the Stowes were hand in glove. Recently, my niece mentioned that young Rupert Stowe is Engaged to marry one of the Pleasaunce girls. This makes me very uneasy, as I am sure you can understand.

Yr Most Obedient—

A coach rattled to a stop outside. Voices carried up to the study window, and one of them was his father's.

Oh, Hades. Alex folded the sheet and tucked it back into its place, and closed and locked the strongbox. Sliding the key into its hiding place took another heart-pounding moment. Then he was closing the door carefully. He heard his father's voice.

"We will be in the library. Bring up a bottle of the claret. Then I do not wish to be disturbed further."

"Very good, sir."

Alex went up the stairs soft-footed and reached his bedchamber unseen.

Chapter 10

Jane was in the kitchen speaking with Mrs. Merry when the scullery maid came in from her half-day holiday.

"I hope your mother is well? And your little brothers?"

"Oh, yes, mistress, thank you. And my brother Jeremy is to attend the Davenant school, that teaches poor boys to read, write, and do their numbers. But I saw the oddest thing when I left my mam."

"What was that?"

"Now, Betty, don't be boring on, taking Mistress Jane's time," Cook said.

"No, no, let Betty tell us. She is great with news, Mrs. Merry."

"I saw Mr. Rupert going into a tavern. I can't think why a gentleman would want to go to a low sailor's public house like that one."

"Foolishness, my girl. Mr. Rupert's gone out of town—even you know that."

Jane said, "Are you sure you saw my brother, Betty?"

The girl was thrown into confusion, but Mrs. Merry said, "She's a silly wench, like all these young girls. They will peep and chatter whenever they can."

"I saw him very clear, and I'd know Mr. Rupert anywhere. He carries himself like a lord." She sighed blissfully.

"You've no call to be thinking about lords or gentlemen, either. And it can't have been Mr. Rupert, as he's gone into the West Country."

"Your family lives in Whitechapel, I think? Can you tell me more precisely where you saw him?"

"Oh, yes, mistress. In Thames Street. The tavern is on the corner, it's—"

"Silly chit," Mrs. Merry interrupted with deep disgust. "Thames Street's Billingsgate, not Whitechapel. You can't have been there if you was coming back here, or if you was, you shouldn't'a been."

"Let the girl explain, Mrs. Merry."

"My sister lives near the fish market there, and I goes by to see her for a little after I sees my mam. That's how I come to be there."

"And you saw Mr. Rupert going into a public house that's on a corner." Betty could not read. Would she know the name of the other street? There must be a score of such places. "Was it before or after you left your sister?"

"After, Mistress Jane. At the Crown and Castle, that I always notices because it has such a pretty sign."

"Did he see you?" Jane heard the cook give a little snort as she turned to measure out barley for barley water.

"No, mistress. But I was on the other side o' the street, and gentlemen don't notice servants anyway."

"Unless they're uncommon handsome," Mrs. Merry muttered.

"I expect once they had accompanied Mrs. Pleasaunce and Mistress Claire to Plymouth and got them settled, Mr. Charles and Mr. Rupert were left to their own devices and went off on their own. Young gentlemen are very likely to do so," Jane said. "I think you should not mention this to anyone else, Betty, and I know Mrs. Merry never gossips. My brother would very likely be embarrassed to have his comings and goings spoken of."

"I'm sorry, Mistress Jane, I didn't mean any harm by it. My lips are sealed."

"I perfectly understand why you thought it remarkable. As long as it goes no further, there's no harm done. But remember in the future that females are expected to ignore the odd things men do. I'm sure your own eventual marriage will be much happier if you do."

"There's no one wants me, mistress," Betty said sadly.

"Some lad will, be sure. You're not sixteen yet. There's time."

The scullery maid flashed a smile, Mrs. Merry made a derisive sound in her throat, and Jane said, "Remember Mrs. Stowe likes a good deal of sugar in her barley water. Please send it up to her maid when it's ready, Mrs. Merry."

Jane was not disposed to imagine her brother was merely out on some sordid male amusement. Gentlemen could perfectly well find those anywhere! Why come back to London, with all the inconvenience travel entailed, if it were not for a sound reason? It must take several days to travel to Plymouth. They could return more quickly on horseback, with no coach to escort, but it would still be days, changing horses often so they could travel fast all the way. It might possible if Rupert had come straight back. *If he, or they, went all the way to Plymouth.* But why would he do it?

And why would Rupert visit Billingsgate? She sat down at the desk in the housekeeper's room—her own office by default—and wrote to Miss Eliza Fairford.

****

Alex lounged at a table, glancing idly at the newspaper. He liked the scented air in coffee and chocolate houses, and the lively conversations. The houses were all different, too, some having their own distinct clientele: writers, men of scientific interests, businessmen, and for all he knew, valets and footmen, while at some coffee houses, you might find a tradesman, a writer, and an earl at the same table. Lloyd's Coffee House published a listing of ship arrivals and was the center for shippers, who went there to arrange insurance for their cargoes. The Cocoa Tree, in Pall Mall, attracted Tories and Jacobites, and being in such a fine neighborhood was elegantly furnished. This was his first visit.

Talk ebbed and flowed around him. He wished he could join in, as a spirited debate was always interesting, but he must not get involved until he found a likely group. He could not follow all the conversations at once, but men often lingered for hours. Eventually, he was bound to catch a few words to lead him to men who might be giving active support to the Young Pretender.

Many who came to the Cocoa Tree would be innocent of any such involvement. Egad, both Oxford and Cambridge were full of Tories, so he himself might see a friend here. *But they're unlikely to see me.* His dark brown wig, his unfashionable old suit, and a few other minor changes to his appearance should be disguise enough, if by chance someone who knew him happened to be present. He used a carefully calculated Scots accent when ordering his chocolate.

The room was rather full, but Alex was the only occupant of his table. Presently, a gentleman entered, glanced around, and approached, to ask if he might share his table.

"Certainly, sir."

The man seated himself, saying, "Ah, a Scot! May I inquire what brings you to London?"

"The same thing that brings all Scots to England," Alex replied. "That is, the hope of mending my fortune."

"Most men, of whatever country, would say the same, I am tolerably sure," the Englishman said with a laugh. He made a sign to a waiter, who acknowledged it with a little bow and hurried off. *He must be well known here.*

"True enough. My country is well supplied with canny, hard-working men, but not as well supplied with opportunities. There is more scope in England for an ambitious man."

"Scotland has seen more than its share of troubles," the other remarked, "which always makes it difficult to prosper."

"Oh, ay. Scots of a martial inclination take service abroad and have for centuries. The Auld Alliance with France was good for us. But more peaceful business is wanting."

The waiter returned and served Alex's companion. "The more recent alliance has not benefitted Scotland?"

Meaning, of course, the Treaty of Union with England. "How good it has been, you may judge by the numbers of Scotsmen in London." That was ambiguous enough.

The exchange continued, less conversation than formal court dance. The other asked if Alex were not of the Lowland landed gentry "as I would guess by your manner of speech, being something of a student of accents."

Alex sighed. "My family had lands once, but over the last hundred years..." He shrugged.

"The Bishops' War, the Scottish Civil War, and all the other risings and unrest have been very hard on your country," the Englishman said.

"You know something of our history," Alex replied.

"I am a student of politics as well as of language. I visited the Borders once or twice, and I cannot but feel sorrow for all Scotland's tribulations."

"They have been many." Alex recounted two or three of the tales he had heard from his grandfather Gordon, giving them a more Jacobitical color than Grandda would have done.

After they had sat sipping their chocolate for a time, the man said, "I think I have not seen you here before, sir. Are you recently come to Town?"

"Yes. I have not been more than a week or two in London."

"Then you have perhaps not yet made many friends here. I am acquainted with some Scots and Englishmen who may be of use to you, including a few who are present. If you would like an introduction, let us join them."

After making him known to a party at a table in the corner, the helpful Englishman melted away, pleading an appointment. It had been easier than Alex had anticipated. Almost too easy. The three Scots and an Englishman, whose name was Warrender, said nothing which could be called seditious. But in their discreetly worded comments and by certain subtle references, Alex deduced that they held opinions that would have appalled the rather broad-minded Anthony Lattimer. Warrender was a Catholic, embittered by the exclusion of Catholics from universities and government posts. One of the Scots was a Highlander, Alex guessed, though it would not have been apparent to anyone not familiar with Scotland. A son or brother of some clan chieftain, well educated, well dressed in a suit of golden-brown, and all but indistinguishable from a Lowlander. Alex wondered who his tailor was. He dared not ask: an impoverished gentleman—as his worn suit testified—would not be able to afford a fashionable tailor. There was something about the third man's dry, precise, grave demeanor that marked him as an attorney. From Edinburgh almost certainly, where Alex had seen many of the species, his mother's family connections having included two or three.

Unfortunately, there was no way to work the conversation around to the subjects in which he was most interested. However, Warrender invited him to supper the next day, and Alex accepted with alacrity. While taking an active role was a bit risky, he stood a good chance of learning more, and more quickly, than his original plan allowed.

****

They were eight at table. The talk was lively and confined to the theater, sport, and gambling. All very enjoyable, Alex thought, but none of it gave him any insight into Jacobite plots. Several of them were interrogating him very subtly, which seemed a hopeful sign. He trusted his apparent candor would allay their suspicions.

With the servants dismissed, the talk turned. Each place was provided with a goblet of water. When all had glasses of port as well, their host raised his over the goblet and offered the toast: "To the King!" All echoed it, including Alex.

The King over the water. James Francis Edward Stuart, Pretender to the thrones of England, Scotland, and Ireland, and father to Prince Charles, the Young Pretender, who was now in Scotland. No proof of actual treason there, his father would say. Talk did not mean action.

The next man raised his glass. "Damn Hanover!"

And so it went around the table, until Alex's turn came. "Confusion to our enemies" seemed adequate. By then, they'd all drunk a good deal, on top of wine at dinner, and one or two had imbibed more heavily than the others. Alex walked a fine line between appearing abstemious and drinking enough to muddle him. Fortunately, he had a hard head for drink, inherited from his Grandfather Gordon.

A certain Mr. Dean, who was seated at Alex's right, had either drunk much more or was very easily fuddled, to judge by his slurred speech.

"I'd ride north tomorrow"—*Hic!*—"if I could not do better for my king and"—*Hic!*—"my prinshe here."

Alex saw several suppressed smiles and also at least one set of compressed lips (the Edinburgh attorney) at this announcement. He would have liked to ask what Mr. Dean was doing for the Cause, but curiosity might be suspect in this group. He settled for an encouraging expression.

"What bushinesh has a fellow like you to be leaving Shcotland at shuch a time as thish, Gordon?" Dean demanded of him suddenly.

Alex responded easily, "I've been nearly a year in England, sir, though I came recently to London. I stopped for a time in several towns and most recently in Bristol. It seemed a place where a man might find opportunities in trade."

"Oh, trade!" someone—an upper class Englishman, of course!—exclaimed scornfully.

"There's no harm in making money," one of the Scots said. "A man must live, and there's little enough for an ambitious man north o' the border—as Gordon said earlier. If you prosper, you can better aid whatever cause is dear to you."

"I'd thought to work my way up in a shipping firm," Alex added. "An island must always need to import goods and export what it produces by sea."

"Verra true, sir. Ye had no luck, I'm thinking."

"No. I worked as a clerk for a shipping agent, and I might have courted the daughter of an importer, but then I heard of events in the North, and thought to come to London to see if I could get better news."

"You must be concerned for family or friends you left in Scotland," a short, intense fellow suggested.

"I have no family left. No, my interest is all for the fate of my country."

"What country?" the heavy-set one—Armstrong?—asked, baldly.

"Scotland, of course," Alex replied, raising his eyebrows. "I'm a Scot born and bred, wherever I may travel."

"Not all of us can say the same," remarked Warrender. "But at least we stand by the principle that a king is chosen by God, not by Parliament. It follows that a king's nearest living heir must be his successor, whatever his religion. James II, son and heir of Charles II, is the true king of England—and Scotland, Ireland, and Wales—" he added with a grin.

"Both sound arguments for supporting his cause," Alex asserted. He found it fatally easy to get into the spirit of the thing.

"We are pledged to support it. Do you stand with us?"

"I drank to the King over the water. I am a Scotsman, and my family took part in the '15 (*never mind on what side!*) and have fought for Scotland since the time of Robert the Bruce, or before. How should I do otherwise than stand with my country now?"

"You'd besht go back to Shcotland and enlisht in the prinshe's army," Dean said morosely, tossing off another half glass.

"Oh, I think Mr. Gordon might be as useful to our king and prince here as there," his host said. "We can always use the help of quick-witted men with energy. Let me think on it. And now…"

The conversation drifted off into other channels. Or not so much drifted as was steered by Warrender. Dean slumped in his chair and began to snore. One by one, the others departed, two of them taking Dean with them. Alex rose also.

"A moment, Gordon," his host said so quietly the last to leave did not hear. "I have thought of a service you might do for us, if you would be so good. Come into my library.

"There is a letter I must send to Oxford. Some urgency attends it, and I have no servant to spare, or none that I would trust with it. It must arrive there either by tomorrow evening or, at worst, by noon the following day. If you would be so good as to take it, I should consider myself in your debt. I will of course be responsible for the hiring of a horse. I think you do not keep one in London?"

"I do not, alas, so I will accept your offer and take your letter."

"Good! That much relieves my mind. It is only a few lines, which I will write now." He took out a sheet, dipped his quill in the standish, and wrote. After sprinkling it with pounce, shaking it off, and folding it carefully, he applied a moistened wafer and pressed it with a wafer stamp.

"Deliver it to Mr. Josiah Brown, tobacconist, to be held until called for by Mr. Peter Arlington. I prefer not to write the direction. Can you remember it?"

"Certainly. I'm accounted to have a very good memory. Josiah Brown, tobacconist, for Mr. Peter Arlington."

"Very good indeed. Here, this should cover hiring the horse and the other costs of the journey. I misdoubt you'll want to ride back the same day."

"Thank you. Barring some calamity, I'll be back in London by midday, the day after tomorrow, and will call upon you."

Chapter 11

He sat up for some time after returning to his lodging, staring at the letter. If its contents were treasonous, he should turn it over to his father, who would know to whom it should be passed on. He would have to confess that he had been carrying on his own, unauthorized inquiry. Another consideration occurred to him. He had encouraged those men to trust him; he had eaten at Warrender's table. To betray them ran against the grain. He could hear his Scottish grandfather saying, *Your fine English gentleman's principles may make a traitor of you, laddie. Have ye no sense at all?* His father would say the same, barring the part about gentleman's principles. At last, with the candle beginning to gutter, he decided that the morning would determine his course of action. He could do nothing further tonight.

****

He rose early, ate a hurried breakfast, and sallied forth to do a little shopping and to hire a horse. On returning to the inn, he locked himself in his room, moved the rickety table over to the window, and set to work.

The green-tinted wafer came off with the careful application of a dampened handkerchief. Heart beating a little fast, he unfolded the sheet.

"The cargo arrives Friday morning, Gregson

warehouse, Narrow Street, Limehouse. Two wagons required."

It could be an innocent message. Certainly there was nothing overtly criminal, let alone treasonous, in it. The cargo could be printed fabric or smuggled spirits or chocolate. Only the most scrupulous, and of course the government, disapproved of smuggled luxury goods. Yet Warrender had made a point of needing a trustworthy man to deliver his message.

Knowing the contents did not clarify matters. He must now decide whether to pass the information on to his father. If the letter had been unambiguous, the decision would have been easy. Those 2500 muskets—

He grinned suddenly, feeling much lighter in spirits. Whatever Warrender's cargo might be, the one thing it could not be was the muskets. While he did not know the weight of a French musket, estimating based on the Brown Bess, such a shipment should weigh…hmm! thirteen tons or thereabouts, not counting whatever they were shipped in. Could such a quantity be transported with two wagons? He recalled reading somewhere that a six-horse team could legally haul six tons. They might scrape by with two wagons at a minimum, assuming teams of six horses. If his calculations were correct, an assumption his old tutor would never have made.

Those considerations aside, bringing two wagonloads of goods of whatever sort into London, if they were actually bound for Scotland, would be foolish. Whatever the freight expected at Gregson's warehouse, Alex thought he could let it go unhindered, in the hope of learning something of greater importance.

He selected a green wafer, moistened it, applied it where the original seal had been, and pressed it down with the wafer seal he had purchased at a stationer's. It bore the common cross-hatched pattern. Thank God Warrender had not used one with his initials or some personal device. If this were not identical to Warrender's, it would pass.

He would deliver it and hope to work himself into a position where he could ascertain whether the group was really dangerous or merely enjoyed the sensation of plotting. He would not place a wager on some of them actually risking anything for the Young Pretender, or the Chevalier, as some called him. They might cheer if he rode into London at the head of an army, and offer hospitality, but while the issue was undecided, they would content themselves with drinking to the king over the water. Warrender and a few of the others might be a more serious matter. Alex had no doubts about Warrender's brains. If he had the steely resolve to match, he would be a threat.

****

He enjoyed the ride to Oxford, familiar to him from his university days. He had always preferred riding to going by coach, not only for the fresh air but because if the road chanced to be muddy, a horse could make better speed and was less likely to overturn or end in a ditch. There was a sort of looking-forward-to-term feeling about the expedition, too; something interesting lay at the end, with the possibility of excitement. Neither of his brothers had ever done anything like this. Gilbert had been a better scholar; Edward had been a natural leader. He himself had been reasonably good at many things without excelling at anything except acting. That was what made it so confoundedly difficult to settle on a career.

The tobacconist's shop was small, dim, and redolent of the scent of tobacco. Alex breathed it in appreciatively. If only the stuff didn't taste so foul. He gave the tobacconist the letter and the verbal instructions. Brown nodded politely, tucked the letter into a drawer, and tried to sell him pipe tobacco or snuff. Alex declined. He had tried smoking the nasty stuff once or twice, and did not like the taste or feeling it left in his mouth. As for snuff, he usually ended with a powdering of it on his coat. He reserved its use for times when he had a head cold. Messy but effective.

Outside, he stood for a few minutes, debating. The day was pleasant, in witness whereof a pair of rustics, small farmers, probably, idled outside the tavern across the street, and people on errands strolled rather than hurrying.

He could hire a fresh horse and ride back to London now. Another six hours in the saddle would see him home in the evening; he did not like the idea of putting up at an inn on Warrender's money. He would dine before starting as he had not eaten since his early, Spartan breakfast at the inn.

This program was speedily put into practice. He crossed the street, catching a few words of the loungers' conversation as he entered the public house.

"The hay, ay?" The speaker puffed on a clay pipe clutched in a hand that was grubby but bore no calluses, scrapes, or scars that Alex could see. He concluded that the fellow managed to avoid a great deal of the work one would expect of even a fairly prosperous farmer. His own family's country manor had only a home farm, but there always seemed to be plenty of work to be done on it by the outdoor staff when the weather was good. Sometimes even when it wasn't. He wondered what had brought them to Oxford.

"Ah, ay. Good crop for certain sure." The second, who was chewing on a straw, gave a sort of shrug with one shoulder as Alex passed.

This time, the horse provided to him by the livery stable had only two gaits: a shuffling walk and an uneven trot. It would make for a long journey, he feared.

Rather less than halfway to London, the animal stumbled and began to limp. Alex dismounted to check its hooves for stones. While he was prying out the pebble that had caused its distress, a rider came into sight around the bend in the road behind him. The man seemed about to pull up, as if to speak, but instead rode on after the briefest check. Alex would have expected him to address some comment to him. When he continued on instead, Alex glanced up. A shy yokel, he concluded from the man's clothing and battered hat, with a canvas bag strapped to the saddle, but with a very handsome horse. That was no plow horse. As he stared after it, the rider's left shoulder twitched.

Gordon led his nag, as it continued to favor its off fore hoof until he came to a coaching inn, two miles farther on. There he was able to hire a mare with some spirit and better paces. As the ostler saddled her, Alex caught sight of a gelding in a stall near the stable door.

"That looks like a good animal," Alex remarked. "I think I saw it on the road a while ago. Is it for hire?"

"No, sir, it come with a man that's taking a pint in the tap. He'll be back for it in a bit."

"A farm laborer or some such?"

"Ay, sir."

"I wonder if he'd sell it."

"I misdoubt it, sir. He's taking it up to London for his master."

Remounted on a horse that was not a slug, he still had plenty of time to think on the homeward journey. On the way to Oxford, his thoughts had all been on handing off the letter and speculations as to who Peter Arlington might be. Gentlemen sometimes received their mail at their usual coffee house, if it did not come through the penny post. But a gentleman engaged in something illicit might well prefer to receive his most secret mail at a tobacco shop, possibly a fellow conspirator's, to conceal his real address and name. Warrender had claimed the matter was urgent, but did Arlington stop in every day to ask for his letters? Perhaps so, if he was in the habit of receiving urgent communications. But if Warrender had such a letter to send, he had been very casual about finding a suitable messenger. How would he have sent it, if he had not met Gordon yesterday and decided he was honest—if he had so decided. Would he have sent to Arlington at all? If it were a test to see if Alex were trustworthy, he hoped he had passed it.

By the time he reached London, he was ready for another meal and a comfortable chair. He had intended to go to his parents' home for the night, but his inn was nearer and he felt disinclined to go where he might be asked questions or expected to converse. Fortunately, he had told his mother he intended to stay with a friend in the country for a few days. As they would be a bachelor establishment, he would have no need of his valet or a trunk full of clothing, merely some body linen, riding dress, and an old suit. So he could go to his inn, eat, drink, and go to bed, which after some twelve hours in the saddle in one day was extremely appealing.

He came down to breakfast after writing to Warrender to assure him of the delivery of the letter the previous day and that he would see him at the Cocoa Tree later. The waiter accepted the letter, promising to have one of the lads carry it, and turned over a letter from Miss Fairford. It stated that J.S. would like to see him at the Place where they had walked at the hour of Ten in the morning at his first Convenience, as she had Important information to Divulge. That had a hopeful sound. He consulted his pocket watch and found he had plenty of time to eat a sustaining meal before meeting her.

With the day shaping up nicely, he gazed idly out the window. At his request, the waiter had opened it, admitting a pleasant breeze and letting out the stale air left over from last night. Alex did not believe that fresh air was unwholesome, even when cold or damp, a view he'd taken from his Scottish grandmother. He had even been known to sleep with his window open when the weather was dry.

Had the window been closed, the thick bull's eye glass panes and the heavy leading between them would have prevented his noticing a man on the other side of the street. He was a tradesman of some kind, a satchel by his feet, lounging near a pie seller and eating a pie in a leisurely manner.

The poor fellow hasn't much business today. It was amazing how many of the common folk seemed to have so much free time, like those farmers back in Oxford—

How prodigious strange that yonder workman should closely resemble one of those idling yokels. No, not strange at all; it was the same man. He was dressed differently and his face was unremarkable, but Alex was not mistaken. He had ever a keen eye for features; it was merely a matter of paying attention. He leaned back in his chair and drank a deep draft of ale. He ate the last of the beefsteak on his plate and summoned the waiter.

When he came downstairs again, he made his bill current, included another two days' rent, and explained that he was called away on business but wished to keep his room. Then he asked the waiter to show him out by the kitchen entrance, tipping him sixpence.

"If you goes 'round to the right, you'll see a little alley, sir. Nobody can see it from the street."

"And there's no one in the stable yard?"

"Nobody as doesn't work in the stable, sir."

Alex glanced around the yard anyway but spotted no one who was not obviously a stable boy or ostler, and at work. He had plenty of time to meet Jane at Lincoln's Inn Fields.

Chapter 12

She had timed her arrival to be only a few minutes early, as a young lady by herself, with no maid—how shocking!—was apt to be the object of unwanted attentions. She took a different route than she would ordinarily have done, leaving the square by Princes Street and turning down Red Lyon Street. Crossing Holborn, she followed Great Turnstile to Holborn Row and the corner of Lincoln's Inn Fields. He would be somewhere along the northern side of the Fields where they had walked that other time. She marched briskly along until she caught sight of a gentleman on a bench near the Great Queen Street corner. Even at a distance she recognized him, and wondered how it was possible.

Mr. Gordon sprang to his feet when he saw her approaching.

Neither of them wasted time on the social niceties.

"My brother's return to London so soon seems very odd to me," she said after relating what Betty had seen.

"Yes, I agree. Suspicious might be an even more appropriate word." He continued, "I went to the Cocoa Tree. What your uncle may have learned there, I cannot guess, but I found myself fallen in with a pack of Jacobites."

"Did you hear anything about the guns? Or about Charles Pleasaunce?" She did not mention Rupert. It seemed impossible that he should have any political convictions of his own unless he'd been led into them by someone else.

"I dared not ask. If I were they, I would distrust a potential new recruit who asked too many questions."

She nodded slowly. "A new recruit? You intended merely to listen and not take chances."

"I think I said 'unnecessary chances.' But it was so easy to be accepted into their circle, it seemed to be an opportunity not to be missed."

He was far more serious today than he had been at their previous meetings, though his face still bore the signs of good humor and liveliness which had initially attracted her. However would a portrait painter capture the rapid change of his expressions? Men who sat for their portraits invariably chose to be depicted as grave, if not stern. She supposed she would never know.

"It cannot be safe," she said at last. "And would conspirators trust you so readily?"

"Ah…their leader, as I take him to be, tested me—I think—by asking me to deliver a message for him."

She looked at him sharply. Something was not quite right. How surprising that she was able to read his tone and face. "What happened, Mr. Gordon?"

He exhaled, and Jane read chagrin in it, but not at her question, she thought. Mayhap at her perception?

"I did deliver the letter. It contained nothing obviously criminal."

"You read it!"

"Well…if it had mentioned the muskets, or a Jacobite plot, I should have had to turn it over to someone who could deal with it. I suppose the thing to do would have been to copy it to be passed on to our government, so the plotters were not warned prematurely."

"That's very clever. But what went wrong?"

"I am not sure it did. I sealed it up again and delivered it. But as I left the tobacconist, I saw a pair of farmers nearby. This morning one of them was outside my lodging. I think the same one rode after me on my return yesterday."

"If they realize you were…were…"

"Not really one of them? Unreliable? Why should they think so? I don't think they can have known I opened it. Warrender may have sent someone to make sure I delivered it. It's strange that the fellow continued to follow me afterward. However. I've lost him now," he added, his usual insouciance reappearing.

"Thank goodness! But what can we do?"

"I wrote Warrender to let him know his message was delivered. I don't think I need do anything but behave as if I had done his chore in good faith. Probably I should not have left my inn as I did this morning, but I really could not meet you with Warrender's creature at my heels. I think I must report it, however, as clearly there's something wrong there."

"Yes, I suppose so." She sighed, thinking of Rupert. He had been a merry child with engaging ways. If this new information must come out, his and Charles Pleasaunce's names would be mentioned as well. While she did not care about Pleasaunce, it would be very hard on her father. And Elvira, of course. "Will you be able to tell me what is decided, after you report?"

"I will—if I'm told. Will you still walk out every morning?"

"Yes. I enjoy the exercise." And the chance of

meeting a strange young man, she admitted to herself.

****

He engaged a hackney to take him to Somerset House, where he thought he might find his father. He could have walked the half mile more quickly, and it was plain the coachman held him in contempt as lazy or a weakling. Alex ignored his disapproval. Best not to approach on foot, lest he be seen by someone he had met at the Cocoa Tree. Sim Banford would scoff at him as over-cautious, but Sim was a cavalryman, perfectly willing to gallop toward men who were shooting at him. The mad fellow was mourning the loss of his elder and only brother less than the fact that as his father's sole surviving heir, Baron Banford had insisted on his transfer to a safe post in London. Though Sim admitted it could have been worse; his papa might have ordered him to sell out.

Alex smiled, remembering some of their boyhood adventures. Sim had always been the one to suggest an exploit. Alex had been the one to extricate them or avert the worst of the consequences. Caution could be useful.

Jane had been looking very pretty today, with a heightened color. Though the dove-gray mantua she wore did not suit her, it did make her inconspicuous, which was an advantage for their public meetings. He wished he might see her attired in something other than a plain gown. She must have better in her wardrobe. A pale or subdued color would do her no sort of justice. She should wear ruby red. Or green or topaz, for her skin was near milk white and would not be made to appear yellow.

They were approaching Somerset House when he

recognized the set of the shoulders, one a bit higher than the other, of a man striding down the street. He was dressed like one of the middling sort, not in the least rustic, but Alex could not be mistaken. He stood and tapped on the panel behind the coachman's seat.

"Don't stop here—I've forgotten something. Take me to…ah, the Two Roses, near where you took me up." He had noticed the roses of Lancaster and York, brightly painted, on a sign creaking over the door of an inn near the hackney stand.

"Ay, sir," the man agreed, with the air of one used to his passengers' peculiarities. "It'll double the fare, mind."

"Yes, yes. That's all right." What a good thing that he had his valise with him! As they passed Somerset House, Alex saw Hitch Shoulder turn into its entrance.

He could not even speculate as to how the man who had dogged his footsteps from Oxford could have turned up on the street here. How could he have known Alex would make for Somerset House? No, impossible. Was he a traitor, planted in a government office to pass along secrets? He could not be combining such a position with surveillance for Warrender's conspiracy, could he? It made no sense.

The Two Roses had a comfortable appearance from the outside, and Alex liked the place immediately. They had no difficulty in accommodating him with a room which was clean and had a soft bed. He wished he might actually stop there. He set out his paper and quill and when the ale and ink he'd requested were brought, sat down to write.

Sir,

I have heard from Mistress Jane Stowe that Rupert

Stowe has been seen in London within the last few Days, which She learned from a kitchen Maid who chanced to see him near Billingsgate. It seems a Suspicious Circumstance that he should so soon be returned, particularly in light of the List which I passed on to you.

Alex frowned over the next bit. He did not wish to alarm his father. Even less did he desire to be ordered to come home—he was really too old for his father to expect him to obey, but he did not wish to create a rift between them, either. How to explain about Warrender? His father would not be pleased to learn that Alex had worked his way into a possible Jacobite conspiracy, but Alex had to warn him that his pursuer had entered Somerset House. His father would know someone who could hunt down a spy in their midst. And he could not explain how he had come by his information without revealing his own activities. But there was no help for it.

Unless…Alex's blood ran cold. Unless Hitch Shoulder was an agent for the government. In which case, he undoubtedly thought Alex was one of Warrender's people and a Jacobite. And he had performed Warrender's errand faithfully as far as anyone knew. That was a fearful thought! Alex thought fleetingly of a grim cell in the Tower, the public execution…his family's grief and humiliation. He could simply go to his father and explain, and his father would clear up the difficulty. Alex had no doubt he could do so. Run to Papa like a child with some minor perplexity? No, by cock and pie! He would have to admit he had been meddling. If Alex could report the details of their plot, it should allay his father's annoyance, and spare him arrest for treason. But he would have to deliver Warrender and scotch—ha!—the gun-smuggling scheme.

He dipped his quill into the ink again and continued.

I hope this finds you and Mother in your customary good Health. I will stay with a friend tonight as we intend to ride out of town to see a horse he thinks of buying and will be late returning.

Yr most Obedient son,

Alex

Obedient? Well…he tried to be. Mostly.

The second missive, to Jane Stowe, gave him a qualm. Her father, stepmother, and the servants would be shocked if she received a letter from a man, and certainly either her father or stepmother would demand to read it. The poor girl had problems enough without that complication!

He wrote his message, let it dry, and folded the sheet. Then he addressed it in the delicate, rather over-ornate hand that Eliza Fairford had taught his sisters, and sealed both letters with wafers, green for his father and pink for Jane Stowe's.

After a moment, he took another sheet, and wrote,

Now that I am returned to Town, I hope we may meet. For reasons Which I will explain then, I suggest the Mall late tomorrow afternoon. Do not reply to my former lodging as I have been forced to leave it.

A.G.

He sealed and addressed it.

Downstairs, he gave careful instructions to a servant to take the first two letters to the nearest penny-post receiving office at once, and have a porter deliver the third. A shilling would pay the postage and messenger fee and leave a tip sufficient to impress the matter's urgency upon the fellow's memory.

He had not long to contemplate the possibility that the servant had tarried. The shilling had done its work well, and shortly after he went down to supper, a reply came. He ripped it open and read the message at once. Then he hurried through his meal, settled his bill, and sprang up the stairs two at a time to pack his few belongings, then clattered down again to send for a hackney.

****

He was wondering whether anyone would answer his knock when the door finally opened. Jessup said, "Ah, the gentleman to catalog Mr. Markham's library. Mistress Jane Stowe sent word to expect you, sir." He showed no sign of recognizing the unemployed jack-of-all-trades who had shared the servants' dinner. Of course, workingman's attire, a yellow wig, and a different way of speaking made a difference.

The front door opened directly into a room rather than an entry hall. With the shutters up over the windows, the only illumination came from the candlestick in Jessup's hand. By its light, he received an impression of a sparsely furnished parlor paneled in dark oak. The house must date back to the time of James I or before, to Queen Elizabeth.

"I will show you up to a bedchamber, as I understand you will be living in. Will you take some refreshment, sir? Or sup?"

"I have eaten already, thank you."

"The library is next to the guest bedchamber you will occupy, though you will want to wait for daylight to begin work, of course."

"Good. Most convenient. It's kind of your mistress to let me have a bed here. That way I can accomplish more than if I came and went from my lodgings." Not to mention that it would make it far, far easier to communicate with Mistress Jane.

The butler led him through a door into a corridor he recognized from his earlier visit, when he had been taken upstairs to help the maid.

After leaving his valise to be unpacked by Jessup, he browsed the packed shelves in the library long enough to determine that the books were in order by subject, then sat down at the desk to plan how to proceed. As his excuse for being in the Markham house was to catalog the books, catalog them he must, or at least begin the project.

Chapter 13

The Mall was less thronged than usual, as the day threatened rain. Yet in spite of the gray sky, there were saunterers enough that Gordon was inconspicuous when he arrived. He had made a circuit, admiring the vista of trees and lawn, before Warrender appeared. He did not approach Gordon directly but strolled idly until he was nearly even with him and only then affected to notice him.

"Ah, Gordon! The Mall is thin of company today."

"You English worry too much about a little damp—it hasn't even come on to rain yet."

"You were out of town, I believe?" Warrender said. By the time Gordon had agreed and mentioned that his excursion had been very agreeable, they were out of earshot of others.

Warrender's voice changed. "You said it was delivered—did you encounter some check?"

"Not in delivering it. But when I left the shop, I noticed a fellow lingering on the street. I think he followed me back to Town."

"Are you sure? Is he following you yet?"

His tone and a certain loss of color in his face confirmed Gordon's suspicions. "No, to both questions. My animal went lame coming back, and while I was tending to its hoof, a horseman passed me. He came upon me unexpectedly, as I'd halted beyond a bend in the road. It looked like the man I'd seen in Oxford. Then yesterday morning I thought I saw him again outside my inn—which reminds me, I must give you back some of your money, as I returned the same day." Alex reached into his pocket for his purse.

"No, no! Never mind the money, it's a pittance. Keep it against future expenses. Outside your inn, you say?"

"I can't be certain, but he was of much the same height and build. He was very ordinary in appearance." If his watcher were employed by His Majesty's government, he must not identify him to Warrender.

"But you were not followed today?" Warrender asked with barely concealed anxiety.

"I spied him through the window as I breakfasted, so I arranged to keep the room for a few more days, but I slipped out the back and found another lodging."

"That was well done. You did not ask whether I had been followed, but I can assure you, I am not—today, at least. Where can I reach you now?"

"The Two Roses." He would not reveal that he was actually staying elsewhere. He had asked the innkeeper to hold any letters he might receive and made it worth his while to agree.

They walked in silence for a few minutes. As the wind came up and the clouds darkened, people melted away. Warrender said, "Dean was wrong. You're of far more use here than in the prince's army."

"That is good to hear, sir. I confess that Mr. Dean's advice caused me some chagrin."

"Dean is...a very ardent supporter of our king, but he is also an ass. And he cannot hold his liquor. I am rather worried about Dean. I believe I must have one of our more responsible members invite him to stay at his country house." Warrender's tone sent a frisson down Alex's spine. Would Dean enjoy a pleasant form of house arrest or would some accident befall him in rustic surroundings where the local magistrate might be a friend of his host?

Warrender continued, "Your instincts are more valuable than your ability to shoot or wield a sword." He glanced sideways at Alex. "I suppose you *can* do those things as well?"

"Oh, ay. Both small-sword and the Scottish basket-hilted sword. The uncle who brought me up was particular about swordplay. And I've done a good deal of hunting, so I'm a fair shot."

"I do not expect it to come to that. But they're useful skills." He smiled, his first genuine expression of pleasure Alex could recall, and said, "I'll send you word soon. There will be some task for you shortly."

Warrender departed by hackney; Alex left on foot. Evidently, Warrender was satisfied that he was trustworthy. Alex hardly knew whether to be glad or worried as he made his way to Bloomsbury Square. It was time to show himself, lest his father begin to wonder where he was and what he was doing. His mother, who took a remarkably cynical view of the activities of young men, was unlikely to inquire, however curious she might be.

After dressing in one of his better suits, he sought out his father in his bookroom. The elder Lattimer was in expansive spirits and poured him a glass of claret.

"It proves to be a useful thing that you are on such good terms with Jane Stowe," he said. "I passed on the information that her brother had been seen in Town.

The…ah…recipient was duly grateful."

"Is Stowe a suspected Jacobite?"

Anthony Lattimer raised his eyebrows. "I have said as much on this subject as I can. I trust you will not feel obligated to mention it to Mistress Jane."

Which was an order not to do so.

"Kinder not to let her know, in any event, sir." If her brother were arrested and ended on the gallows—surely it would not be the more extreme penalty!—the shock would be sudden and quickly over. If she knew, rather than merely suspected, she might live in fear and uncertainty for weeks or even months. Alex pitied Jane, but he had no sympathy for Rupert Stowe, less because he was probably a traitor than because it must have been he who tried to implicate Jane in Markham's murder.

His father steepled his fingers. "I think I may have misjudged your Jane. I do not like the family's connections on her father's side, and I hope you will take no action until her brother's affair is resolved, but it appears she cannot be involved in any plotting. If she were supporting the Young Pretender, she would certainly never have passed on that list or have told you Stowe had returned to London. Roger Markham was a fine man and a good friend of mine, and he had a high opinion of her. No doubt she takes after that side of the family. Her mother was a very lovely girl, though perhaps too trusting. I fear she paid dearly for it, as I do not think her marriage was a happy one. If in due course you wish to make the young lady an offer of marriage, I believe I should not oppose it."

His father did not mention that Jane's inheritance was another point in her favor. He did not regard marriages based solely on financial gain with approval, but he would certainly consider it an added benefit.

****

Her father had been in unusually good humor for days, and the house benefitted. Even Elvira was less fidgety and anxious, although she did occasionally voice a hope that Mistress Pleasaunce's aunt's servants aired the bedding adequately and did not serve Rupert anything that might disagree with him, and that he might not catch a chill. But she too seemed quite in charity with Jane.

Jane returned from her morning stroll, brief because she had not seen Mr. Gordon and had no shopping to do. In the late morning, a scruffy lad arrived at the kitchen door saying he had a message for Mr. Stowe. He refused to give it to Cook or even Wilson, claiming he'd been promised a shilling on delivery, though he could provide no proof of such a promise, and it was a perfectly exorbitant amount. Without it, Mr. Wilson refused to pay out a shilling "for how would it look in the household accounts, if it proves to be only a trick?" So Jane was asked to decide.

"You could have taken the boy up to my father's study," she pointed out. "He could have decided whether to buy a pig in a poke or—" She peered at the folded, sealed sheet the street urchin held possessively and saw what neither Mrs. Merry or the butler had noticed. Her father's name, although inscribed on the letter in an awkward, back-slanting hand, had undoubtedly been written by Rupert.

"Well, we'll accept it. Wilson, give the boy his shilling."

The exchange of hostages complete, Jane herself

carried it up to her father.

"The boy who brought it wanted a shilling," she said. "I gave it to him."

"Highway robbery," he grumbled, tearing it open. "Who the devil can be—" The sentence broke off.

"I hope it's not bad news, sir?" It should be safe to ask that much. It was always risky to ask her father questions. He had no patience with foolish queries, and he could be very touchy about anything that he took to be criticism of himself.

When he did not respond, she said, "I'll be planning the menus with Cook, if there's anything you want," and turned to go.

"Wait. Sit down, Jane. Don't fidget." He read the letter again, sighed, and then tossed it onto the embers in the fireplace and watched while the sheet caught fire.

Finally, he said, "Rupert has gotten himself into a foolish tangle."

Jane found she felt sick with apprehension, even though she had suspected he was deep in some dangerous matter. "Foolish tangle" seemed a monumental understatement.

"I shall not go into details. You need only know that it involved a young lady and a hot-tempered aspirant to her hand."

Her first, unguarded response would have been, *My goodness, that was quick work on his part.* However, that remark would have earned her a sharp rebuke, so she kept it to herself. She didn't believe it anyway. Her father's lips compressed, as they did when he was thinking hard. "Oh, dear," she murmured prosaically.

"Your brother felt it best to return to London. But when he stopped at an inn to refresh himself and change horses, he espied a fellow he had seen in the West Country beau's company—a hanger-on of some sort. The suitor's father made his fortune in tin mines or some such thing, and this young sprig of a midden heap is said to have an unsavory reputation. Rupert fears he has sent a cutthroat after him."

"I see." She did not believe it for a moment.

He looked annoyed, either at her lack of agitation or as if he sensed her disbelief. She had never learned to counterfeit emotion, only to suppress it.

"He eluded the scoundrel and went to earth in some squalid inn here in town. He is almost out of funds—of course!—and he dare not come home, as the fellow can easily find out his direction, if he does not already know it. If he can but remain hidden for a time, no doubt the pursuit will be discontinued. He cannot have any serious intentions about the girl, who is the daughter of some middling prosperous farmer. Young men will dally with pretty chits. There's no harm in it."

Jane nodded encouragingly.

"Which brings me to your part, Jane. I propose to collect Rupert from his current lair. Would you be so good as to let him stay in your uncle's—I suppose I should say, your—house?"

It was not really a request, though phrased as one. "Why…" Rupert and Alex in the same house, with Alex so very interested in Charles and Rupert's activities? It took her a few seconds too long to answer.

"I do not think it a great favor to ask, and no inconvenience to you, as I think you still have staff in the house? A waste of money, but fortunate in the circumstances."

"Mr. Harris did not disapprove of it. An empty

house might be robbed, and there is still work to be done to ready it to be leased out. Of course Rupert may stay there. In fact, a gentleman is at present cataloging the library, in case there should be some rare volumes worth selling before a tenant moves in." Really, the number of lies she found herself telling of late reflected sadly upon her character.

"The presence of the servants is a convenience with Rupert to be staying there," he allowed. "Thank you, Jane. You're a good, dutiful girl."

Jane smiled dryly. She had found, since recently having her father's approval, that it no longer meant as much to her as it would have when she was a child. She could not remember her own mother; her father had married Elvira within a year of her mother's death. Her stepmother's dislike she understood and it had never bothered her. But her father had never been an affectionate parent, whether because she was not a son or from some anger at her mother, she did not know. It did not matter now.

He went on, "Send to the butler—what's his name, Jessup?—to expect your brother this afternoon. I'll take him there myself."

Chapter 14

Alex received Jane's note, enclosed in the sheet directed to Jessup, with pleasure—until he read it.

...I could not well refuse to let Rupert stay, although I fear it may cause some awkwardness.

There was an understatement!

But perhaps if you and he meet, you may learn something from him by discreet questioning which will assist you.

And exculpate Rupert? Gordon feared she would be disappointed. What was behind Rupert's flight? This tale of a murderous henchman must be pure drivel. It was like something from a play. Had the letter Stowe received told the true story? If so, it was hardly surprising Jane's papa had burned it. Though a man might throw a letter on the fire in a fit of exasperation.

Toward the middle of the afternoon, as he finished listing all the volumes of poetry, he heard a stirring downstairs. He would not take any notice of it; someone who was in the house to perform a presumably paid service would not do so. But it was very hard to turn his mind to cataloging the next section, history, with so much to distract his thoughts.

It might be that Rupert would confine himself to his chamber, like a creature (perhaps a stoat?) hiding from hunters. If he and Rupert never met, he need not worry about discovering some truth which would hurt

Jane. It was too bad it wasn't Charles Pleasaunce come to stay instead. Alex would have had no hesitation about squeezing him for information, like a lemon for juice.

Markham had arranged the house with an eye to what suited him, the needs of a modern gentleman being rather different than those of a tradesman of the previous century. The drawing room, dining room, bookroom, and a spare bedchamber were all on the same floor, so when Alex put aside his pen and list at supper time, he needed only to stroll down the hall to find Rupert.

Alex paused in the door to the drawing room. Stowe, clad in a pale blue coat with a brocade waistcoat of blue and silver, sprawled in a chair, a half-empty decanter on the table beside him and a glass in his hand. His neckcloth was loosened. Alex's nose detected a stronger scent of brandy than could be expected from one glass. Stowe must have been saturating himself with it. He stared at Gordon blankly for a moment before saying, "I'm Stowe. Rupert Stowe. This is m' half sister's house. Inherited it from her uncle. You must be the book fellow. Said someone was, what-do-y'call-it, going through the library. What's your name?" Altogether, a young man on an alcohol-fueled spree.

"Alexander Gordon. Yes, I'm cataloging the books." He added a cool smile and sat down to wait for Jessup to call them to the dining room next door. But for Jane, he would not have found himself in a predicament; he would have sought to draw Rupert out. But he did not want to cause Jane unhappiness, so the less Rupert had to say to him, the better. A hired "book fellow," little above an upper servant, would hardly rate a greeting from a fashionable young man, let alone conversation. To be ignored as beneath notice was agreeable to Alex, especially since at some future date Rupert might meet him in his own identity.

But Rupert kept darting glances at him. "You sound like a gentleman," he mumbled.

"My father is a magistrate in Hampshire. Our family have been gentry there forever."

"What are you doing here?" Stowe peered at him owlishly.

"Cataloging the late Roger Markham's library."

"I mean...working. Like...like..."

"Like a third son with no expectations. Though I do expect to be taken on as confidential secretary to a government minister in the near future." He thought it unnecessary to be more specific, considering the amount of drink Stowe had taken.

"Oh. Well, a gentleman, anyway." Stowe nodded.

In the dining room, the fellow uttered bursts of disjointed observations interspersed by periods of abstracted silence. The weather—a little cool for August? He'd been out of town for a few days. Devilish good to be back, even if not at home. Not a genteel area, this, but a comfortable enough house.

Whatever had brought him back to London, Stowe must be worried. He was drinking heavily and talkative.

"Jessup! Brandy in the drawing room."

Jessup murmured, "Very good, sir."

"We'll sit there a while." Stowe stood up, leaning on the table to steady himself, and shambled out of the room.

He cast himself into an armchair with a sigh as Jessup entered with a bottle and two glasses on a tray.

Stowe tossed off half his glass as soon as it was poured but did not speak until Jessup had left the room, rolling the glass back and forth between his palms. Alex had said very little during the evening, only answering questions and occasionally making encouraging noises. His desire to spare Jane grief for her brother warred with his memory of Grandfather Gordon's tales of the Highland Host of 1678, and the daunting prospect of a similar army supplied with 2500 muskets. Rupert might be beyond his aid. He asked sympathetically, "Troubles?"

"Oh, God! Yes!" Stowe burst out. He did not continue.

Alex waited until he was sure Stowe would not go on unprompted. "Would talking about it help?"

Rupert Stowe poured himself another glass of brandy. "I don't see how. I-I lost some money."

"Cards or dice?"

"Both."

"And of course since it's a debt of honor, you must settle up. I know it's very hard to admit something like that to one's father. They always roar so. But on the other hand, they always come through, in my experience." Not that he himself had ever had to ask his papa to pay such a debt, thank God! "One can't let one's son be known for reneging on a gaming debt. Or sometimes it's possible to borrow on the expectation of inheriting, though I don't recommend it unless...ah, inheritance is imminent. The interest would be ruinous in the long run."

Stowe gazed at him blearily. "It's worse than that. Can't tell m'father. Never understand. It's not a gaming debt. Worse."

"Extortion?"

Stowe shook his head and apparently found it a mistake. He looked so green, Gordon wondered whether he should help him to the window before he was sick. Happily, the queasiness seemed to pass off. After a moment, Stowe said, "I gambled with someone else's money. I thought I was sure to win, and then I'd have the money he entrusted to me to…to…well, it's not important. And I'd have some extra for m'self. Can't go to m'father to make it good. I'm a dead man." He dropped his head in his hands and groaned.

"Surely your friend wouldn't challenge you? No doubt he'll be angry but to duel over a monetary matter? No, really, Stowe, no gentleman would do so. He'll simply have to give you time to pay him back."

"Won't be a duel. Worse. Much worse. 'M afraid he already knows. Saw a fellow following me. There's no time, either. Need to have the money in…ummm…what day is this?"

"Tuesday. Almost Wednesday, now."

"…three…four…five days. Have to have it by Monday night."

"That's not impossible," Alex said. "It gives you a little time to raise the money."

"No, because I have to deliver it in the north. Up in Scotland."

"Perhaps I can help." Alex took a slow sip from his almost untouched glass.

Stowe raised his head and muttered, "Don't know what anyone can do."

"Er…how much money do you need?"

"Eight hundred pounds." He groaned again.

"Hmmm. It could be worse. I might be able to find

a way to get it."

"You?" Incredulously.

"I might be able to raise it. We could work something out. What's it for, if it's not a gaming debt?"

"Can't tell you. Shhhecret. Need money to get there, too."

"Ah. Well, even so. You should go to bed. In the morning, I'll see what I can do."

"No hope for it. Have to die, that's all. Not as if I don't have a couple of brothers."

"Don't die tonight. I'll help you upstairs now. No, don't take the brandy with you. You'll need a clear head in the morning." Or as clear as Rupert's head ever was, he supposed.

****

"I believe I instructed you not to pursue the Stowe matter—the political Stowe matter, that is—any further," Anthony Lattimer said austerely the next morning, when Alex told him he had additional information about Rupert Stowe's activities. He had left Markham's house early, to catch his father at breakfast. The footman had been dismissed when Alex murmured that he had a matter to discuss. He helped himself to cold beef and pickle and took a reviving draught of coffee.

"It was the purest chance that I encountered him, sir. He was worried, drunk as a sow, and fairly panting to pour it all out to a sympathetic listener."

His father gave a bark of laughter. "It's odd how often you find yourself in such situations, Alex. Is it the behavior of a gentleman to let another gentleman incriminate himself? It's not as if you were a magistrate."

"He's Mistress Jane's brother, and given the way his nerves were all to pieces and he was trying to settle them with drink, I supposed his trouble was what you'd expect of a man of three-and-twenty. Gaming debts or bills he couldn't pay, even a predatory courtesan. The Stowes are not fabulously wealthy, after all. When I realized it appeared to involve that other thing, it was too late to extricate myself. Besides, can a gentleman stand by when he learns a crime is afoot? What were you and Mr. Markham doing in Scotland in 1715?"

"Never mind that now. I grant you it was a difficult position to find yourself in. You have now performed your duty, and we must let those who are paid to do it manage the rest. How did you happen to be at Markham's anyway?"

"I was looking at some of the books in the library on Mistress Jane's behalf. There might be some rare volume worth selling. Naturally, when Rupert came to stay—hiding from his creditors, as I believed—we met."

"Naturally." Dryly.

"Perhaps you know, sir. Was some government agent watching Rupert? Or can it have been someone of Pleasaunce's? It affects what plan I suggest."

His father gave him a satirical look. "I don't know why you think your opinion will be consulted. Though since you have talked with the young viper..." After a longish pause, he went on. "As it happens, I knew Stowe was being kept under observation. They lost his trail the day before yesterday. They can pick it up again now, of course."

"I think perhaps it won't be necessary, sir. I have an idea."

"When you were younger, I learned to dread that phrase. You never got into ordinary mischief. What is it this time?"

"I think I can extricate Stowe and prevent the delivery of the weapons—assuming this is about the weapons, for why else deliver money to Scotland?—if you can make certain arrangements, sir."

"I would not give a groat to save Stowe's soul. I suppose I can guess why you wish to do so."

"It's not because of Mistress Jane, sir. Not solely because of her, anyway. I think he's too stupid to be a full partner in it. An innocent? No. Harmless without a stronger personality to push him? Yes."

His father grunted. "I hope Mistress Jane appreciates your championing her scapegrace brother."

"Only a half brother, sir. Thank God."

It required all his arts of persuasion, but his father finally assented to his plan. Or plans: he had an alternative, in case the better of the two proved to be unworkable, though it seemed unwise to mention that possibility. "I will need to know as soon as possible if you've persuaded your friends in the government to agree. Because of the travel, you know."

"Oh, they'll agree." His father smiled, but it was more than half a grimace. "Come, we will pay a call on those who can facilitate the matter."

****

Alex returned to Wych Street in the early afternoon from a long and rather confusing appointment at Somerset House. There, his father had left him in a plain, scantly furnished room for near an hour. Then he was taken to another room where—of all things he had expected—a tailor took his measurements, mumbling under his breath, "It will do me no credit, nor you neither, but no help for it. Mind you bring another suit. You'll need it, as this will never fit, after..." He had been conducted to another room to wait yet again. Finally, his father returned and bore him off, saying, "A case marked 'books' will be delivered to Markham's house late this afternoon. Tell the servants to expect it. Open it immediately, in private. It will contain instructions, including your travel arrangements, and...er...other things."

To his inquiry, Jessup reported Rupert had not yet left his chamber.

"Mr. Rupert does not possess a hard head for drink," the butler observed dispassionately.

"When he stirs, let me know, please. Oh, and I'm expecting a delivery, and I'll want that as soon as it comes."

Gordon beguiled the time by repacking his valise, then attempting to continue his work in the library, though without much success. He began a letter to his father, leaving space to fill in the details he did not yet possess.

When Jessup came to let him know Stowe had rung for tea and toast, he hastily put the letter aside. He found Rupert sitting slumped in bed, wrapped in a banyan, dispiritedly nibbling toast between sips of tea.

"We must talk."

Rupert raised bloodshot eyes. "Oh. It's you...what's your name, again?"

"Alexander Gordon, at your service. Ah...do you remember last night?"

"...did I talk? About anything?"

"You told me you'd lost the money a friend

entrusted to you to pay for something."

Something that sounded like a moan escaped him. "Oh, damn it all to hell." Stowe closed his eyes.

"You were in despair. Does the situation look less dire this morning?"

Stowe pushed the tray aside. "No."

"And you're sure your father can't help you?"

"My God, no. He'd disown me. And Ch—my friend will murder me. If I could borrow enough money to buy passage to the Colonies…but how would I live there? I haven't a penny of my own."

Stowe's father had helped him hide, but if he were aware of the plot, and he'd had any suspicion of the kind of trouble Rupert was in, he would surely have paid the money to save the plan—if it were the muskets this muddle involved. *Remember to add that to the letter.*

"May I ask how your friend came to entrust this, ah, transaction to you? It seems a great imposition on a friend."

"He had a…a family obligation that took him to Plymouth. The shipment was arranged before we left, but then the shipper wanted more money. Someone had to meet the ship and deliver the payment to the captain. As my friend could not leave his business in Plymouth, he asked me to act for him. And now I haven't the money. He'll kill me if I can't get the cargo."

"He may be very angry, of course, but he'll hardly murder you," Alex said bracingly.

"You don't understand. I'm a dead man if he finds me, I tell you."

"If that's so, I believe I can't let you be done to death. I may be able to help you."

"Can you? How?"

"I think I can get the money."

"If you could—!"

Alex saw the beginnings of hope, suddenly dashed.

"But I would still have to arrive in time to meet the ship. If I hadn't lost the money, and my own, too, I would have had time to get there. Assuming I could afford to change horses, I still might not be able to make it before the cargo arrives."

"I know of a skipper who intends to take his schooner north. If we went with him, we could be there in time. Faster to sail than to go by road."

"You'd help me?"

"Yes."

"You could arrange my passage as well as get me the money?" What a good thing Rupert was so gullible, he did not think to ask how a man who was cataloging a library might be able to lay hands on such a sum.

"I can. I've made provisional arrangements with the ship's master. He's almost ready to sail from a small harbor well downstream—to avoid the adverse winds often met with on the river. We will have to hire horses and leave early tomorrow morning."

Rupert looked momentarily perplexed. *Not sure whether he wants to prevent me from witnessing his very dubious business or wants me to go with him to hold his hand*, Alex guessed. The latter won.

"But your work here? Can you leave it?"

"Oh, I think Mistress Jane won't object, since I'll be aiding her brother."

"She must not know!"

"Then I'll tell her I have a family crisis to attend to. There's no great hurry about the cataloging."

He left Rupert to his own devices then and wrote a carefully composed letter to Jane, to be left with the butler, of which the most important line was, "I have been called away to deal with that family problem of which we spoke, and I hope to have news of its satisfactory conclusion in a few days." After a moment's perplexed thought, he added a hasty postscript.

Chapter 15

As they ate dinner the first day, the *Lark*'s captain said, "Your friend is no sailor."

"He'd had a bit to drink before we came on board," Alex explained. Rupert was laid on his bunk recovering from both the brandy and the nausea that struck him almost as soon as they sailed. Alex chewed a mouthful of beef stewed with turnip and onion. "His stomach is a trifle uneasy."

"Are you always this bad on the water?" Alex had inquired during one of Rupert's periods of consciousness.

"Don't know. Never been on a boat but to cross the Thames to Vauxhall Gardens. The last few days I've been dipping a little deep, too."

"Sick as a wench who's increasing, is he? Is it drink or the sea?" Captain Sykes asked.

"Both, I think. He was drunk to insensibility the day before yesterday, then fortified himself somewhat before we boarded today. The action of the waves has not helped."

By way of comment, the table-sized board, suspended by ropes at the corners, swayed. Evidently, it could be hauled up to the ceiling to make more floor space when not in use, turning the officers' mess into the officers' common room. The captain and first mate sat at the head and foot of the table, on chairs. The second mate and Alex sat on sea chests at the long sides. The *Lark*, a small two-masted schooner, had only a captain and first and second mates for officers. The five crewmen and the cook had their own mess, but it would not be crowded, as one or two of them would be on duty while the others ate.

"He would be the better for food." Sykes took a long swallow of beer.

"Stowe did not feel he could manage it, sir."

"Too bad, for we're eating like lords. That's the advantage of coasting. We can take on fresh provisions in port, and it's money well spent, for we sailors like our food. In the Navy and on long voyages, one lives on salt beef, salt pork, ship's biscuit, dried peas, and oatmeal. Tomorrow, perhaps the men will catch a few fish for our dinner. For today, I will have the cook send Stowe a tumbler of brandy and some ship's biscuit. That is always settling to the stomach."

If they were not eating like lords, as the captain avowed, accommodations on the *Lark* were at least better than expected. He and Rupert each had a tiny cabin, barely big enough in which to dress, with a narrow bed against the bulkhead and cabinets above and below. The first mate had one, also, and the captain had a larger cabin. The second mate, cook, and seamen slept in hammocks in one room (if that was what one called a space on a ship) with their belongings stowed in sea chests. Below deck was confined and dim, illuminated only by whatever light came through the portholes and from candle lanterns. At least it was warm, compared to the deck, where the wind cut like a dagger of ice.

"When do you think we'll reach St. Andrews,

Captain?"

"We're making good time. Sunday afternoon, as we're going." Alex was glad for the captain's conversation, not that the man said more than he needed to. The crew were civil but discouraged conversation. However, they kept a very clean, disciplined ship. The *Lark* was fast, too, with a shallow draft for coastal waters, making it an excellent choice for a ship which might pick up freight or passengers at places not thought of as ports.

The instructions which had come in that crate innocently marked "books" implied they were simply a ship and crew for hire to carry whatever cargoes they could get. Discretion required him to pretend to believe it, though the instructions in the packet (conspicuously marked *Most Secret*) also advised him the captain was aware of their mission and might be trusted. Alex wished he had been able to question the source of the instructions about the latter, but there had been no time and no signature. The other letter had been sealed with a thick red wax seal. His instructions were to carry it on his person at all times, and "present it to any Lawful Authority in the event of serious Difficulties."

"Do you know anything about the place? I suppose there's an inn? Or some old woman who takes in travelers?"

"There are inns. It was once a thriving town. It won't matter which you choose, *he*"—the captain jerked his chin in the direction of their cabins—"won't like it. One piece of counsel I can give you."

"I'd be glad of it."

"You came aboard plainly dressed, and that will do well. I would suggest you conduct yourselves as grave as curates, as there's a mort of very fierce Presbyterians there. I believe they take the Sabbath seriously. Ah, and mayhap the landlord will invite you to dine at his own table. It's a custom some of them have, of a Sunday."

"We will certainly heed your advice, sir."

****

Rupert had still not emerged the following day, except presumably for brief visits to the deck. He had managed to avoid meeting Alex.

When Alex visited him in his cabin, he was either asleep or too ill to talk.

Sykes offered to show Alex a map to assist in planning his and Stowe's trip. As he was sure the captain knew their visit was not merely a tour of picturesque countryside, Alex accepted the invitation to the captain's cabin. It was far enough from Rupert's cabin that there was no chance of being overheard.

"We will be putting in at Leith later today," the captain said.

They were bent over a fairly detailed map spread out on the captain's desk. "Near Edinburgh," Alex agreed.

"You've done fine, portraying a feckless young gentleman off to see North Britain, Mr. Gordon. Now we must make plans. At Leith, I have a little cargo to unload. At the same time, it will be necessary to send a message to the garrison with the final destination of your companion's cargo."

"That is rather a difficulty, Captain."

"Is it?" Sykes looked at him in a way that reminded Alex of various headmasters—or his papa.

"Stowe has not told me where the shipment is to go."

Sykes straightened. "You don't know where it's going?"

"I believed he would confide in me before this." Seeing that the captain was bereft of speech, he added, "There were reasons why..." He let it trail off. He could not think of any reason that the Spy Office, as he thought of the department which had arranged passage to St. Andrews, would have done so without knowing in advance where to spring the trap. In his letter to his father, Alex had implied that Stowe was waiting for word as to the muskets' disposition; perhaps they had believed it.

"There's always some reason for the most crackbrained scheme." The captain sighed. "Stowe has hardly stirred from his bed. It might be sickness or it might be to avoid talking to you."

"I fear it is the latter, sir."

Sykes drummed his fingers on the map. "Well, the place is likely somewhere near St. Andrews." He peered at the bulge of land between the Firth of Forth and the Firth of Tay. "It will be too late to send to the garrison at Edinburgh if we do not do it when we dock at Leith. One of my men who goes ashore will hand off a message to be delivered to the garrison. We can but choose a place for the dragoons to wait for word and hope we do not hit too near the mark."

"I realize not knowing where the arms are to be delivered makes planning difficult—"

Sykes's explosive laugh took him by surprise. "These things seldom go exactly as planned. My command, thank God, is not quite as hidebound as the Navy. We shall do well enough, I think."

****

They had lain at anchor overnight to approach St. Andrew's in daylight. Alex listened to the water purl and hiss around the ship's bow, watching for the first sight of the town. He found he was not overfond of shipboard life. Thank God he had not taken it into his head to run away to sea!

An hour or two after the captain had read the Sunday service and the men scattered to their tasks, Sykes came up beside him. "The two spires there belong to the old cathedral. They and the square tower of St. Rule's are a useful landmark as the bay can be dangerous. Ridges of rock run out from the shore, and a ship driven upon them in an easterly wind is lost. But we'll have no trouble today. Have you had any success yet?"

"No."

"Ah. Well, if your smuggler is not yet here, perchance you'll have a day or two to work on the matter. If you learn where the cargo is to go, get word to me, and I will pass it on."

"Captain, what if I have to contact the authorities myself? My instructions did not include any information as to who should be apprised in St. Andrews."

"I can give you no local contact. Don't worry about it overmuch. Stowe may tell you where the cargo is to go once you are ashore, and you will pass the word to me. Or one of my men will find out when the goods are taken off the smuggler's ship. The carters will know where they're going, after all. Either way, I will send word on to the fishing village where the lobsterbacks will be waiting."

The captain's calm good sense was reassuring.

"Good. I suppose those receiving the muskets cannot intend to take them far, for fear of detection."

"More because of Scotland's roads than for fear of being caught," Sykes said. "There are garrisons in the north and one at Edinburgh Castle, but there's not much military presence apart from those. With the war on the Continent…" He let the thought trail off.

That explained a great deal. The soothing newspaper pronouncements about how the Young Pretender's ragtag army would fade away might be merely optimism, or they might be meant to prevent panic in England.

****

Stowe came up on deck when they docked, pasty-faced but not unwell. "We'll have to find lodging," Alex said. "The captain told me of an inn—"

Stowe said, "We will stay at the Star. It came highly recommended by a friend."

As they disembarked, Captain Sykes wished them a pleasant stay in Scotland. He added jovially, "There's a Scotch game they play hereabouts called golf. They hit a little ball around with a stick. I've a mind to try it myself, if we stay long enough."

"Oh…are you not going on now?" Stowe asked. "I thought you were sailing farther north."

"There's one or two little matters I want to see repaired before sailing. And I hope to take on a cargo here. I suppose you gentlemen will be hiring horses to continue your tour?"

"Yes. I suppose the Star Inn can direct us to a livery stable," Alex replied. "We would not wish to be shut up in a coach in such fine weather."

Sykes grinned and remarked brutally, "It's fine

140

weather now, to be sure. But when it changes, you can shelter in some public house or cottage, if there chances to be one nearby."

His first impression was of a gray town—houses of fieldstone with dressed stone framing the doors and windows. Captain Sykes's remarks about St. Andrews had led Alex to expect ramshackle buildings and an air of depression and poverty. Yet though the buildings must be of some age—St. Andrews's prosperity had declined well over a century ago, according to Sykes— they seemed more solid than London houses of similar antiquity. Being built of stone, they showed their age less than timber and plaster and did not appear as ancient as some in London, in Wych Street, for example.

As they walked, Alex asked, "What are the arrangements for meeting the ship?"

"I'm to wait at the Star until they've docked."

Alex chewed his lower lip.

The inn proved to be a respectable one, if only moderately comfortable. Dinner was spent in the company of the innkeeper and the other guests, as the captain had predicted. Alex found the experience interesting. He asked the questions an Englishman visiting Scotland for the first time would be expected to ask and enjoyed the sound of Lowlands Scots. Rupert was rather silent. Afterward, they strolled up North Street, then down South Street for some welcome exercise after their confined shipboard quarters. Perhaps "strolled" was not quite the right word. "Reeled" more nearly conveyed the gait that resulted from their brief voyage on a vessel her skipper described as "lively." Alex had an additional cause for unbalance. This must be how ladies far gone in pregnancy felt.

Afterward, they went to Rupert's bedchamber, there being no private parlor available for rent. Either customs were different in Scotland or the inn did not cater to finical guests. Alex could not imagine most English gentry sitting down to dinner with the innkeep, but he could imagine very vividly the reaction of English gentlefolk to such an invitation.

Rupert commenced to pace. He was clearly nervous but refused Alex's suggestion that they order brandy. Either he still felt queasy or he had enough sense to realize he must be sober for the ship's arrival. Eventually, he sat and became lost in thought, turning down the offer of a game of cards.

"What is this cargo, anyway? Do you have to store it or send it on?"

Rupert shrugged. "All that is arranged. Nothing for me to do except deliver the payment." He ignored Alex's first question. The near-panic he'd shown in London seemed to be gone now that he could believe he would succeed in securing the shipment. When not under stress, Rupert Stowe might pass as a man with a backbone.

"This seems a prodigious inconvenient port at which to receive a shipment."

Stowe twitched. "Ah…my friend owns a small property nearby. There's furnishings needed."

"I see. It would not make sense to ship them overland, then."

"No. No, it wouldn't," Rupert agreed.

****

When they walked out after dinner the next

afternoon, he saw that the *Sea Mew* had made port.

Like the *Lark*, it was a schooner, though rather larger. Gordon heard his companion draw in his breath sharply when he saw the vessel's name. His own heart beat faster. He must not reveal that he knew anything of the *Sea Mew* and its captain.

"That's a fine-looking ship." A fair-haired man his own age or a little less stood in the bow, hands on hips, grinning and shouting orders to several of the tars. Alex could not see his eyes but guessed they were blue as sapphire.

"Yes." Rupert added, "Ships are best admired from a distance, I find. The only voyage I look forward to with pleasure is the one across the Channel to France, when we can visit France again. I suppose you have never seen Paris? I intend to do so, once we are no longer at war. I'm told it's marvelous sophisticated—London is to Paris as some provincial town is to London." He prattled on, spending more words than Alex had heard from him since his drunken confidences in Town. Alex smiled agreeably and made encouraging noises at intervals. Stowe meant to distract his attention from the *Sea Mew*.

They came to the *Lark*, farther on, its crew bustling about. Sykes was standing at the rail; when he saw them, he gave a curt nod, which Stowe civilly returned. Alex grinned and gave the captain a little salute.

"You're no military man, I see," Sykes called out.

"No, sir. According to my father, I'm a good-for-naught and a scapegrace."

The captain barked a laugh and turned away to call some unintelligible seafaring command to one of the men.

Rupert's flow of chat dried up before they returned to the Star Inn some time later. He agreed to play piquet but did so absentmindedly. *Not a man I would choose as a fellow conspirator. He has no acting ability.*

Abruptly, after supper, Stowe announced that he meant to go out for some fresh air. He clearly did not want company and was trying to think of a reason for Alex not to come with him. Obligingly, Alex yawned and murmured, "Oh…ay? I got my fill of Scots air earlier. I mean to read the *Scots Magazine* I bought."

Rupert departed, and Alex made no attempt to follow him. He was tolerably sure he knew where Rupert was going. The young idiot could not pay the captain of the *Sea Mew* without getting the money from him. It must be a preliminary visit to appoint a time for Stowe to bring the final payment.

Stowe returned sooner than Alex had expected. The *Sea Mew*'s captain could not have offered him refreshment as he had not been gone long enough to drink a leisurely glass with his host. Would they have tossed off a tumbler of spirits by way of celebrating the bargain? He would expect a smuggler coming from France to have at least a cask of good brandy which would call for sipping.

Rupert greeted him with a jerky nod and stood just inside the door as if undecided. He reopened the door at a brisk double tap to admit a servant with a bottle and two glasses. While the man's back was turned to set out the glasses and bottle on the table, Rupert cleared his throat to catch Alex's attention, raised his eyebrows inquiringly, and held out his hand.

Ah. He needed to tip the waiter and had no money—or preferred not to spend whatever coin he possessed. Alex dug in his own pocket and tossed Rupert a penny. He passed it on to the waiter, looking somewhat embarrassed. The waiter, after a discreet glance, thanked him and begged the gentleman not be slow to ask for anything else he might need.

"I thought it too small a gratuity, but he seemed pleased with it." Rupert gave Alex a glass and subsided into the other chair.

Alex looked at him over the top of the magazine. "Well he might. Scots money is worth only one-twelfth of ours."

"You gave him the equivalent of a Scotch shilling! No wonder he was pleased." Rupert laughed. The light-hearted moment was only that, a moment. Then Rupert recalled his cares and took a swallow of brandy.

Alex returned to his reading.

"Ah…Gordon…"

Alex looked up.

"The ship I have been waiting for has come in. I must have the money. It is too late in the day for the wagons to set out, but I have sent a message to the carter to be ready in the morning."

"Very good. What time shall we deliver it?"

Rupert stared into his glass. For all he had ordered the bottle of brandy (which the government was paying for), he had not finished his first glass. "About tomorrow…I think I should visit the ship alone. The captain expects me. If you come along, he may think it odd."

"Then in the morning you can take this damned uncomfortable corset." Fourteen pounds of golden guineas, double or triple layers sewn compactly into a canvas girdle that reached from his waist to chest, made

Alex bulky through the torso and gave him a round belly. The tailor at Somerset House had supplied him with a coat, waistcoat, and breeches, as his own clothing would not button over it. He would be exceeding glad to be rid of the corset; after wearing it next his skin continually for days, he was sure he had guinea-shaped impressions on his body. It was also hot and itchy. He wondered how Rupert could safely transport it. He was slighter than Alex, and it certainly would not fit under his clothing. He could carry it in a valise or box, but Gordon could easily envision the jackanapes dropping it in the harbor when he crossed the gangboard to the *Sea Mew*. Well, they would have to risk it.

"You could give it to me tonight. It would save time in the morning." Rupert did not sound optimistic.

"Better to leave it until you are ready to go. No one suspects its presence now, whereas when I go to my room, someone might notice the plump Englishman has lost bulk suddenly and wonder." He would not trust Rupert with the money any farther than the distance between the inn and the *Sea Mew*, even though Rupert could hardly abscond with the gold tonight. "You'll have to carry it in your portmanteau tomorrow."

Rupert nodded, looked longingly at the bottle, and put down his glass.

"I'm for bed, Stowe. Would you like me to take the brandy? You'll want an early start in the morning."

"I expect that's a good idea. Take it."

Doubts his ability to abstain from it, or hopes I will drink deep and be in no condition to hinder him. And there had been no way to gain his confidence and persuade him to report the muskets.

Alex left him at the end of the street the next morning and watched Stowe stride away, swinging the valise jauntily. Rupert intended to see the wagons loaded before returning to the inn, an unexpected show of responsibility, but useful.

"I mean to explore the ruins," Alex had told him. "They are said to be worth viewing." And on the way, he would pause to send a message to Captain Sykes, although he suspected it would be redundant. The captain and his crew did not miss much and would have seen Stowe go aboard the previous day.

He walked back the way he had come, then continued past the end of North Street to the ruins of the old castle that had been the bishop's residence before the Reformation. The façade was impressive, but Alex had seen the side of the castle that rose up from the sea, which was grim enough to give one nightmares. It had been a prison as well as the bishop's palace. He walked a little farther then went through a wynd or narrow lane to return to North Street.

There, he paused to gaze at the medieval buildings of St. Salvator's College. The chapel was a graceful thing, though it had suffered defacement at the hands of reformers. The niches set into the buttresses would once have held the statues of saints. Stained-glass windows would have filled the interior of the chapel with glowing colors—at least when the sun was shining—before the Protestant reformers vandalized them out of existence. As he gazed at the tower, a thin-lipped, dour man informed him that one Patrick Hamilton, a member of the university, had been burned outside St. Salvator's in 1528.

"And it was but eighteen years later that George

Wishart, another martyr, was burned. Cardinal Beaton, the de'il who ordered it, was murdered soon thereafter and hung from the castle wall like a side o' beef. And is burning in hell now, I am sure."

A bloody-minded race, the Scots, with long memories, as he knew from his Scottish grandparents' tales, though they themselves had not been extreme in their views. Gordon wondered idly whether it was the religious temper of the town or the difficult approach to the harbor that caused the *Sea Mew*'s captain to insist on more pay.

He idled through the spacious cathedral grounds and admired its twin spires and the tower of St. Rule. After a while, he emerged through an opening in the broken wall. A short walk took him to a point from which he could see wagons pulled up beside the *Sea Mew*. In addition to a freight dray, there were several farm wagons. They must intend to take all the cargo in one trip, rather than having to return for a second or third load. That was how he would have planned it, to allow less chance of discovery. Heavily laden wagons could not move as fast as a coach, which might travel five miles an hour, or more if it were light, well made, and the roads good. As the dray pulled away, a crane was already hoisting a crate over the side of the ship and down onto the next wagon. He made out the markings on some of the stout wooden crates on the dray: *Boiseries*. That would be decorative wood paneling. Fireplace surrounds and the like. Other crates bore the names *Martin Frères* and *Charles Cressent, Ébéniste*. *Ébéniste* meant cabinetmaker. If the contents were as marked, their destination would be furnished in the latest style. A little indiscreet to use French cabinetmakers' crates.

A sailor paused to puff on a clay pipe and admire the sight of work going forward. He muttered, "Our Jem's heard the cargo is to go to a house some ten miles west, on the way to Cupar. Bought within the year by an Englishman."

"Do you know his name?"

"Pleasant, or some such thing, they say."

"Has Captain Sykes taken any action?"

"He's sent a man to the dragoons as are standing by."

"Thank you. And thank Captain Sykes on my behalf."

"Ay." The tar ambled off down the street.

Alex continued his tour of the town in a fit of abstraction. He was almost surprised the affair was over, but for the arrival of the troops to capture the cargo and arrest anyone in the house. His part and Stowe's was complete; it would be wise to leave St. Andrews as soon as possible. They had made no plans, not knowing when the *Sea Mew* would arrive. The *Lark*'s remaining in port to make repairs had been meant to give them time to meet the *Sea Mew*, with the idea that they would then go back aboard, apparently to sail farther north but in reality to return to London. There was no need to wait about longer and every reason to go. All the same...He ought to feel satisfied with the outcome. He had persuaded Rupert to trust him somewhat and betrayed Rupert's errand to the proper authorities, not that he regretted doing so. The thought of good muskets in the hands of Highlanders and Jacobites did not bear thinking of. But he had hoped to persuade him to turn Crown evidence, saving him from prosecution. Jane would be heartsick if the fool were punished as he deserved.

He toyed with the idea of hiring a horse and riding out in the direction of Cupar. Charles Pleasaunce would not be there. Surely he would have met the ship with the additional payment rather than entrusting the work to Rupert Stowe. If he had known Rupert long, he must be aware of his weakness of character. Or would he? Rupert was the follower to Pleasaunce's leader. Maybe the strength of his character had never been tested before, leaving Pleasaunce to believe him a reliable subordinate. With no stress upon him and no opportunity to make free with someone else's money, he must appear no less reliable than any other young man of good family. Alex admitted to himself he had not seen Rupert at his best.

He rejected the idea of riding out to look at the house on the Cupar road. If the conspirators should see him and take fright, the dragoons' raid might be jeopardized. Worse, the Jacobites might be able to transfer the cargo to some other location. This was a perfect occasion to heed his father's instruction to leave the job to those paid to do it.

It was midafternoon when Rupert returned to the inn. Alex had been trying to calculate how many wagonloads the muskets would fill, given that one was a freight dray pulled by a pair of Shire horses and the others were farm carts, drawn by one or two horses. If one horse could pull a load of a thousand pounds.... But Shire horses—or whatever the Scottish equivalent was called—could pull amazing heavy loads. The law regarding legal freight loads would not necessarily apply in Scotland, which had its own laws. The limiting factor was more likely to be the wagons and the roads than the horses. Why had his schoolmasters never set them arithmetical problems which might have been of some practical use? He might have paid more attention.

Stowe entered, looking hot and rather anxious. "Gordon, I think I must ride out to my friend's house and make sure his new furnishings are safely bestowed. I shall be staying there a few days." He rushed on, "I would be glad of your company, but I can hardly invite you in my friend's absence, and with the renovations in progress and only two or three servants to act as caretakers, the house will be in turmoil. And no doubt you will wish to return to your employment."

"I see. But would it not be better to lodge at an inn nearby? I misdoubt the servants will be able to give you a tolerable dinner or well-aired bedding, with repairs in progress and the owner not in residence."

"Oh, well," said Stowe airily, "It can hardly be worse than the accommodations on shipboard. Ah…how do you mean to travel back to London?"

"I believe I will hire a horse, rather than be packed into a stage coach, like salt cod in a keg. A ship would be best, but St. Andrews appears not to be a busy port."

"A capital notion. No doubt I'll see you back in Town."

Alex smiled a little at Stowe's evident relief, while thinking, *Now how the devil am I to drag the fool clear of this?*

Chapter 16

"Papa?" She slipped into his study and closed the door behind her.

"What is it, Jane?" Her father looked up from the litter of tradesmen's bills on his desk. One of the bills was from a fashionable perfumer. The amount made her wince.

"I've just come from Uncle Markham's house—"

"Your house now, my dear."

"Yes, of course. Were you aware Rupert has left for Scotland?"

Evidently not, to judge from her father's blank stare. "Scotland? How's this?"

On reading the message Mr. Gordon had left for her, she had at first been at a loss to know what to do. Not that he had asked her to take any action immediately or hinted at what he must have suspected, but really! Obviously, this sudden journey must be connected to the importation of those muskets for…call it criminal purposes.

She had decided she must mention Rupert's absence because, if her father had known of his plans, it would have seemed very peculiar if she had said nothing. Even if he were unaware of Rupert's activities, when he eventually learned of Rupert's absence, she would have to explain why she had not told him and how could she? It would be necessary to reveal

Rupert's involvement in some mad scheme involving smuggled muskets and her own meetings with Mr. Gordon. No, impossible! Her father might well not believe in Rupert's misdeeds, but he would surely censure her own behavior. Yet how could she have done other than assist Mr. Gordon?

"I learned he had left when I went there to make a list of draperies and bed curtains that must be replaced. Some of them are very old and worn," she added.

"But why?"

"The house will fetch a better rent if the hangings—" She faltered a little at the last word, and cleared her throat to cover it. "—are not faded and worn thin."

"I mean, why go to Scotland?" her papa rapped out.

"He did not tell the staff nor leave me any message. Could he have believed the fellow who was following him had discovered his whereabouts and thought it best to flee?"

"Good God, he could be lying dead in an alley!"

"Oh, I don't think so, sir, as he took with him the gentleman hired to catalog the library."

"What use would some cursed librarian be to him?"

"Mr. Gordon appears to have a good deal of common sense and to be quite athletic. At the least, if Rupert were attacked and murdered, Mr. Gordon would report it to us. It's more likely yet he would be able to thwart such an attempt."

"You seem to know a great deal about the fellow." Her father's brows drew together in suspicion.

"Mr. Harris brought him to Wych Street when I

was present, thinking it proper I should know who he had hired. I formed my opinion of him then. I believe Mr. Gordon has relatives in Scotland. Perhaps he suggested some place of safety there." How she hoped Papa never mentioned Alex to Mr. Harris, who would be surprised to hear he had hired anyone to catalogue the library.

"Jane, I hardly think Scotland can be considered a refuge. Mayhap you do not know it, but there is a good deal of unrest there at the moment."

"I had heard something of Highland clans gathering. It's said some expect war."

"Rebellion," he corrected, repressively.

"Would Rupert know it?"

"In fact, he did. He mentioned it a month or two past." Her father snorted, and added dryly, "Young men are always excited by such things."

"That is no doubt why so many of them are eager to don a uniform and take arms."

"I am sure your mama has told you gentlemen do not care for young ladies to display too much perception."

Stepmama.

"Papa, if a gentleman is disgusted by a young lady's intelligence, the young lady is better off not to engage his interest."

"A sensible young lady does not display her intelligence—if she has any! Her place in life is to make her husband and family comfortable, not to air her opinions. Claire Pleasaunce is a pattern of feminine behavior. You should try to emulate her. However! I am extremely concerned about Rupert. To go to Scotland—and drag your librarian fellow along—is very strange. Though if you are correct, Gordon may be some protection. I don't suppose Rupert or he had the wit to mention to the servants where in Scotland they were going."

She dared not admit knowing they were bound for St. Andrews. Papa would surely not gallop off to Scotland in pursuit...but he might mention Rupert's destination to his good friend, Mr. Pleasaunce. It seemed unwise to share her knowledge.

"No, sir."

"Well, I would as soon he were not in London, if he is in the right about this cutthroat pursuing him. I expect he'll do well enough and have a little adventure for entertainment." Jane recognized this as her father's attempt to convince himself.

A little adventure, indeed.

It occurred to her suddenly that she should not have mentioned Gordon. If her father should repeat it to Mr. Pleasaunce, it might get back to Charles and cause him to wonder why her brother had taken a stranger along on a most secret errand. Yet another thing to worry about!

Chapter 17

Alex watched Stowe ride up North Street. *Damnation!* If Stowe were at the house when the dragoons arrived, he would be taken with whatever other conspirators were there. If only Rupert had confided fully in him. Then Alex could have offered him the safety of testifying against Pleasaunce and the others. He could have preserved Jane's brother with no fuss. It would not have sat well with Alex to turn on his co-conspirators, but Stowe did not seem to be a man of very tender conscience.

Now it would be more difficult. Troops would probably be in place tonight, after dark. It seemed unlikely anyone would try to move the muskets from the house immediately, with the area so full of ardent Presbyterians. There could not be enough Jacobite sympathizers nearby to need so many guns and collect them discreetly, a few at a time. They must intend to send the arms on farther north. What a feather-brained idea! Had he planned it, he would have had the *Sea Mew* make its delivery at some more northerly port. If all their planning was equally bad, the London papers might be correct that there was no danger. That was a cheering thought. Rupert, however, remained a problem. His problem, unfortunately.

Rupert must be induced to leave that house. Therefore, Alex must set out soon himself. He could allege an urgent message for Rupert and tell him that he had overheard a plan for the house to be searched. That would be fraught with risk. Rupert might tell the others, causing them to fly. He wanted to save Stowe, but he did not want the rest to escape to continue their schemes.

If Alex turned up to speak to Stowe, the real miscreants might suspect Alex and...er...what was his father's phrase? *Cut your throat or drop you in the Solway.* Or the Firth of Tay, of course. He could approach the officer in charge of the dragoon detachment and explain the matter. On the whole, that seemed the wisest choice.

He hired a horse at the livery stable and set out only half an hour after Rupert, who had already provided himself with a mount before parting from Gordon. His one concern at the moment was not catching up to Rupert, as the fellow who had followed him from Oxford had done.

The stableman had given him directions. Alex had no doubt of being able to find the house: a two-story stone house with outbuildings, set well back from the road but visible from it. As twilight came on, he was within a quarter mile of it and dismounted in a copse near the road, where the horse could be concealed. At dusk, he moved cautiously toward the rear of the house, stooping to take advantage of the cover of a low wall that ran some hundred yards behind it. One of the outbuildings stood just on the other side of his wall, on a diagonal from the house. A few paces farther on, the wall ended at another wall. Scotland was rich in stones, if nothing else. He squatted to consider his next move and rest the muscles unaccustomed to traveling in a crouch.

Alex had surveyed the surrounding area while some daylight remained. It was difficult to know how the soldiers could approach the place undetected. Apart from some small spinneys, the house was surrounded by neat fields crisscrossed at intervals by low stone walls. The troops must know this countryside and plan to arrive after the occupants of the house had gone to bed.

What if Captain Sykes's message to the garrison had miscarried or had been ignored? Sometimes things go wrong: Sykes's contact might be away, or sick, or dead, with no one else briefed on the captain's identity as a government agent. Worrying about such things was madness. He must assume the authorities would arrive, because he could do nothing by himself. If a party did come to take the cases away, he could not stop them. They were likely to be more suspicious than Rupert or even the household would be and unlikely to be convinced by any story he could spin.

The thing to do was meet the soldiers far enough from the house to be able to talk to their officer. From which direction would they come? Sykes had not mentioned where the detachment would wait, but surely they'd come by the road from one direction or the other. If he waited there, he must surely hear their approach—the horses' snorting, the clop of hooves, the clink and jingle of metal—however quietly they tried to move.

He took a quick look over his wall toward the house. A faint glow escaped chinks in the shutters in several windows of the house. No lights shone from the buildings that were probably the stable, barn, and dairy.

No servant would be doing chores in the dark. Rising again to a crouch, he followed his wall toward the one ahead, rather than go back the way he'd come. He would get back to the road from the other side of the property. There was a hut near the meeting of his wall with the one that ran east-west. It would give him a little cover from anyone who might be looking out of the house when he went over.

Coming to the end of the wall, he took a deep breath, unfolded himself and hopped over—

—and came down on something that was remarkably uneven.

"Umphf!"

It gave way with a thud and an almost musical jingling. And that muffled "Umphf!" It wriggled. Trying to disentangle himself and scramble to his feet, Alex felt something chilly and tube-like under his hand: the barrel of a musket. Now he heard furtive noises around him. *Oh, damn.*

"Make a sound, and you are a dead man," whispered a husky voice behind him. "My bayonet's at your throat. You—pull him off Riggs."

The struggling man under him had to be helped to rise. "Caught me in me privates with his knee, he did," he muttered, voice muffled as he was bent almost double.

"Never mind that now," Husky Voice said. "Keep quiet. We don't want to alert them."

Feeling the cool edge of sharp steel a quarter inch above his neckcloth, Alex forbore to struggle. He tried not even to breathe. His captor's breathing, by contrast, was the more audible. A bird gave a chirrup or two in a tree. Rough hands pulled him to his feet, and the steel followed, never leaving his Adam's apple.

"Move."

The man who had helped him up twisted his arms behind him. The other, whose blade was against his throat, said in his ear, "We are going over the wall, carefully this time, do you understand?"

Alex gave a minuscule nod.

The maneuver was awkward as clearly none of them wanted to risk a fall which might be noisy or fatal…for someone.

The door was on the side nearest them. As it opened, Alex heard a faint rustling in the shed.

The new voice was almost too low to make out. "In here, Corporal."

There was something like a dance as the corporal circled to face him, the bayonet leaving Alex's neck only for a moment, and backed through the door. More hands grabbed him, and the door closed behind him. The second voice addressed someone. "Gag him and bind him with his neckcloth. We'll deal with him after we've rounded up the rest."

"Ay, sir."

"You, fellow—Corporal Fisk will withdraw his bayonet. But if you struggle or shout, you'll find it's still close enough."

A hand succeeded in freeing his neckcloth.

Alex cleared his throat and said softly, "Sir? I am no Jacobite. My name is Alex Gordon, and it was I who sent to the garrison to come here. I must speak with you about—"

Fabric ripped.

"I've no time now," came the well-bred drawl. "You're a civilian, you've a Scots name, and you're a damned nuisance. I'll sort you out after. Private, get on with it."

"I've a letter from the highest authority, bearing upon your actions here tonight. It's in an inner pocket of my coat on the left side."

"I can't read it by starlight, and I'll be damned if I light a lantern to warn that nest of vipers we're here."

A wad of more-or-less clean linen was stuffed into his mouth. A length of his mutilated stock secured it. Alex held his hands at an angle that he hoped would provide enough slack in the bindings to let him free them later.

He was pushed into a corner. "Private, you'll remain here to guard him. If he moves, knock him out." One of the men opened the door, and the officer strode out, followed by the corporal and the other private.

As his eyes adapted to the darkness, he distinguished the figure of the private, standing nearby. From the man's occasional twitch, it seemed he was nervous. *So am I.* Yet he was in no danger. He had his letter of authority to prove his identity and his mission, and once the officer in charge read it, he would be released. Rupert...Jane's brother would be captured with whoever else was with him. It was too late for him to inform against his fellow conspirators present in the house. He might still have a chance of leniency if he offered up Charles Pleasaunce and anyone else who was not caught in the raid, but Alex feared Rupert would be too stupid and panicky to think of it. *I did the best I could.* He hoped Jane would think it enough.

At length, he heard the rush of feet and the ringing of metal on metal outside the shed. Then shouting and breaking glass. Easier to go in through windows, if they were not shuttered; the doors were likely too thick to kick in and bolted or barred. Two or three shots were fired—not by the soldiers, he thought. Alex sat glumly, waiting upon events.

Which took a long time coming. There was a gray light around the door before the sound of men milling around and shouted orders died down. Various parts of his body ached, or were stiff, or had gone to sleep. His mouth felt dry although the linen gag was damp with saliva, and he urgently needed to relieve himself. The private had made use of the opposite corner of the shed hours ago.

The door swung open and silhouetted a tricorned figure.

"Bring the prisoner out, Private."

The private used his bayonet to cut the strip binding his feet and Alex was hauled up—not without difficulty, for the private was shorter than he and not burly—and aimed toward the door. He uttered a stifled groan.

"You may remove the gag, Private."

Alex gasped as it was taken out and croaked his request.

"Ah…you may free his hands, too. The army is a hard service, but there's limits to what we'll ask of a man," the lieutenant said with a grin.

His most pressing need taken care of, Gordon said, "I must speak with your commanding officer. I am here on behalf of the government and have an order authorizing—"

"Ay, so you said last night. The captain is ready to see you now. Mind you don't try to escape."

"Nothing would induce me to do so, as I have no

reason to fear His Majesty's forces."

"That's as may be." The lieutenant snorted.

"It would be best if the people you have taken into custody did not see me, however."

"No fear of that. They're on their way to Dundee."

Captain Sloane had set up his command post in a back room of the house. He regarded Alex without favor.

"Gordon, is it? What were you about last night, skulking around this place?"

"Sir, as I tried to explain, I supplied the information about the smuggled shipment which I expect you've found. I came to intercept you with information of use to you. I have a letter which will make everything clear." He reached up to pull it out of his coat's inner pocket. Sloane and the others stiffened, and Gordon heard a pistol being cocked behind him.

"Raise your hands," the captain said. "Corporal, see what he's got inside his coat."

The tension eased somewhat when the corporal brought out the letter and presented it to the captain. The latter took it then levelled a glance somewhere behind Alex's left shoulder.

"You will oblige me, Lieutenant, by clearing the pan. It hardly seems that it will be necessary to fire. I do not want the prisoner's brains on my desk."

Alex heard and felt the puff of breath as the man blew the priming gunpowder out. He sighed with relief himself. Captain Sloane studied the thick red seal on the letter before breaking it. He read the letter, frowned, and reread it more slowly. Then he squinted suspiciously at the signature. It was not quite the reaction Gordon had expected. Sloane seemed lost in thought. At length, he said, "I can take no action based on this remarkable document, except to pass it on to my superior." He folded it up and tucked it into his pocket. "You will be held pending Colonel Tate's decision."

"But no action is called for, now that the house has been raided. Except that one of the men you arrested can be persuaded to give evidence against other conspirators, and his cooperation should be secured as soon as possible, before the ones still at large come to hear of this and scatter. And I am sure the order you have just now read identifies me as an agent of our government."

"It does. But I have no way of knowing if the document is genuine. Even if I recognized the signature, it might be a clever forgery. I've never seen such a thing as this: 'The bearer, Alexander Gordon, is acting by my Order, and you are Instructed to give him Any aid he may request.' If it had come through official channels, I should have to trust its authenticity. This is too serious a matter for me to take any action except to refer it to a higher level."

"But—"

"There is no more to be said. Private, lock the prisoner up in the cellar until he can be sent to join the others."

"Captain Sloane, I would ask that you keep me away from the other prisoners. Only one of them knows me, but if he encounters me here, when he supposes me gone back to England, he may guess I am an intelligencer."

"Hmmm. Well, you won't be less comfortable in the cellar than you would be in a cell in Dundee. See that he's provided a blanket and some straw, Private

Bates. If confirmation of your document can be obtained, or Colonel Tate chooses to trust it, your stay may not be overlong."

"Thank you, sir. And if you could pass the word that the prisoner Rupert Stowe would probably be willing to give evidence—if someone suggests it to him? He's a fool, and I believe was led into this...this—"

"Treason," Sloane finished, succinctly.

"By men of stronger character than he, who would be the more worth catching."

"Very well. I see no harm in that, as I must send a messenger in any case."

Even with a blanket, a pile of straw, and a bucket, the cellar room to which Alex was escorted was not appealing. There was a small ventilation grate high up on the outer wall, and the unexpected bonus of a pair of packing crates, one empty, one half full of kitchen utensils. He would at least be able to sit on one box and use the other for a table. No doubt they would feed him eventually.

Dinner proved to be a thin stew or thick soup containing some sort of meat and root vegetables, accompanied by beer. Supper was cheese, crackers, and beer. In the intervening hours, he speculated as to what was happening, or more specifically, why nothing seemed to be happening. Why had he not heard wagons arriving to impound the cases of muskets? Unless Captain Sloane was waiting for Jacobites to come for them. There were several problems with that strategy. For one, the word of the raid must have already spread for miles around and would have come to the ears of someone who would pass it to whoever was supposed to move the weapons along on their journey. He well recalled from his visits to Scotland as a boy how word spread in these country places. He dwelt for a while on memories of roaming the fields and hills with his cousins, who were all but bilingual in the Oxford English drilled into them by their tutor and the Lowland Scots dialect. There was a ruinous little tower, its floors and roof gone, they'd used as a fort to fight the many battles of Scottish history as related by their grandsire. They caught fish in a stream nearby and cooked them, pretending to be under siege by Edward I or some rival Border lord. Those grilled trout and the oatcakes they had brought with them had seemed a feast.

He sighed and forced his mind back to the present. He really could not believe the Jacobites planned to send a procession of freight wagons to collect the muskets. Transporting the cases from St. Andrews to the house, marked as imported furnishings, might pass unremarked. A string of wagons moving them away again could only arouse curiosity. If he were planning to distribute them, he would do it a few cases at a time in a farm cart, well covered with hay or turnips, or in a visiting gentleman's carriage.

The light penetrating the ventilation grate was fading. As no one had provided him with a candle, his tinderbox having been confiscated, he would be spending the night in the dark. He hoped there were no rats, but the certainty that there would be preyed on his mind until he moved one crate over against the other, piled the straw and blanket on them and curled up on top to await the morning.

He finally fell asleep, thinking of a ramble he and Cousin Hugh had taken the year before Hugh entered the University of Edinburgh and he went to Oxford. They had traveled on foot cross-country to the coast, sleeping outdoors wrapped in plaids at night. One day, they discussed the *Meditations* of Marcus Aurelius and the application of Stoic doctrine to modern life. When they realized they were doing so in the broadest Scots, they laughed until their sides ached. "We must not do so at university," Hugh had said, wiping his eyes.

A pair of redcoats arrived shortly after he finished his breakfast of oat porridge and bread.

"Out o' there, you," the older one ordered brusquely. "The captain wants to see you."

Gordon did not regret leaving his cell. The soldier might have shown a little common civility to an agent of His Majesty's government, however. He would go back to the inn, wash thoroughly, have his coat and breeches brushed, put on clean linen, trade his hired horse for a fresh one, if the *Lark* had sailed, and start his homeward journey. What a heartening prospect! He'd done what he could for Stowe, passing on the word that he might be willing to give evidence. Perhaps the young fool would learn something from his misadventure.

The doors of the barn stood open, he noticed. Several redcoats were prying cases open, while another set out paper, ink, and quills on a table. Of course they would want an inventory. It was the British army at its best, though he was now quite glad his father had not bought him a commission.

It was not until he was shown into the back parlor and saw Sloane's expression that he realized his plans might have suffered a setback.

"I almost believed you were an honest man," the

captain said. "It's fortunate I'm cautious by nature. I'm sending you on your way to Dundee."

"Why? If your colonel hasn't had time to respond, why not keep me here?"

"He has responded. Your fellow conspirator— Stowe, is it?—was indeed willing to give evidence. He swears that you organized this business, provided the money and arranged your and his shipboard passage to St. Andrews. The navy will be advised to board and search the *Lark* if they sight her, and ascertain whether her crew are smugglers, traitors, or innocents. As innocent as sailors ever are," he added sourly.

"Unbeknownst to Stowe, our government supplied the money, Stowe having gambled away the sum he was entrusted by Charles Pleasaunce, who apparently owns this house. No doubt Stowe hit upon this outrageous lie as a way of repudiating his supposed debt to me and diverting blame from himself. And you'd do better to stop the *Sea Mew*, captained by Daniel O'Brien. The cargo came on board that ship. The *Lark* is—" He stopped. Captain Sloane was ignorant of the *Lark*'s connection to the government. To call off the search for the *Lark*, Sloane would have to send word to his colonel who would forward the message to his navy contact through who knew how many intermediaries? There were the two privates present, as well. Once the secret was out in this room, it would soon be up and down the coast, putting the *Lark*'s usefulness in jeopardy and mayhap endangering its captain and crew.

"We took passage on the *Lark* because when Stowe lost the money, he panicked. By the time he confided his troubles to me and I had made arrangements with the, ah, correct department, it was too late to travel by coach or horse."

"You are welcome to explain all that to Colonel Tate, though I doubt he will believe such a manifest Scot as yourself."

"It's true I'm half Scottish, on my mother's side, but no one has ever mistaken me for a Scot." Not since boyhood, anyway. And not that there was anything shameful in being Scottish, but just now it might be inconvenient to be taken for one.

"What, with such an accent as yours? If I'd noticed it yesterday, I'd not have been so trusting."

"I don't have an accent," Alex started to say and then heard himself. Being in Scotland and remembering earlier visits, the burr had slipped into his speech, as it had during his boyhood visits.

"Take him away."

They rode north by the highway that ran from Kirkcaldy to Newport, where a ferry crossed the Tay to Dundee. Through the whole journey, some fifteen or eighteen miles, Alex tried to decide what to do. He was guarded by a corporal and several privates, making any attempt to escape a forlorn hope. He would have to persuade the colonel to send to London to confirm his identity and mission. A few days' imprisonment, or perhaps a week or two, and he would be free. Also, the *Lark*'s captain might come to hear of his arrest and take action. What, Alex could not guess. The captain would hardly care to reveal his status as an agent of the Admiralty. If he had no more pressing business, possibly he would sail back to London to notify that body, and that discreet office in Somerset House.

****

"It's a fine, new building," the corporal said chattily as they reined in before a great, steepled building fronted by an arcade. A number of men were idling there, talking in low voices. Even without being able to make out the words, there was an air of palpable tension. He'd sensed something very like it as they had ridden through the town: a sensation like that when amber is rubbed on silk.

"They call this the Town House, and the official offices are here. I'm told the cells are not bad. As cells go," Corporal Fisk added.

He asked to speak with the colonel and was told Colonel Tate was too busy to be bothered, meeting with the provost and bailies of Dundee. "When he wants to question you, you'll be sent for."

Alex was escorted up a set of exterior stairs to an upper floor and shown into a cell containing several other men. None was Rupert Stowe. They fell silent when he entered. Once the guard had gone, there was a brief exchange of greetings. Alex took care to sound Scots, but no one offered any explanation of why they had been arrested. He noted they were dressed decently and spoke like men of some education. None appeared to be common criminals. He would have to rely on their recognizing his speech as a gentleman's, for his appearance did not testify to it: no neckcloth and his coat and waistcoat dusty and bearing bits of straw from his imprisonment in shed and cellar, in spite of his attempt to brush them off.

Conversation was desultory, and he noticed a certain constraint, because of his presence, perhaps. Or mayhap they were worried. Which, in the absence of such proof as he had, would be very understandable, if they were rebels. It then occurred to him that he no longer had his letter. It was in Colonel Tate's possession. Or not. He might have sent it on to London. He might have thrown it on the fire. That possibility gave him very uncomfortable cause for reflection, taking his mind off his fellow prisoners.

By the next morning, if his mind was not at ease, he had at least regained his powers of observation. As they ate their oatmeal porridge (rather cool by the time it was served out), he realized the other three men were very nearly as relaxed as if they sat at their own tables with no prospect of trial or hanging before them. They seemed to apprehend no more danger than if they had been taken up by the watch for some street brawl and would pay a trifling fine and be released. He remembered the feeling clearly, from his college days, when he and a few friends had spent a night in a cell over some silly prank.

He learned a little about the other men over the following two days. One was the owner of a small manor, one owned a linen manufactory, and the youngest was an attorney. Political discussion was avoided. They might be Jacobites or they might not. Their stoicism compelled all his respect. Would that he himself were as able to ignore the filthy condition of his clothing and the itching, which he feared was lice. He chose not to look beyond those minor discomforts.

That afternoon, he felt again the skin-crawling tension of the day of his arrival. They could hear the jailers whispering together when they passed in the corridor, and the afternoon meal was late. Then they heard the ringing of church bells. Alex's cellmates exchanged glances and tight smiles. Even through the building's thick walls they began to hear some commotion and shouting. Heavily shod feet ran past their door.

"Not long now, I think," one man muttered to another.

Chapter 18

When she received the discreetly worded note from Jessup (*"The chimney sweep failed to arrive today, as expected."*), Jane read once again the last paragraph of the letter Alex Gordon had left for her.

I expect to return to London with your brother no later than 7 September, on the schooner Lark. We may be delayed by bad weather or other circumstances, but in the event I do not contact you by the end of the aforementioned date, please convey the enclosed to the address inscribed thereon, to the hand of Anthony Lattimer and no other.

Your most obedient,
Alex Gordon

No message had come from Mr. Gordon at her papa's house (which would have been awkward, but oh, she wished it had!) or at her uncle's, as Jessup's message had informed her. It need not mean that he— and Rupert, of course—had met with difficulties. Not dangerous difficulties. Storms might have delayed the ship they were to meet or kept the *Lark* from beginning its return voyage. It might have sunk. *No, not that, please.* Travel was often slow. Still, it was Scotland. Certain items in the last issue of *The Gentleman's Magazine* occurred to her. She must fulfill Mr. Gordon's request.

It was too late in the day to do so. With both her

stepmother and her father at home, she could not go out to deliver it, or even send it by a servant without it being noticed and questions being asked. The next morning, 8 September, was Sunday, and she could do nothing until they had attended church.

After church they dined, and her father retired to his bookroom to doze over a copy of *The London Gazette*, and Elvira went to her chamber to rest her eyes.

Mrs. Merry, too, was resting. Supper on Sundays was a simple cold collation requiring minimal preparation. Betty was sitting by the hearth in the kitchen, mending a petticoat. The girl was happy to set her sewing aside in favor of accompanying her on a call. Betty was the one servant Jane felt sure would be willing to lie about their errand, should the necessity arise.

Thank goodness, the address to which she had been directed was close by, and it was not raining; they had no need to go by hackney. Leaving the house on foot, Jane would appear to anyone who noticed to be a young lady going out for a walk, properly accompanied by a maid (*for once!*). Betty, who had scrambled into her best gown to impersonate a proper lady's maid, trailed a step or two behind her. Even with Betty's presence, Jane could imagine what her stepmother would say of a young lady visiting a gentleman, and one she did not even know. But Stepmama would never know, she hoped.

She was prepared to do battle with the butler over the letter but to her surprise, he accepted her statement that while her name was unlikely to be known to Mr. Lattimer, she had been told to deliver the message to him directly. She was asked to wait in a small salon while the butler announced her presence to his master.

"This is a terrible fine house," Betty said timidly. "The gentleman must be rich."

The houses on Bloomsbury Square were finer than those on Red Lyon Square, as was obvious even from the outside. Inside...Jane sighed. The walls of the small parlor were a pale gray, with draperies and upholstery to match. It might have seemed drab if not for the glowing red and blue Turkey carpet on the floor, and the Chinese porcelain displayed on the mantle and in a pretty walnut bookcase with glass doors. The blue-and-white plates and the red sang-de-boeuf vase echoed the main colors in the carpet, and a few smaller pieces—bowls, saucers, and pots—picked up the minor colors. It was restrained, lovely, and soothing.

"Or else he—or his wife—has extremely good taste." But good taste alone would not be enough. She could not imagine how much it had all cost. Though she did feel that the great open space of Bloomsbury Square, which the salon's windows faced, would be the better for a few trees or decorative plantings.

A middle-aged man, well though not ostentatiously dressed in pale green, with a salmon pink waistcoat, entered the room.

"Mistress Jane Stowe? I am Anthony Lattimer."

"Why, you were present at my uncle Markham's funeral!"

"I was. We were old friends, and I was saddened to hear of his death. May I extend my condolences, as I should have done at the funeral? There were reasons why I felt I could not approach you and your father."

She inclined her head in acknowledgment. "Thank

you. About my coming here…I realize it must seem very odd…" And really, there was no way to explain *why or how*.

"Not at all. May I peruse the letter while you wait? I may have questions."

"Certainly." She gave him the letter.

As he read it, although he betrayed no expression, she thought he was surprised.

"Mistress Jane, as it happens, there is a point or two upon which you might be able to inform me. But as the matter is confidential…" He glanced at her maid.

"Oh! Yes, I understand, but…"

"And I understand how improper it must appear. There is a garden at the back of the house. If your maid will wait in one corner, and we sit in the one diagonal, I think we may converse without being overheard and without impropriety. I would not request such an interview if it were not of the utmost importance."

"In that case, of course."

When they were seated under a well-pruned and cared for mulberry tree—for there were no dropped berries to stain one's shoes or clothing—Mr. Lattimer said, "I know Gordon expected to return before this. Given the difficulties of travel, I have not been concerned. But from his remarks, it appears he believed he might encounter setbacks beyond what one anticipates on any journey. I do not quite understand why, for his errand was to be a simple one. I usually expect the worst in any situation, and even I could not foresee any great problem arising. Apart from adverse winds, *mal de mer*, terrible roads, bad food, and dreadful inns, of course," he added with a slight smile. "Do you know of any reason he might have been worried?"

"I must first ask you what he told you he proposed to do," Jane replied. It was rather bold of her, but she did not care to divulge anything that Mr. Lattimer should not know, although he was apparently Mr. Gordon's superior. Which was peculiar, now that she thought of it, because she had understood Mr. Gordon was not employed.

Mr. Lattimer looked somewhat amused. "He was to accompany your brother Rupert to a small port in Scotland where young Mr. Stowe was to make payment and accept a cargo. The goods almost certainly consisted of muskets, as you must already know. Your brother would then communicate with the nearest English garrison, informing them of the place to which the guns were to be transported, in return for which, his part in the smuggling would be overlooked. Alex went with him to, er, make sure the money was not stolen on the way. Then they were to return directly by the same vessel, if possible."

"Did Mr. Gordon actually say that Rupert intended to go to the authorities?" Jane asked, startled. "I wonder why he thought Rupert would?"

"That was the plan, or so I understood. I suppose your brother must have agreed to it."

"That is very puzzling to me, sir, as I have never known Rupert to admit to any fault or wrongdoing. He will deny the most minor misdeeds and be indignant if you do not believe him, as I told Mr. Gordon, because he hoped to persuade Rupert to confide in him. Granted, Rupert did tell him he'd lost the money with which he was to pay the ship's captain, but from what Alex—Mr. Gordon—told me, my half brother was very drunk and terrified at the time. I warned him he should not expect further admissions, except perhaps under the same circumstances, but he said he had a plan in reserve."

"Did he," Mr. Lattimer said in a flattened tone. He went on slowly. "What would you have expected Rupert Stowe to do? Once they reached their destination and met the smuggler?"

"I think he would deliver the payment and remove himself as quickly as possible. I would expect him to return home, or mayhap go back to Plymouth, as he interrupted his stay there, and not give it another thought—including the need to repay whoever lent him the money. I hope it wasn't yours, sir? Or Alex's, but I don't think he could raise such a sum. The lender must be repaid somehow."

"Do not trouble yourself, Mistress Jane. No person will sustain the loss."

Whatever that means. Mr. Lattimer's slight evasion did not go unnoticed by her.

Lattimer continued, "I defer to your knowledge of your half brother. My...Gordon told me you were a keen and unsentimental observer of humanity. But we are speaking of men and a few women, too, I am sure, who are conniving at treason. Are you certain Rupert Stowe would not remain in Scotland to throw in his lot with the Pretender's son?"

Jane sighed. "Since we are being blunt, sir, yes. A stronger personality than his might lead him into trouble, but as soon as he perceived real danger, Rupert would absent himself."

"The Young Pretender appears to have cast a spell over quite a surprising number of Scots and a few

Englishmen. Though it's hard to know how Stowe would have caught the infection."

"Rupert might support him passionately under someone else's influence, if he could do so without inconvenience to himself. At a distance, most likely. If he found himself in actual jeopardy, it would only be because he does not always foresee the consequences of his actions."

"Then could he have failed to foresee the likely end of an act of treason?"

"I know Rupert. He might be optimistic and believe things would all turn out well, and he would not expect any consequences to himself if they did not. His nanny was indulgent, and my stepmother has always been delicate."

"Enjoys poor health?" Lattimer interpolated.

Jane tried to suppress a smile. "Exactly. I tried to correct his behavior if you can conceive of a child of eight years attempting to instill good behavior in a child of six. By the time he went away to school, I had given up, though I hoped Eton might succeed where I had failed."

"The guidance of firm-minded men and a few sound drubbings from other boys do sometimes work wonders."

"They appear to have failed in this case. I don't wish you to think Rupert is—is *steeped in vice*, as I suppose a writer would put it. Some suffer from weak lungs or feeble intellect. Rupert's affliction is weak character. I should not say such things of a member of my family, but truth is more important than loyalty. Family loyalty, I mean." She sighed. "The only way I can explain my reasoning is this: Rupert would take part in a brawl with his friends, because no one takes young men brawling seriously. He might strike someone in the heat of the moment if he believed he could get away with it. He has enough sense of self-preservation not to strike a man who would call him out or who looked as if he could give a good account of himself in a fight."

"A cornered rat will fight for its life."

"If we are drawing on the animal kingdom for comparisons, my brother is neither a rabbit nor a rat. He's a weasel and would eel his way out of trouble."

Mr. Lattimer appeared nonplussed. "Would the rebellion count as a brawl with friends?"

"It might seem so to him at first. I have no experience of military life, but I suspect that an army on campaign is very disagreeable. Dirty, with uncertain supplies of food, and harsh discipline. If Rupert actually joined the Highland forces, I cannot think he would enjoy it. I imagine he would take to his bed with some debilitating malady until they left him behind to recover, and then take to his heels."

"Then I do not quite understand why he and Gordon have not reappeared. If all had gone well, the authorities there would have expedited their return."

Jane bit her lip. "Mr. Gordon must have formed a tolerably accurate notion of Rupert's reliability. It does explain why he instructed me to bring you this letter."

"Let us think it through. Can we assume the money was delivered? Is there a chance your brother might have made off with it? You did say he lacked foresight."

"I don't think so. According to Mr. Gordon, Rupert was terrified Charles Pleasaunce would murder him for the loss of the money."

"Then presumably the payment was delivered and the authorities notified. Is it possible Stowe feared to return to London immediately and fled Gordon's company? I wonder if Gordon would have felt obliged to hunt him down and bring him back?"

"I hope not, Mr. Lattimer. With the North in such a ferment, I hope Mr. Gordon would not risk himself merely to return Rupert. However, I cannot imagine Rupert striking off on his own with no money, and I'm perfectly sure he cannot have had more than a crown or two with him. He never does."

"I must confess I hope the same, as Gordon is very…useful."

"And intelligent, and…" And amusing and attractive and he appeared to enjoy her company, but she could not say so to a virtual stranger. She could not think of anyone to whom she could confide such a thing. Lattimer smiled at her, but the smile faded quickly. They stared at each other.

"What can be done?" Jane asked.

"I fear there is nothing much to be hoped for your brother, if he carried through on the delivery of the payment and did not agree to give evidence against the conspirators. As for Gordon, I can pass word to some connections of mine in North Britain. Something must have gone wrong indeed."

"What can I do?"

"Nothing but inform me if you hear from your brother. It has been a pleasure to meet you, and thank you for bringing me Gordon's letter." He apparently took note of her distress, in spite of her attempt to conceal it. "Very likely we're worrying too soon. There might be a dozen reasons he has not returned. It might be he—they—could not return by sea and are even now plodding along by coach." He stood up, and Jane, perforce, did also. Mr. Lattimer offered his arm.

"On second thought, there is one thing," he said. "You reported one of your servants had seen your brother in Billingsgate when he was supposed to be in Plymouth. Can you tell me—or find out—precisely where he was? The nearest building or the name of the street?"

"Certainly. Betty said he was going into a tavern called the Crown and Castle. She passes that way regularly. It was on a corner in Lower Thames Street. Would you like to ask her any questions, as she is here with me?"

"I think not. Better she not realize there was any significance to his presence there."

"Yes, I thought as much at the time and impressed upon her that she should not talk of it, to spare Rupert embarrassment, as young men do not care to have their less savory activities gossiped about."

"Very good, indeed, Mistress Jane. The information will be helpful. And I commend your foresight."

Not until Jane had returned home did she wonder what connections an old friend of her uncle could have in Scotland who could inquire into Mr. Gordon's whereabouts. And whose money had gone to pay the balance due on the guns?

Chapter 19

Voices and footsteps sounded in the corridor, and a key grated in the lock. The door was flung open by a man with a white cockade pinned to his hat. He greeted them with a jubilant "Dundee's in our hands. When we reached Perth four days ago, Lord George Murray was given charge of the army instead of the Irishman, O'Sullivan. Who knows where we will be in a week?"

They surged out of the cell, calling out to other freed prisoners, one of whom was Rupert Stowe. Seeing Alex, he looked a little conscious—*as well he might!*—and approached, stammering, "So you were arrested also? I thought you had got away."

"Alack, no."

A burly, ruddy-faced fellow clapped Rupert on the shoulder as he passed and inquired, "Are you coming, Stowe? I'm off to seek a commission from the Prince."

"I'll be along presently. I've some arrangements to make with my friend here, first."

"We'll share a bottle tonight, then." The fellow hurried off, calling boisterously to others.

"What are your plans?" Stowe asked Gordon.

"I had best return to England. I was gone longer than I anticipated. I was not expecting to be arrested on charges connected with the smuggling of your friend's French furniture."

"Furniture? Oh, ah. Furniture, of course. Is that

what you were told when you were arrested?"

"The officer did not specify the charge, though smuggling was mentioned. He seemed to believe I was a Jacobite. I can't think why."

"Odd," Stowe mumbled. "They thought the same of me." He frowned thoughtfully. "I should return to England with you. There's a great deal of unrest here at the moment. We don't want to be caught up in it."

By which Gordon concluded that Stowe was not enthusiastic about joining the Highland army. Alex would as soon leave the spineless, treacherous dog to stand or fall on his own in Scotland, but he had Jane to consider. Although Rupert might not be any safer in England, if word made its way back that he'd been jailed as a supporter of the Prince.

"We may as well travel together," he agreed. "And I think we should start immediately." Stowe looked relieved. "By the way, what's the date? I've lost count of the days."

"Someone said it was the seventh day of September. He suggested it be made a holiday in Dundee hereafter. How will we get home? If the *Lark* is still at St. Andrews…but I don't really want to go back there."

Neither did Alex. "I can't imagine Captain Sykes has tarried so long over his repairs. No, I think we should take the ferry to Newport. When I was brought from St. Andrews, I noticed there was a house that offered lodging and horses for hire."

"I think," Stowe began tentatively, "they may not have any horses by now. The Prince's men are said to be scouring Dundee for arms and mounts. Someone is bound to make off with them one way or another."

"Then we will walk." Fortunately, he had paid attention to how he had been brought from the ferry to the Town House; he would hardly care to ask directions of any of the locals. He led Stowe down the roughly cobbled St. Clement's Lane to the waterside.

"How are we to get across, Gordon?"

"We will hire some boatman to carry us over and farther down the firth. If you are correct that there are likely no horses for hire at Newport, there is no advantage to going there." They would also be able to avoid the highway, on which they might meet British troops.

"But have you any money? Mine is spent."

"I've a few coins yet." The stiffened skirts of his coat, and its collar, held both guineas and smaller coins, some of which he had worked free his first night in the gaol, while his cellmates slept. "It's perfectly essential to one's survival to have the ready if one should get into difficulties," the tailor at Somerset House had told him. "One may need the wherewithal to hire lodgings or a horse or pay a bribe. I'll send along a coat containing some hidden assets with the rest." He had sewn a reassuring number of crowns and guineas and smaller coins into it.

"I think you should avoid speaking, at least when people are about," he told Rupert. "You sound like an Englishman. We must pass as unremarked as we can."

"How is it you sound like a Scotchman? I never noticed it in London. Or on the schooner."

"I spent some time with my Scottish grandparents as a child. Their way of speaking comes back very easily if I'm around Scots."

The question, Alex considered when Stowe fell

silent, was not whether they could cross the firth. It was whether it would be better to get someone to take them down the firth to the coast, and then south. They must find a small fishing boat whose master would oblige them. If that fellow who had opened his cell was correct, the Jacobite army was moving at speed. They'd entered Perth four days before; today they were in Dundee, a distance of some twenty miles, no difficulty for a man on horseback, but impressive for a force he had heard described as undisciplined and ragtag. Still, two men on foot should be able to travel fast enough to outdistance the Highlanders. Besides, the Jacobites surely would not try to move their army across the Firth of Tay. Ferrying men and baggage carts and horses across would take too long. Even if they did so and took the highway from Newport to Kirkaldy, they would then have to cross the Firth of Forth. The Jacobite army would most likely go by land, west of the route Alex had travelled under guard several days ago. It should be safe enough for them to take the highway. Except, of course, for possible detachments of English troops, who must by now know how close the Prince's army was.

And what of the muskets? He would like to know whether the boxes were still in the barn at the Pleasaunces' Scottish property or if they had been removed or destroyed by the English. If they were still there, they might yet fall into the rebels' hands. But he would very much like not to encounter Captain Sloane, or indeed, any English officer or soldier to whom Gordon's or Stowe's name might have been mentioned.

He had come to Scotland to make sure delivery of the muskets was thwarted. If they fell into the rebels' hands, it would be a material aid to the Young

Pretender. Now that Alex had seen the situation here, the article in *The Gentleman's Magazine* dismissing the risk of invasion of England seemed a little optimistic. While many of the Highlanders and the Young Pretender's other adherents were said to be badly armed and equipped, they had swept down to Perth with little or no opposition. Who knew what they might be capable of, better armed?

The fishing boat landed them a little north of St. Andrews. Rupert Stowe complained. He wanted to bypass St. Andrews entirely.

"We will," Alex assured him. "We will find another boat south of the town to take us down the coast." *After we've gone by way of the Pleasaunce property, to see if the muskets are still there.*

Gordon had a fair idea of how to find the place again, having taken careful note of his route from St. Andrews. The thought of encountering Captain Sloane again made his blood run cold, but the possibility of the muskets falling into the hands of the Young Pretender's army made it necessary to chance it. He grinned, remembering Jane's acerbic "What would be a necessary chance?" His father would say that he should leave that business to the British army, which had no doubt already taken care of it. He hoped they had. What would Jane say? Most young ladies, if they were fond of one, would probably urge a strategic retreat. Was Jane fond of him? There was Rupert as an offsetting factor, too. She might feel greater concern about Rupert, even if she had seemed rather exasperated with him at whiles.

"We're walking inland," Rupert objected. "How will that take us south?"

"We're circling around St. Andrews on the landward side. We can't stroll through the town. Do you want to meet Captain Sloane again?"

"By Jove, no," Jane's brother breathed. "Once was quite enough."

They kept to whatever cover was near, which added to the distance. They also skirted a field containing a bull. However, Alex's rough calculations, made with a stick in a patch of dirt, were not far wrong and brought them only a little way north of their goal. His tutor had been correct: geometry could be useful in real life.

He saw the house before Rupert did.

"That's the house Charles—" Stowe left the rest of the sentence unspoken. "I don't want to go back there."

"I'm not fond of the idea, myself, but I want to see what's become of your cargo."

"Why?" Stowe inquired, warily.

"We both know it wasn't French furniture and gewgaws. I want to know if Sloane has taken them away or if they're still there. He may have thought he'd round up whoever came to collect them, if word didn't get out that the shipment had been discovered. Given what we heard and saw on our way out of Dundee, it seems at most a small detachment captured the town, or else merely local supporters of the Pretender managed it. The army itself was probably some distance away, as we saw no sign of it. It may still have been at Perth, or marching south from that town."

"The fellow who let us out of the cell I was in said the army was some way to the west," Rupert admitted. "I wasn't paying much attention. My chief interest was in getting out of that pigsty."

"I have it on good authority the cells aren't bad, as cells go."

"Ha!"

"If they keep marching south, on their way to either Glasgow or Edinburgh, they could send a company of men to fetch the muskets. They'd need freight wagons, but they could appropriate them, as they seem to have done with the horses." It was not at all apparent that the Young Pretender's army would meet with any opposition. He recalled hearing two regiments under the command of General Cope at Edinburgh were said to have gone north to engage the Highland force. How could the Young Pretender's rabble of an army have reached Perth in the face of well-trained British troops? It did not affect his own plans. The Jacobite army was on the move. It seemed unlikely that General Cope, or anyone else, would make sure those muskets were not used against His Majesty's troops or loyal subjects.

Stowe was not attending. He slumped to the ground with his back to a tree. "How did you find out? Did Charles send you?"

"If he had, I wouldn't have needed to drag you along with me, would I?"

"But you were just cataloguing books for m' half sister…" Rupert's voice trailed off.

"Well…more or less. But your plan came to the attention of certain men in London who take an interest in such things. Captain O'Brien is watched, you know." Let the young fool suppose that was how the scheme was discovered, rather than by Jane's acute observations.

"I feel sick."

As well he might. "If you had confessed the whole to me, as I gave you every opportunity to do, you would have informed the nearest garrison and would have been forgiven your earlier part in the matter. Now..." Alex made a casting-away gesture. "Mayhap your testimony against your accomplices will be enough to win you leniency."

At the sight of Stowe's face, Alex almost felt sorry for him, until he remembered Jane. "Was it you who tried to make it appear that Mistress Jane poisoned her uncle?"

Rupert gaped at him in evident surprise. "No! Of course not. Disgrace our family? Are you mad?"

"Someone knew your sister's name and that Markham was her uncle. And someone arranged for poisoned potted shrimps to be delivered to him in her name."

"So that's why they suspected Jane? I thought it was only a rumor. Or that maybe she had sent them. You never know what an old maid will do anyway, and the prospect of being an heiress might have been tempting."

"Who knew she was Markham's niece and his heiress, Stowe?"

"My friend, Charles P...Charles, would know."

"Charles Pleasaunce, yes. Who else besides?"

"I think I mentioned it to Captain O'Brien's son. He's first mate on the *Sea Mew*."

"So you told Pleasaunce and young O'Brien."

"I didn't tell Charles. Our families are friendly. We thought it would be a good thing if he married her, though Jane's not to his taste, since she would inherit from her uncle. Jane behaved ridiculously and turned him down flat. We thought she'd change her mind when she was more desperate for a husband."

"What about O'Brien?"

"I told him because Markham sent me a letter, asking me to explain what I was doing on the *Sea Mew*. He claimed it was a smuggler's ship." Rupert smiled ruefully, revealing what must be considerable charm when he wasn't being petulant. "Well, she is, but how inconvenient that Markham guessed it. I thought O'Brien should be warned. It was no business of Markham's if I visited a ship, the meddling old fool," Rupert added sulkily. "Gabriel told me not to concern myself about it. He's an excellent fellow, good company and very understanding."

"Does he have fair hair and very blue eyes and an open, friendly manner?"

Stowe stared at him as if he had grown wings and flown. "How did you know?"

"He delivered the shrimps."

Neither of them had much more to say after that, although Stowe protested when Alex announced he was going to approach the house.

"I don't ask you to come with me," Gordon said. Rupert would be an encumbrance. "Stay here if you prefer." He might, of course, run off instead, but Gordon thought not. Stowe had no money. He would only abandon Alex if Gordon were taken.

Alex sheltered behind the same wall that had concealed the redcoats when he had last approached the house. The barn was some thirty yards farther on, and he could not see the great double doors which faced the house. But a small door on the side facing him was equipped with a fine new padlock.

It would have been better to wait until twilight, but Alex feared Rupert's nerve would break. Too, accomplishing his errand in daylight might conceal it longer, giving them more time to get away. He fished in his pocket and found the threads he'd snipped to make a little concealed pocket before leaving London.

Picking the lock was easy. It was new and well-greased, with no rust at all. He took the padlock from its staple—the thought of someone coming along and relocking it, with him inside, was not one he liked to contemplate—and pulled the door shut behind him. There was enough light from two or three windows high in the wall to make a lantern unnecessary.

The big crates were at one side, lying open, packing straw scattered around. Three, somewhat smaller, apparently were still sealed. The muskets' original packing cases had been removed and laid out in several rows, in layers two deep. Their lids had been replaced but were not nailed down. He peered into a randomly chosen half a dozen. The soldiers who had inventoried the contents had opened each but not removed the guns. Circling the rows of muskets and the debris, he paused to look at the unopened boxes. It was strange they had not been opened.

Then he noticed that on one side, two or three of the nails had been hammered in askew, and there were empty nail holes as well. The box had been opened and inexpertly closed up again. Looking with greater attention, he saw the other two had also been reassembled, though with greater care. He returned to the first and wished he had a tool of some sort. He could not take time to search for one. He pulled irritably at the edge of the crate's side. The lower part gave a little. He squatted and studied it, wishing for more light.

None of the nail holes in the bottom half of the crate's side contained nails. With a fierce grin, he stood again and tugged the edge hard, hoping to make a gap big enough to see what was inside. When the panel pulled entirely free, he almost fell over. Alex shoved it aside and stared into the crate.

Dear God. It was a cannon.

Even in the dimness, he could see what it was. A smallish one: a French eight-pounder, he supposed. But a cannon. The other two crates looked identical. He would not take time to open them. Alex thought he would not lose his money if he wagered they also held artillery.

He turned to continue his circuit of the boxes and crates. The panel he had pried off had fallen against a pile of hay and was propped against it at an angle, the hay having compressed not at all.

What unusually solid hay.

He brushed away swathes of it until his fingers felt something hard and wooden. Stacked casks of gunpowder.

Better still.

There was a deal more hay—bundled—up in the loft, and it was the work of minutes to toss it down onto the crates. Then he descended and listened at the door by which he'd entered. No sound. A candle lantern stood on a small shelf by the door, and a tinderbox with flint and steel. *Convenient!* His own tinderbox had been taken from him when Sloane's soldiers searched him. He struck sparks until the shreds of hemp ignited, took the candle from the lantern, and lit it.

Starting on the far side of the barn, he touched the flame to piles of hay at intervals, moving quickly toward the door. When he reached it, he tossed the candle toward the crates he had not set alight and then threw the smoldering contents of the tinder box, too, before slipping out the door. He paused only to replace the padlock before sprinting back the way he'd come. He wished he could be sure the fire would actually catch, but he would have to trust to luck. Staying to make sure would be to risk capture.

Alex leaned against a tree to catch his breath. Rupert was sitting where Alex had left him, idly scratching patterns in the litter of decayed leaves.

"What's happened?" Rupert demanded, white-faced.

"Oh...nothing much. But we should leave now." He was still breathing heavily. He'd been at university the last time he'd run like that. Perhaps he should make a regular effort to do so, to increase his stamina. Or take up some sport as a regular pastime.

"But why did you insist on coming here? And come running back as if the Devil were on your tail?"

Alex hauled him up. "Come on. We won't wish to be here when they notice the barn's afire." He wondered whether the gunpowder would burn or explode when—

"Good God!" Rupert's cry needed no explanation. The blast answered Alex's half-formed question. The casks had exploded. Flame gouted from the barn's shattered windows, and part of the roof fell in.

"This way! Before they think to send out search parties, Stowe!"

Stowe needed no further urging.

Alex hoped the blast and fire would be assumed to have been caused by spontaneous combustion, but they could not count on it. Rupert kept glancing back until the barn was out of sight but matched Alex's pace. Even Stowe was not foolish enough to want to be found in proximity to the conflagration.

"Where are we going?" Rupert asked. He was breathing heavily. Not a sportsman, clearly.

"South. After we're past St. Andrews, we'll turn east and find a fishing village where we can hire someone to take us down the coast. Or we may be able to find a farmer taking a wagonload south who will take us up for a few miles, or buy horses. Then we'll find a boat to take us across the Firth of Forth. Did you hear anything to suggest whether the Pretender's army will march to Glasgow or to Edinburgh?"

"No. I don't believe the locals at Dundee knew, Gordon. Or if they did, I didn't hear them talk of it."

"It's too bad. It would be helpful to know." If Stowe did know, he might keep silent, anyway. "But even if their goal is Edinburgh, I think they will keep well inland so they need not move their forces across the Forth."

"Can we afford to purchase horses? And we'll need food and lodging. And to pay for passage on a boat. It's a long way to England."

"I have some money, fortunately. And we won't be staying at inns or eating in public houses. We can buy bread and cheese at some farm or village, and we'll sleep out."

"Sleep out? In the open? It will be damned cold. And what if it rains?"

"I expect we'll find a byre to shelter in." If they

were fortunate. There was no point in discouraging Rupert.

"Stay a moment. I've a stitch in my side."

Alex had pushed Rupert hard across the open fields until they were again in a grove of trees, the ground littered with brush and branches fallen in some recent wind. It seemed safe enough to rest for a few minutes. Rupert bent over, hands on his knees, panting. He raised his head and asked, "What's that over there? Behind you?"

Alex turned to look.

Chapter 20

Jane paid a visit to her house. Had anyone asked, she would have said it was because she wished to see how the cleaning was progressing, but no one did. In fact, she was curious to see the Crown and Castle. It was easy to enlist Molly, whose work was far lighter with no one living in the house but the servants, and get a hackney from the nearest hackney stand. To be sure, Mrs. Harrow wanted to know her errand.

"I've heard there is a merchant with a shipment of Turkish rugs. The one in my uncle's study is sadly worn. Even I cannot be sentimental about it. If I can find one of the same size and general appearance, I will replace it."

That satisfied Mrs. Harrow, who graciously ceded Molly to Jane for the morning.

Her uncle had once mentioned an importer of carpets, and Jane recalled the name. It was perhaps a little odd to request that the coachman take them to the Turkish Emporium by way of Lower Thames Street, but it was not far out of the way. Having inquired of Betty with some particularity for landmarks near the Crown and Castle, she was able to sight it without difficulty. She leaned close to the window to peer at it, wondering what could have taken her brother there. As they passed, the coach came abreast of a gentleman waiting to cross the street. Jane's eyes widened. In the moment that he recognized her, his ordinarily impassive face took on an arrested expression. And then the coach was past, and Jane sank back on the seat, half glad and half alarmed.

Dear Mr. Lattimer,

I passed the Crown and Castle near the corner of Lower Thames Street and Pudding Lane today in a hackney, on my way to shop for a carpet. You may imagine my surprise to see Mr. Charles Pleasaunce near the public house. I suspect you will find the fact of interest. I am sorry to say he saw me, as I chanced to be looking out the window as he was waiting to cross. I hope I may not have frightened him away.

****

Papa having been irritable since Rupert's flight to Scotland, Jane had composed a series of menus which included his favorite dishes and told Mrs. Merry to begin preparing scarlet beef, as that would take several days.

However, Wilson sought her out in the housekeeper's office and cleared his throat before murmuring, "Mistress Jane? The master has returned early from his club and requests that you attend him in his bookroom."

This could not be good news. She set aside the schedule of draperies to be taken down for thorough shaking and airing in the little back garden. It was a chore which gave some trouble every year, as it must be done in good weather, and without inconveniencing the family: the drawing room must be done on a day when no one was expected to call, the dining room when the family was invited to dine elsewhere, and the project depended on the weather being dry.

When she arrived in her papa's lair, his compressed lips and livid face suggested that even such present treats as artichoke pie and sweetbreads, and the future prospect of cured beef, would not soothe his temper.

This is become a thought tiresome. Jane was beginning to yearn for the days—years!—when her father had paid her little attention. "Yes, Papa?"

"There is a letter," he began without preface, picking up a folded newspaper and slapping it down smartly on the desk, "demanding to know why Markham's slayer has not been arrested. It asserts there is an obvious suspect, but that Mistress J—S—, a 'young lady of good family,' has been ignored by the authorities. The writer, some poxy meddler who styles himself 'A Friend of Justice,' writes 'while few enjoy the idea of a gentlewoman being hanged, justice must be done, whosoever the murderer's friends may be.' "

Did the rest of the paragraph imply that, however reluctant the authorities were to prosecute a lady, justice should be the same for a gently-bred female as for a laundress? If so, she wondered at its being published, for many would consider that a radical notion.

"Anyone who reads it will assume you are being overlooked as a suspect because of bribery or some other favor. I hardly knew how to hold up my head. God knows what we can expect next."

"But Sir Thomas de Veil—"

"Will he produce the letter he told us he had received? As I recall, he said the murder of your uncle touched upon secret affairs of the government. If that is the case, will he be permitted to make it public? I fear His Majesty's government will consider its secrets take precedence over our reputation."

"And my life?"

"We will hope it does not come to that," he said, with an obvious effort to be reassuring. "If it does, de Veil may be able to arrange a pardon. If de Veil has such a letter, that is."

"He said he did and showed it to the coroner, too. Why would he lie?"

Her father fiddled with his pen stand. "Do you swear you have never met Sir Thomas before he visited us that evening?"

"I never saw him before in my life."

"I hope you are not lying, Jane. This is a serious matter."

"Why would I lie, sir?"

"If you had a close acquaintance with Sir Thomas, it might explain why he would exert himself to deflect suspicion from you."

The statement took her breath away. "Sir, are you suggesting some improper relationship between Sir Thomas de Veil and myself? And that he lied about there being a more likely suspect to oblige me?"

He still did not look at her. "You often go out unaccompanied, I am told. Perhaps you only go shopping, but you do not always buy anything. You went out every week, supposedly to visit your uncle, also unaccompanied. Who's to say where you went or what you do? Or who you see? I consider your mother to blame for failing to chaperon you adequately."

Stepmother, Jane thought. Her heart thumped, and her face felt warm. With an effort, she suppressed the flood of anger, finding it more difficult than usual. What it would be like to let it go? She drew in a steadying breath.

"And how she will endure this business I do not know," her father continued.

"I swear I never met Sir Thomas de Veil before he called upon us." The answer felt evasive. If she had not slipped out to—to *tryst* with the magistrate (as if she would! Why, he was older than Papa!), she had certainly done so to meet Mr. Gordon and Mr. Lattimer, too, but not for any immoral purpose in either case. Though she did enjoy talking with Mr. Gordon: sensible men of wit seemed to be in short supply. She certainly did not intend to confess those lapses of propriety, when they had nothing to do with this matter.

…Except that they were related. Should she tell her father what she knew? She could not well explain about her uncle's death and its probable connection to smuggled arms without mentioning Rupert. Her father would be shocked, less perhaps by the plot than by the potential humiliation of having his son arrested for involvement in it. He would be angry that Jane had alerted Mr. Gordon to the existence of the muskets; if he himself had discovered what Rupert was about, he would have forbidden him to continue, and perhaps have shipped him off to the Colonies to ensure his obedience.

She could understand his first concern would be to protect his son. On the other hand, that would not have prevented the muskets from falling into Jacobite hands, potentially to kill who knew how many? Although no one but Mr. Gordon (and perhaps Mr. Lattimer) seemed to take the unrest in the north very seriously.

"Is there some other man? One who could influence de Veil?"

"To the best of my knowledge, he was acting under no influence but that of the government, as he said, sir."

"Well, that's something to be thankful for. It's bad enough you are suspected of murder. To have it thought you were immoral as well would be insupportable. Then, too, perhaps nothing will come of this curst letter. It's not as if we had nothing else to worry about, with Rupert off on some madcap jaunt in the north. He should have sent me a message. He could have visited Ireland or stayed with friends of mine in the country."

Chapter 21

The ground was chilly. Damp, too. Silly place to nap. The lack of a pillow made his head hurt. Alex opened his eyes and found he had a worm's-eye view of last year's fallen leaves. It was dim under the trees…no, by Jove, it was dusky everywhere. He sat up and explored the back of his head with a cautious hand. It was tender, but he didn't feel the stickiness of blood. He didn't feel sick, either, and his memory seemed to be intact. Fortunate! His brother Gilbert had cracked his skull falling out of a tree and had forgotten the previous several days.

His wig must have protected him from the worst of the blow—curse Stowe, anyway! He peered around and spotted something that was either his fallen wig or a dozing woodland creature and patted it tentatively. *Eureka.* Shaking leaf mold from it, he set it upon his head. His hat was nearby.

He fished in his pocket for his handkerchief to wipe his face and hands and found his pockets had been rifled while he was unconscious. His handkerchief was there, but the purse containing a few shillings and pence and two guineas was gone. There had been nothing in his left pocket but the flint and steel he'd taken from the barn, together with a little tinder, and they were still present.

He stood up. He felt odd and off-balance, and it

was not the dizziness alone. His coat was hanging askew. The left side felt heavier than the right, and— were those shreds of cloth? Alex cursed Stowe again, with a richness and fluency which would have appalled most of his acquaintance. Stowe! That Jacobite, idiot, traitor, *thief*! Stowe must have pushed back the coat's skirt to reach his breeches pocket and noted the weight of its front facing. He'd torn it open and removed the remaining guineas.

Stowe had had no money with him, bar a shilling or two, so he'd helped himself to Gordon's, leaving Alex with none. Damn! It would make his return to London a hundred times more difficult.

No, he was being foolish, more shaken by the blow to his head than he'd realized. The left side of the coat was intact—probably because Stowe had been in too much of a hurry or was too squeamish to roll him over. Alex tugged a few threads loose and transferred several guineas and some smaller coins to his pocket. It would have been awkward to be literally penniless when he needed to return to England quickly.

Although the light was failing and the air seemed misty, he thought he recognized the dimming landscape to his right as the direction in which they'd been travelling. No, not mist. Fog was rolling in.

He dared not try to wait it out and risk being captured by a patrol if any were out. Alex wished he knew more about the state of military affairs. Wouldn't whatever troops were available be on their way to intercept the Young Pretender's army? There was no point in wondering when he should be making use of his time.

He gazed around the copse until he spied a fallen

branch almost four feet long and broke off its smaller branches, then stepped out as briskly as he could, given his aching head, which throbbed at every step. He wanted to get as far as possible before the fog was too thick. He would like to find a road or a track before it was too dark, or too foggy, to see his way.

The fog thickened to impenetrability even before full dark, and it became necessary to use his stick to feel his way. Going cross-country, there was no knowing what might lie in his path. A quick sweep of the ground before each step assured him he was not about to run into a wall or tree or fall into a ditch. He could not go fast, but on the other hand, no British patrol or Jacobite detachment would be able to move faster, assuming any were out in this gray nothingness. No sensible person would be abroad. He continued to feel his way. And every yard he traveled was one step farther from pursuit. He hoped. *Unless I'm going in circles.*

The tip of the branch dragged through stubble, as it had for the last hundreds of steps. At the next sweep, it met no resistance. Alex did not move for a moment. He prodded downward with the end. It met resistance, and he moved it back and forth. He squatted and felt with his hand, discovering a bare, packed, slightly concave surface. He edged forward and groped. The stubble resumed. It must be a footpath, exactly what he wanted. He would still need to feel his way with the stick, for while a well-worn path was not likely to end suddenly at a cliff or river, it might run into a gate or door, or turn suddenly at a tree or wall. But it would lead somewhere.

****

He had been walking for half his life. His head pounded, he was cold and hungry, and his shoes were not as comfortable as he might have wished. At least, being on a path, he couldn't be going in circles. Probably.

The faint odor of a stable or byre alerted him. The damp, chilly air muffled sounds as well as blinding eyes, but it did not deaden the nose. Where horses and cattle are kept, there is certain to be a heap of used straw and manure. *Or vice versa.* Further, where horses and cattle are kept, there is human habitation. His tutor had been very fond of logick. Alex congratulated himself on having made good use of what Mr. Thorpe had called "the logickal faculty." In the midst of admiring his deductions, it occurred to him that this was not the schoolroom nor yet university, and the presence of livestock and people bore greater significance than a tutor's praise. His aching head, lack of food since— when?—and weariness were as dangerous in their way as actual pursuit.

He listened, trying to get a feeling for how close he was to the midden and outbuildings. Now that he was not moving, he heard faint rustlings and the whuffle of cows or horses breathing a little ahead and to his right. A cottage must be near, but where? He would not expect to find it too close to the stable, but he would bet his eyes it would be on the path. He couldn't have passed without sensing it. Odds were it lay ahead. If anyone were awake within, there would be a glimmer of light to guide him. If anyone were awake. They might all have gone to bed, as folk kept early hours in the country and he must have been trudging along for half the night, if not half his life.

The stable was behind him when he saw a faint glowing line, like candlelight through a gap in curtains or shutters, a little way ahead. He was moving toward it when a little farther on, a brighter, longer line appeared and grew as a door opened. The gates of Heaven could not be more welcome. Warmth, light, something to eat, a place to sit or lie down beckoned. With a sigh, he felt around with his stick, found bare, solid ground, and took a step to the side. Then several more careful steps. He was now around the corner of the house from the door and a little beyond the window he had seen first. Alex dropped to the ground, bending his knees so that the skirt of his coat would conceal his stockings and buried his face in his crossed arms. His clothing was dark. It was only his hands, face, and white stockings that could betray him if a glint of light penetrated the fog.

"…private must fetch it if there's yet more water to be drawn tonight. This is no inn, and you're no paying guests," a woman said. A deeper voice sounded from inside, the words indistinguishable.

The door closed, and an English voice said, "I'm that sorry for the work we've made you, mistress, but you'd not turn the Devil out on such a night, would you?"

He stole a peek. There was a faint, diffuse glow from the lantern one of them must be carrying. It grew fainter. They were walking away from him along the path.

"Yon lieutenant should have had more sense than to bring you all out with fog rising, for a burning barn."

"They say the fire was set deliberate-like. Our captain was hot to get the one as done it, and there was no fog when we set out."

The woman spoke, but Alex could not make out her answer as voices and light receded to vanishing. The well was a good distance away from the stable.

Alex waited. After a time, he heard them return. The door opened and closed. After an eternity—but mayhap it was only an hour or so—the glow between the crack in the shutters disappeared. A faint light appeared in the gable end window above him. He waited a little longer, and it disappeared. He finally risked getting to his feet. If he could get past the house and avoid falling into the well...it was going to be a long night.

****

The footpath led, eventually, to a road. Having found it, Alex waited nearby for morning, chafing to be on his way in spite of weariness and sore feet. There was no use going on until the sun rose. Even if the fog lasted, it should be possible to determine where the sun was. He did not want to find himself walking north or west. In the gray murk, with neither sun nor stars to guide him, there had been no hope of keeping his bearings.

He was walking again before the last of the fog lifted, though he paralleled the road, keeping as much to the cover of trees, rises, and the occasional wall as he could. His head had given up aching, though now he had blisters on both feet and probably holes in the heels of his stockings. He was hungry, in damp garments, his stockings filthy, and his coat not much better. But he forgot all his discomforts when he reached the outskirts of a village and saw a small inn.

It was not a posting inn, or "change house" as such

things were called in Scotland, or a place that well-to-do travelers would stop. Good.

"A room and a meal, and hot water to wash with," Alex drawled. His best aristocratic manner had often entertained his college friends in their amateur theatricals. He had no reason to suppose he was being sought, but also no reason to assume he wasn't. The talk he'd overhead last night—that the army was hunting for the arsonist—caused him some alarm. How had they come to suppose the fire had been set? Barns did burn unassisted. But likely it was only suspicion. If he were guarding a barn full of muskets, with a rebel army on the march, he'd suspect sabotage, too.

The innkeep ran a knowledgeable eye over Gordon, no doubt noting his days-unshaven face, dishevelment, and his middling suit. "And will you be needing stabling for your horse, sir?"

Alex laughed sourly. "No, blast it. A ruffian hit me on the head, robbed me, and stole my nag yesterday evening. I came to myself in the dark and lost my way. Ah...he did not get quite all my money, fortunately." He displayed a guinea.

"Och, these are terrible lawless times. You'll want your shirt washed. And your stockings as well?"

"If you'd be so good. But first a meal."

"It will be ready as quick as a cat can blink her eye. There is minced pie of beef, soup, and a dish of egg and onion, simple for an English gentleman's taste, but my gudewife is a braw cook. There's only the taproom for a dining salon, unless you'd be served in your chamber, Mr....?"

"Thomas Elphinstone. The tap will do well enough." Elphinstone, his old college friend, would not mind the appropriation of his family name. He'd a peck of brothers, cousins, uncles, and nephews, after all. Better to be someone else until he was safe back in England.

He sat in the taproom again after his meal and a few hours' sleep and listened to the locals' gossip. No one mentioned the barn fire, so he must have come far enough to be outside the area the soldiers had been searching. His first impulse had been to find transportation away as soon as he'd woken. On reflection, it seemed better to behave like an innocent traveler, rather than a fleeing felon. By the time he'd eaten and slept and eaten again, the afternoon was too advanced to be setting out. He would have visited a barber to be shaved, had there been such a convenience. Failing that, he thought he would wait.

The publican asked whether he wished to report the robbery.

"Is there a justice of the peace or magistrate here to whom I can report it?"

"Och, well, no. The nearest is in Kirkaldy, I'm thinking. We're decent, law-abiding folk here."

Alex sighed. "And where is Kirkaldy from this place?"

"South, sir. It may be three or four Scots miles or a wee bit more in English miles."

"Then I will go to Kirkaldy in the morning, though I misdoubt it will do me any good to report the matter, and I do not want to linger long, waiting to hear of the rogue's apprehension. I have already been delayed and am expected at home."

"But to be robbed of a horse and money and not report it will only hearten such rascals. My father used to say, 'If you hang a thief when he's young, he will not steal when he's old.' "

"Will I get my horse and my money back if the fellow's taken? Hardly!"

"The horse, mayhap. Money aye goes fast."

"The horse was no great loss. It was an evil-tempered brute I bought at Tayport. An excellent bargain, I thought, until I found he would not go faster than a trot, which is how I fell prey to that villain. On the whole, he's welcome to the beast. I hope it throws him and breaks his neck. 'Twould save the cost of hanging. I chiefly regret the loss of my valise."

The man chuckled though he tutted at Alex's lack of zeal in prosecuting the crime. Of course, he could not know there was no horse or valise. "You'll have had business in Tayport, then, sir?

"No, I accompanied a friend who meant to make his way to Perth, and we parted at Tayport. I did not have time for a leisurely tour of Scotland. It seemed an easy enough thing to ride to the Firth of Forth and find a ship to take me south."

"There's many a slip 'twixt the cup and the lip. But you'll find a boat at Kirkaldy to carry you across the firth. Or there might be a ship, though there is not much shipping there now. And you would be able to buy another shirt and stockings, as well, if you wish. Even a coat."

"Oh, ay. I would be tired indeed of the ones I'm wearing by the time I reach home." He looked a veritable ragamuffin. Even laundering had not restored his shirt and stockings to their original state. His coat and breeches were unbrushed because the inn was unaccustomed to offering such services for the country folk and laborers who stayed there. And he could not have let someone brush his coat anyway lest the remaining coins be discovered. Alex had shaken both garments thoroughly and trimmed the dangling threads that had secured the facings and the guineas within, but their look was not much improved.

"If you cross the firth, you will likely find a ship at Leith."

"First I must go to Kirkaldy then."

Then he had to spin a skein of lies about his manor in Lincolnshire and the obligations that called him home. It was lucky he'd once visited Elphinstone's family property in that county and knew something of it. It was a fine line between giving so little explanation that the hearer's suspicions were roused and giving so many details that one was caught out in a lie.

Chapter 22

The next day was not better.

She was heavy-eyed in the morning and trying to decide whether to write to Mr. Lattimer in the hope that he would know what to do. When her papa strode into the housekeeper's room where she was writing out a list of household sundries to be purchased, she was so startled, she dropped her pen, spotting both the list and her gown with ink. He flung a newspaper down on the desk, to the further detriment of her shopping list. It would be necessary to write it out anew.

"You might have told me, when I asked you about de Veil." The words were spoken quite softly, a sign that Papa was very angry indeed.

"Told you what, sir?"

"By God, I don't know which is worse: the accusation that you poisoned your uncle or this! Read it!" He indicated a paragraph with a shaking finger. Rage, not fear, she concluded.

It has now been revealed that the young lady who seemed so likely a suspect in the death by arsenical poisoning of a relative has not been prosecuted because the true murderer is known, though currently not in England. Several witnesses who are deemed reliable, and who are unconnected with the young lady, Mistress J—S—, and with each other, have given statements that a certain merchant ship's officer posed as a messenger to deliver poisoned potted shrimp to the late Roger Markham, giving the lady's name as the sender. The officer, strongly attracted to the lady, who had rebuffed his advances, chose to avenge his wounded pride by making it appear she was guilty of murder. His ship having sailed soon after the evil deed, it has not been possible to arrest him, but port authorities have been notified that when his ship next makes port, he is to be detained.

There was a good deal more, both leading up to the passage and afterward, but Jane read no more, partly because she was overwhelmed by relief and gratitude, and partly because her father snatched the paper away again. Someone had acted to save her.

"How do you explain this, Jane?" Her father's voice was ominously soft.

This would be an excellent time to swoon. She had no notion how much she dare say about the imaginary suitor, in case there should be another fragment or two of information in the paper. And what witnesses? Alas, fainting was an art she had never learned and did not feel she could feign successfully.

"My acquaintance with this person was of the slightest and came about only through the mischance of my losing my balance on uneven cobbles in the street. I encountered him again in the neighborhood on two or three other occasions. He was civil and well-spoken, but it never occurred to me he had any romantical interest in me. We hardly exchanged more than polite greetings on those occasions, until the last, when he proposed marriage. I fear my first impulse was to laugh, thinking it was merely banter. On realizing he was serious, I tried to decline as courteously as I could, but I must have injured his feelings. Though how he could suppose any lady would accept an offer of marriage on such short acquaintance and without the agreement of her family, I cannot think." The man's behavior as she had described it sounded perfectly demented—but then, men were often rather odd creatures. And to poison in revenge for a slighted proposal, and not even the lady, but a relative of hers, was the work of a madman. From that perspective, the tale made some sense.

"I did not bring my children up to lie. You may have been sworn to secrecy, but that cannot apply to your father."

Jane found herself speechless. It almost sounded as if he knew the story in the paper was a ruse. Yet how could he? *Another scold is coming.*

He sighed. "It is all of a piece with your behavior in general. I really do not know what the world is coming to! Everything seems turned upside down. All the Whigs' doing, make no mistake." He frowned at her for a moment as if it were her fault, which it probably was. "This sort of mishap does not occur to girls who do not go out unaccompanied. In the future, you will not go out without a maid."

She opened her mouth to protest that she would either have to take Betty away from the kitchen, which would raise Mrs. Merry's ire, or take the parlor maid, which would inconvenience everyone else. It was easier to argue that suggestion than to counter his accusation she had lied, which was impossible.

"I do not care to discuss it, my dear. You must nearly have completed whatever is required at Markham's—your—house. It can hardly be necessary to visit that part of town often. When you must…" His forehead creased in annoyance. "You must take a maid, or I must accompany you. If the church were closer, you might interest yourself in parish activities. However, you should ask the parson if there is some sewing to be done for the church or the poor that you might occupy yourself with at home." He grunted, which made Jane think of some irritable large animal— a boar, perhaps. "Though that is all beside the main point at the moment." Her father's expression did not encourage her to expect it would be good news.

"A Mr. Lattimer approached me at my club and requested a private interview. I almost felt I'd seen him before, but I cannot think where it could have been."

Jane, with years of practice in keeping her face agreeable or at least bland, did not show surprise at the name.

"He is connected with the government. I am not perfectly sure how, as the document he showed me was quite circumspect. From what he said, I think it must be either the excise, as the affair involves smuggling, or perhaps the War Office, as he mentioned it touched upon the security of the realm. I was extremely sorry to learn you were not truthful with me from the beginning, Jane. Although, given what Lattimer told me, I understand you were sworn to secrecy. Quite improper for a young lady to—but I have already expressed myself upon that topic. I could wish they had spun some other tale to account for the murderer claiming you had sent the shrimps. I suppose the defense of our country must take precedence even over a young lady's reputation. But I do not see why you should not have told me of the suspicious activity you witnessed. I could then have communicated it to the appropriate office, and your name would not have come into public notice."

"I should have done so, sir," Jane agreed mendaciously.

"Ay, well, enough said of that matter. Mr. Lattimer is of the opinion you should go out of town for a time. He tells me some members of the smugglers' ring you exposed escaped capture and may seek revenge. In the morning you will be called for by Mr. and Mrs. Lattimer, who will take you to their country home, where you will be safe. I can scarcely imagine a scurvy pack of smugglers would make an attempt on your life, but Lattimer claims smugglers have murdered witnesses before, and your testimony as to what you saw may be required in court. More humiliation for our family! You had best pack now, so as to be ready."

"Yes, indeed, Papa. How very vexing."

"I hope spending two weeks, or perhaps more, as the Lattimers' guest will not turn your head. Our family is well born enough to consort with any society, but we do not aspire to mix with the aristocracy. Not that Lattimer comes of any better stock than we do, but I believe he comes in contact even with the highest levels of society. His home is in Bloomsbury Square."

She returned some vague reply and whisked out, several ideas revolving in her head.

How exceeding strange. As she folded the best of her chemises and petticoats and sorted out her stockings (some being too much mended to be taken), she concluded Mr. Lattimer must be more important than she had supposed. Clearly, he was responsible for the tale he had told her father, which was at least a distorted version of the truth. She doubted he had orchestrated the embarrassing story in the papers which publicly absolved her of involvement in her uncle's murder. He would have managed to do it with greater subtlety. Now he proposed to spirit her away to protect her from "smugglers." Was it really necessary for any purpose except to add verisimilitude to the smuggling gang story? Remembering Charles Pleasaunce's cold eyes, Jane decided she was not sorry to be hidden away somewhere.

If only the Lattimers' home was a country gentleman's house, a simple establishment. It would be ridiculous to hide her among fashionable people who entertained when the idea was to keep her out of sight. Which was fortunate, as her wardrobe was not extensive. She had her yellow brocade taffeta, of course. It was three years old but still pretty. She had one each of a mantua, a *robe à l'anglaise*, and a *robe à la française* which were not too worn, as well as the assorted accessories necessary to them. Stays. Panniers to hold the skirts out. Her simple cotton gowns needed no panniers, only petticoats. Shoes, handkerchiefs, fichus, caps, hats, gloves. She sent the footman up to the attic for two trunks.

She spent the rest of the afternoon and evening inspecting the household accounts and giving the cook and butler instructions. Several tiresome cleaning projects to be done before autumn set in would have to be postponed until her return. She and Mrs. Merry consulted *The Compleat City and Country Cook* to find a new way to dress mutton, as her father had been complaining of lack of variety in Mrs. Merry's dinners. The cook did not like to attempt new dishes unless she was told to do so, and even then liked to discuss them thoroughly with Jane first. The frayed drapery in the drawing room needed mending (which Elvira could do better than Jane if only she would), but it could wait. Airing the draperies would have to wait. The remaining time until she retired she spent in making a list of all the other chores which she would have to attend to when she came back from her stay with the Lattimers and writing to Jessup to let him know she would be out of town.

Jane awoke in the middle of the night with her heart pounding. At first she thought a nightmare had wakened her, though she could not remember one. Then she wondered if she had been startled back to consciousness by some noise. She listened for another sound, then threw back the covers and tiptoed to the door of her chamber. She opened it gingerly, stepped into the corridor, and padded toward the stair despite the darkness. She had lived here her entire life. She stopped at the head of the stairs, straining to hear. If someone had broken in, she would have heard something different from its normal repertory of creaks and rattles. The wind sighed around the house when it blew from a certain quarter. When she conceded to herself that nothing was stirring within (bar the occasional mouse, possibly), she returned to bed, now too wide awake to sleep.

Only after she had lain down and tried to compose herself to sleep did it occur to her that she was afraid. Not for herself: Alex Gordon had assured her she was safe when she was first suspected of causing her uncle's death, and so she had not really feared she would be tried for the crime. Somehow, he and Sir Thomas de Veil and Mr. Lattimer among them had averted the danger. Now Mr. Lattimer felt Charles Pleasaunce might be a danger to her and meant to hide her. Having formed a high opinion of his good sense, she was willing to be guided by him. No, she was not afraid for herself.

But Mr. Gordon was in Scotland now—if he were not dead, which was a terrible thought. She hoped fervently he was only suffering the normal delays of travel. Was anyone taking as much interest in his safety as Mr. Lattimer was showing in hers? If she were staying at the Lattimers' home, it would be easy for Mr. Lattimer to let her know when he had news of Alex, which was another reason to be perfectly willing to leave town for a visit in the country. Finally, she drifted back to sleep, imagining she had received word from her host that Mr. Gordon was returned, none the worse for his journey. Or that he arrived at the Lattimers' country house, tired and dusty and smiling, to assure her of his safety and...

Chapter 23

A farmer friend of the innkeeper gave him a ride to Kirkaldy. He no longer looked like a gentleman, and after parting with the farmer, he changed his upper-class speech for that of a clerk or tradesman. Alex gave the Kirkaldy Town House a wide berth; he felt wary of the authorities at the moment. From a seller of secondhand clothing, he bought a coarse shirt and a well-worn coat of the sort a small farmer might wear and an old valise in which to carry the shirt and his old coat. At the first opportunity, he would remove the remaining coins from it.

He decided against going to Leith. In its favor, it was near Edinburgh, where his cousin Hugh lived. Hugh might be able to help him, but Edinburgh would be dangerous for a fugitive. And Stowe would likely have made for Leith to find a ship.

The stagecoach would take about a week from Edinburgh to London, and that assuming the weather held. If he wanted to go by sea, which was really the only practical means of getting back to London, he must find another port. If he went west, he might sail from Glasgow, which would mean a longer voyage. Worse, going to Glasgow carried the risk of crossing the path of the Jacobite army. He might gather some useful intelligence, but he would have no way of passing it on—and he might be taken as a spy. So he had best find a ship here.

There was no ship at dock in Kirkaldy, but a warehouseman directed him to a carrier who had a shipment of striped and checked linen to deliver to the *Susan McKay*, lying at Burntisland, half a dozen miles away.

"Too bad it could not be shipped directly from Kirkaldy," Alex said to the freightman, "although it's money for you."

"Ay, and it should have gone from here, but the linen must be inspected and stamped, you'll ken, and the stampmaster being gey slow to do it, it missed the sailing. Cheaper for the manufactory to pay me to haul it to Burntisland than to pay the fine for unstamped linen. And you are paying me a bit, so 'tis a good day for me."

Alex was prepared to explain that he had been sent north on an errand by his employer, but the Scot was chatty and incurious and had a good deal to say about the loss of foreign trade resulting from the union with England and about the odd things he had sometimes been hired to transport.

He went with the carrier to the ship to arrange for his passage and was told he might come aboard immediately.

"Though if I was you, I'd have a meal ashore first," the mate said.

While finishing dinner in a tavern near the docks, he picked up a copy of the *Newcastle Courant* someone had left on the bench and glanced idly at it. One of the items captured his attention:

It is reported by our Correspondent in Scotland that a follower of the Young Pretender has been captured. One Alec or Alexander Gordon, believed to be attempting to smuggle arms to the rebel cause, is being held in gaol at Dundee.

The newspaper was days old, having been published on the sixth of September, before the prisoners had been freed. Fortunate that he'd given Elphinstone's name at that inn. But if news of his arrest had appeared in a provincial English journal, it might be reprinted in one of the London papers. He must continue to be Thomas Elphinstone until he returned to London, resumed his own name, and reported the confusion to his father. He did not look forward to that meeting. He could imagine the high points: *secretive, deceitful, no sense, reckless, ship you off to the Colonies…*

It was all a tangle. He had done what he could for Rupert Stowe, and Stowe had scorned his help and even cast suspicion on him. It was not surprising. Alex had formed a fair notion of the fellow's character before they left London. He hoped Jane—Mistress Jane— would understand. She was a practical young lady, and probably knew her half brother tolerably well.

On the other hand, he had destroyed the muskets and the cannon, though he could not be certain about the latter. The cannon barrels might have survived the explosion and fire, having been made to survive repeated firing of cannon balls. At the very least, the wooden wheels and carriages which supported the cannon barrels would have to be replaced. The gunpowder had been destroyed. He had accomplished something.

Chapter 24

For once, Elvira had bestirred herself to leave her bedroom early. She and Jane's father were entertaining the Lattimers in the morning room, while the Stowes' footman loaded Jane's trunks. Jane hurried down from one last inspection of her bedchamber to make sure she had forgotten nothing.

Stepmama, all agoggle, said, "Here are Mr. and Mrs. Lattimer, come to take you for a visit, Jane. I was never so surprised. Of course, I never knew any of your mother's friends."

Jane interpreted this as meaning that her papa had not confided to her the real reason for her "visit" with the Lattimers.

The lady, whose face bore a few freckles which she was at no pains to conceal, replied, "I fear Jane will not recall me, as I have not seen her since she was three or four years of age."

Strangely, she did seem somehow familiar. She was neither beautiful nor conventionally pretty, having a rather long, thin face, and with freckles, too. In fact, everything about her was long and thin, or tall and slender to put it more kindly, and she had long, graceful hands. Jane, relinquishing truthfulness—for it had become all but impossible since her uncle's death—said, "I believe I do remember you a little, ma'am. Thank you for inviting me to stay with you."

Her stepmother attempted to prolong their stay by offering refreshments, but the Lattimers, seconded by Jane's father, succeeded in making their adieus and carrying Jane off to their coach. As it rolled away from the door, Jane wondered if she would have an opportunity in private to ask Mr. Lattimer several pressing questions.

Anticipating her thought, he said, "I apologize for the story that was published. There had been some discussion of how best to lay to rest the rumors about your culpability and clear your name, but nothing had been decided. Someone"—his voice chilled—"took it upon himself to act without further consultation, feeling our hand was forced by a malicious letter which was published. I did not know the *someone* had acted until I saw the article in the *Evening Post*. It's true the tale was the best anyone had suggested, but I...the group considering the matter hoped to find one less sensational. The rejected-suitor explanation did have the advantage of being titillating enough to capture the public's imagination. Young men who persecute young ladies who do not reciprocate their sentiments are not unknown."

"Oh! I see. While it was a little awkward, I confess I was worried after that letter appeared in the newspaper. I suppose this must seem outrageous to you, ma'am," she added.

With a look of pure merriment, Mrs. Lattimer raised her eyebrows. "No, Mistress Jane. My standard for the outrageous is rather high."

"Of necessity, my wife is fully aware of the underlying matter," Mr. Lattimer said.

"That is a great relief to me. I was not brought up

to deceive people—except socially, I mean."

For some reason, Mrs. Lattimer found that funny, to judge by her quirking lips. Mr. Lattimer kept his face admirably bland.

"I am hopeful you will not have to remain in concealment very long, Mistress Jane. With luck, the matter will be speedily settled, or at the least, Charles Pleasaunce and his associates will be too busy to bother further about you. I should mention that the 'Friend of Justice' who reignited the question of Markham's death is being investigated as a possible conspirator. Pleasaunce likely set him on to discredit anything you might say about him or about conspiracies."

The property to which the Lattimers took her was a small one, on the outskirts of a village some twenty or twenty-five miles from London. It seemed even more distant, well removed from any of the main roads into the city. The house, like something a prosperous farmer might occupy, enchanted her. It was of mellow brick, with many small-paned windows, and half a dozen dormer windows that made odd humps in the thatched roof. It sat a little back from the road, with the prettiest garden she had ever seen. It was not laid out in orderly beds, and included honeysuckle, cornflowers, lily of the valley, roses, snapdragons, hollyhocks, and a host of flowers she could not identify.

"The owner lives in Town for the most part, but sometimes lets friends stay here," Mr. Lattimer said. "The servants are accustomed to guests, and you may repose complete trust in Cheddle, the butler. No…ah…smugglers need worry you here."

She had understood she was going to the Lattimers' country home.

"If you leave the grounds, I ask that you take a maid and one of the outdoor servants with you."

"Certainly, sir."

"There is one other thing. I trust you will not mind being known by another name while you are here? For the duration of your stay, the staff will know you as Evelyn Ashton. I hope you do not dislike the name, for there was not time to ask your preference. The servants will ask no questions of you. If you should be asked by anyone else—if you go into the village, for example—you will say you are related to Lionel Ashton, the owner, and have come to stay until you secure another post as a governess." Lattimer added with a twinkle, "I'm sure you know how to discourage the impertinent from asking more than that."

"I believe I can do so. But if I am to be Evelyn Ashton here, if my father should send a letter to me addressed to my own name, will it not cause confusion?"

"I was guilty of a little deception there, Mistress Jane. I told your father you were to be our guest and gave him the direction of our manor, which is some distance away. If he or anyone else sends you a letter, one of my servants will bring it here within a cover addressed to your *nom de guerre*. And if you must write to your family, Cheddle will make sure 'tis dispatched discreetly."

Clearly, Mr. Lattimer possessed a devious mind and some experience in misdirection. She found herself exceedingly curious about how he had come by it.

She and the Lattimers passed a pleasant evening playing cards and retired to bed at an unfashionably early hour, by London standards. She fell asleep easily, tired by travel and lulled by the quaint little room with its slanting, beamed ceiling, simple old furniture, and patchwork counterpane. By the time the Lattimers left in the morning to go to their own manor, Jane felt quite at home. No, better, except she wondered how she would occupy herself without her ordinary chores. The house was well staffed, with enough servants, gardeners, and stable hands to serve a family, but with no family in residence. The servants took care of everything, with no need of direction. She feared her days would be boring without her usual tasks, until she discovered the fascinating activities of country life. There was a vegetable and herb garden to explore, fruit trees, chickens, a pig or two, and a cow to admire. Jane watched the dairymaid milk the cow and make cheese and clotted cream and butter. She helped the cook pickle green walnuts which Jane herself had helped gather.

Her own family did not own a country property. Papa usually rented a house in Bath or at one of the other spas in the hottest part of the summer, though this year they had stayed in Town. He had not explained his decision, and Elvira had not questioned it, at least in Jane's hearing, which suggested that Rupert or possibly Matthew had run up debts which made it impracticable to spend the money. The season had been wet in London, eliminating the heat, stenches, and dust which were the usual reasons for abandoning Town in summer, and as her father had observed, it might well be rainy wherever they went.

For evenings and damp days, there was a well-stocked library containing works on geography, history, foreign dictionaries, and a good many less easily classified works, even recent novels. Jane suppressed a feeling of guilt at such a temptation and steeled her heart to enjoy herself.

She was cutting flowers in the garden when Cheddle himself, rather than the footman, brought her a letter.

"Mistress," he said with a deprecating throat-clearing sound.

"For me?" She was surprised. Surely it was too soon for mail to have come from her family. Unless it was some domestic emergency. Heaven forbid Elvira or her father had offended Mrs. Merry, causing her to give notice. Or mayhap it was from Mr. Lattimer, with news of Alex?

"Please take these into the house. I'll arrange them as soon as I've read the message." She held out her hand, and the butler said, "Mistress…this was brought by a stranger. Not someone who should bring the mail. It's not directed to Mistress Evelyn Ashton."

It took her a moment to understand. Mr. Lattimer had said that if a letter came to his home for her, it would be sent on with one of his servants, under separate cover addressed to Evelyn Ashton. She glanced at Cheddle. He was looking very directly at her with a most unbutler-like expression. He was correctly garbed and deferential and ran the household to perfection—better than her own family's Wilson did, in fact. Yet there was something different about Cheddle; it was not his size, for he was not conspicuously taller or broader than most male servants. He might have begun as a footman. They were expected to be well set up. Cheddle might have spent a great deal of time outdoors, doing something energetic; it was in his weathered face, his nose obviously broken at some time, his large, strong-looking hands, and his brisk movements. And he had very sharp, watchful gray eyes.

Taking her pause for incomprehension, he said, "I'm charged by my employer to keep you safe. Please open it, Mistress Evelyn. I must know who sent this, and what it says."

Did the staff here know who she really was? They called her Mistress Evelyn, and Anthony Lattimer had not said whether they knew her real name, but Cheddle had had no doubt the letter addressed to Jane Stowe was meant for her. She sat down on the rustic bench beside a damask rose bush, now bare of blooms, and broke the seal.

Your presence is required in London with some urgency to give Testimony in a matter related to the Death of your uncle, Roger Markham. I confidently Expect that this will complete the investigation and Result in your absolute exoneration. I will send a Coach within the next day to fetch you.

Sir Thomas de Veil
Magistrate
Bow Street Magistrate's Court

That was good news. Jane wondered why she was a little disappointed. She wished it had been word of Alex's—Mr. Gordon's—safety. Though once she was back in London, she could ask Mr. Lattimer if he had heard anything. She must tell the maid to pack her trunks.

"Cheddle, I'm summoned back to Town to give evidence at Bow Street. Sir Thomas de Veil is sending a coach for me. I don't know whether I will be returning or not, but I can discuss that with Mr.

Lattimer. If you'll have my trunks brought to my room—"

"Begging your pardon for interrupting you, mistress, but how would Sir Thomas know you was here?"

"Why, I suppose Mr. Lattimer told him. Surely he would trust a magistrate? Sir Thomas de Veil has been investigating a…a suspicious death of—of someone I knew." Why would Mr. Lattimer tell him? Or how would Sir Thomas know to inquire of him? They might have a connection through the government, of course. Clearly, Mr. Lattimer held some sort of office, and in addition to his duties as a magistrate, de Veil was now hunting out Jacobites.

"It would still have come by the usual method, mistress. Are you familiar with Sir Thomas's hand?"

"No, I've never seen a specimen of his handwriting," she admitted.

"It's easy enough to sign any name you please to a letter. Mr. Lattimer wanted you safe out of London at present. I'm responsible for you."

Cheddle's clipped words and ramrod posture were almost military at times…and this was one of them. Not an officer, but perhaps a sergeant?

Cheddle went on, "The letter did not come by the usual means. It was delivered direct, to your true name. Someone knows you are here, apart from those who should know."

"Then 'tis a trick?"

The butler inclined his head slightly.

"Then should we not send a message to ask for instructions, by the fastest possible means?"

"I do not think we have time to receive an answer

before someone comes to take you away. And I am reluctant to send any of the menservants. They may be needed here. I will apprise the appropriate gentleman, and he will no doubt ascertain whether the message did somehow come from Sir Thomas. In the meantime, we must move you to a new refuge. If Sir Thomas did send for you, which I do not apprehend, we will produce you."

"And if there is someone watching, will he not follow if I leave here?"

"He will not see you leave, mistress."

****

The farm cart bumped over the road, and Jane bumped with it. The groom driving it commented occasionally to the horse and sometimes to her. There was a large barrel with a broken stave in the back of the cart, to make it plain that they were on their way to the nearest cooper.

Jane, wearing a maid's plain gown, with a plain round-eared cap and wide-brimmed straw hat, sat with a basket on her lap, a servant on her way to make some purchase. At the cottage, the gown's owner, wearing Jane's third-best gown, was sitting by a front window. She would also flit past other windows from time to time so any watcher would have plenty of opportunity to conclude Jane was present. The ease with which Cheddle had organized the ruse was disquieting. One would think such things were commonplace in Lionel Ashton's country cottage. If there were a Lionel Ashton. It must be all right because Mr. Lattimer had arranged her visit and she trusted him. He had been her uncle's friend. *Or so he said.* He knew Alex, and that was certainly true because Alex's message had directed her to Mr. Lattimer. *But what do I know of Mr. Gordon except that he has eyes that crinkle at the corners when he smiles and a sense of humor? And a lean, strong body?* as she had deduced from walking arm in arm with him. His arm was reassuringly hard.

Still, it appeared Alex and Mr. Lattimer were not Charles Pleasaunce's allies. Alex—Mr. Gordon! She should not be thinking of him so familiarly, or the next time she saw him, it might slip out—had sought her out to tell her not to fear and had gone north to try to save Rupert. How kind, how good he was! Though his and Mr. Lattimer's ability to arrange things, like preventing her arrest, obtaining money and transport, and fabricating tales to clear her name, were a trifle puzzling. How had they managed such feats? She would not think further about it.

Yet her mind kept returning to it. Given the political situation, and Rupert and Mr. Gordon having gone to Scotland, it was obvious the smuggled muskets were destined to assist a Jacobite rebellion. Mr. Lattimer (and Alex) were attempting to stop it. Which must mean they represented the government, a theory supported by Sir Thomas de Veil's involvement in preventing her prosecution for murder. But if they were government agents, had Alex been acting only on the government's behalf in assisting Rupert? Perhaps even not to protect Rupert from the consequences of his actions but to arrest him when he had incriminated himself beyond hope by delivering the payment?

Remembering his evident enjoyment of her company, his approval, the light banter, she could not bear to think it intended only to gain her trust. He was utterly unlike Charles Pleasaunce, whose cool compliments might have come directly from a book on how to woo a lady. She had had years to study Elvira's methods for gaining her own ends: the flattery and flirtation, the feigned helplessness that invited others to take care of her, the fits of vapors, the subtle use of guilt. Jane was immune.

Or was she? Her stepmother had never tried to manipulate her. Elvira's targets were generally male. She was far more likely to criticize Jane than to praise. Or Mr. Gordon might simply be more skillful than Elvira. She was unaccustomed to receiving admiration. Might it have swayed her judgment?

She sighed. Oh, yes. The attention of an attractive man would affect her as easily as it would any spinster. How lowering to realize her previously unrecognized craving for appreciation could blind her.

She uttered "Phoo!" startling the groom.

"Mistress?"

"Nothing, Jack. I only had a vexing thought."

Jack nodded and clucked to the horse.

These thoughts (and worry about Alex in spite of her new suspicion) occupied her mind until Jack Ridgley drew in a harsh breath. All the bucolic good humor had vanished from his face, and his lips were set in a thin line. A coach approached, driven at a brisk pace.

When it had passed and the sound of its progress was no longer audible, he urged their own horse to a faster pace. "Mayhap it's nothing," Jack muttered. But he did not permit the mare to slow until they had turned into a rutted lane marked by a fingerpost with the paint worn illegible.

"A stranger would find that sign of little

assistance," Jane remarked, squinting at it doubtfully.

Jack gave her a sidelong look. "Ay, none at all, unless someone gave him directions."

"All to our benefit, no doubt." If Jack feared the coach was the one sent to fetch her. "It's fortunate it's not readable."

"Ay. Some magistrates are particular about keeping the fingerposts in repair and some aren't. When it's only a bit of a village that's not on the way to some important town, there's no urgency about it."

Littlefield certainly qualified as "a bit of a village," with no more than the cooperage, a small public house, and a shop in the front room of one of a handful of cottages.

"I'll walk you to the shop when I'm done here." Very softly he added, "Recall that you are Susan."

She waited while he unloaded the barrel and talked quietly at some length to the grizzled cooper.

They stopped in at the little shop that sold the things the country folk hereabout might need most urgently, and Jane purchased a paper of pins, as Cheddle had instructed her, and added them to her basket.

"New maid at Hawthorn Cottage?" the woman asked Jack.

"Ah, nay. Susan is a cousin of Cook's, on her way to service."

"Well, I hope you'll like the place you're going, Susan."

Jane gave a little smile and bobbed a curtsey.

"She's shy, is Susan," Jack said. Cheddle had found Jane had no ability to mimic lower-class speech or any regional accent for more than a word or two.

When they came out, the cooper was standing in front of his workshop, smoking a clay pipe. He nodded a greeting at Jack and gazed at the sky. Business must not be brisk.

Jack led her into the yard behind the cooperage, where a cart loaded with several casks and firkins stood. A hatchet-faced woman, wisps of grizzled hair poking out from under her linen cap, was at the horse's head. Her short gown, worn over a brown petticoat, had faded to the color of cooked celery, and her stockings were blue. She gave the animal a pat on its shoulder and approached.

"Susan, this is Alice. She'll take you to my auntie's to stay for a bit. 'Til things are sorted out, like."

The woman gave her a friendly nod. "Come along, then, Susan."

She did not like feeling like a parcel, to be handed on without knowing her destination or having any control. But there was really no choice.

"Tell my auntie I'll come see her my next free day."

"Ay." Alice clambered up onto the wagon seat, followed more slowly by Jane, with Jack Ridgeley's assistance. She hoped she could get down without help.

Alice drove out of the yard and into the road. Before Jane had had time to accustom herself to the height of the wagon seat above the ground, they had passed the last of the cottages. Hedgerows grew on either side, cutting off any view of fields or herds. *We are deep in the country. No one could possibly find me here.*

Alice, for all her hard-bitten appearance, was good company. She kept up a flow of observations about the weather, the crops, the reason she never wore a hat ("They flap around and get in the way. Try milking in a broad-brimmed hat."), and how it was no use for a countrywoman to expect to keep a white complexion. Jane uttered an occasional "Oh?" or "Ah!" which was encouragement enough for Alice and concealed Jane's upper-class speech.

"I'm pleased to have a reason to visit my daughter," Alice remarked. "She lives only a mile or two from Jack's aunt." She added, "My daughter's new baby is Susan, too. I've always liked that name. It makes me think of daisies; I don't know why."

They had come several miles and left the hedgerows behind, affording a view of fields broken by bands of trees, with distant hills for a background.

"A few more miles to go," Alice was saying when Jane, glancing back, saw a rider approaching at a gallop. She nudged Alice and gave a quick jerk of her head back the way they'd come. The woman turned her head to look.

" 'Tis Jack."

Alice must be very farsighted, Jane thought. She would not have recognized the groom at such a distance, though it would help that Alice must know him well. The rider waved his hat over his head and shouted something. By then, the cooper's wife had pulled up. Jack brought his horse to a halt and looked over his shoulder.

"Jack?" Alice and Jane traded glances.

"Sorry...Susan is needed at home. Your mother is ill."

"She is?" Her voice squeaked a little.

He cast her a meaningful look. "Terrible ill, and

wants to see you before…"

Oh. "That ill?" She gathered her wits. Of course he wasn't talking about her late mother or even her stepmother.

"Ay, and you're sent for. There's no time to waste. You'll ride back behind me to catch the stage."

"That's a good horse," Alice remarked.

"I borrowed it of Farmer Mason. Breeds good stock. I left the wagon and Bessie as security for it. Mason knows Mr. Ashton would pay up for any harm to his horse."

"Mr. Ashton is one of the best. Then Susan must go. Just bring that nag closer, boy, and she can get up behind you with no trouble."

Jane murmured her thanks to Alice and stood as Jack's mount sidled close beside the cart. The wagon was steady, and the horse content to stand and rest, but the prospect of making the transition to the back of Jack's horse was a little daunting. It wasn't actually moving, but it looked as if it might do so at any moment. Jack swiveled in the saddle and extended a hand to steady her. If they had to travel fast, she could not perch sideways on the horse's rump, not without falling off. He evidently did not mean her to ride before him, for which she was grateful; that would have been uncomfortably intimate. The horse's rump was directly before her.

She swung her leg out and over the animal, feeling awkward. The front of her skirt and petticoats caught between her legs so they were between her bare skin and the glossy brown hide when she dropped onto the horse. It felt very strange to bestride the horse, and because the front of her skirts was between her legs and under her, her limbs were outlined, almost as if she were wearing breeches. At least she had not slid backward to land ignominiously on the ground. The back of her skirt fell over the horse's tail, and she must hope the horse did not produce droppings.

Riding astride was not something she had ever done, although she had seen country girls do it. They seemed to have less difficulty controlling their skirts. Did she appear indecent? It all felt terribly immodest, especially when she wrapped her arms around Jack's torso to hold on. If the male body she was hugging had been Alex's, it would have been different. Embarrassing, perhaps, but…different. She ended the thought abruptly. She smiled her farewell to Alice and hoped her face was not pink, or if it were, that the woman would think it was excitement or exertion.

With a nod to Alice and a brief "Are you secure, Susan?" to her, Jack turned their mount, and they cantered away.

As soon as they were out of sight of the cart, Jack spurred the horse.

"What's amiss, Jack?"

"After I saw you off from Littlefield, I heard a fellow had been asking about the maid I brought there this morning. Seemingly someone picked up your trail right quick. If he kept asking, he may have found someone who saw you leave with Alice."

They came to a tidy farm Jane had admired when they passed it, and Jack reined the horse in to a trot and turned into the track to the house, then branched off onto a path past the fields toward woodland. The leaves were beginning to turn, harbinger of autumn and cold, dark nights. She shivered with apprehension rather chill.

"We ride cross-country from here. I want to be off the roads." Jack's manner was no longer that of a bashful young groom. He sounded older and more decisive. His previous rustic manner might go no deeper than her own disguise as a maid or her earlier pose as an unemployed governess.

"What shall we do?"

"That's what I don't know. I've no orders to guide me. It never seemed I'd need them, only to deliver you to Littlefield and pass you on. Mr. Cheddle's needle-sharp, but he can't have expected them to see through our plan. All I *do* know is I've got to get you away to some safe place. They must want you desperate bad, whoever they are."

They followed the path and then a cart track without seeing another village or even a house or cottage, except at a distance. A great deal of the country seemed to be almost empty, a startling discovery for one who had always lived in London. Even when her family went to Bath or Tunbridge Wells in the summer, they seldom left the main coaching roads and signs of civilization.

"Haymaking's finished. It's as well for us."

The fields they passed were down to stubble, with no laborers in sight, and no one to see their passage, Jane understood. "You must know this countryside very well."

"Ay, I grew up not far from Littlefield. Maybe ten miles north from where we are now. We'll go there. If the master's there, he'll know what to do."

"Should we involve someone else? We would have to explain the situation. Mr. Lattimer might not approve."

A pause. "My old master, Mr. Grantham, knows Mr. Lattimer. Mr. Grantham will understand. And if he's not in residence, we'll still have a place to stay, and I'll send a message to Mr. Lattimer."

They passed from ordinary countryside into a wood with huge, gnarled trees, following a narrow, dim track overhung by branches. It might have led them from the modern world to some earlier period. She almost expected a troop of King John's men or a procession of druids to pass and suppressed a shiver. Their gradual emergence from deep forest into a scattering of trees and then into a sunlit meadow came as a relief.

Her legs and thighs ached before Jack reined in at the top of a rise. A road in good repair lay before them, though clearly not a coaching road.

"A'most there," he said, jerking his chin to the right.

A large house stood off to the side of the road beyond a small lake. Of light gray stone, its long façade was broken by evenly-spaced windows pedimented in the Palladian style, and tall columns flanked the entrance. "Is that where we're going? It's very impressive."

Jack chuckled. "Ay, Mr. Grantham built it a few years since, when he came into some money. Mind, it's not half as deep as it is wide. Not much land, either. He didn't want to be bothered with a pack of tenants, so there's only a home farm and some parkland. The building in back is the stable and carriage house. They say it's made to look like a Roman temple or some such thing."

"I see," she said faintly. She had supposed the

smaller building to be the dower house.

****

Mr. Grantham stared at Jane, who stared back. Jack had introduced her and given a concise account of who she was and why she needed help, and then was dismissed, to her dismay.

Grantham said, "I can't think why Lattimer chose to involve a lady in such a matter. It was quite improper, and this is what comes of it."

She did not explain that she had no choice but to be involved. Jack and the Hawthorn Cottage folk did not know how it had come about, and Mr. Lattimer had instructed her not to tell them. Would he have agreed that Grantham should be told? She didn't know, and she was reluctant to do so. She had not taken a liking to him.

"And you cannot remain here," he went on, "as my wife is not in residence. It seems to me the Hawthorn Cottage staff took fright too easily. Jack Ridgeley was always sensible enough when he was employed here, but servants take their tone from their employers."

Ridgeley was a servant of Mr. Ashton, surely? Yet Grantham's disdain was for Lattimer.

"Then I will have to write to Mr. Lattimer," she said briskly. "Is there somewhere I can stay while I wait for him to tell me what he would like me to do? Some woman who would take me as a lodger for a few days or a week? I saw an inn, but it would certainly be unsuitable for me to stay there without a maid."

"As it happens, I know Lattimer is away at the moment. I don't know when he will return to London. I believe the only possible course of action is for you to go back to Town. Surely you have family or friends to

242

whom you can return?"

"It would be awkward to explain, as I am supposed to be staying in the country. However, I could go—" She had meant to say *to my uncle's house*, but changed her mind. "—to the home of a friend."

"Very good. I've no doubt you'll be perfectly safe there."

If indeed there was any danger to you, he must be thinking.

"If you wish, I will send you in my coach."

The grudging note in his voice was plain. "I will not put you to such inconvenience, sir. If Jack can take me to the nearest posting inn, I will go by stage. No one will notice me, dressed like a maidservant."

Chapter 25

She was exhausted and sore when she arrived at the Oxford Arms, the stage's London terminus. Since Ridgeley had seen her safely aboard the stage hours previously she had been jolted and bounced over rough roads, beside a woman with a crying baby and a little girl suffering from travel sickness who had vomited out the window several times. She would almost have preferred sitting next to the man with breath like an open sewer or the young man who stared at her as if he were undressing her. The coach stopped to change horses, but such pauses were brief—enough time for a male passenger to pour a pint of ale down his throat or for a visit to the necessary house behind the inn, but not to really stretch one's legs or eat.

Thank goodness it had been only a day's journey. Many travelled long distances in such vehicles, spending several days on the road. She had heard from her uncle that in his youth the trip from Edinburgh to London had taken as much as ten days. Thank goodness, too, she had had a seat inside. Those with less money rode on the roof, which must be extremely uncomfortable. It would often be necessary to keep a tight grip on the low rail around the top, choked by dust in dry weather or drenched if it rained. Horrid!

At least no one except the leering young man had paid the slightest attention to her. Ridgeley had contrived to deliver her not long before the stage's arrival and paid her fare so she would not betray herself by her upper-class diction. He had stayed to see her off, as though she were his sister or sweetheart, to discourage anyone from trying to strike up an acquaintance with her. And now she was back in London and almost home.

The inn yard was bustling with passersby and travelers coming and going or waiting for their belongings to be unloaded from the coach. But she had only her basket, with the pot of jam, wedge of cheese, and loaf of brown bread supplied by Grantham's cook, at Jack Ridgeley's request. It gave her the look of a maid or country woman on an errand and meant she need not linger to wait for a bundle or valise, as others were doing. Would her two trunks of clothing at Hawthorn Cottage ever be sent back to her? It was foolish to worry about such a thing when she had so many more important matters to occupy her mind, but she was very fond of that yellow taffeta, and she really could not spare those clothes.

She glanced around the courtyard, overlooked by its railed galleries, gawking like a raw country girl. No one appeared to be paying attention to anything but his own luggage or duties. It was foolish to fear someone might be watching for her arrival. How could the man or men who had meant to abduct her from Hawthorn Cottage, or the man who had followed her trail to Littlefield know where she had gone? But they had known of Hawthorn Cottage. And if she had been pursued to Littlefield, might the pursuer be able to find out that Ridgeley had taken her to Mr. Grantham's manor, where he had once worked? If she were not to be found there, the nearest town where a coach stopped might seem her obvious next destination. It would be simple to ask if a young woman had boarded at that stage. And then it would only be a matter of riding to the London inn and waiting for her. It was unlikely, but she could not help but be a little nervous. Mr. Grantham had obviously felt she was in no danger. He might be correct—but gentlemen had been mistaken before on any number of subjects.

She tied her straw hat over her cap and followed an elderly couple when they began plodding toward Fleet Street, hoping it might appear that she was with them. Darkness had fallen, but it was early enough in the evening that people were still going home or out on errands. When the couple turned east, she detached herself, trusting the darkness would deceive anyone watching for her if there were such a person. She turned west, onto Ludgate Street, setting off briskly, glad to be walking rather than still rattling along in the coach. She needed to stretch her legs—and the wild gallop behind Jack Ridgeley had exercised quite unsuspected muscles which had now tightened up. The Oxford Arms, near St. Paul's, was less than a mile from her uncle's house.

She crossed the Fleet Ditch, holding her breath at the stench of sewage and rotting debris of all sorts. The bridge marked the end of Ludgate and the beginning of Fleet Street.

No, the distance was not far, except to the mind: some twelve hours ago she had been jouncing along in the wagon with Jack, sure that they had gotten away from Hawthorn Cottage unremarked. How she wished to reach the safety and comfort of Uncle Markham's house!

At Temple Bar, she passed through one of the small arches meant for those on foot. Where Fleet Street ended, she took the left-hand way to the Strand and then went through St. Clement's Yard, to avoid Butchers Row and the Back Side of St. Clement's, both of which had an unsavory reputation. There was a public house at the beginning of Wych Street, but it did not worry her. Its patrons were local folk; indeed, Mr. Eales, the upholsterer, was standing outside the tavern, talking to the old man whose shop sold a bit of everything: used household goods, tallow candles, secondhand hardware, and a little gin.

Eales broke off in the middle of a sentence to say, "You hadn't ought to be out by yourself, Mistress Jane—at night, too!"

"I know, Mr. Eales. I was delayed."

He tutted. "Joshua and I will see you to your door. That's not to say this is a bad neighborhood, but best to be careful." And the two of them ambled beside her until she reached the kitchen door, and they saw it open. Now she was home.

The kitchen maid stood gaping at her.

"Yes, I've come at an odd time, dressed like a countrywoman. Let me in, Molly." Jane pushed into the kitchen. Mrs. Harrow looked up from the chair by the hearth where she was knitting. "Mistress Jane! Why ever...?" The rest of the staff, also in the kitchen, as they often were in the evenings, looked up.

"Mrs. Harrow, will you make tea for us? I've been wishing for a cup for hours, and I have something to tell you all."

On the stagecoach, she had had plenty of time to reflect upon her best course of action. She was glad she had not told Mr. Grantham where she would be staying. She could not quite like him, and he did not appear to take her concern seriously. To be fair, he had not known all the facts, but still, he seemed to know something of Mr. Lattimer. He knew he was out of town, which was troublesome. Although perhaps Mr. Lattimer had gone to do something about the Pleasaunce matter or to find out why Alex had not returned.

Or perhaps he was in town, and Grantham had lied. Her stepmama would say that was a ridiculous idea, for Mr. Grantham was obviously a gentleman and a gentleman would never lie. Which was the commonly accepted view, except that even ladies knew that they did lie, easily and often, though perhaps some preferred not to acknowledge it. That might make married life pleasanter or less humiliating, but as her own situation was more serious than a matter of gaming debts or mistresses, she chose to be a realist.

They sat around the long table where they ate their meals, and Mrs. Jennings poured out cups of bohea, then took the chair left empty by Uncle Markham's departed valet, ceding her own place to Jane. No Covent Garden audience was ever as quiet.

She took a deep breath and began.

****

"Murdered by Jacobites!" Mrs. Harrow exclaimed. "What has the world come to?"

"Or perhaps only smugglers, though it seems they were hand in glove with Jacobites, certainly."

"It explains a good deal, Mistress Jane," the butler said. "We did wonder at Mr. Gordon going away so sudden. And Mr. Stowe as well."

She had not mentioned Charles Pleasaunce's or Rupert's involvement, in spite of being quite out of charity with the latter. She had avoided explaining Alex Gordon's precise role because—well, because she was not at all sure what it was, though he must be some sort of government agent. It was apparent that at least Mr. Jessup suspected the connection.

They were watching her expectantly, hoping she would explain further. "This is a very serious business. I was instructed to keep it secret because if it were widely known, foolish people might panic. But given that the official with whom I spoke may be out of town, and it appears someone may wish to harm me, I am confiding in you because…" How to explain that she could not go to her father's home?

"Because you need somewhere to hide, Mistress Jane," Mrs. Jennings said.

"Yes."

"With no one knowing," Jessup added. He, Mrs. Jennings, and Mrs. Harrow all looked sharply at Molly. "With no mention of it to anyone—not the grocer's boy or the servants next door or a beau or family."

"I'll never say a word," Molly squeaked. "I never did that time I went with you to look at carpets, mistress."

"Which is true enough, as it took everyone by surprise when the new carpet for the bookroom was delivered," Mrs. Harrow said.

Mrs. Jennings tapped a finger against her lips. "It would be easy enough to conceal you, if you could pass as a new maid. We wouldn't mention you at all, but if someone chanced to spy you at a window, that's what we would say. You'd have been hired to help with the cleaning, as Fannie left us to take a post in one of the grand houses on Grosvenor Square, where her brother is a footman. It would mean wearing a maid's gown and cap and apron, but Fannie's would fit you. And if you wouldn't mind eating in the kitchen, for someone might notice if you took your meals in the dining room, which would look peculiar. Or you could dine in your chamber, of course."

"On the top floor, where you all have your rooms," Jane pointed out. "That would make a great many stairs for someone to climb with my meals. I couldn't sleep on the floor with the family bedrooms: the light might be seen even through the draperies and reveal someone was in residence, other than all of you."

"That's well thought on, Mistress Jane. Though it will make it uncomfortable for you, as well as unsuitable, to live like a servant."

"Not nearly as uncomfortable as I've been today, Jessup."

"Ay, well, there's that," he agreed.

****

Alex could have fallen to his knees and kissed the filthy paving stones. After the fresh sea air, the smell of London assaulted his nose, but oh, he was glad to be home. They'd had rough seas and then been delayed by adverse winds when they were coming up the Thames. The brig *Fair Weather* was not notable for cleanliness, and the food was bad. Alex did not really enjoy sailing.

He wanted a good meal. He wanted a bath and a change of clothing and a comfortable bed and to sit in front of a fire with his feet up and a good book and a glass of brandy. He wanted to see Jane and explain. He wanted…well, no. He *needed* to see his father.

Everything else would have to wait.

It was not much over a mile to Somerset House, where he suspected he would find his sire at this time of day, and he wanted to stretch his legs. It was unfortunate that he must present himself in filthy linen and shabby, stained suit—and smelling ripe, too—but it could not be helped. He was striding toward the entrance when a fellow coming out glanced at him and broke stride. He had forgotten his old friend Hitch-Shoulder.

"Here, you! Halt—" And Hitch-Shoulder sprang at him.

He had spent days in cells, days of playing the fox in Scotland, and far too much time on shipboard worrying about matters ranging from his own possible execution as a traitor to Rupert's fate (or Jane's reaction to it) to whether some Somerset House clerk would demand an accounting and repayment of the money Rupert had stolen from him. Salt beef and ship's biscuit lay leaden in his stomach. He was desperate to explain to his father what he had done and why it had seemed the only thing to do. He could almost see his brother Edward's pained expression. Ned was rising in the diplomatic service and never put a foot wrong. Their younger brother, Gilbert, who might one day be either a bishop or else merely a beloved vicar, would suppress a sigh.

Gordon's fist shot out by reflex. His blow caught the man in the stomach, doubling him over. His next blow connected with Hitch-Shoulder's chin, stretching him full length on the ground. Alex dropped his valise and ran like a hare.

He would wager the next words after "Halt"—

would have been—"in the king's name." He must keep out of the authorities' hands until he could communicate with his father.

He sprinted for his life into the entrance of Swan Yard across from Somerset House, almost knocking over a peddler with a barrow, who swore vilely. His immediate impulse was to get home. His second thought as he pelted over the cobbles was that the used clothing he'd bought in Burntisland would make him an object of suspicion in Bloomsbury Square. He should get out of sight and send a message to his father.

He swerved into White Hart Yard. It ended at Drury Lane. He turned right, then left to the Craven Buildings, going through their stable yard at the back, which debouched into Maypole Alley. Should he go left or right? Left would take him north to Stanhope and Haughton streets. If he went right…He hesitated, trying to recall everything he could of the area. It was one with which he was not very familiar. Maypole Alley led roughly north and south. If he went to the right, south, he would come either directly or indirectly to the Strand, a little way east of Somerset House. Not a direction in which he wished to go! But to the right, the mouth of the alley ended at some small street lined with old houses which must date back to Queen Elizabeth's day. His several visits to New Inn, when he had contemplated without enthusiasm a career in the law, came back to him. The entrance of New Inn was in Wych Street.

His heart leapt inexplicably. Jane's house. Refuge. He trotted down the alley, then turned east on Wych Street, past Lyons Inn on the right and New Inn on the left, to Jane Stowe's house, with the relief a hunted fox might feel on going to earth in his den.

How was he to explain his tatterdemalion appearance, he wondered, tapping at the back door. He hardly looked like a respectable if poor gentleman hired to catalog a library. Not that his dress was in any way remarkable in this area. No one passing had looked twice at him.

As the door opened, a grumbled "It never fails! The chit's away just when I'm rolling pastry" warned of an irritable reception. Then the cook's round, ordinarily good-natured face stared at him.

"Mrs. Harrow, it's I, Alex Gordon. I thought I'd best come to the tradesman's entrance, given my—"

"Quick! In with you, sir." She pulled the door wide and stood back to let him enter, shutting it behind him and throwing the bolts. Molly emerged from the pantry, tea canister in hand.

"Go tell Jessup Mr. Gordon's here, girl." To him she said, "You're looking pinched, Mr. Gordon. As soon as you're settled, there will be a bite to eat."

"Thank you. Ah...I realize I am not correctly attired for a call. I must look like a vagabond."

"Think nothing of it, sir. We all understand. Mistress Jane explained it to us."

"She did?"

The butler appeared, followed by the kitchen maid.

"I'll take you upstairs, sir. Mistress Jane will see you in the bookroom. The windows do not look out upon the street. These are unconventional circumstances and, I fear, call for putting aside some conventional behavior. This way, please."

"I'll put together a tray and send it up. Mr. Gordon, would you like ale? Or Mr. Jessup will fetch the brandy."

"Ale would be most welcome." How fortunate he had arrived when she was actually in the house. It would have been awkward to explain to the servants that he must stay until he had dispatched a note to her and she replied. Or perhaps they would have understood: she had explained something to them. The question was, exactly what?

The library was well lit, with windows on two sides; two overlooked the little back yard, for you could not call it a garden. It contained a necessary house and was clearly utilitarian rather than decorative, though one corner sheltered a tiny kitchen garden and a tree grew near the back wall. Another window opened on the passage beside Markham's house, but it gave no view of the bookroom door to anyone looking out its neighbor's windows. The room had been rearranged also, with the desk and chairs as far from the windows as possible, out of any line of sight from the house on the other side of the yard. He mentally applauded the forethought which had suggested the changes. Jane and her staff were taking no chance of someone next door or in the house across the yard seeing someone in the room.

Jane stood tensely by the chairs, twisting a handkerchief.

"I will leave the door open, Mistress Jane." Jessup executed a half bow to her and retreated down the hall on silent feet.

"Thank God you are safe. When you did not return by the eighth, I—Mr. Lattimer and I were concerned."

Not a word about her brother? He thought of saying, "So you went to Mr. Lattimer then?" and dismissed the idea. Of course she had; he had asked her to do so, and she was sensible and not timid.

"I fear I have failed you, Mistress Jane. I was unable to bring your brother back with me." He wondered how to explain what had occurred. Better, perhaps, to say they had been separated.

"Oh, Rupert! I suppose he would not let himself be saved from his error. That would be just like him."

Evidently, she was not going to be grieved that he had lost Stowe.

"I think he was too frightened to trust me."

"At least you are safe. I could never have forgiven myself if you'd come to harm through trying to help Rupert."

"Thank you, Mistress Jane." Did she feel a certain partiality for him, or would she have felt the same whoever had gone with Stowe? The latter, he supposed, though he hoped otherwise. "But why was my—Mr. Lattimer concerned? I did not expect him to worry over my being a little delayed. It was only that—"

Mrs. Harrow bustled in with a tray holding a pitcher of ale, a mug, a teapot, and its accoutrements, and a dish of cakes and biscuits. She set it on a side table. "Is there anything else, mistress?" He would have expected the task would be Molly's. Either the cook was curious or Molly was not to be trusted to overhear even a word or two. Well! Molly did tend to chatter, as he knew from his visit to the house soon after Markham's death.

"No, that will be all."

As she left, Jane said, "Please serve yourself, and do sit down." She poured herself a cup of tea and seated herself in one of the leather chairs in front of the desk.

When he was seated and had taken a long draft of ale, he decided what he had meant to say, "—if I never returned, he would know why," sounded over-dramatic. "The letter was intended only to supply a few bits of information I had not had time to report to him."

She gave him a skeptical look. "For some reason, Mr. Lattimer believed Rupert was cooperating with you."

"I wonder where he got that idea."

"Apparently from you, Mr. Gordon. When he read the letter, he could not understand why you would think what he described as a simple errand should become complicated. He was quite surprised when I told him my brother had not confided fully in you. Then he asked me why I was worried."

"May I inquire what you told him?"

"I gave him to understand that Rupert's character is not strong, and he could not be relied upon if there were any danger or even inconvenience to himself."

"Ah."

"You lied to him, Mr. Gordon. Or at least misled him."

"I admit it. But if I'd told him Stowe might not agree to inform the authorities there, the matter would have been handled differently, and there would have been no chance to get your brother out of the situation."

She sighed. "Thank you for trying to help him, wretch that he is. I hope you won't be in difficulties because of it."

"Probably not," Alex said. What could his father do? Dismiss him? A very fine, thorough raking-down was the worst he could expect, apart from the problem that brought him here.

"And thank you for bringing me word, sir. I think you must have come directly from shipboard? For I believe I see a smear of tar on your coat sleeve, rather than the dust of the highway."

"I did. I did not come solely to let you know about Stowe, however."

"Oh?" She blushed a little and looked down at the tea bowl in her hands.

This would be a good time to tell her he had come straight to see her, except that, unlike many young ladies, she would soon see through such a blatant falsehood and despise him. How could he have known she would be here? The truth was a better policy with Jane Stowe.

"There was a little difficulty. We were both taken into custody, though we were freed when Dundee went over to the Jacobites. Then after I burned the barn in which the muskets were stored, I became aware I might be hunted."

She gave him a long look. "I think you had better give me a full account of your adventures, sir."

Ah. Yes, perhaps so. She and her servants were so deeply entangled in the affair now, she had a right to know. Boiled down to the relevant facts, it hardly seemed so much activity could be described in so few minutes.

When he finished, she said, "They might well wish to avenge themselves, if you destroyed their arms. They must have been counting upon those weapons."

He realized he had possibly not been specific enough. "...not by the Jacobites, Mistress Jane. Our own troops. Because they thought I was a Jacobite." Perhaps they were not searching for him. The army very likely had enough to do in Scotland without pursuing one escaped suspected Jacobite. "The thing is, my arrest as a supporter of the Pretender was mentioned in the *Newcastle Courant*. So I may be liable to arrest here. I'll write to…er…Mr. Lattimer. I merely need a place to stay while he clears up the misunderstanding."

"Oh! Oh, dear. But Mr. Lattimer—" She frowned, evidently in perplexity rather than annoyance.

"As I'd been staying here to catalog the library, it seemed a logical place to take shelter." He smiled. "Though I was a bit surprised your staff let me in, looking as I do."

She was biting her lip. "I wrote to Mr. Lattimer this very morning. His butler told my messenger that he is not in London at the moment. Which may be true or not. You see, I am supposed to be staying with Mr. and Mrs. Lattimer at their country house."

They regarded each other blankly. "Your cook said you'd explained to them. I wondered about that. What has happened?"

She told him. His tankard was empty and the tea was cold in the pot before she finished.

"This is a confounded coil. I cannot like it that Pleasaunce's confederates have tried to seek you out. If you are already hiding here, Mistress Jane, I must find somewhere else and write to Mr. Lattimer at his country home. He should be informed of this as soon as possible, and also of my return."

"I have already dispatched a letter to Mrs. Lattimer. She was aware of what was going on, when she and Mr. Lattimer escorted me to Hawthorn Cottage. If her husband is not there, she will probably know where he is. But, of course, I have not yet received a reply." She chewed her lower lip. "I know it would be shockingly improper for you to stay, Mr. Gordon, but I think you must. To write to Mr. Lattimer, I had Mrs. Harrow take my letter to her brother's haberdashery to have him send it with one of his boys. The boy came here to report rather than passing it through his papa. It is not a convenient way to communicate, but I did not like to send one of my servants, and I am not sure I would trust the penny post. Foolish as it may sound, men will gossip and take bribes, too, and if someone should pass on word that a letter from this house was being sent to Mr. Lattimer..."

"What admirable instincts you possess, Mistress Jane. I would have done the same." He watched her blush with pleasure before adding, "I particularly dislike that they found you, in spite of Mr. Lattimer's precautions."

"The thought makes me quite nervous, I vow."

"While it's improper, I think I must remain here in case those villains track you this far."

"Your room is as you left it. I will have hot water sent up so you may bathe, if you wish."

He laughed. "I certainly need to do so. I haven't had a good wash since Stowe and I sailed for St. Andrews. I left a change of clothing here, fortunately. But I will sleep on the servants' floor. That may make my presence marginally more acceptable."

"I am already occupying a room on that floor, however. You were living here while cataloging the books, and you have returned, so you can resume your old bedchamber, and I will have Molly sleep in the second bed in my room."

Few would consider that adequate chaperonage. If

he stayed in the house, almost any decent person would consider that he had compromised her reputation, which would necessitate making her an offer of marriage. Not that he was in any way opposed to doing so, as he had never met a young lady he liked as well.

"If this house is under observation, the watchers may not know you employed a librarian to live in. Why should they? They probably were not set to watch until you and Pleasaunce saw each other, after I was gone. If they see a chamber not on the servants' floor is occupied, they may suppose you are here and break in. But if they have heard one Alex Gordon was staying here, they might also have heard that an Alex Gordon was in Scotland in company with Rupert Stowe and was detained by His Majesty's forces."

"But if the watchers are Jacobites, that is no difficulty. They would think you one of themselves."

"They may be aware I was not working on behalf of their cause," he said cautiously.

"How—oh, my *curst* brother! Could he do such a thing?" But the question sounded rhetorical.

"Shocking language, Mistress Jane!"

"You are laughing at me, Mr. Gordon, but I assure you, if I'd had any idea he would betray you when you were trying to save him, I would never, never have let you go with him."

"It would still have been my duty to prevent the delivery of those muskets."

"Which might more easily have been accomplished by advising your superiors and their not supplying the money Rupert needed. I—"

A thought occurred to her, arresting her expression.

"We are making this too difficult," she said after a

moment. "You are an agent of the government. Can you not contact someone else in your department? Mr. Lattimer's whereabouts must be known, or perhaps there is another who could help us."

"I am not actually employed by the War Office. Mr. Lattimer sent me to investigate your uncle's death unofficially. Then, when I told him about your half brother's dilemma, he let me continue because Stowe had already confided in me to some degree and an official agent could not be substituted. I have no connections in the department. Apart from Mr. Lattimer, the only person I met there was the tailor who outfitted me." News of Alex Gordon's arrest in Scotland might have reached the War Office and the odd, discreet little offices to be found at Somerset House. And Hitch-Shoulder, who had meant to arrest him, was to be found at Somerset House. Alex had not mentioned their recent encounter to Jane. What was the penalty for assault on a government agent?

"That is too bad; it would have made everything easy."

"There is also the possibility someone in the War Office passes on information to the Jacobites, either intentionally or through carelessness. How else could Pleasaunce's friends discover your whereabouts?"

"It did occur to me to suspect as much," Jane admitted. She nibbled a slice of seed cake. Her teeth were small and white, and her lips looked soft as rose petals. He could imagine what they'd feel like, nibbling on his own lips, or on his ear. He dragged his mind away from the vision. He was in danger of seriously embarrassing both of them,

"There is someone who might provide me with a

place to stay," Alex said slowly. He had forgotten Warrender. If he had no connection with Pleasaunce, it would be perfectly safe to contact Warrender. Even if he did, there should be little danger, unless Stowe contacted Pleasaunce. "What do you think your brother will have done?"

"My half brother. After he abandoned you? He'll make for safety. I'm surprised he has not arrived back in Town yet. Unless he went to my father and is being concealed by him."

"Or perhaps he would go to Pleasaunce?"

Jane shook her head. "Rupert may have sent him a letter, which I imagine would merely state the arms had been delivered. He would certainly not mention you or the rest of it because if he did, he would have to admit that you were with him, which would have to be explained. No, I believe he will keep clear of Mr. Pleasaunce."

"Then I will write to someone I met at the Cocoa Tree."

Chapter 26

The possibility that the house might be watched made her very nervous. Mrs. Harrow announced she was going out to buy a foreleg of mutton for a mock-venison pasty for dinner the following day, it being a dish that required a day's preparation. She would not trust Molly to buy meat or fish. This gave her an excuse to go out so she could stop in at a friend's home, to have her daughter deliver Alex's letter. The cook agreed with Jane that using her brother's son to carry another letter might be unwise. Alex had not wished to send it by the penny post because he feared the mail of suspected Jacobites might be inspected. According to Alex, Warrender claimed to be under surveillance, making it likely that if anyone's mail were being intercepted, his would be a high priority.

"Nan will have her girl take it to Mr. Gordon's friend's kitchen door. She'll have a basket, as if she were delivering vegetables or the like," Mrs. Harrow said.

"It's only a question now of waiting for a reply." Jane rather hoped Mr. Warrender would be unable to help Alex. On the whole, she would prefer he remain in the house, even though he was right about its being somewhat scandalous. But if no one but her servants knew, propriety was not irredeemably breached. And even though she was not living alone, she would feel safer with him present. She did wish she might hear from Mr. or Mrs. Lattimer. She had written to the former both at his manor and at Bloomsbury Square before Jack Ridgeley took her to the coaching inn to set things in motion. Unfortunately, mail delivery to and from the country could be very slow, though London's penny post was a marvel of efficiency. Yet it might not be wasted effort, as when those letters arrived, perhaps his staff would send them on even if they would not tell someone who inquired where their master had gone.

She was reading in the housekeeper's room when Molly tapped on the door and then peeked in.

"Mistress, Cook is asking for you and Mr. Gordon, too. I'm just on my way to fetch him next. She says as it's important."

Alex caught up with her in the downstairs corridor and was one step behind her in reaching the kitchen.

Mrs. Harrow was wiping her hands on a dish clout, preparations for supper suspended.

"Nan Turk, that sent on Mr. Gordon's letter by her daughter, was here a moment ago. She come to tell me she couldn't deliver it." The cook pulled the letter, now a little crumpled, from her pocket and held it out to Gordon, who took it without comment but with raised eyebrows.

"The girl took it to the kitchen entrance, like you said, sir, but their cook wouldn't take it, nor the butler nor housekeeper, neither. They was all in the kitchen and looking grim as death. 'In't the master at home, then?' Nan's little girl asks. At first, they wouldn't say, but then she says, 'I'll be beat if I can't deliver this here letter and can't say why.' That's when the butler tells her the master's been took up by a pair o' King's

Messengers, and the house searched. And then he says, 'We don't want your letter in this house, whether it's from some lady or the Archbishop of Canterbury himself—*or anyone else*.' So she took it back to her ma, who come to explain why she couldn't leave it. And I knew you'd want to know," she said with a meaningful glance at them both, "as soon as she was gone."

"I see. Thank you, Mrs. Harrow. Ah…does Jessup know? And Mrs. Jennings?"

"Ay, and Mr. Jessup's up the attics to fetch down footman's livery, and she's putting Molly to work sorting through the linen cabinet."

Alex raised his eyebrows, puzzled.

"To keep Molly out of the way for a bit."

"Where do you suppose Warrender is, then?" Jane asked.

"Probably in the Tower."

" 'Tis too bad it wasn't Mr. Pleasaunce instead."

"For all we know, they're sharing a cell," Alex replied. "What does Jessup want with livery?" he asked the cook.

"Why, in livery and the white wig, your own lady mother wouldn't know you, sir. Or even notice you. It seemed a clever notion to have it ready, should you need it."

So they spent the night under the same roof, in defiance of conventional behavior. She could not feel compromised by it, though if it became known, only marriage would make it right. But her reputation was safe as long as the indiscretion was unknown in good society. While the wealthy and aristocratic might live no more than a few minutes' walk from the poorest tradesmen and laborers, the social distance was an ocean wide. The inhabitants of Wych Street and their few servants could not spread gossip to Red Lyon Square. Her uncle's servants, who did have friends in better parts of town, would not speak of her peculiar conduct. Marrying to save one's reputation would be horrid if one did not at least like the man. Certainly the man would dislike being forced into marriage—unless he had arranged the scandal with marriage in mind, as sometimes occurred when the lady was well dowered. That thought gave her a moment's pause, before she acquitted Mr. Gordon of such a stratagem. He was clever, amusing, and capable; he might even be devious, but she trusted him. If Mr. Gordon should feel at some point that he had to make her an offer, she would be happy to accept. But they really must get through the current difficulty first. It would make no sort of sense to make future plans with a man who ran the risk of being clapped up in the Tower.

****

Alex and Jessup were in the hall outside the reception parlor at the front of the house. Past the door into the parlor was the flight of stairs up to the floors containing the drawing room, dining room, library, and bedchambers. This had been some well-to-do tradesman's home in earlier, simpler times. The upstairs withdrawing room was an afterthought, converted from some other use. Originally, the family's parlor and dining room must have been located on the ground floor where the butler's pantry and housekeeper's room were now, between the kitchen and the front room. The tradesman's doubtless practical wife would have overseen the household.

Jessup had moved a chair and small table to hold a candlestick to the hall near the foot of the stair. It led up in a series of right-angle turns, meant to take up as little floor and wall space as possible, not for elegant ladies and gentleman to sweep down, making a grand entrance. The woodwork was of carved dark oak, although a small window on the first landing gave some light. The shutters had been left open, so anyone using the stairs would not have to grope his way up or down in the dark.

"When Mr. Markham was still engaged in business," Jessup said, "a footman was on duty in the front during the nights and on Sundays, those being times when Mr. Markham sometimes received messengers or visitors, not being in his office on Thames Street then. I doubt you'll have much to do, and you can sit and read if you wish, sir, as there's some light from the window on the stair, as well as the candle if you need it. The front room is more comfortable"—he tilted his head toward the parlor— "but you'd need to use the candle, the shutters being in place."

The butler had shown him the reception area earlier. It was comfortably furnished with several armchairs, a cabinet for liquor and glasses, and a bookcase. A copy of *Lloyd's List*, now several weeks old, still lay on a side table. All things considered, however, he thought he would be happy to remain in the corridor, where he might catch a glimpse and a word with Jane Stowe if she chanced to go upstairs.

"If you leave the door into the front room ajar, you can hear if someone should come. You need not worry overmuch, sir. No one will expect a footman in this household to be as polished as what you'd find in the better parts of town. This is the only household in this neighborhood to possess such a servant."

Jessup must assume Alex had little experience of footmen. Admittedly, he didn't look like one. The *beau monde* hired footmen for appearance—broad shoulders, well-muscled legs, handsome, or at least unremarkable, faces. But he could certainly mimic the proper stance and demeanor, even if his livery was worn and his wig needed resetting. He would not be out of place here. He almost regretted that his acting skills were unlikely to be called upon.

It took them both by surprise when there was an authoritative rap at the front door. They traded glances and both went into the front parlor. Alex froze into immobility against the wall, while Jessup went to the door.

Who would be paying a visit? The knocker having been removed from the door should be ample notice that the family was not in residence. A tradesman would go to the kitchen door. He heard a voice murmur, "For Mr. Markham."

"Mr. Markham is a month dead, God rest his soul," Jessup replied.

"If the old gentleman's dead, maybe it should go to his next of kin or his heir. No business of mine, is it?"

Jessup closed the door and shot the bolt, before turning to Alex.

"Might you be expecting a letter addressed to Mr. Markham, sir?"

"You should probably call me 'William,' " Alex said. "Lest you make a slip in front of a stranger. But no, it can't be for me." He withdrew into the corridor and peered at the inscription by the light from the high window on the stair. He recognized it instantly. "You had better give it to Mistress Jane."

But he accompanied Jessup to the housekeeper's room where Jane was mending a sheet.

"Mrs. Lattimer has written," she said, when she had broken the wafer that sealed it.

...I write to you having had a very disquieting letter from Cheddle at Hawthorn Cottage. I have had no occasion thus far to send on any letter to you. *[A double, very emphatic underscore.] So the letter you mention came from someone who learned of your whereabouts by some unknown Method, and certainly neither my husband nor I revealed them, nor should anyone else. I have secured your letter, which Mr. Lattimer will wish to read for himself, in a place no one else can come at it, and I will not divulge that you have gone to visit other friends. I should also mention the gentleman you met has had occasional business dealings with my husband, but we are not close friends. It was probably for the best that you did not go into detail about your plans. Mr. Lattimer is not Here, nor in London, at the moment. He is travelling on the Business that caused You and Myself some concern recently, and I do not know where I could Send to him. I do not quite know what to do if you receive any Letters from your Family which are sent to you here. It seems unwise to send them on to your current location, for reasons which you will understand, I am sure. If one comes, I think I must open it and pen a reply, stating that as you have sprained your wrist and cannot write, I am writing at your dictation. I think it would be a mistake for us to write each other again* except at

greatest need. *[The phrase was underlined.] If you should hear from A., pray tell him to conduct himself discreetly and dress plainly, so as not to be of interest to footpads and to take all necessary precautions against the same...*

Before she had finished reading the missive, Alex was laughing. Jane looked at him with raised eyebrows.

"Mrs. Lattimer has a talent for obscurity," he said, still chuckling. "It would puzzle anyone who did not knew of your recent activities, if they should happen to find her letter."

"I'm glad you can derive amusement from it." Her tone was tart. Of course, Jane could not see quite the same humor in it. "Someone else knew where to find me, when no one should have."

"That thought did cross my mind, Mistress Jane. Either there is a spy in Mr. Lattimer's household or in—" He stopped. He felt a reluctance to discuss those odd offices at Somerset House. What a sad reflection upon him to be so secretive, and with a lady closely concerned in this business and whose intelligence he increasingly respected.

"Mr. Gordon?"

"Or in the War Office or one of its, ah, illegitimate offspring."

A long pause ensued. "I had no idea the War Office had relations of That Sort." Her voice quivered with amusement. Then she compressed her lips and blushed.

"By War Office, out of Trickery and Guile, as they would say in horse breeding circles?"

"I meant connections, Mr. Gordon. Family connections. Not...ummm..."

He grinned at her. "Those are family connections,

are they not? Though I apologize for such an indelicate reference. To return to the issue—I beg your pardon! No pun intended!—the problem at hand, when the Lattimers took you to Hawthorn Cottage, how many servants and retainers accompanied the coach?"

"There was only the coachman and a footman."

"Can you describe them? I know that one doesn't notice servants, but if you can remember anything, it might help. I would wager the pair of them were the only others who knew where you were going."

She sucked her lower lip, a sight which almost distracted him. "The coachman was middle-aged and really had no outstanding characteristics. He was not particularly tall, or short, or fat. I am not sure I would be able to recognize him again. He did talk like a West Country man, though I realize that's not much help. The footman was large." She went on hurriedly, "Footmen always are well set up and usually tall, but this one was, how shall I put it, more so. Not conspicuously, but he was not quite as smooth as one expects. I thought he might serve the same function as the outriders who travel with some nobles' or rich men's coaches. For protection, you know."

"As it happens, I know both men. They've been with Mr. Lattimer for many years. And neither is loose-lipped. It must be someone in one of the War Office's...family connections."

"But what has Mr. Lattimer to do with the War Office?"

Jane Stowe was so deeply involved at this point, he could not justify secrecy.

"While he is not officially employed by the War Office, he serves as a sort of intermediary between several of its…small, detached divisions. That is how he was able to arrange for the money and the ship passage for your brother and me."

"Half brother, Mr. Gordon. And I am considering striking him from my family tree."

"Ah." On his behalf? Flattering!

"Do you know if Mr. Grantham is connected to the War Office or its offspring? Mrs. Lattimer's letter was not clear upon that point. It may be unfair of me, but I could not quite like him or trust him."

"I believe he is associated with one of the Somerset House offices. It appears he was unaware you were at the cottage until you arrived on his doorstep, so he is presumably innocent of divulging your whereabouts to whoever tried to kidnap you. Unfortunately, determining who is responsible for passing on your presence at Hawthorn Cottage may not be easy. It may only be that someone was indiscreet. M-Mr. Lattimer will have a better idea of how to ferret out the gossip or spy than I do." He would not care to put money on Grantham's holding his tongue about the young lady who had fled Hawthorn Cottage, convinced she was in danger of abduction. The man obviously did not believe in Jane's danger and would consider it merely an amusing story. Alex recalled an acid comment of his mother's regarding Grantham: "If a man and a woman made exactly the same suggestion, he would dismiss the woman's, while endorsing the man's."

Chapter 27

Jane took a candle and went up to her room on the servants' floor. She needed time to compose herself.

She was glad Mr. Gordon had no choice but to stay in her house. While her stepmother would go off in a fit of the vapors and her father would rant, she could not refuse to harbor him—even if she had wanted to do so. He had assured her she was in no danger even before she had found she was suspected of murdering her uncle. He had been more reassuring than her own family, who might at least have shown they believed in her innocence.

He had even tried to extricate Rupert from the consequences of his stupidity and lack of character and had endangered himself in doing it. And she suspected there had been somewhat more to Mr. Gordon's adventures than he had revealed.

And he was extremely attractive. He could not be called handsome, though there was nothing wrong with his face, but its kindliness and humor had drawn her from the first. He was quick-witted, and his conversation was lively. There was no fault to be found in his body, either, which was lean and gave an appearance of strength and whip-like energy. The men she met at the parties and assemblies her family attended seemed flat by comparison. Their humor, if they had it, was too often shallow. If they were serious and worthy, they were boring. There might have been charming, interesting men at those entertainments. They would not be drawn to her. She had never been vivacious. Her stepmother claimed she was too plain, too like a governess, too conceited to pander to the conceit of gentlemen—not that Elvira had phrased it in those words. If she were like a governess, it was perhaps because she had taken responsibility for the household when she was too young. Someone had to do it, after all! Stepmama claimed that any young lady who was not ugly could make an eligible match if only she would make the effort to flatter gentlemen, smile at them, laugh at their jokes, and practice some wiles. Yet if she did so, someone for whom she felt no respect or partiality might make her an offer, and then what would she do?

"Though I believe you would do best to secure a widower, Jane, some older man, more interested in a lady who will manage his house and rear his children than in romance. I must think who in our circle might suit." But that had been several years ago, and she had heard no more on the subject. Perhaps it had occurred to Elvira what it would mean if she did marry. Or because soon after, Uncle Markham had let it be known Jane was his heir. Could her stepmother be so calculating? Very likely! While Elvira could not—or would not—add a column of figures, she had managed to marry Jane's father, when she was only the daughter of the third son of a purse-pinched baronet. Papa's small fortune would have been adequate, had it not been for the expenses of rearing three sons and clothing a fashion-conscious wife.

Would Mr. Gordon feel he had to offer for her?

Like her, he had a practical turn. He was also either a gentleman or mimicked one convincingly. If he were not a gentleman born, would she consider marrying him? Perhaps she would have no choice. If his presence here came to her father's attention, he would bellow and reproach her for loose conduct, then sigh heavily and say Mr. Gordon must marry her or she would be ruined. It would not be a disaster, she thought, not for her. Having made her bed, she would lie in it willingly. Oh, yes. Even if she did not love him (but she thought perhaps she did), she liked him very well, and that might be enough. Or would it? They could be comfortable together. Only, she did not want him to be forced to marry her when perhaps he would have preferred some other lady.

Would she have to marry him? Unlike some girl fresh out of the schoolroom, who would have no recourse but to run away to a very uncertain future in order to avoid an unwelcome marriage, she was of age. She owned a house and she had a fortune, all her own, on which she could live comfortably. It would also make her a target for fortune hunters if it became known.

If Mr. Gordon were clever enough to counterfeit the manner of a gentleman as easily as he did that of a footman, could he also be only pretending to admire her? While he did not display the conventional signs of interest like fulsome compliments and languishing glances, she had no doubt at all that he was flirting with her. But was he attracted to her or was it only playacting? She knew nothing of his background. He might be the son of a tradesman or even a criminal. He claimed his father could have bought him a commission, which might be true—or not. He made a very convincing footman, all his whimsical humor gone, his face impassive. He was a skilled actor, then. And how had he become involved in the mystery of her uncle's murder? He said he had been asked to look into it by Mr. Lattimer. Then she had pulled him into her brother's and Charles Pleasaunce's plot. He said Mr. Lattimer had contacts in the War Office and other government departments and implied that Lattimer was his superior. Alex had been able by some sleight of hand to produce a great deal of money and passage on a ship at short notice. That fact might support his claim. He had useful connections of some sort, at least. But really, she had no proof that any part of his story was true. He might be a criminal who had intended to divert those muskets in order to sell them to someone else. The thought congealed into a lump in her chest.

But he had been right that she had not been charged in her uncle's death in spite of testimony that she had sent the shrimps. Colonel Sir Thomas de Veil had prevented it twice. According to him, the instruction to do so came from the government. And Uncle Markham's attorney had obviously suspected her, when he came to inform them of Uncle Markham's death, though she only realized it after learning that he had been poisoned. Yet Harris had changed his mind and begun the process of transferring the house and fortune to her. So she thought she could assume the government was concerned in the matter and that Alex was not merely a criminal.

Supporting this theory was Mr. Lattimer's evident respectability, and his connection to her uncle, which she considered proven by the note in Uncle Markham's commonplace book: "Write A.L. again."

If Alex Gordon were an agent of one of those unnamed divisions of the War Office, an intelligencer, he must be lowborn. Gentlemen did not spy for a living. If a man serving in such a capacity were able to marry an heiress, he could give up a job that must be dangerous and set up as a gentleman. He might not be able to travel in the best society, for with no social connections, he would be frozen out as a social climber. But her own family did not mingle with the *beau monde*, as one needed both birth and fortune to do so. Her uncle had not done so, either, although he was a gentleman and rich, because he had been in business.

Would she be willing to ally herself with a man of low origins who was a spy?

Yes, if he loved her. The difficulty was, how would she know, when he was such a good mimic?

Then she found herself remembering a phrase from Mrs. Lattimer's letter: *If you should hear from A., pray tell him...* How did she know about Alex? Or, if she were so deeply in her husband's confidence, was it not strange that she referred to him by his first initial, with a personal message? Unless it were some sort of code, of course. Alex Gordon had laughed after she read that line.

Chapter 28

Doing a footman's duty, without the advantage of having any actual work, was a little frustrating. Alex was not accustomed to idleness. At least he did not have to stand motionless but ready in the front hall. Markham had kept a man on duty in the front parlor during the hours when Markham's office was closed. "The shipping business being one in which difficulties sometimes arose outside the business day," Jessup explained. Alex gathered the footman had been permitted to sit during his watch. Clearly, Markham had been an indulgent employer. Jessup seemed to feel this called for an explanation.

"There were many nights when no messages came, and there were no other callers, of course, Mr. Markham not being a member of the fashionable set."

Alex turned his attention back to the book he was reading, Drury's account of his captivity in Madagascar. Jessup, who had the makings of a first-class schemer, had pointed out that if he stayed in the kitchen, there was the danger of his being noticed by the butcher's or greengrocer's lad. "The boy would mention it to someone, and everyone would wonder what we needed with a footman, the master being dead, and none but us servants here," the butler said.

If someone did come to the door, he need only put down his book and go into the reception parlor, not that any caller was likely. Though there had been that messenger, of course. His post here did not actually limit his access to the rest of the house (and Jane). He could go up the stairs a few feet away to the family living areas and up another flight to the family bedchambers. Jane, however, was spending most of her time in the housekeeper's room near the butler's pantry and kitchen. The staff clearly meant to preserve the decencies as much as they could even if some unconventionalities were unavoidable.

He alternated between reading, thinking, walking back and forth, and practicing fencing positions. To be immured in a house with a pretty girl and only a handful of servants (not that they were lax in their chaperonage) and a devilish plot for seasoning was a foolish lad's daydream. Jane in a topaz silk gown, with emeralds at her throat and ears, looked on, smiling, while their grateful sovereign proclaimed, "Arise, Sir Alexander…"

A pounding at the door jolted him out of his reverie. He answered the summons wearing his bland servant's demeanor.

A pale, distraught face thrust into his as the caller tried to force his way past.

"M' sister owns this house. Let me in—quick, damn you!"

Alex reached out, grabbed Stowe's neckcloth, and hauled him inside, shutting the door so fast an edge of Stowe's coat caught in it.

"Awwwk!"

Gordon reopened the door, freeing the coat, slammed it shut, and planted his fist in Stowe's chin.

Stowe staggered, caught his balance, and felt his

jaw gingerly. "What the devil—? What's the meaning of this, you scoundrel? I'll have you taken up for..." The threat trailed off weakly as Stowe must have realized he could not act on it, if he meant to hide in Jane's house. Gordon hit him again, and this time Stowe folded slowly to the floor. As he stripped him of his neckcloth and looted his pockets for his handkerchief, Alex reflected that he had learned a great deal from his visit to Scotland. He now knew how useful such accessories were for binding and gagging a captive.

Then he bolted the door and went to find Jessup.

****

"It's dry enough, and there's no rats, I don't think," the butler said. "Tib's a terror for the rats and mice. The master had it built to hold valuable cargo, if ever he should have small goods of great value in the house. He wouldn't trust those to a warehouse."

The little brick-walled room in the cellar was not a place Alex would have cared to spend much time, but the heavy oaken door with its padlock should certainly keep Stowe safely. Their prisoner was sitting on the straight chair Jessup had brought down, mumbling curses and holding his jaw.

"You'll be comfortable enough, sir. The bucket's in the far corner, there's a good pile of blankets, and you've got tallow dips and a tinder box on the table, when you need another light. And here's Mistress Jane with your supper."

"Jane! You can't mean to keep me in this dungeon! I'm your brother!"

"Half brother." She set the tray on the side table, carefully edging the candle holder and tinderbox aside.

"It's more comfortable than lodgings in the Tower," Alex said.

Stowe stared at him. "Gordon?"

Stowe had not recognized him until now. "Ay, Stowe, the man you—abandoned." He had intended to say "implicated in the smuggling of the muskets, then struck down and robbed," but remembered in time that Jane was present. Jessup need not know the whole truth, either.

"I had to borrow your money to get away! You'd just fired a barn! I couldn't be caught with you. Sorry I had to knock you out, but I knew you wouldn't give me any, and…" He seemed to become aware that his half sister and her butler were staring at him. He went on in scrambling haste. "Jane, my dear, your Mr. Gordon is a d-desperate rogue. He's a—a Jacobite plotter. I discovered it in Scotland. He attacked me when I came to your door to w-warn you about him, not that I expected he'd come back h-here, as the authorities were searching for him when I left him, but I thought you should know. You must send to a m-magistrate to have him taken up. Of course, there's nothing we can do to prevent him from f-fleeing before the bailiffs arrive—"

"I know all about the smuggled muskets and for what they were intended and the money you lost at cards and why you wanted to hide here, Rupert." The words fell like icicles. "If I send for the bailiffs, it will be for you."

Gordon moved out of Stowe's line of sight and gave a slight head shake.

Jane continued after a barely perceptible pause, "…but it would grieve my father to have you sent to the Tower."

"You can't trust him, Jane! He's a Scot, for God's sake. I suppose he's lied to you and wheedled you. Those tricks always soften old maids. Let me go, and I'll lie low somewhere until this is all over. I'll need some money to find a safe place for a few weeks—it's why I came; I ran out of money, and the innkeeper tossed me out and kept the clothing I'd bought—but you can give me some, can't you? Then—"

"I think you will be most safe here, if Mistress Jane decides to keep you."

"Yes, Mr. Gordon, I agree. My half brother may come to harm if he is allowed to wander London on his own."

Stowe looked from one to the other and to Jessup in the background and buried his head in his hands.

Jane said, "You have everything you need until morning. You might spend some time reflecting upon your errors."

"Jane! Please let Father know. He'll help me."

"I do not wish to see Father implicated in your and Charles Pleasaunce's schemes. Mr. Gordon and I will consider what other steps we might take. Good evening, Rupert."

Upstairs, Gordon said, "You are very frightening when you are ice-cold with rage. I sincerely hope you never have cause to be so angry with me."

She pursed her lips before replying, "I hope so, too." Which was not totally reassuring.

In the housekeeper's room with the door left open for propriety, she asked, "What are we to do with Rupert, Mr. Gordon? How long can we keep him confined?"

Alex's forehead creased. "I have been wondering

that very thing. If I could contact Mr. Lattimer, we could refer the matter to him, but he might feel obligated to hand your brother over to the Crown. Although if your brother—half brother—agreed to bear witness against Pleasaunce and any other plotter he knew of, he might even now escape—"

"Hanging? Imprisonment? Transportation to the Colonies?"

"Jane, I am not an authority on the law. I don't know. He might be pardoned, if he were even charged."

He had called her Jane. She liked the sound of her name in his voice. It was almost enough to distract her from her worry.

"I beg your pardon. I should not have addressed you in so familiar a manner."

"I took no offense, Mr. Gordon. I liked it."

"Oh." His smile was glorious, like the sun rising. Her heart rose with it. They gazed at each other for a warm moment, before Alex gave a little shake of his head. "If we could find someone in authority, it might go well or ill for Stowe. I don't know who we could trust, apart from Mr. Lattimer."

Jane said, "I think I know someone who might be able to help. Cheddle, the butler at Hawthorn Cottage, was obviously in Mr. Lattimer's confidence. It seemed to me that Cheddle, and indeed the whole staff, were accustomed to serving guests who were there under assumed names or who were in hiding. It seemed a very practiced household, if you take my meaning."

"I do. Should we send a message to Cheddle explaining as much as we can of our difficulty, and requesting that he advise us of someone with sufficient authority either to send to Mr. Lattimer or to deal with the matter himself?"

"Yes, I think we must. But it might be days before we received a reply. It takes two days to send to Bath, for my stepmother regularly communicates with a friend there. Mail to villages that are not directly on a post road often takes much longer."

"It does. That is why I will send a messenger."

"Can you find one who is trustworthy, Mr. Gordon?"

"Yes. I will have to go out tonight, and I may be gone for several hours. But a reliable man will be on the road with it in the morning, and he will return with a reply."

"Please do not take chances, sir," she said, remembering what he'd said about necessary chances before visiting the Cocoa Tree.

The staff retired to bed early as they usually did when there was no master or mistress for whom to wait up, either to admit them on their return or to serve if they chanced to be at home. Jane and Alex composed a letter to Cheddle as they waited until the house had been silent and dark long enough to deceive anyone who might be watching. She intended to wait for his return. He had changed into the poor, travel-stained clothing in which he had arrived from Scotland, though the coarse linen shirt had been washed.

"I may not be back until shortly before dawn. Jessup or Mrs. Harrow can let me in when they come down in the morning. You should go to bed."

"I can sleep during the day. I have nothing better to do with my time."

"I will not argue with you. Do not open the door unless I tap three times, then three times again."

She had to smile at the theatricality of it, in spite of recognizing it as a sensible precaution. She could not forget Charles Pleasaunce's cold eyes or the attempt to abduct her from Hawthorn Cottage. They were dealing with desperate men. She shivered, though the kitchen was pleasantly warm. Alex took her hands, which were folded at her waist, and lifted them to his lips, one at a time. Oh!

Gentlemen had occasionally kissed her hand at balls or assemblies. That had been mere elaborate courtesy, meaningless. This was something more. She gazed into his eyes and found herself hoping he would kiss her lips, too.

He flashed her a reassuring smile. "I'm only going half a mile or a little more. Most of the time I'm gone, I'll be making the arrangements with the messenger and others."

Then Gordon drew back the heavy bolt and slipped out the door. Jane bolted it behind him and sat down near the banked kitchen fire to wait. Would Alex be safe? While he was very plainly dressed, he might still be a target for a robber.

She was glad he had not told her not to worry, because how could she help it? Men were always giving women empty assurances and promises that turned out to be false. That he need not go far and would be in company the rest of the time was reassuring, however. And he had survived Scotland and her half brother's attack on him. She suspected that rendering Alex unconscious and robbing him had not been the full tale of Rupert's duplicity.

What was to be done with Rupert? It would break her father's heart if Rupert were arrested or worse. Or if he had to flee the country. How long would they have to worry about Charles Pleasaunce's schemes? She herself might no longer be in danger from him. He must realize she would already have divulged his presence in town to others. Or would he? For all their families' long friendship, she could not claim to know him well, and she doubted he understood her. He had always seemed rather contemptuous of females.

Or he might want to learn if she knew her brother's whereabouts. Charles had known he had lost the money, hadn't he? She tried to remember what Alex had told her. Rupert had been terrified; was it because he knew his gambling loss was known or only feared what would happen when he could not get the guns? It had not been clear from her half brother's drunken confession to Alex, at least as reported to her. But the payment had been made. Rupert must have written Charles that the muskets were received. Then why had he come here to hide?

She could not concentrate on the problem. Her mind kept drifting to other matters, and too much had occurred in the last few weeks. Her uncle's death, the accusations against her, meeting Mr. Gordon, that wild ride across country, and her surreptitious return to London.

The more she saw of Mr. Gordon, the better she liked him. She hoped he was not in difficulties for helping Rupert, who was not worth it, not to her. No doubt her papa would be properly grateful if he knew what Alex had done to help his son. But he would be horrified to learn why Rupert had needed such assistance. Families! They could be one of the greatest sources of annoyance known to man—and woman. Or one of the greatest pleasures?

She would not mind seeing Alex's face over the breakfast table every morning. He did not seem to suffer from bad moods, and he could converse on frivolous as well as serious topics. What would it be like to kiss him? She wished he had taken advantage of the opportunity.

A tapping woke her from a drowse in which she was trying to dress for some great occasion and was unable to find her shoes. The tapping came again, very distinctly: one, two, three. She jumped up and hurried to unbolt the door.

Chapter 29

His luck was in. He found the head groom in the public house favored by the local stable hands, ostlers, and grooms. He bought himself an ale and glanced around the room, before drifting toward the fireplace, which was swept clean and unlit, the weather not being cold enough today to require a fire. He propped himself against the mantle and waited. Cuddie was sitting on a bench nearby, lecturing a stable lad—not one of Lattimer's—on glanders.

"...better to keep the stable clean and air it well than to treat the horse after it's sick. Most o' those receipts for cures do no good, anyhow," Cuddie said. The groom's eyes passed over him.

"That is my advice to you, young Tom." Then he drained his tankard, and nodded to his table mates. "I'll be off now."

Gordon finished his ale in a leisurely way, set the tankard down, and wandered out the door, turning in the direction that Cuddie would have gone. He heard a soft whistle and "What mischief are you up to, Master Sandy?"

"That's put me in my place," Alex said with a grin, as Cuddie slid out of the shadows into the slightly less dark alley. A few of the residents had hung out lanterns, in the old way. London was said to possess no fewer than 15,000 oil-lit street lamps, though more in wealthy neighborhoods and correspondingly fewer in poor streets. The next street had its fair share of lamp standards, making it tolerably easy to see the flagway underfoot, though the light did little to illuminate the center of the street.

He had known Cuddie all his life. The man had thrown him up onto his first pony. Well, his only pony, as he had graduated to a horse a few years later. A small horse, but still a promotion from a pony.

"You'll be in trouble, no doubt. Are you just now back from wherever you'd gone?—not but what it's like asking a tomcat where he's been. Ah, your mother and da's away, too."

"I know they're out of town. If my father were home, I'd go to him. Now that you've had your grumble at me, I'll tell you what I need."

"And mayhap what the trouble is? Your da was right worried for you—not that he owned to it."

They had been speaking in low tones. Now Alex whispered, "I cannot go into much detail. It has to do with the trouble in Scotland."

Cuddie grunted.

"I need to find someone to deal with a matter related to that trouble. To do that, I need a letter carried to a place about twenty-five miles away. With my parents both gone, it should be easy enough for you to take it and bring back the response."

"Ay, if you make it right with that stiff-necked butler. Jed can take my place for a day or two, and we'll see what he's made of, left on his own."

Cuddie turned off to go to the stable yard. Alex continued on to Great Russell Street and around the corner to the door of a house facing the square. There was a footman on duty all night, not the case in all wealthy houses. His papa, like the late Markham, sometimes received messages at odd times. He had once wondered what could require his attention in the middle of the night. Surely, the messengers could as well wait for morning and save everyone a great deal of trouble. He now appreciated the convenience.

"Welcome home, sir." The young footman on duty took in Alex's suit, much the worse for wear, and forbore to comment even by a twitch of his eyebrow.

"I've not come to stay, Peter. I only need to pack a few things and leave a letter for my father. I'll write it in the library."

"I will summon your man, sir."

"No, that's not necessary. I can manage on my own."

How fortunate that he was not a slave to his valet. He knew where the trunks and valises and portmanteaux were kept, and he was perfectly able to pack the things he needed. Or at least to stuff them into a portmanteau. Two pair of shirts and drawers. Stockings. Another pair of shoes. He chose a decent plain suit and a fawn-colored waistcoat from the pegs on the dressing room wall, and then glanced down at himself. Both the suit he was wearing and the one he'd brought back from Scotland had suffered too much wear and tear to be of use to anyone but a street scavenger. He added a second suit and waistcoat. He had to mash them a little to fit into the valise, but no doubt someone at Jane's could press them. He added an old wig, left over from a college theatrical, and stuffed it in, as well.

As he packed, he composed the letter he would

write. It must be short and not easily understood by anyone but his father.

Sir,

The visit did not go quite as planned. My companion's luggage arrived, but some confusion and excitement ensued and his goods were then destroyed in a fire. We were invited to stay in a Town House [Alex hoped his parent recalled that in Scotland the term referred to the town hall and gaol] *in Dundee but departed to return home, although separately. He is now returned and is staying in the home of your old friend, as am I. So also is my friend's relative, who came back early from a visit to the countryside, the neighbors not having been congenial.*

A.

How surprisingly difficult to write something which would confound strange eyes and yet convey one's exact meaning to the intended recipient. Inwardly, he apologized to his mama for his amusement at her attempt and hoped that Anthony Lattimer would come back soon. He seldom left London for any length of time unless he were staying somewhere he could receive forwarded messages.

Good Lord! Had Father gone north to look for him? Surely not. How utterly humiliating that would be. But Cuddie had said he was worried.

After folding and sealing the letter, he wrote a note for their butler, telling him Cuddie would be gone on an errand for two or three days.

The door had no sooner closed behind Alex than Cuddie intercepted him. "I'll be going along with you, Master Sandy, by your leave."

"Or without it, I make no doubt." Not a bad idea,

perhaps. Cuddie would be able to find the Markham house again without having to ask directions in the neighborhood.

On the way, they passed an alehouse in Butchers Row, near St. Clement Danes, not far from the end of Wych Street. The area was poor, with a reputation for rowdiness.

Cuddie spoke in his ear. "Let us take a little rest in yon pot-house."

"We are nearly at our destination. We can get a tankard of ale—or something stronger, if you wish—there."

"Oh, ay. It's not for the drink or the rest we'd be stopping. I'm thinking it might be wise to make a few acquaintances hereabouts. Dressed as you are, you will draw no notice to yourself, if you can still sound like a low fellow."

Alex grinned. "A'course I can."

****

"I've come back," he said, dropping the portmanteau as Jane pushed the kitchen door shut. She was flushed, slightly tousled, and remarkably appealing.

"Did you find your man?"

"Ay. At the worst, Cuddie should be back tomorrow afternoon. He has access to a good horse"—from the Lattimer stable—"and will leave early this morning. He won't risk injuring his mount, but even so, he should reach Hawthorn Cottage by early afternoon. He will not likely start out on the return journey until tomorrow morning, to rest the horse."

"At least we have set things in motion. Would you like a warm drink? I've ale here, with sugar and nutmeg

292

and a little brandy."

He accepted gratefully. He did not really need a drink, but if he refused, he would have to bid her good night. She wrapped the handle of the poker in a towel to remove it from the fireplace where it had been propped up on one of the andirons, pulled it out and gave the end a quick swipe with a wadded wet rag before plunging it in the tankard. An inviting odor of ale, spirits, and burnt sugar wafted up with a hiss.

"It smells wonderful," he said. "And tastes better." It also took away the taste of the rather inferior ale he and Cuddie had swigged down.

"I thought you would want something warm, coming back this late. I would have worried if I'd known you meant to be a packhorse, with all the crime in the streets. How could you have run, weighed down so?"

It seemed almost a *domestic* moment, a foretaste of what marriage might be like: a pretty woman waiting by the fire with a warm drink and concern for one's safety. Damned if he knew why some men spoke slightingly of matrimony.

He wanted to respond, "I? Run from a footpad?" but he knew she would not be impressed, and worse, would think him a fool. And he would be, even in his own estimation. "Cuddie came with me. He will carry our letter to Hawthorn Cottage tomorrow." He drained the tankard. "This is very good. I've never had anything like it before."

"I'm afraid it's not a gentleman's beverage. My uncle called it 'flip,' and was fond of it on cold nights or when he wanted to sleep. It's a sailor's drink." She lit a candle from an ember. "Come, I'll lead you

293

upstairs."

She took him up to the door of the little bedchamber between the library and the dining room. "Take the candle, and light yours while I wait."

He put his valise down inside the door and lighted the candle on the table near his bed.

Returning her candle, he asked, "Should you not sleep in your own chamber tonight? You may wake the servants, if you're sleeping in a maid's room."

"I intend to sleep in my own chamber tonight."

It would hardly be decent, their being separated by only one floor. "If anyone knew—" he said. If anyone knew he was staying in the same house with an unmarried lady and no one to chaperon her but the servants—no matter how many floors separated their beds—Jane would be ruined. She was not known in the upper levels of society, but her family would know and their friends would come to hear of it. It would be ruination.

"Why should they? My servants won't tell. I certainly won't."

"If it does become known, or if you should feel your reputation is compromised, I will gladly make you an offer of marriage. It would be no hardship at all, Mistress Jane."

In the light of the candle she held, outside his chamber door, he saw her bite her lower lip and look down.

"I will bear it in mind, sir. And to assure your peace of mind—in case you should be a sleepwalker—I will lock my door."

Not embarrassed but insulted. He was an idiot. A lady wanted a romantic proposal, with a declaration of love, in a garden, perhaps, with a suitor who was not dusty, sweaty, and inarticulate. And worse, he had implied the only reason he would offer marriage was in case he might have compromised her reputation.

****

She was quite out of charity with him. Admittedly, if his presence ruined her, as it might do, marriage would be the only respectable choice for her and the only honorable amends he could make. If some other lady found herself in this situation, Jane would have agreed no other solution was possible. But she did not feel compromised, and how could she have refused to give him shelter?

She had lost count of her place in the one hundred strokes she brushed her hair every night. It was too bad she could not curse like a man: it must be an excellent outlet for one's annoyance.

She did not want an offer from him out of his sense of duty. If he had folded her in his arms and kissed her…She could understand how a girl might find herself in difficulties when alone with a man. No wonder such tête-à-têtes were discouraged!

Jane sighed. If he had embraced her, the candle she was holding would probably have set her clothing alight and it would all have been very ridiculous and uncomfortable. And potentially deadly—she had been wearing a silk gown, wishing to look pretty for him. Mrs. Jennings had purchased a few replacements for the clothing left at Hawthorn Cottage from a secondhand clothing merchant who resold garments given to ladies' dressers and maids as vails.

He would have thrown himself on her to smother the flames, knocking her to the ground and covering her burning gown (and her) with his body. One of them would have overset the little hall table near the door, and the noise would have waked the servants. She laughed a little at the thought. It would not be at all romantic and would certainly require an instant offer of marriage.

If he did propose marriage, she wanted it to be because he loved her. And yet if he claimed he did, she would wonder if he were sincere, or if it were her fortune he loved. Not that there was anything wrong with marrying for practical reasons. Women usually did, to avoid being alone in the world with neither family nor resources, or a dependent in a relative's home, or if one wanted children, marriage was the only choice for a woman, even though everyone knew a husband gave no guarantee of security. Men married for practical reasons, too. But oh, it would be so much better if there were love as well.

She snuffed the candle and opened the heavy draperies over the windows an inch or two, before padding over to the bed. In the morning, the chink in the draperies would admit enough dawn light to wake her, if she left the harrateen bed curtains open.

As she snuggled into the warmth of the blanket and counterpane, she wondered if she would accept Alex's offer even if she knew he did not love her. She was of age, wealthy, and free. She did not need to marry. He was pleasant company and he was attractive, if not classically handsome. He seemed even-tempered and kind—though one could not always be sure until after marriage. On the other hand, he was unquestionably intelligent and possessed a sense of humor, which were important qualifications, to her, at least. Besides, he was not haughty, which was a trait impossible to conceal. She had heard him speaking with chairmen and servants much as her uncle would have done.

Slipping into sleep among the lavender-scented sheets, she wondered whether Alex would be willing to live in her house. Would he insist on a more fashionable or at least genteel neighborhood? If what she suspected about his origins were correct, he would not be accepted in the best circles. Uncle Markham's house was not ideal, though her fond memories made it dear to her. Her last conscious thought was of a scale, with house and freedom on one side and love— perhaps—on the other. The pans dipped one way, then the other.

Chapter 30

They had gathered in the kitchen for their midday meal when a sharp rap at the door made Molly squeak and jump. She and Alex exchanged a look. Jessup rose, unbolted the door, and opened it cautiously. Alex sat looking down at his plate, as his place at the table faced the door. Jane understood his motive: even someone who knew his face would hardly recognize him, dressed as a footman, eyes lowered. She herself, with her back to the door, in a maid's gown and wearing a large cap, was even less recognizable.

"I've a message for your footman, William."

Jane glanced across the table at Alex, who had raised his head.

"Let him in," he said softly. "He's the one we've been waiting for."

"Cuddie?" he said after the door was again secured. "Do you have—"

The man, almost elderly, though still tough and sinewy, shook his head. "'Twasn't thought safe to put anything down on paper."

"By your leave, mistress," Alex said, "I would like to withdraw to the butler's pantry with Cuddie."

"Certainly," she said. "Mrs. Harrow, I am sure Mr. Cuddie would like a draught of ale while he speaks with William. With dinner after he and William are done."

"Thank'ee, mistress."

She ruthlessly suppressed an urge to ask if she might be a party to Alex's interview with him. It would be humiliating to be refused, which, if government secrets were to be discussed, was quite likely. Alex gave her a friendly nod and a smile, took a candlestick from a shelf and lighted it at the hearth. They would need it in the windowless butler's pantry. The men withdrew, Alex with the candle and Cuddie with a tankard.

Conversation died at the table. They all knew Alex had sent a messenger somewhere and was awaiting a reply, though only Jane knew the details. Although there had been a feeling of being in a fortress under siege since her return, they had managed to go about their daily tasks in almost a normal manner. The feeling had intensified with the arrival and captivity of Rupert, but now the sensation of something impending was impossible to ignore.

"Well," Mrs. Harrow said at last, to break the silence, "Moll, I think we will make the almond sort of Portugal cakes tomorrow. You must blanch and peel the almonds today, and pound them in the morning. I'll weigh them out for you while you clear away."

Molly bobbed her head.

"What a good idea," Jane said. "I am very partial to them."

When Alex and the groom returned, Mrs. Harrow dished up a large serving of pork pie for Cuddie, with cheese and pickled onions for relish, and another tankard of ale. Alex said he had a letter to write and deliver that evening, and added in a low voice, "I'll explain before I leave."

"I'll go with you," Cuddie volunteered from his

seat at the table.

"Better not, I think. You'd best go home when you've done eating."

Cuddie, his mouth full of pork and apple and Mrs. Harrow's good crust, nodded reluctantly.

The last few days—no, the whole of the last month—had been shockingly informal, Jane reflected. However would she reaccustom herself to servants being invisible and nearly silent but for a "Yes, madam" or "No, madam"? And go back to the dull routine of her father's home and the occasional party or ball at which nothing important was said or done?

Perhaps she would not have to do so.

****

The footman wanted to take the letter.

"My orders are to give it into Sir Howard's own hand and wait for a reply," he said. Compared to Sir Howard Dampers's footman, Alex felt quite shabby. The man's livery fitted as if tailored for him—which it probably was—and his white wig must have been recently reset. His shoes shone. The housekeeper had done some alterations to Alex's coat and breeches, but they had clearly seen long usage.

"Wait here. I will inform Sir Howard."

Dampers, like Anthony Lattimer, must be accustomed to secretive messengers for the footman returned almost at once, to show Alex to the master's study.

Dampers, a stocky man with bulldog jowls, extended his hand for the letter, asking, "Who sent you?"

"It's…complicated to explain, sir. It would be best if you read the letter. It's all set forth very plain."

"You know the contents?" Dampers asked, eyebrows arching.

"I'm in his confidence as you might say, Sir Howard."

The bulldog growled and broke the seal. The letter ran to three pages, two written close on both sides, and the third on only one side. Alex watched rather nervously as Sir Howard read, sometimes rereading a paragraph, intermittently sipping from a glass of brandy, and once or twice muttering, "Hmmm!"

Finally, he refolded the sheets and tucked them under the blotter. "This is a confounded business. What's your name, and how do you come to be involved in it?"

He had had the foresight to come up with a name for himself, and that different from the name he used in Wych Street. Lucky he had thought of it. No, not lucky, precisely. One must be thorough in acting a part.

"Hubertus Canty, sir." It was the name of a character in a short play a friend had written in their college days. His own performance as the sly footman had reduced the audience to tears of merriment. Admittedly, a good deal of alcohol had been consumed beforehand.

Unfortunately, he had not foreseen the second part of the question. "I'd better not say, sir. It's not really important, is it?"

Dampers gave a snort of laughter. "Ay, you're a deep one, right enough. Well, I can't put you in touch with Lattimer, because he's pursuing inquiries out of town. However, I may be able to help. Who told you to come to me?"

"Mr. Lattimer's second son, sir."

"Idiot! How did he know to send you to me?"

Alex mentioned the Hawthorn Cottage butler.

"The former Sergeant Cheddle, hey? Who's your master?"

"Better if I don't say, sir."

The bulldog eyed him broodingly. "Hmmm. Well, perhaps that's true. If you're in young Mr. Lattimer's confidence, tell me the two things he's asked me to do, in his father's absence."

"First, to make sure he is safe from arrest as a Jacobite or smuggler, or for having burned a barn containing smuggled guns. Second, to secure the arrest of Charles Pleasaunce, who is a Jacobite, which may be accomplished by the third, though you have not mentioned it, which is to take charge of an unwitting accomplice of Pleasaunce's, who is currently being detained by a...er...private party. Mr. Alexander Lattimer believes he can be induced to turn king's evidence."

Dampers steepled his fingers. "So young Lattimer became, by some undisclosed means, his father's deputy. But I am dealing instead with his—or someone's—servant. Or agent. I would prefer to speak with young Lattimer directly."

"It would not be safe for Mr. Alex Lattimer to come into town, given that he may be arrested, as he nearly was at Somerset House recently."

While Sir Howard's jaw did not drop nor did his eyebrows meet his hairline, he was clearly surprised, judging by the delay in his response.

"That was young Lattimer, was it?" Dampers shook his head, more in wonder than denial, and said, "I am always filled with amazement at Tony Lattimer's methods. They are seldom tidy, they ignore established procedure, and yet they usually accomplish the desired end. Well, I can assist with part of the problem. I can take this 'unwitting accomplice' in charge and see he's turned over to the right people. If he reveals the identity of currently unknown Jacobites and is willing to give testimony against any, I can see to it that his assistance will be taken into consideration, though I cannot promise he will escape all punishment. I assume that is young Mr. Lattimer's wish?"

"Yes, sir." That would be a relief to Jane Stowe.

"I'll need to know where to collect him, then."

"He will be delivered, sir."

"Where? When?"

"Mr. Alexander Lattimer will advise you of the particulars after arrangements have been made."

"Canty, I believe my department would be pleased to hire you, if you should wish to change your employment."

"I'm flattered, sir. About the other matters…?"

"If your 'unwitting accomplice' implicates him, Pleasaunce will be taken into custody. His family's connections make it damned awkward to arrest him without evidence."

"And Mr. Alex…?"

"Now, that is a problem, indeed. I can pass word on that he is acting on behalf of his father. However, that may not do much good. It depends on who is seeking him. Tony Lattimer's connections reach farther than mine, even up to the First Lord of the Treasury. Mine, alas, do not. Young Lattimer will do best to stay out of sight until his father returns. I can send on a message which may find him—or not. I know he expected to be on the move."

"Thank you, sir. I will urge Alexander Lattimer to stay out of sight."

"How soon can I expect delivery of the 'unwitting accomplice'?"

"Most likely tomorrow night, Sir Howard."

"Good. Are you aware that Edinburgh is in the rebels' hands? Except for the garrison in the castle, of course."

"We had not heard that news, sir."

"We received it only today."

On leaving Sir Howard's elegant house, he strode briskly to the Whitehall Stairs as if he had no fear of being followed. While there was a nearer watermen's plying place, Whitehall was likely to be busy, even at night, given the political situation, insuring a boat would be available. The south side of the river was mostly unfamiliar to him, so he asked the waterman to take him to the nearest stairs opposite the Three Crane Stairs.

"I can't call to mind the name, but I do remember it was across from Three Crane Stairs, or near, anyway."

"Ah! That'd be Horseshoe Alley Stairs. "

The fellow kept up a patter of ribald commentary on the way downriver, sometimes addressed to him and sometimes to watermen in other wherries and barges, many of which were bound to Vauxhall Gardens, or returning from there. No doubt any lady passengers covered their ears in horror at the language used. Though anyone who had been on the river at least once should be prepared for it: watermen were famous for taunts and jests bawled back and forth.

At Horseshoe Alley Stairs, Alex paid the man the

set fare and added tuppence. Although Southwark was mostly *terra incognita* to him, London Bridge was not far to the east. He turned at the first street he came to, and found it ended, leaving him a choice of turning toward the Thames or away from it. Choosing the first, he learned that the south side of the river had fewer streets and lanes, and many alleys were not cut through. On the other hand, his roundabout route made it less likely anyone could follow him. When at last he found the road leading to London Bridge, he crossed it and dove into a convenient alley where there appeared to be a number of people coming and going.

It led to the Ship Inn and a maze of narrow passages by which he found his way out to Tooly Street, the last thoroughfare before the bridge. On the other side, he'd find a hackney.

"That went fairly well," he told Jane on his return.

"You were so late I feared something had gone amiss, Mr. Gordon."

"It occurred to me to make sure I could not be followed. I crossed the river by wherry, lost myself in Southwark, and came back by the bridge."

"Will the man you saw help?"

"As much as he can. He'll take your half brother, who, if he has sense, will testify against Pleasaunce and any other conspirator he knows. If he won't…"

Jane sighed. "I don't want my father hurt, which he would be if Rupert were brought to trial and transported or worse. Rupert is self-centered and foolish—and often perfectly exasperating—but he is my part of my family. Yet it seems wrong to hope he will betray Charles Pleasaunce, who has been his friend since they were little boys."

"I'm sorry there's no really satisfactory outcome to be had. We can only trust your half brother will make the most of his opportunity."

"How and when is he to be turned over?"

"I told Sir Howard we would deliver Stowe. I would rather he not connect Stowe or me with you or this house."

"Rupert will tell him, I apprehend," Jane pointed out.

"He may. But I hope he will limit his disclosures to what he knows about Pleasaunce, to spare his parents humiliation." He was quite sure Rupert Stowe did not give a rap for Jane.

Well after midnight the following night, Jessup helped him lug the inert body of Rupert Stowe out to the waiting cart. The butler's nostrils were pinched, either in disapproval or at the smell, but he made no comment beyond, "Have a care, sir." He went back into the house, and Alex heard the bolt slide home.

The wagon rattled along the street. Even the few people they passed paid them no attention. All they saw, if they looked at all, were two men on a night-soil cart laden with the usual barrels. No one would care to get too close. Cox had dropped his assistant off before meeting Gordon and moved his buckets, shovel, and other equipment around, to make room for Stowe, who was now propped up against a barrel in the wagon bed. If anyone did see him, he would be taken for another Tom Turd. Gordon swallowed saliva and wondered how long it had taken Abel Cox to grow accustomed to the smell of the privies he cleaned and whether his wife's nose had also grown jaded.

They had gone some distance before Abel Cox

said, "You was right about the cully. He's dead drunk. Not a peep or a move he's made...I reckon he is drunk and not dead? 'Coz if it's the second, I know a doctor, a 'natomist, he calls himself, what cuts up bodies at St. George's Hospital who'd take him off our hands and pay us for the favor, too."

"He's not dead."

Cox clucked his tongue. "Ah, well, and if he's a friend o' yours, I wouldn't wish him to be. Wouldn't wish to *be* him, neither, when he wakes up, with a bad head, sick as a cat, *and* smelling of night soil."

"He brought it on himself by annoying me," Alex said. "Besides, I put an old sheet down in the wagon. Pull up, Cox. It's right along here. We'll take him down the area way and leave him by the door."

"His cook will be right happy to see him first thing in the morning." Cox chuckled evilly.

Alex mentally saluted Cuddie's foresight. Without their visit to that low public house, he would never have made the night-soil man's acquaintance.

Rupert's clothes probably stank. So did his own, Alex suspected, glad he'd worn his old travel- and tar-stained suit. He wondered if Mrs. Harrow would let him into the house—probably about the time she came down to start her day's work—or whether she would make him sluice himself off out in the narrow passage leading to the kitchen door. The suit—and the shirt and shoes as well—were probably fit only for burning. Or burying or dropping in the Thames.

The horse stood patiently while he and Cox manhandled Stowe's inert body off the wagon—*faugh!*—and back to the tradesman's entrance.

"We'll prop him against the door."

"Ay."

They trod briskly back to the street. The nag and wagon were still waiting, as why would they not be? This was a quiet, respectable neighborhood at any time, and at four in the morning no one was stirring. Few men would be returning from late carouses. Besides, even the wildest young gentleman on a spree would not steal a night-soil cart.

"Cox, take the wagon down around the next turning and wait for me there. I'll only be a moment."

The night-man darted him a look: wondering if Gordon planned to go back and cut their passenger's throat, perhaps?

"Don't get caught," was all he said before urging the horse to move.

When he was out of sight, Alex ran back down the areaway, pulling a folded, sealed sheet of paper from an inner pocket and a pin, supplied by Jane, from under his collar. It took only a moment to skewer to Stowe's coat the letter addressed to Sir Howard. Then Alex made for the street and ran light-footed to catch up to Cox.

"I'll keep in mind not to get crossways of you, Canty," the man said as Alex climbed up to the seat. "Ah, will you be wanting that sheet you put down in the back?"

"No. It's an old one anyway, with two or three rents in it."

"I'll take it, then. Plenty of wear in it, looks like, and nice quality linen. My wife can darn it. She'll like it."

Chapter 31

"Mr....the new footman has returned," Mrs. Jennings said when Jane passed the housekeeper's room on her way to the kitchen early that morning, hoping to find Mr. Gordon.

"Oh, thank you. Did he...was he successful, do you know?"

Mrs. Jennings said primly, "I could not say, mistress. He is down the cellar with a tub of hot water and soap. Mr. Jessup has taken him a change of clothing." At Jane's inquiring expression, she added, "There's not a stitch he was wearing that's fit for anything but burning."

"What happened to him? To them, I mean."

"Perhaps he is telling Jessup, and we will find out later. Mrs. Harrow did not let him linger in the kitchen, you may be sure." The housekeeper thinned her lips. "Mistress Jane, he smelled like a...a *necessary house*."

"Oh! No wonder Mrs. Harrow did not want him in the kitchen. We will leave him to his bath and wait to hear how his errand prospered." If it had. But surely if he had returned with Rupert, Mrs. Harrow would have said so.

Alex emerged from the cellar as Mrs. Harrow was setting out the bread, meat, and tea for breakfast. His close-cropped hair looked damp and when he took his place at the table, Jane detected a rather strong scent of eau de Cologne. He must hope to disguise any lingering aroma of privy. She wanted to ask what had happened, but while Jessup, Mrs. Harrow, and Mrs. Jennings were aware of his nighttime excursion, Molly was not. The less the kitchen maid knew, the better.

He gave her a meaningful look presumably signifying he would give her a more complete account later.

In the housekeeper's room after breakfast—but with the door ajar for decency—she merely looked at him, with raised eyebrows.

Mr. Gordon's account of his night's activities was as good as a novel.

"However did you think of employing a night-soil cart? Such a thing would never have occurred to me."

"I first thought of hiring a barrow from a street vendor, but I'd met Cox in an alehouse after taking our letter to Cuddie to deliver to Hawthorn Cottage. No one thinks anything of seeing a night-soil wagon in the middle of the night—they only work at night, after all, while a peddler on the street at three in the morning would be hard to explain."

"What if Rupert woke after you left him and wandered off?"

"Where could he go but here or to your papa? Don't worry. The brandy and laudanum kept him docile."

Jane laughed at the understatement. "Mr. Gordon, when you left here, Rupert was laid out like a flounder at the fish market."

"And so he remained, when I delivered him to Sir Howard's areaway. There is not a chance he regained sufficient consciousness to move before the kitchen staff opened the door. He drained a pint of brandy laced with laudanum almost at one swallow. And Stowe has no great tolerance for spirits, as I observed earlier."

Jane realized they were both still standing and seated herself in one of the armchairs. "Please be seated, sir. We need to talk. Will this soon be over?"

"I don't know. We have careened from one crisis to another. If your half brother is frightened enough— when he sobers—I hope he will turn king's evidence and offer up everything he knows of Pleasaunce, including his hiding place."

"If he knows it," Jane said. "I do not think I would entrust Rupert with a secret if I had any choice in the matter."

"Does Pleasaunce know him as well as you do?"

That was a point. Men behaved differently together than they did with women, as any woman with sense knew. When Rupert and Charles Pleasaunce were children, Pleasaunce had always been the leader and Rupert the follower. In those days, there had been no test of her half brother's allegiance, as far as she knew. Mayhap Pleasaunce assumed his loyalty, based on their boyhood scrapes. This was supported by his having put a large sum of money in his charge. Jane would not have trusted him with as much money as would buy the meat for dinner.

"Perhaps not," she admitted. "I wish Mr. Lattimer would return to Town."

"So do I."

The door from the passage to the front hall being open, they both heard the rapping. She glanced uneasily at Alex. He rose and strode into the dim corridor. Heart thumping, Jane followed. By the time she reached the door into the entrance hall, he had closed it behind him. Standing behind it, she reopened it a bare inch to listen, unseen by the visitor. Now that Rupert was gone, who would be coming to call at a house with the knocker off the door?

"…Captain Daniel O'Brien to see Mr. Markham on business."

The captain of the *Sea Mew*? Why would he come here asking for her uncle?

"I'm sorry, sir, but Mr. Markham took sick and died." Alex's voice was no longer that of a gentleman. He sounded exactly like a footman of the less accomplished sort.

A long pause. "I am sorry to hear it. It has been many years since I last saw him, but he was a strong, healthy man then, like to live four score."

Jane thought she heard both surprise and sorrow in the faint Irish lilt. So long a pause followed before Alex answered that she wondered if he would say anything.

"The coroner found as he was poisoned, sir. So it wasn't what you might call a natural death or to be expected."

"God in heaven."

Jane heard real anguish in the utterance.

"Sir, mayhap you should sit and catch your breath."

There was a measured tapping—a cane on the floor?—and then a deep sigh as he lowered himself into a chair. "My leg was broken badly several months ago, and I have only recently recovered enough to get around on it. I would have thought I would be buried before Markham."

Jane realized she was holding her breath, waiting

for one of them to speak again.

Alex said, "At the inquest, they claimed his niece put arsenic into some shrimps and sent them to the master. But none of us that worked for Mr. Markham believe it." If he had been a servant in fact, she would have chastised him later for gossiping with a visitor. However, Mr. Gordon's remark was not idle; he must be offering a little information in hopes of learning something from the man Jane thought of as "the pirate captain."

"Was she arrested, then, the poor woman?"

"N-no. Not yet, anyway."

"Thank God for that mercy." Jane heard what sounded like a shuddering sigh and risked a peek around the edge of the door. She could see Alex, standing almost at attention, like a proper footman, and a man sitting, head down, forehead resting on the clasped hands that clutched the head of his cane.

"Would you have me summon a doctor, sir?"

O'Brien drew a long breath and sat up. Jane pulled her head back just in time.

"No. It's sick at heart I am, not ill. Will you supply me the lady's name and direction? I wish to write her to offer my sympathy. Markham did me a great kindness many years ago. It may chance I can be of assistance to her now."

"...I don't rightly know if—"

Jane slipped into the room. Both men stared at the intrusion. Alex started to speak, then thought better of it.

"I am Jane Stowe, Roger Markham's niece."

Captain O'Brien had very sharp blue eyes in a tanned, weather-beaten face, and hair the color of ivory.

He began to rise, awkwardly bracing his hands on the chair's arms, while still clutching the cane.

"Please don't trouble to stand. I heard you had broken your leg." She seated herself on one of the other chairs. Alex froze into immobility.

"Ah, it's that way, is it?" O'Brien muttered. "You have not been arrested—yet—because they cannot find you."

"Not exactly, sir. Though I am in hiding from someone else."

He stared at her. "Not a simple matter, I think. I owed your uncle a debt, and I fear I also owe you amends for another thing. I may be able to help you, one way or another, if you will tell me your trouble. Though your footman has mentioned the…legal difficulty."

Jane laughed. "That is certainly one way to describe it. William, please pour some brandy for Captain O'Brien, and bring us tea as well."

"Mistress—"

Their eyes met. She could read the message in his: *Don't trust him. We know what he is.* Jane hoped Alex could interpret her look as well: *He is genuinely distressed. And we need whatever help we can get.*

"Ay, Mistress Jane." He took a decanter of brandy and a glass from the lacquered cabinet, filled it three-quarters full and set it on the table by the captain's side.

He left the door into the rear of the house ajar when he went to fetch the tea.

"We will wait for the tea to arrive, sir, before I begin to explain. I fear it will take some time."

"I have time in plenty for my old acquaintance's niece."

"I believe you met my uncle in Scotland in 1715?"

"You know that, do you, mistress?"

"I discovered it in connection with my uncle's death."

"You would be his sister's child?"

"Yes."

"Did he have the rearing of you? How does it come about that you are hiding in his house?"

"My mother died many years ago. My father is still alive and remarried. But my uncle and I were always close. Why I am here will become clear."

"Stepmothers can be a terrible affliction to a child," he said. "I had one, myself."

Alex Gordon returned with another small table and placed it in front of Jane's chair, and marched out, returning with the tea tray. He took a position out of O'Brien's line of sight.

The captain did not fail to notice his inconspicuous presence. He gave her a searching look. "Mistress Jane?"

"William is in my confidence and is to be trusted," she said.

The captain drained his glass and accepted a cup of tea. "A trustworthy crew is a treasure. Will you tell me?"

Even refreshing herself at intervals with increasingly tepid bohea, her throat grew scratchy. There was a great deal of background to be provided. She had to fill in additional details, too, and several times the captain asked for clarification of one point or another, particularly regarding the muskets' arrival in St. Andrews. Talking about the guns to the man she knew had brought them from France was a little awkward, as she could not let him know she was aware of his involvement. She did not mention Lattimer or Gordon by name, referring to both as simply friends. She suppressed mention of Hawthorn Cottage, saying that she had been staying in the country with acquaintances, and skimmed lightly over how she had left it and returned to London. Captain O'Brien could not be considered a friend to England, making her account of the murder and its connection to the muskets a verbal minuet.

He watched her keenly. He evidently understood how carefully she was editing the story. When she finished, her shoulders slumped. She had been holding herself very rigid, more even than her stays and good posture would have required. She had tiptoed around Rupert's return and delivery to a government authority.

He set his tea bowl down and poured himself more brandy, Alex having left the decanter on the table, conveniently to hand.

"So the possible charge of murder against you has been quashed by the magistrate, though one might wish whoever instructed him had made up a different story. Though people do love scandal, and unrequited love and murder by a slighted aspirant to a young lady's hand is certainly scandalous. That story will be more readily believed than any true account would be."

She smiled wryly. "That is precisely what Sir Thomas de Veil said."

"This 'friend'—or is it your beau?—who is being unjustly sought for smuggling and treasonous activities: you will not want him to have to flee the country, permanently, at least?"

Jane's face warmed; she must be blushing. "A

friend." She did not let her eyes stray to where Alex stood. "But I do not think he would wish to have to live in hiding for the rest of his life."

"Then he must be cleared. I am not sure, either, that we should be waiting for your half brother to betray Charles Pleasaunce, who is a dangerous fellow. Oh, ay, I've met the man. But I believe I know someone who can deal with both problems, if he is still alive. He is another old acquaintance of mine and was a friend of Markham's."

"Mr. Anthony Lattimer?"

"You know him?" O'Brien's eyebrows rose.

"His name came up in passing," Jane replied. "I know he was in Scotland with my uncle."

"I do not think he was employed by the government at that time, or I should likely not be here today. But I heard later he might have been offered a post in some government department. Even if not, he had many good friends in office and can help us, if he will. If he lives."

"He does, in fact. But he is out of town."

O'Brien regarded her thoughtfully. "Can you write to him?"

"He is said to be travelling, and his exact route is not known."

O'Brien grinned, rather wolfishly. "Then we can assume he will be able to help—once we find him."

"I fear that may be more easily said than done. Though we have put out word through one or two channels that he is needed here."

"This reminds me of my youth," he said finally. "I had forgotten what it was like. And now perhaps I should be on my way and see if Pleasaunce's fangs can be pulled."

"Before you go, sir, pray tell me what brought you here today? I have told you a vast number of secrets, and you have told me almost nothing."

O'Brien sat lost in thought. Jane sat without fidgeting, as she had been taught. Alex might have fidgeted if it were not out of character for a well-trained footman. But he did very quietly refill O'Brien's glass.

"Secret for secret," the captain agreed finally. "I do not do much smuggling now, for that's a young man's occupation, and I mostly gave it up when I married. I did not wish to leave my wife a widow and my children orphans. The ordinary risks of the sea are bad enough, but Marie was accustomed to those, being a sea captain's daughter herself. I did not wish to double or triple them and mayhap be hanged at Execution Dock."

He sighed. "You must understand, when I was young, I hated the English Crown, which has never been kind to Ireland. If I had stayed at home, likely I would still be full of hatred—or dead. But I settled in France after I married, so there was less to rub on the old sore, and I let most of my anger go. Then a man approached me four or five months since and asked me to deliver a cargo of muskets to Scotland. My wife is dead and my children are grown, and so I agreed, not for the money, but for a chance at a little revenge on your Crown, and because the Scots, like the Irish, are Celts, and like them, are oppressed by the English government, as are Catholics. Even some of your good Anglicans believe the fat little German had no God-given right to be king over them, when there was nearer royal blood."

"So I have heard, sir. I know Catholics and the

Irish and Scots have few more rights under English law than English women. Though to be a male is always preferable, even if one is not permitted to attend university because of one's religion."

The captain appeared to be struck momentarily dumb. "But ladies—women of all degrees—are designed to be mothers and wives and to support and comfort their men. To cheer men's lives and not to strain their bodies and minds with too much study."

"That is the common view," she agreed. "As the Irish are lazy, the Lowland Scots clutch-fisted, and the Highland Scots savages."

Alex Gordon coughed.

"Do you suffer from a congestion of the lungs, William? I am sure either Mrs. Harrow or Mrs. Jennings has an effective remedy."

"It's only a little scratchiness, mistress. Nothing that needs dosing."

"I am certain my dear late wife did not feel slighted or confined in her role," Captain O'Brien said, ignoring the issue of the footman's health.

"Really?"

He looked discomfited. "There were occasions when she waxed a little satirical. I cannot believe women feel themselves oppressed. Men cherish and protect them. The ladies, God bless them, would speak out if they believed they had a grievance."

"To whom would they address their complaint, Captain? To their husbands whose property they are? Or to Parliament, which consists only of men and makes the laws?"

O'Brien laughed heartily. "You have bested me, Mistress Jane. Your argument sounds reasonable, and I am no orator or philosopher to counter it."

Jane smiled sourly. *Sounds reasonable, indeed.* Out of the corner of her eye, she noted that Alex's lips were compressed—but the corners definitely quirked up.

"Mistress, I bear no anger against the English in general. I liked and respected your uncle and Tony Lattimer, and many other Englishmen, though there were English landlords in Ireland I would have killed as I would a rabid dog. Well! I agreed to transport the muskets, and soon after the arrangements were made, I fell on the deck. Over forty years I spent at sea, from a lad of ten or twelve, and nothing worse than cuts, bruises, a broken nose, and a pistol ball in the arm. 'Twas sheer bad luck." He shook his head and gave a crack of laughter. And took another drink.

"Bad luck indeed. I expected it to heal in time for me to sail with the cargo. Since having a ship of my own, I never failed to deliver a cargo, and I saw no reason to suppose I would do so this time. But the doctor thought I might lose my leg entirely, and I was sick with the fever, as well. I was too ill to do more than instruct my first mate to contact the shipper and explain that he would have to find other transport. There was plenty of time for him to do so. While I was abed, I let my first mate take charge of the *Sea Mew.* We had no other business at hand, without the shipment of muskets, so I told him to inspect her and set to rights anything that needed work. There's always something needs doing on a ship. I had been thinking for some time I should buy him a sloop or schooner or else go ashore permanently myself and turn the *Sea Mew* over to him. But I did not want him involved in the matter of the muskets. He has had little experience of smuggling, and he had never sailed into St. Andrews. In an easterly wind, the approach is treacherous." His voice shook a little on the last word. He drank again, and Alex stepped forward and poured him another glass of brandy.

O'Brien paused, then drank again, and held the glass against his chest. "He told me we had been offered a cargo of fine furniture to be taken to London, if I cared to let him take it. He wanted to prove himself. I agreed. I would not have him think I did not trust his ability. Not until I was finally on my feet and able to leave the house did I find out from a friend that he had not cancelled the musket shipment."

Alex Gordon was maintaining the impassive face of a good servant, but his ears were on the prick. Her own must resemble those of a cat who has heard mouse feet in the pantry. "That is very interesting, Captain O'Brien. I can understand that you must have been very worried for your ship. Has it not returned? Did you come to London to seek news of it?"

"Oh, she returned. My first mate reported to me that his voyage had gone well, and the furniture was delivered. There was not a great profit, shipping charges being as they are, but profit was not the object, after all. Before I could ask him about the muskets, he said those had been delivered also, with no trouble at all."

Jane glanced surreptitiously at Alex, whose eyebrows had climbed toward his wig. "You must have been very angry with him."

"I was. When I told him to cancel the shipment, he did not argue with me. By way of excuse, he said he did not want me to lose my reputation for reliability, and he was certain he could make the delivery. He has done the like before, though never such a serious thing. He would do what he was warned against and rely on success to win forgiveness.

"I was not easy in my mind about it. I paid a call on the second mate's woman and left word I wanted to see him without anyone else knowing. I learned that Gabriel—my first mate—had demanded more money before delivering the arms. Sébastien said he was surprised, but thought I had ordered it, because Gabriel was not familiar with the difficult approach to the harbor. But there was something worse than Gabriel's cheat. There had been some difficulty in London though Sébastien did not know the details. But he had heard that someone knew my ship had been a smuggler's vessel, and there was a rumor aboard the *Sea Mew* that Gabriel had taken care of the problem with a gift and seen to it someone else paid the bill. Sébastien was worried about that, though he did not know why. 'It sounded wrong' was all he could tell me. He could not come by a true report of how the rumor started, and we all know what is said is not always true."

Jane swallowed hard, trying to clear the lump in her throat before speaking. "It does sound very peculiar, Captain." Her hands clasped tight in her lap, mimicking the hard weight in her chest.

"I came to London to make my own inquiries, because I did not want to question any other crew member, lest it should come to Gabriel's attention. If he took some...desperate action here, I thought I could find out from one of my old partners or friends. I came to see Markham first, and now I have learned he is dead, perhaps by a poisoned gift, said to have come from you."

"So the man who delivered the shrimps claimed. But the magistrate was able to cast enough doubt on it that I was not arrested, and then the story about my supposed suitor was put about."

O'Brien sighed and leaned back in his chair. "Could they obtain no description of the sender of the shrimps from the delivery boy?"

"They were unable to locate the man who brought them, although they had a good description of him. He made a very favorable impression upon the kitchen maid."

"What did he look like?"

Jane obliged with a verbal sketch of the handsome, smiling young man with sapphire-blue eyes, who had so charmed Molly.

O'Brien closed his eyes. "God in heaven."

"Was it your first mate, sir?"

"Ay."

"You are not responsible for his misdeed, Captain O'Brien, and if you have known him for many years, I'm sure you are fond of him. I can understand you would not want to inform the authorities or give evidence against him. There is no need, I believe, as the authorities are apparently satisfied I did not cause my uncle's death. Though it must be hurtful that he betrayed your trust. Do you mean to dismiss him?"

The captain regarded her with no expression whatsoever. "You are kind to say I am not responsible, but in my heart, I know I am. Gabriel is my son."

Alex poured more brandy into the captain's glass. A great deal more, and Jane could not feel he was wrong to do it.

"He would not have known Markham was someone I owed a favor. I would not have mentioned his name, when I told Gabriel and his brothers about my wild youth. If he had known, he might not have murdered poor Markham."

Or perhaps he would have.

"But to throw suspicion on you, Mistress Jane. That, I cannot forgive. How could he even know you existed, when I did not—and I have occasionally heard news of Markham, over the years." He took a long drink.

I have never been a weeper. I will not start now.

When she was sure her voice would not break, she said, "My half brother, Rupert, may have mentioned my name."

"But there was no need to give anyone's name as sender of the shrimps. To implicate you seems like pure malice. It would have been a mystery, and no one would have been in serious danger of prosecution."

She sighed. "My family is not wealthy, merely comfortable. They all knew I was my uncle's heir. Possibly Rupert mentioned as much, and your son simply thought to benefit him." *Or Rupert suggested casting the blame on me.* The thought was deeply dismaying but not unimaginable. Both her stepmother and Rupert regarded her expectations from Uncle Markham as being their own. She remembered hints that she should ask for money from her uncle for this or that, or that he should make her an allowance. She had always refused to do so; her father had the means to support the family, and she herself was not a spendthrift. Her family would only come to rely upon the extra income and feel pinched when she eventually married. Which led to the question: did that explain why Stepmama had ceased making the slightest push to find her a husband once Uncle Markham let it be known she would inherit a fortune? It might be annoying to have an adult stepdaughter underfoot—although that stepdaughter's services as housekeeper were an economy—but if she remained a spinster, living at home, she would quite likely contribute to the family budget once she inherited. If she chanced to die unmarried before her father or half brothers, the fortune would pass to them. She must think longer about that possibility, but not right now.

"Family can be a source of great happiness," O'Brien said sadly. "Or of great pain. I suppose I must take comfort that my other sons and daughters turned out well." He bowed his head, lost in thought. She knew how he must feel. She could not bear to look at his private grief. Alex was watching him closely, though he could not see O'Brien's face from his position. Now why—?

The captain's hand, still holding his empty glass, was resting on the arm of the chair. She did not even realize it was sliding off until Alex sprang forward and caught the tumbler near the top between thumb and forefinger, a second before O'Brien's hand slipped off to hang limply over the side. His eyes were closed, his jaw had dropped, and Jane heard a faint, purring snore.

The decanter was empty. Alex drew her away to the far corner of the room.

"He did not show any sign of the amount he had taken, did he? I wondered how much more he could hold," he murmured, keeping his eyes on the slumped figure in the armchair.

"Did you intend this, Mr. Gordon? I noticed how assiduous you were in keeping his glass filled, but I thought you meant to loosen his tongue."

"That, too, mistress. I believe he was telling the truth, but I did not want him leaving here and perhaps divulging your presence to someone. By the time he wakes, I hope to have decided what to do."

"I hope *we* have decided what to do."

"Ah, quite. Certainly. I don't want to turn him over to Sir Howard."

"No, I agree, Mr. Gordon."

"But if the choice is between his son and you, I fear love of his son will prevail."

"Do you think so? Why would he have told us, then? And Gabriel is not here, is he? I'm sure Captain O'Brien implied that he was not, when he said he had come here secretly so Gabriel should not know."

"However angry he may have been at his son's disobedience, the captain is not likely to testify against him, is he? And he himself was the one to agree to transport the muskets."

"He would be incriminating himself," Jane agreed. "Yes, I can see that it would be too much to expect of him. But what will he do?"

"If I were he, I'd go back to France and turn the *Sea Mew* over to Gabriel."

"And wait for him to come to a bad end?"

"Ay."

She gazed at him unhappily. She was resigned to that outcome with Rupert now, but she liked Captain O'Brien. And he had had two shocks: the murder of her uncle and the fact that his own son had committed it.

Mr. Gordon chewed on his lower lip. "I think he should stay here, until he's slept off the brandy, if you do not object, though having two strange men sleeping under your roof is surely more than twice as improper as one. By then, we may have had news of Mr. Lattimer, who would know what to do. Or we may have devised some clever idea of our own."

"Pray, how can it be improper, sir, when there are none here but servants who have permitted an old friend of their late employer to stay when he was overcome with travel weariness and grief? Mistress Jane Stowe is not here, for she is visiting in the country."

He grinned at her and her heart gave a thump. He had a very infectious grin, better even than his smile.

"I will have Jessup assist you in taking him upstairs."

"No need. He is a sailor. If he can be waked, he will probably be able to walk with my assistance."

Chapter 32

He looked in on Captain O'Brien shortly before supper. Their guest was sleeping soundly; it would be a pity to wake him. Not only had he had a great deal of brandy, but he must still be recovering from his injury, and he was not a young man. He could eat when he woke.

Conversation at supper was subdued. The senior members of the staff were feeling the tension as much as he and Jane were, though for different reasons, perhaps. They were serving in a house in which shocking improprieties had become the rule rather than the exception.

The only one who spoke much was Molly, who under ordinary circumstances would have been hushed by either the cook or the housekeeper. There was as strict an order of precedence among servants as among the gentry, and kitchen maids were near the bottom. Under the strain of the last few days, the social order had broken down: the mistress dressed as a maid, eating with them in the kitchen, an unrelated man living in the house, mysterious comings and goings. What did it matter if Molly chattered on? Besides, it filled the silence.

"There was a peddler came to the door this afternoon, with such a smile. I wished I could have bought something of him."

"You'll buy yourself only trouble and that without a penny to your name, if you encourage strange men," Jessup said.

Alex saw Jane struggling to suppress a smile. She must be thinking of his admitting to being a strange young man, early on in their acquaintance. Was it only a month ago? It seemed longer.

"When was this?" Mrs. Harrow asked. "I don't recall a peddler coming today."

Molly blushed and looked down at her plate. "You was out of the kitchen, on personal business, like."

Ah, a visit to the necessary house in the yard.

This time the cook's face reddened. "Oh! Ay, there was a few minutes I was gone."

And perhaps a few minutes spent chatting with one of the servants in the house next door, over the backyard wall.

"What was he selling?" Mrs. Jennings asked. "I need some green embroidery silk."

"He hadn't any o' that. But he had thread and buttons and ribbon and some broadside ballads and pins and all manner of things."

"Trumpery, it sounds like," Jessup said.

"He give me a ribbon as blue as his eyes." Mollie sighed.

"You shouldn't take gifts from a man that's not your father, brother, or husband, girl," Mrs. Harrow pronounced.

"He must have expected to get something in return," Mrs. Jennings said.

"What was it?" the butler asked. "I'm sure Mrs. Harrow wasn't gone long enough for you to have done something that'd make your ma weep, but peddlers don't give things away for free."

"He didn't touch me…hardly. He did kiss me, but only to thank me for being so friendly and not turning him away, he said. And the ribbon was a bit frayed at the ends, and wrinkled."

With a feeling of foreboding, Alex asked, "Did he ask you who else was here that might buy from him?"

"He's new to the neighborhood and wondered if he could get any business here." The girl's chin trembled.

Which meant that he had indeed questioned her about the inhabitants.

"And what did you tell him, Molly?" Jane asked, as if it were not important at all.

"I only told him there's Mrs. Jennings and Mrs. Harrow and Mr. Jessup and me. I didn't mention you, Mistress Jane, nor Mr. Gordon, only that we had a new maid and footman."

Jane glanced at him. Alex heard Jessup make a sort of throat-clearing sound.

Molly seemed to find her mistress less intimidating than her fellow servants—they would be the ones who scolded and disciplined her, after all—and he was trying to think how to prompt Jane to ask the question that had occurred to him several minutes ago. He had not asked it himself, so as not to alarm the maid or cut off the flow of information. But Jane had thought of it, too.

"Had you ever seen him before? Or someone like him?"

"I can't have, mistress, for he said he was new to the area. He did remind me of the man that delivered those potted shrimps that killed poor Mr. Markham. I'm that partial to men with blue eyes and blond hair."

"Molly! That blackguard told a terrible lie about Mistress Jane!"

Alex wished Mrs. Jennings had not spoken out. She might silence Molly.

"P'raps he was told by whoever did send them, Mrs. Jennings," Molly said timidly.

"Very likely that's true." His response appeared to reassure her. She flashed him a little smile. "Were they much alike? Or was it only that their hair and eyes were similar?"

She puzzled over the question, while Alex fancied he could see gears turning in her head.

"N-n-o-o-o. They looked as if they'd spent time out in the sun without a hat." Then she added, "He—they both—talked a bit funny, too."

Mrs. Harrow said, "I'd forgotten that, about the fellow that came with the shrimps. He did have an accent. It sounded almost French but different. Some kind of foreigner, anyway."

Molly sucked on her lower lip. "It couldn't have been the same man? Could it?"

Alex locked gazes with the others. "No, it doesn't seem likely, does it? It's an odd coincidence, but London's full of all sorts of people. I'd wager there's some girl who looks like you and someone who looks like me, or Mrs. Harrow, or any of us."

"Ohhh," Molly sighed. "That must be it."

"Mrs. Jennings," the butler said. "Perhaps you would give our Molly a lesson in fine sewing? You do it so well, and it's a good thing for young staff to be taught a bit outside their usual duties, and with things as they are, there's not much work."

The housekeeper raised her eyebrows, then caught

his meaning and smiled. "What an excellent idea, Mr. Jessup. Come, Moll, we've finished our meal. We'll sit in my room, and I'll show you how to mend net and lace before you go up to bed."

When they were gone, Jessup said, "That girl has no sense. Not a thought in her head but men and courting." Mrs. Harrow began to do Molly's chore, clearing the table. They all understood that there were things to discuss that Molly should not hear.

"To be fair," Jane remarked, "that's true of many girls of all classes."

"What's to be expected and no harm in a young lady is a fault in a servant, mistress. A maid has to be practical."

"I concede the point, Mr. Jessup. What I would like to know is why he would come back, if it were the same man?"

"You would think he would avoid coming back," Alex agreed.

"It can't be to do with Rupert, can it? Would he come here seeking my brother?"

"I can't think why he would. Their business was done, and returning to London could only endanger the fellow."

Mrs. Harrow put the dishes in a pan of hot water to wait Molly's attention.

"Mrs. Harrow? Could you deliver a letter to the penny post?" Alex asked apologetically.

While she went up to her chamber to fetch her shawl, he penned a few lines and waited impatiently for the ink to dry. Jane peered over his shoulder. When the cook came down, he sealed it and inscribed the outside "Cuthbert (Cuddie) McDonald, in care of Mr. Anthony

Lattimer, Bloomsbury Square."

Jessup had gone about his duties, and Mrs. Jennings and Molly were still in the housekeeper's room.

"Mr. Gordon…is it possible Charles Pleasaunce sent him?"

He stared at her. "They could be acquainted, I suppose. Captain O'Brien had met him, so it's not impossible." After a pause for reflection, he went on, "Your brother can't have arranged the matter by himself. Not if what I saw of him was representative of his—" He broke off.

"His abilities? His intelligence? His reliability? No. He must have been doing some errand for Pleasaunce when my uncle saw him leaving the *Sea Mew*. Pleasaunce—or someone else—must have negotiated the muskets' delivery."

"Your brother went out of town with Pleasaunce, and they both came back. I suppose it's possible that Pleasaunce and…well, it must be Gabriel O'Brien…are in contact. Unless O'Brien came looking for his father."

"Would you, in the same circumstances? I'm a female, so it may be I don't understand these matters, but I think I'd give my papa time to regain his temper."

Talking with Mistress Jane was unexpectedly helpful as well as enjoyable. Now that she pointed it out, he did not think he would want to confront his father, either. In fact, there were any number of times he had made a point of not seeing his own papa. "That assumes he understood that his father was angry. Did you get the impression Captain O'Brien let him know he was displeased?"

"That is well thought of," she confessed. "I don't

think he told his son Uncle Markham was a friend. He did leave France without telling Gabriel he was going, so I suppose if he found out, he might have come looking for him, if he believed the captain was in danger."

"At least he did not learn he was here. Molly did not mention him. She didn't know he had come to call and stayed."

"She didn't, did she? So he'll go and look elsewhere."

"That would certainly be desirable. It's too bad this is all mere speculation on our part. We can't assume there's no risk of his coming back. What if he's a committed Jacobite himself and a conspirator with Pleasaunce?"

"Then would he have increased the price for delivering the guns, sir?"

"That might not have been greed. The captain of the ship Rupert and I took told me the approach to St. Andrews is dangerous, and we have heard Captain O'Brien confirm it. A higher fee may have seemed justified."

****

She was in the attic storeroom, going through the trunks and boxes to see if there were anything useful stored there. It might be a vain hope, but rummaging through old draperies and antique clothing and furniture was a pleasant occupation, when she could not settle to read, and had no mending to do. She need not compose menus. With no family supposed to be in residence, Mrs. Harrow was capable of planning meals for the staff. Though she had also been adding a few treats: marmalade and coffee or chocolate (at five shillings the pound!) for breakfast in addition to the usual cold meat, cheese, and bread and beer the staff would ordinarily eat. Her pride would not allow her to feed the mistress and Mr. Gordon upon ordinary servants' fare, and Jane agreed. She would not want Mr. Gordon to think her spendthrift—but she also did not want him deprived of his usual breakfast.

The cook had gone out to buy some nice haddock or cod for dinner and some peas. Jessup was in the butler's pantry, very likely having a little rest. What an old-fashioned ladies' jacket! From portraits she had seen, it must be seventy or eighty years out of date. Too old, surely, to belong to Uncle Markham's late wife. Perhaps it had been her mother's? People kept such odd things out of sentiment. But underneath it, carefully wrapped in a piece of worn linen was a collection of pretty old lace. She put it aside to be used for something. Perhaps on her bride-clothes—if ever she had any need of them.

If she could find a pair of draperies that were not too worn, she might replace the faded, frayed ones in the odd little chamber next to the bookroom. Being in the middle of the floor, it had but one window, looking out on the narrow passage that led to the kitchen entrance and the yard in the back.

Or perhaps she would find the kind of pistol Alex had hoped for.

After hearing about Molly's handsome "peddler," he had asked whether her uncle had owned a pistol. She did not pretend to misunderstand his concern, and they had searched his chamber and the library. They found a flintlock pistol in an old valise Jane had not previously gone through, as it appeared to contain nothing but odds and ends. Alex had loaded it and taken it with him to the reception parlor. But he had hoped for a "coat pocket pistol." The flintlock was too long to carry on his person, and there was, apart from size, something very desirable about the pocket pistol.

Mrs. Harrow had taken Alex's letter to the penny post the previous evening. Alex had not seemed particularly worried last night, but by midmorning, it was obvious that something was weighing upon him.

At least Captain O'Brien was now awake though feeling the effects of his clandestine journey to London. And the brandy, too, no doubt. But he had drunk the tea Alex took up to him and found himself able to eat ham and porridge and bread and even to tell Alex to compliment the cook. "For I have never grown accustomed to the way the French eat in the morning, as long as I have lived there. My poor wife could never understand why I would want more than a roll or two, a cup of chocolate and mayhap a bit of fruit or cheese." Alex reported his words verbatim, lilt included. The captain had, however, kept to the guest bedchamber, asking Alex to apologize to his hostess that after drinking so deep on top of a tiresome journey and very evil news, he was fairly laid low.

She wondered what Mr. Gordon was doing. He was probably pacing, wondering why he had not received an answer to his letter. She hoped his footman's wig, a little too large for him, was not askew again.

Chapter 33

The flintlock was out of sight under a shawl he had begged from Jane and draped over the arm and seat of one of the chairs. The effect was of a wrap taken off hurriedly, dropped, and forgotten; it concealed the pistol reasonably well, considering the gun's fourteen-inch length.

He had taken up a post in the reception parlor, rather than in the passage leading to the stairs and the kitchen. The servants were in the rear of the house, with the kitchen door bolted and Jane was upstairs. It seemed well to keep watch at the front, though he hardly expected O'Brien or Pleasaunce to break in through the shuttered windows. It would not be impossible, but breaking them open in broad daylight in a street full of businesses and their customers would attract attention. Mr. Markham had been on excellent terms with the other residents of Wych Street.

Why would Gabriel O'Brien have returned to London? He might believe his part in Markham's murder was not known but even so, why return? This was not his home port, and to return to Markham's house was to court discovery.

He wished an answer would come to his letter. Where could Cuddie be? He wished he might leave the house and go to Sir Howard, but he would be at the War Office in Whitehall now. He could not visit him at his home tonight and leave the house unprotected but for Jessup. He wished Jane would come downstairs with some question or suggestion.

The hours seemed to be dawdling along. They always did, when one was waiting for something. Surely it must be time for the servants' dinner? After that, he would try to have a private talk with Jane. He would have to think of some reasonable excuse for doing so, as the servants were as good as the most diligent chaperon, though he did not think they disapproved of him. Having the servants on one's side is always good, when courting a lady.

The muffled shriek, "She's not here!" carried even through the closed door to the back of the house. Alex sprang for the chair where he had left the pistol, but he was too far from it. The door was thrown open, and a man pushed Mrs. Jennings through roughly. She fell hard on the wooden floor. He levelled his pistol at her heart as she lay gasping.

"If you move, she dies."

Another man edged past him, pulling Molly into the room.

Alex, frozen halfway to the chair, had no doubt at all about the second man's identity: the fair hair and blue eyes marked him as Gabriel O'Brien.

"Molly, you stupid girl." Mrs. Jennings sat up cautiously, keeping her eyes on the man who had threatened her. He wore a plain suit that was still too fine and well-cut for a tradesman or common criminal. He had the air and accent of a gentleman, as well. Charles Pleasaunce, at a guess.

"I'm sorry, I didn't mean to tell him about Mr.— about William!" Molly sobbed. Mrs. Jennings sniffed, a lady-like equivalent to a man's snort.

"Sit over there with her, now." O'Brien let go of the girl's arm and gave her a gentle shove. Then he moved to take a position at an angle to Pleasaunce, opposite Alex. His faint Irish inflection was overlaid with a cadence that sounded French. No wonder Molly and Mrs. Harrow had found something un-English about his speech.

"Keep your pistol on the footman," Pleasaunce ordered. "The devil take him, he's not Stowe. You, fellow—where is Rupert Stowe?"

"Mistress Jane's brother, would that be? I haven't never seen the gentleman, sir." The slightly unpolished diction of a footman who would never be hired by one of the *beau monde* was easy enough. Deciding on the right facial expression was harder. A really good footman would probably show no surprise. He settled for inquiring and slightly stupid.

"And Jane Stowe? Find her and I'll find her brother. Or she'll tell me where he is."

"I don't rightly know, sir. She lives with her parents, though she comes at whiles to make sure all's well and the repairs and such are going forward."

Pleasaunce swore sulfurously. Molly clapped her hands over her ears.

Mrs. Jennings and Molly must have denied her presence, too. Where were Jessup and Mrs. Harrow?

"She's not been at her father's house in days. She was said to have gone to stay with 'friends' in the country, but she's not there. Quick, woman! Who else might shelter her?"

Mrs. Jennings clearly had more to her than primness and efficiency at running a household. "Why,

I think I once heard she has a cousin in Dorset, but that's as much as I know about it."

Pleasaunce seemed the more dangerous of the two men, in spite of the other being a murderer, but Gordon kept an eye on young O'Brien as well.

He saw Molly, huddled against Mrs. Jennings, give a little twitch, in reaction to what she must know was a lie. But she was not looking at the housekeeper or even Pleasaunce. She was looking in the direction of the open door behind Pleasaunce. The stair was beyond it, only just out of Alex's sight. Was it possible Jane had come downstairs without anyone hearing?

"*Mon ami*," O'Brien said softly, and continued in the same language, "ask the woman how it happens they have been dining so well. Coffee and chocolate? Rice and sugar and chickens? My *maman* would have stared to hear of such fare for servants."

Mrs. Jennings put her arm around Molly and gave her shoulders a squeeze.

"If there are but the five of you, who is drinking coffee and chocolate and supping on chicken, woman?"

The devil take O'Brien for noticing their grocery purchases. Thank God neither had realized there should be another maid as well. He kept his face wooden, but their position was worrisome. If Jane had come downstairs, she must be aware of Pleasaunce and O'Brien; she might well have heard them speaking as she descended. She might have paused to assess the situation. If she thought both intruders were facing away from the door, her logical move would be to go past silently and out the kitchen door. He would not be able to see if she passed the door into the reception hall; Pleasaunce stood squarely in front of it, blocking his view. She might have slipped past—or she might be lingering in the hall. Molly's eyes were focused either on Charles Pleasaunce's elegantly stockinged legs, or on something behind him. Surely Jane could not be intending some desperate attempt to rescue them? It would be doomed.

Even if he had his hand on Markham's old flintlock and succeeded in shooting one or the other, there would still be one armed, dangerous man who would undoubtedly shoot him.

The sensible thing would be for Jane to leave the house and summon assistance…but it would take time to seek out a magistrate and convince him to send constables. Especially as she was dressed as a maid.

In the meantime, what would Pleasaunce and O'Brien do? For they would not simply leave. The very best outcome he could imagine was that they would shut the staff in the cellar and sit down to wait for Jane or Rupert Stowe to return. If only one or two constables came, the Jacobite and the smuggler could shoot them and escape.

The housekeeper said, "Mr. Markham was always generous with our household allowance, and Mistress Jane increased it, too, as she sometimes takes a meal or a cup of chocolate or coffee when she comes to oversee the furbishing up of the house. And she has had a literary gentleman come in to work at listing all the books in the library, to see if there's aught of value, so he must be provided for, as well."

"Where is he? Why didn't you mention there was someone else in the house?" Pleasaunce's voice went harsh.

Yes, it would be nerve-wracking to realize there

might be another man in the house.

"He is not here today, sir. He is a tutor to several young gentlemen who will be going to university soon. He comes in to work on the library as he has time. Today is not his day to work here." She hugged Molly to her side.

Jane's housekeeper should be writing novels. The explanation had tripped off her tongue without hesitation. If only—

A darkness obscured some of the faint light from the passage and stair behind Pleasaunce. Molly buried her face in Mrs. Jennings's shoulder, and the housekeeper murmured reassurances to the girl. Pleasaunce stood with his back to the door, and Gabriel O'Brien faced the candle near Alex and both had their attention fixed on him. If his expression changed, they did not notice it.

Then the darkness moved. Alex did not hear the flint and hammer strike the frizzen but saw the faint flare behind Pleasaunce's head as the priming charge caught. In the light of the candle, Pleasaunce's eyes widened with terrible knowledge. If he tried to move in the moment before the main charge ignited with a deafening report, the attempt came too late.

Time and Alex's heartbeat seemed to stop while Pleasaunce collapsed like a marionette with its strings severed. His pistol discharged as it hit the floor. Alex wondered where the shot from Pleasaunce's weapon had gone—not into either of the women, praise the Lord! The women's screams were strangely muffled, but they were both sitting up, arms around each other, as they had been before the shots. But there was no time to think; he sprang to the armchair and tore Markham's flintlock free of the shawl and cocked it. Pleasaunce was no threat; the singed hair smell was proof of that. A shot fired at close range to the back of the skull left no possibility that Pleasaunce was still alive. But Gabriel O'Brien was still armed, and whoever had shot Pleasaunce might have a second pistol—

Gabriel O'Brien's arm swung like a compass needle toward the figure standing over Pleasaunce. Before Alex could bring his own pistol to bear on either, the man in the doorway spoke in French.

"I am quite annoyed with you, *mon fils*."

The other recognized his target even as his finger tightened on the trigger. Gabriel O'Brien jerked his arm to one side. There was a third onslaught on their ears—how did soldiers avoid losing their hearing entirely?—and the ball smashed into the wall several feet to Alex's left. The room was thick with smoke and the reek of burnt powder. Captain O'Brien recoiled slightly.

"Papa! Beware the footman—he is armed!" Gabriel exclaimed. His arm dropped to his side, pistol hanging disregarded in his grasp. He looked suddenly younger, and uncertain, a feeling Alex knew well. He had often felt the same with his own father. Though never, fortunately, in such a situation as this.

O'Brien spared Alex a glance and switched to English. "He will not shoot me. He might shoot you. I would not be able to blame him, I think."

O'Brien's son had evidently not yet noticed that his ball had ripped through the older man's sleeve. Alex cleared his throat. "Captain O'Brien, I fear you are hit."

The women had stopped shrieking—although he was not sure Mrs. Jennings had ever done more than gasp—though Molly was sobbing loudly. His ears felt stuffed with wool, but he heard hasty footsteps on the stairs. O'Brien looked over his shoulder.

Chapter 34

Jane paused in the doorway, trying to make sense of the scene, half distracted by the sobbing, the smell and smoke of gunpowder, and fear. A tall, thickset man stood a few steps inside the room, his face turned toward her: Captain O'Brien. Beyond him, Alex stood near one wall, another young man almost directly opposite him against the other, both holding pistols pointed down at the floor, like mirror images. For one ghastly moment, she wondered if they had been engaged in a duel.

She struggled to gather her wits, now that she knew Alex was unharmed. Someone was lying face down beyond the captain. Molly and Mrs. Jennings crouched together on the floor beyond the motionless figure, white-faced. As she saw them, Mrs. Jennings began struggling up from the floor, leaning on Molly's shoulder. The kitchen maid was—*of course!*—weeping and hiccuping into her apron.

Daniel O'Brien spoke. "Mistress Jane. My apologies for the trouble here."

Jane looked to the captain, who appeared to be the only composed person present. He too held a pistol down at his side, though his left arm was held against his body rather awkwardly.

"Captain, you are wounded."

"My coat more than my skin, I believe."

"M—William…help the captain to a chair. Molly, stop crying, stand up, and—and go heat some water. Mrs. Jennings…"

"Ay, mistress. I'll fetch scissors and an old sheet for bandages, should they be needed. Mayhap a needle and thread, too, so I can mend the gentleman's sleeve?"

"Yes, please. That would be very helpful. And where are Mrs. Harrow and Jessup?"

"Locked in the cellar, mistress. That one"—she nodded at the body on the floor—"said Cook was insolent, by which I suspect he feared she would fly at him armed with her best frying pan. Our Mr. Jessup, being a man, might be dangerous, too." With a tight-lipped smile, she hurried out, followed by the still-sniffling Molly.

"It's a tricky thing, for two men to hold four at pistol point," Gabriel O'Brien remarked. "It seemed best to reduce the odds."

Captain O'Brien glanced at him coldly, as Alex assisted him toward an armchair, and his son looked down, abashed.

That the captain permitted himself to lean on Alex Gordon's arm made her fear that he had been gravely wounded.

"Ah…Mistress Jane…Captain O'Brien," Alex ventured, "it's possible that the shots will have attracted attention."

"Well thought on, but unlikely. You've the shutters up, and this is a thick-walled old house."

"You are correct, sir, but what's to do now?" Jane asked.

Mrs. Jennings returned then, bearing a tray with a bowl of steaming water, scissors, a needle, thread, and a soft old linen sheet. Jessup came in on her heels.

He looked none the worse for wear, except that his coat and breeches were dusty and there was a cobweb on his shoulder. One could not expect a cellar to be clean, after all.

"Jessup, help Captain O'Brien off with his coat, gently, if you please, before he sits. Mrs. Jennings, if you will see to the sleeve? How fortunate it's a dark color. You will sponge it, I know, if there's any blood—oh, there isn't. Good. And pour some brandy, Jessup."

"Thank you, I will take a glass. Though only one today. I had a glass too many yesterday, and I'm out of practice."

Jessup, after a quick appraisal, poured the younger O'Brien a glass as well. He had approached to stand a few feet away, his face whiter than his father's. Jessup's eyes slid to Gordon and evidently decided it would appear peculiar to offer the footman spirits. Jane noticed what Jessup, perhaps, had not: Alex was standing back from the group around the captain, positioned to have a clear shot at Gabriel O'Brien. No, Alex did not require a sustaining dram, even if he was a little pale.

"It appears your wound is not as serious as it might have been." Jane eyed the torn, blood-stained shirt sleeve. "Do you think you can raise your arm, sir? If you can, we might remove your shirt rather than cutting it."

"If someone—" He glanced around, and Jane saw him register Alex's position and understand its significance. "—ah, Gabriel! You will help me to stand while I take it off. I would rather save the shirt, for 'tis one of the last my late wife made for me." The younger O'Brien hastened to his side, realized he was yet holding his pistol, and set it upon the sideboard. He bent to allow his father to put his left arm around his shoulders, and put his own arm around the captain's torso, to aid him to rise. He must have done something similar many times during the captain's recovery.

Jane, taking the shirt once they'd pulled it free, looked at O'Brien again. "Where is your cane, sir? How did you come to be here?"

He sank back onto the chair. "I was up in your pleasant guest chamber, feeling the better for a long sleep and a good breakfast and time to collect my thoughts, when I heard a woman squall. I listened at the door, and I could hear men's voices, though not what they were saying. It sounded like trouble, and I never was good at avoiding that commodity. So I made certain preparations, such as leaving my cane, and slipped along the passage to the head of the stair. There, I heard enough to know you and your household were in need of assistance."

"But however did you manage the stairs, with your bad leg?"

"Like a toddling child: by lowering myself to the floor and going down one at a time, on my backside. Then I hobbled the few steps to the door. Lucky the villain had his back to me, and his attention upon your people. As soon as I stood up, I took my pistol from my pocket, so…" He shrugged in a very Gallic manner.

Jane had given the shirt to Mrs. Jennings with instructions to rinse out the blood and bring it back when it had dried by the kitchen fire. "And you will be more comfortable there, to mend the coat sleeve. And make sure Molly is all right."

She washed the deep graze with warm water before folding a pad from the torn sheet. "Jessup, will you fetch one of my uncle's shirts? He was much of a size with Captain O'Brien. There are several bundled up in his chamber. They are somewhat worn, I fear, but at least they are whole." They were among the older garments she had meant to send to the parish for distribution to the poor. She glanced at the captain's stockinged but unshod feet, and added, "And fetch the captain's shoes and cane. Wait in the kitchen or your pantry until I send for you. Close the door as you go."

"It's clever you were to send them out, Mistress Jane. You will have realized I wished to speak with my son."

"Papa—"

"And you've a right to hear, mistress. And your trusted servant, I suppose, if you wish?"

"Yes, Captain."

O'Brien nodded. "Gabriel, I wish with all my heart you had not murdered my friend, Markham, but I console myself that you did not know he saved my neck in the '15."

"Ah, Papa, if I had known—but I wish I had not, in any case."

"There is no remedy for it. But why in God's name did you cast suspicion upon his poor niece?"

"I am most sorry. But Pleasaunce was a good fellow, or I thought he was. Stowe—this lady's brother—who was a friend of Pleasaunce, said that Monsieur Markham had seen and questioned him about his visit to the *Sea Mew*. It worried Pleasaunce that the plan might be discovered. He said she was a harpy, only waiting for her uncle's death, and was a trial to her papa and mama and brothers, and if she were thought guilty of murdering him, no one would look further for a reason Markham had died. It seemed a most sensible solution. Now I wish I had not let him persuade me to do it."

"Which?"

"Either. Killing someone in a fight...eh, these things happen. To murder? That is different. I did not understand. And to cast the blame on someone else, a woman, that was worse. Afterward, when I had thought it through, I knew I had done wrong. It has gnawed at me, like the story you told us about the Spartan boy and the fox."

The elder O'Brien sighed gustily. "You also went against my orders, Gabriel."

"When you broke your leg and said we could not make the delivery, I was sorry to miss such an adventure with you. Also, I did not like it that your reputation would suffer. But when I met Pleasaunce to cancel the arrangement, he had so many good reasons the delivery should be made, they overbore my reluctance and I agreed to help. The true king would rule England; Catholics would be free to worship and to own property and hold government offices; Ireland would no longer suffer under brutal Protestant landlords. It seemed right."

"Why did you ask him for another £800?" Jane inquired. The captain winced. "Was it because of the difficulty of approaching the harbor?"

Gabriel O'Brien looked at her for the first time. "*Mais non!* It was the cannon. The seller came to me and told me he had been able to get the cannon after all.

He would send them with the muskets, but he must receive payment first. He could not reach Pleasaunce to inform him. I knew the cannon had been wanted for the Chevalier's campaign, so I said I would pay and collect the money on delivery. *Maman* taught us thrift, so I had money set aside, and I sent a message to Pleasaunce, saying he could have the cannon at the price I had paid for them." Gabriel's expression turned grim. "Then Pleasaunce insulted me, which is how I began to suspect he was not a man of honor. He offered to compensate me for my trouble and risk in, ah..." His eyes slid toward Jane. "I refused, of course."

"Your trouble and risk in murdering Markham." Captain O'Brien completed the unfinished thought. "Then in the name of all the saints, what brought you here with him?"

"When I learned you had come to England, I worried for your safety. I followed you and sought out F—the man you know of and found him gone. Arrested or fled, I could not discover. I had no choice but to contact that *canaille*. He told me his friends might have news of you, but I must help him find Rupert Stowe, who had betrayed him. Stowe had sent word that the transaction was complete, but Pleasaunce believed it was a lie because he had heard Stowe had gambled away the money. I did not wish to assist him, but what else could I do?"

O'Brien shook his head. "You could have considered that I do not need a nursemaid, much as I appreciate your concern for me. For trying to throw the guilt upon this lady, I find it hard to forgive you. *Mon fils,* you are impulsive, as I was at your age. For all of that, I usually calculated the odds before acting.

Gabriel, I have had the honor of meeting Prince Charles. He is charming. I am sure he believes in his very soul in his father's divine right to rule England, Ireland, and Scotland. However, I am not sure he is intelligent in the way a good leader must be, and God does not necessarily aid the stupid. I was willing to transport arms for the cause, but I do not expect it to prosper."

"I am sorry," Gabriel whispered.

"I, also. I told you too much when you were a boy—about my life in Ireland, about my youth, and not enough about what I have learned since."

Jane finished binding the wound. She did not expect it to bleed much more.

"Well," O'Brien said, "mistress, what's to be done depends upon your wishes, I think. Do you intend to send your man here to the magistrate? I know there is a watch house not far away and law courts as well."

Alex cast her a meaningful glance and shook his head ever so slightly. It would have made no difference if he had nodded.

"While it might be justice, the true instigator of my uncle's death is now dead, is he not? I would be sorry for your sake for your son to end on the gallows. May I leave you to deal with him as you think fit?"

Captain O'Brien inclined his head. "Thank you. I am more grateful than I can say."

He straightened. "Gabriel, did you bring the *Sea Mew* here?"

"No, sir. She is safe at Lannion. I feared there might be a hue and cry for her. I came over in a friend's fishing boat."

"Good. Go home. When I return, I will transfer the

Sea Mew to you. And then I will not wish to see you again for some time. Go now, and be quick and careful. As Mistress Jane has a mind to spare your life, it would be a pity to lose it by recklessness."

Gabriel bowed. In French, he thanked his father, assured him of his undying love, and took formal leave of him. Then he bowed to Jane as well, and said in English, "I truly am sorry, Mistress Jane."

Alex said, "If you put on my wig, waistcoat, and coat, you may pass as a footman."

Both men stared at him in surprise. The captain glanced at Jane.

"A very good idea," she said.

With his own blond hair hidden, and the livery coat on, Gabriel walked out the front door, a down-at-heels servant from a shabby household sent on an errand.

Alex bolted the door behind him.

Captain O'Brien turned to Jane. "It puzzles me what to do with the carcass, I confess."

"By your leave, sir, I can deal with it. After you've gone," Alex added.

O'Brien smiled wryly. "I can see why your uncle's footman enjoys your confidence, mistress."

"I could not do without him, sir." She smiled.

Alex forgot to keep his face impassive.

Her own face turned warm. She hoped to divert attention from it by saying crisply, "William, please bring the captain's shoes, cane, and coat from the kitchen. Oh, and his own shirt. Perhaps it could be done up in a parcel. And then summon a hackney or a chair for him."

"No, no, I will walk to the end of the street. There is certain to be a rattler there. The exercise of the last two days is doing my leg good."

When Alex had gone out, he said, "Hmmpf. It's not my place to advise you, but I hope you will do nothing your uncle Markham would not approve."

"Certainly not, Captain." She was blushing again.

"He seems a sensible fellow and good-hearted."

The door opened, and the captain did not pursue the subject. Alex acted as valet, assisting him into his shoes and coat. The captain took his cane and the brown paper parcel containing his mended shirt.

"Good day to you, mistress." He paused and turned at the door as Alex opened it. "If there is ever a favor I can do for you, everyone in Lannion in Brittany knows Captain O'Brien's house in the rue Geoffroy-de-Pontblanc."

After he had gone, they gazed at each other blankly until Jane took a deep breath and said, "And what is your plan for the late Mr. Charles Pleasaunce?"

"There are two possibilities. I can go to Sir Howard who so obligingly took care of your half brother for us—but not until this evening, when he will be at home. Or I can ask Abel Cox, the night-soil man, to help me with him, but that would be even later tonight."

"I cannot like the idea of leaving him on the floor all day. So untidy! And if someone chanced to come to the door, it would have a very strange appearance."

Alex laughed aloud. "It certainly would. Jessup and I might move him down to the cellar. Or I could send a message to Sir Howard at the War Department, though there would be the danger of someone else seeing it."

"After what happened at Hawthorn Cottage, I hardly like to trust to that department's secrecy."

They had been standing almost shoulder to

shoulder as they regarded the remains. Alex turned and placed his hands gently on her shoulders and said, "Jane, there is really no need to look at it any longer. Let us go to the kitchen. Jessup and I will put it out of sight somewhere until tonight." The familiarity startled her, but she did not object. When he bent to kiss her, she did not hesitate to wrap her arms around him and lean into the embrace, luxuriating in the sensation of safety and warmth. When they pulled apart, awkwardly, he appeared as stunned as she felt. The upper half of his body was clad only in shirt and neckcloth. Which brought to mind a question she had been pondering.

"Mr. Gordon?"

"I do beg your pardon, mistress. I did not intend to take advantage—"

"Never mind that. I was very willing to kiss you. I want to ask you about your hair. When we first met, you wore your own. Do you intend to let it grow again? Or have you resolved to wear a wig?"

"What would the correct answer be, Mistress Jane?"

"If a man were going quite bald, a wig would be a sensible choice." How could she phrase it? "However, he would have to wear it all the time, except in his chamber, and then if it were cold, he would have to wear a nightcap—"

"Which most do in bed in any case," he pointed out, guilelessly, introducing a subject she had hoped to avoid. Although it did indicate he was following her thought.

"But when a man has perfectly good hair of his own, it seems a pity to sacrifice it merely for, for…" Why did men wear wigs but for baldness? It seemed such an affectation.

"Fashion. Or convenience. One need not have one's hair fussed over and curled, or even powdered. One simply positions a wig of the desired style on one's head and is ready for the most formal occasion. I cropped my hair because a different wig can alter one's appearance mightily, which seemed a good idea at the time. But it makes my scalp itch, and I believe I will dispense with the wearing of wigs in the future."

"Oh! Good."

They beamed at each other. She thought they were beginning to lean toward each other, presaging another kiss—*would* Uncle Markham have approved? He would certainly have understood. The scream shattered the moment.

Chapter 35

"Back of the house!" Alex snatched the old dragoon pistol from the sideboard where he had left it before retrieving the captain's belongings, then ran out. Jane glanced around for a weapon and grabbed the brandy decanter by its neck and hurried after him as fast as her petticoats would allow.

She caught up to him where he stood in the door to the kitchen, blocking her view into the room. His right arm hung down by his side, the pistol, uncocked, pointing at the floor. Was someone pointing a weapon at him? Could it be more of Pleasaunce's gang?

Mrs. Harrow's voice rang out. "Molly, you baggage! I make allowance for your having had a fright earlier, but I swear you've no sense at all. Here's Cuddie, that we all know, come with a gentleman to the back door, polite as you please, and you shriek out like a mouse caught in a cat's jaws, though much louder. And here's William—Mr. Gordon, that is—come to save you, thinking murder's being done."

Jessup's precise voice added, "Sir? Mr. Gordon? I am sorry for the kitchen maid's outburst. She has had an upsetting day."

"Sir," Alex said on an oddly tentative note.

"We must talk, Gordon. In...ah...private."

"It's hardly worthwhile, sir. Everyone here—almost everyone—knows almost everything."

Mrs. Harrow spoke out. "I am going to send you up to your room with a bit of my cherry cordial and some wigg buns, Molly. Stay there until you've calmed. Or better, until you're summoned downstairs. Here is my market basket, with the buns wrapped in a towel and a little bottle of cordial, and there's a tumbler. And if you carry them up careful, you won't drop or spill them."

Alex perforce moved into the kitchen to let Molly pass, and Jane followed him. Alex's man, or friend, Cuddie—whatever he was—stood out of the way by the door. He grinned and dipped his head in her direction.

" 'Almost everything' is not 'all.' Mistress Jane." Anthony Lattimer acknowledged her with a bow. His clothing was creased, and his boots dull with dust. He was thinner than she recalled, and his face was tired.

Mrs. Harrow was arranging more wiggs on a serving tray.

"If I may relieve you of the brandy, mistress," Jessup suggested.

"We might remove to another room later, sir, to discuss certain other matters, but everyone here is aware of a great deal and should be present to explain today's events."

"I see." Lattimer did not sound as if he saw, but he did not disagree.

"Mr. Lattimer, won't you take a seat at the table? Here, between Mrs. Jennings, my housekeeper, and me?" She smiled as winningly as she knew how. Manipulating gentlemen was a skill she had never acquired, possibly in reaction to her stepmother's example.

The gathering defied the conventions. Gentlemen (and ladies) did not usually sit with their staff in the kitchen, the men, including Jessup, drinking brandy and the women sipping Mrs. Harrow's cherry cordial. How fortunate she had had another bottle at hand. A certain constraint reigned.

Alex said, "Thank you for coming, sir. We are faced with a...mmm...transport difficulty with which I am sure you can help."

Lattimer, mellowing under the influence of brandy and wiggs—he had eaten two—asked cautiously, "Who or what requires transport?"

"The body of Charles Pleasaunce." His voice was level.

"I think perhaps you had better begin at the point at which you sent the note to Cuddie which he did not receive until this morning. I had sent for him to meet me on my way back to Town, with whatever messages might have come in my absence. I was relieved to hear you were alive on the one hand and worried by your urgent summons on the other."

Alex outlined the events of the past several days, with an interpolation by Jane as to how she had had to flee Hawthorn Cottage. Mrs. Harrow described being accosted by Pleasaunce and Gabriel O'Brien as she returned from buying fish. O'Brien had held a knife to her eye to make her call out to Molly to open the door, and once inside, the two men had forced Jessup and the cook into the cellar by threatening Molly and Mrs. Jennings.

Lattimer listened without interruption to Alex's account of the arrival of Pleasaunce and O'Brien in the front parlor and its noisy resolution.

"Excuse me for one moment." Lattimer strode to the kitchen door, opened it, and gave a piercing whistle.

A man in decent but nondescript clothing appeared in the doorway in a matter of seconds, tilting his head as his master issued low-voiced instructions. A quick nod and he was gone.

"I suppose it will take as much as two hours to remove your embarrassing guest, Mistress Jane. I trust you have somewhere an old, shabby carpet of some size which you are willing to give up?"

"As it happens, I recently replaced the bookroom carpet, and the old one is stored in the attic."

"Very good." He turned back to Alex. "Where are the O'Briens? For I do not see them here, and you have not mentioned confining them to the cellar. Clearly, you did not give them in charge to a magistrate, or you would not need me to relieve you of Pleasaunce. And thank you for not involving the authorities, by the way. That would have made it much more complicated."

"You are very welcome, sir." Alex cleared his throat. "Gabriel O'Brien was hardly more guilty than Rupert Stowe. They were both cozened by Pleasaunce, who seems to have been a remarkably persuasive fellow—"

"He could convince almost anyone that black was white and that the sun rose in the west," Jane interrupted. Except herself, fortunately. Imagine being married to such a man. It did not bear thinking of.

"But not you?" Alex inquired.

"He seemed always to be calculating his next word or action. He courted me once—soon after Uncle Markham let it be known that I could expect a sizable inheritance."

"Ay, ay, no doubt that explains a great deal, though it is not really relevant to the topic under discussion."

Lattimer was sounding testy again. "The O'Briens?"

"If Captain O'Brien had not shot Pleasaunce, I suspect the staff and I would have been locked up, and Pleasaunce and O'Brien would have been waiting Mistress Jane's—or Rupert Stowe's—return. They might have taken you prisoner, too, when you came to find out why I had sent an urgent letter to Cuddie for help."

"Well, I won't deny the possibility, though when Cuddie or I did not emerge or whistle for him, my other fellow would have taken action. You let them go?"

"Yes, sir. Wouldn't you?"

Lattimer grinned. At any rate, the expression drew his lips back over his teeth. Jane chose to consider it a grin.

"While not strictly according to procedure, it makes no real difference. I do not know how young O'Brien could have been tried for Markham's murder without certain facts emerging which are best kept secret. I would have liked to meet O'Brien again, but I would have had to deal with the matter in my official capacity, which would have been distasteful." He was lost in thought for a moment, while Jane decided she liked Anthony Lattimer very much.

"And now, young man," he continued in an ominous voice, "what are you doing in your shirt and no wig in the presence of a lady? You look the veriest ruffian."

Before Alex could speak, Jane said, "When you arrived, sir, we were discussing the removal of the body to the cellar. Rather than risk staining them, Mr. Gordon took off his coat and waistcoat, with my permission. And the wig persisted in slipping around, which would not have been helpful at all." She saw no reason to let him know that Gabriel O'Brien was now dressed as a footman.

Lattimer waved away the explanation dismissively. "I think Mr. Gordon and I must have a private conference. If you will attend for a few minutes also, Mistress Jane?"

"Mistress, my room might be suitable to the purpose," Mrs. Jennings said.

Settled in the housekeeper's room, Lattimer said, "Mistress Jane, you have rendered as good service to our country as any military officer. Thank you. As sometimes happens in battle, you have suffered injury for it. The accusation of murder and the accounts in the newspapers must affect your reputation for some time to come. Unfortunately, the clumsiness of our efforts to exonerate you did not greatly help, for reasons I cannot discuss."

"Because they are most secret, Mr. Lattimer?"

"Just so, Mistress Jane. Young O'Brien's trial would have done much to erase the suspicion against you, and yet I confess letting him escape is a better outcome in other ways."

"I quite agree, sir."

"Then there is the matter of your living here with Gordon in residence, as I suspect has been the case. While perfectly understandable—even necessary for the safety of you both—the world would still regard you as ruined if it ever became known. Your servants appear to be loyal and discreet—"

"Except perhaps for Molly, whose tongue sometimes runs away with her," Alex added.

"I would like to find Molly a position in the

country with some nice family," Jane said. "She is a good girl, but she is silly."

"I believe I know someone who needs another kitchen maid, who would not be inconvenienced by her garrulity. Still, I wish it had not been necessary for Gordon to stay here. There is a degree of impropriety about it...enough said of that. But there is nothing I or even the First Lord of the Treasury can do to stop whatever gossip may arise. I am heartily sorry. You deserve recognition and reward for your actions. But that too would reveal matters which are best concealed. Our government will not publicly thank you. I fear you must make do with my thanks on its behalf. If there is anything I can do for you, you need only ask. I do have some influence. And thank you for aiding my son."

My son?

Both men noticed her expression at the same time. She closed her mouth, but her eyebrows remained elevated. *At least Mr. Gordon's father is a gentleman.*

"Not my natural son," Lattimer said hastily. "I gather he did not explain our relationship."

"I introduced myself as Gordon, as you instructed me, sir." To Jane: "There are a few who know my father has a connection with the War Office and some other departments, and if they heard that a Lattimer had called upon your uncle, someone might have speculated. Later it would have been awkward to explain."

"We do make rather a cult of secrecy, except when the members of some departments are as loose-tongued as your Molly. Alex is my second son. Until recently, he displayed no great talent for anything except acting, not that there is anything amiss with his brains. I now perceive that he has a turn for intrigue." Lattimer rose. "Again, thank you."

Jane took it as dismissal. No doubt the two had state secrets to discuss, and she certainly needed to think about other matters.

"Thank you, Mr. Lattimer. I'm very pleased you came—and even more so that Charles Pleasaunce will be leaving in the near future, rather than late tonight. Good day, sir." She curtsied, and Lattimer laughed outright and bowed. She dipped a curtsy to Alex, smiling. My goodness, it would be hard to think of him as Alex Lattimer rather than Gordon!

****

Jane swept out. His father's eyes skewered him.

"You were rather smitten with Mistress Jane, as I recall. Do you intend to court her? Or perhaps I should ask if you believe you have a chance if you do court her?" He added, "I don't say you must make her an offer, although in ordinary circumstances there would be no other recourse."

"I think she likes me. I have some reason to hope she would accept my offer. But can I make one in good conscience when I have no profession—which is my own fault, I know. It would look as if I wanted to marry her for her money. If you are still willing, sir, I will set myself to make my fortune in whatever merchant house or bank will have me. That would at least show I was not merely a fortune-hunter. She would not object to my engaging in business. Her uncle did."

"No," his father said deliberately. "I now realize you would be wasted in the commercial field, unless your heart is set upon being a banker or trader. Did you find the excitement of your month as an intelligencer to your liking?"

Oh, no. "I could do the work, sir, though often plaguey uncomfortable, and I could feel the shadow of the gallows the entire time. And if Mistress Jane is willing to marry me, how could I ask her to endure my absences and the risk that she might be left a widow unexpectedly?"

"I would not ask it of any woman, myself. I feared you might have acquired a taste for the danger. Some do. But spying is no work for a gentleman or a husband. We have men of lower degree for that. There is a position for which you might be very well suited."

Alex sat up straighter.

"Two men will be vacating their offices in Somerset House. They were far too fond of boasting to friends how important their posts were and how many secrets they knew. I could have some respect for a man who gave our secrets away out of political or moral conviction, but fiend take all loose-lipped braggarts! I have thought for years they should be removed, though not because I suspected them of passing on information." He sighed and leaned back in the housekeeper's armchair.

"Positions of authority are always held by men of birth and breeding. That is the way of the world. However, I have noticed that men who have no experience with...say, casting cannon...cannot effectively command those who do the work. One needs an understanding of the processes involved, rather than social graces. The men in question have been responsible for directing the activities of intelligencers and making recommendations based on their reports."

"I see, sir." It seemed necessary to say something, to make it clear he was listening with rapt fascination.

"It would be best if both men's positions were combined into one, and that held by a man who knows what it's like to have to make his own decisions when things go wrong, with no way to contact his superior. The First Lord agrees on the ground that one man would be less costly than two and more efficient, which is also true. You would be able to sleep in your own—ahem! or your wife's—bed at night, except for rare exceptions like my recent journey north to either find you or recover your body. Would you consider such work? The pay is not munificent, but then, Mistress Jane's fortune is more than adequate. If I'm not mistaken, Markham's income was several thousand a year."

"Hang the pay and Jane's fortune, too," Alex said. "Well—no, not that. But being employed by the government would be respectable, useful work, and I think I would enjoy it. If she will agree…"

"That's settled, then. Why should she not? She must be attached to you, judging by her concern when you failed to return as expected. And your prospects are better now than they were a month ago. I trust you will call upon Mr. Stowe, for courtesy's sake, if not for permission."

"Certainly, sir." Alex paused. "If there is nothing more, may I be excused?"

His father gave him a knowing smile. "You may. With any luck, Pleasaunce's transport will be here soon, and I think you should depart with it, as if you were one of the freightmen. The order regarding your status as an accredited agent of the government may not yet have been passed to all the relevant departments. You will no doubt have time enough to speak with Mistress Jane first."

His father paused, and Alex chafed a little at the delay.

"Thank God you destroyed those muskets and cannon, Alex. I stopped at Whitehall on my way here to give orders to end the search for you. Word was received today that General Cope's two regiments were defeated near Edinburgh on the 21st—and that with only such weapons as the Highlanders had. With more and better arms, who knows what they might do? You deserve recognition for your work, but that's not the way of our service. Though I've been told I can expect a knighthood when I retire," he added with a laugh. "Go along to Mistress Jane, now. I'll see you at home, later."

In the kitchen, he was met by the news that Jane and Jessup had gone up to the attic to fetch down the old carpet.

"I'll help Jessup," Alex said.

"I doubt you will be too late to do much," Mrs. Jennings said. "Though you may meet them coming down the stairs."

They were indeed almost all of the way downstairs.

"Let me take that, mistress."

She relinquished her end of the roll of carpet.

"I was not sure how long you might be closeted with your papa. I wanted to be ready for the removal."

He grinned at her as he and Jessup set the roll down parallel to Pleasaunce's corpse. Jessup kept his eyes averted from the body. Alex looked; he had not done so at the time of the shooting or did not recall doing so. Too much else had been happening. The sight was not as nasty as he expected. There was not much blood…or anything else. O'Brien had chosen his shot well, killing Pleasaunce instantly. Better than hanging, surely.

He looked at Jane, who seemed not unduly upset by the presence of Pleasaunce's mortal remains. A very practical young lady.

"Mistress?" Jessup asked. "As we are done here…?"

"You may go," she said. "I will be along shortly to speak with Mrs. Harrow about tomorrow's menu. Faith, about tonight's supper, too! Which should be early as we have not had our midday meal yet."

"Very good, mistress."

With rare tact, even for a butler, Jessup shut the door behind him.

How did one propose marriage? Kneeling at the lady's feet and taking her hand was supposed to be the romantic thing to do, but he thought he would feel like a fool. Particularly given their surroundings. If they were at Vauxhall Gardens, he might find a secluded spot to make his addresses to her. But that would require addressing himself to her papa first, which would involve finding a way to introduce himself and explain how he had come to know Jane…And she was gazing at him expectantly right now. The devil fly away with Pleasaunce's corpse! If its presence did not bother Jane, why should he delay?

"At last we are free of this business, Mistress Jane." What does a fellow say? Perhaps he ought to have consulted an etiquette book, but the opportunity had come up without warning. "This is not the place or circumstances I would have chosen to..." *Ah! Inspiration!* "...to lay my heart at your feet, but I find I cannot wait any longer. Will you do me the honor to be my bride? I have no fortune, though I will eventually inherit a competence, but I have been offered employment in the government." Possibly he should stop there, but there were so many other things he needed to say. "I know your father is unlikely to look upon me with favor. Please don't think I offer because of our recent living arrangements. I was drawn to you from our first meeting, like iron filings to a magnet." That was a nice, poetical touch. "I have found new qualities to admire at our every meeting. May I—" He halted before saying, *May I ask your hand of your father?* Fool that he might be, he suspected it would be the wrong thing to say to a strong-minded young lady of five-and-twenty who had managed her papa's household for years and more recently helped thwart treasonous activities. No, he *knew* it would be a mistake. His own father had certainly not approached Grandfather Gordon before proposing to Mama. "May I ask for your hand in marriage, my dear Jane?"

"Oh, yes. Yes, you may." Her eyes were shining. For the second time in the day, he found himself passionately embracing a young lady in proximity to a dead body. And, if he were not mistaken, it was drawing flies. He breathed in the scent of lavender water on Jane's skin and rosemary on her hair. They were not strong enough to overcome the tang of gunpowder and a more human stench, which was probably what was attracting the flies.

When they drew apart, he could not help glancing toward the mortal remains again. Her eyes followed his.

"It seems wrong to be happy," she said, looking down at what had been Charles Pleasaunce.

"Surely not." He put his arms around her again, hoping to distract her.

"I mean, about him. I've known him all my life, he was my brother's friend—not that that was a recommendation—and now he is suddenly dead by violence, and what I feel is relief. It seems callous and unladylike."

He himself was conscious of no such qualms. "Are you sure you have not been persuaded by sentiment and novels to believe you should pity him? Does he deserve it as much as your uncle, whose murder he caused? If you had fired the shot, 'twould be reasonable to be affected by it. I'm sure I would, had I killed him. But neither of us bears any guilt in this matter, and I, for one, am glad he's dead. He led your brother into treason and meant you to hang. If Pleasaunce were alive, he would almost certainly be executed for his crimes. And if he somehow escaped prosecution, I would call him out."

"Would you?" She sounded surprised.

"What sort of fellow do you take me for? Of course I would."

"But the danger!"

"I am considered accomplished with a sword. My grandfather was particular about swordplay. Pleasaunce would be as dead as he is now."

"Oh." After a pause during which she rested her head against his shoulder, she remarked, "I fear embracing in such surroundings is sadly lacking in decorum." She did not sound overly concerned.

"Not at all. If we had gone beyond the kind of kiss

and embrace suitable to a newly betrothed couple, that would have shown a want of decorum. And this is the only place in the house we could achieve the privacy necessary to kiss, without being so private as to outrage decency."

"And you could not have offered for my hand in the kitchen. That would have been ridiculous. With the servants there as an audience, you know."

They both considered the corpse again. The flies seemed to be increasing in numbers. Alex stole a glance at her and found that she was looking back at him. They both burst into laughter.

"What a relief that it's over!" Jane sighed when they were able to control themselves.

"Let's go to the kitchen," Alex suggested. "While the privacy here is enticing, the atmosphere is not." And they both laughed again.

What a tale to tell our children and grandchildren!

A word about the author...

When she was three years old, Kathleen Buckley's father bought a set of the *Encyclopaedia Britannica*. Big books! With all kinds of words (and pictures) in them!

By the age of twelve, she knew she wanted to write fiction (she also wanted to be a journalist, a spy, and a spaceperson—but NASA wasn't accepting female spacepersons then).

She never became a journalist because she hates asking pushy questions, nor a spy, because she's not good with foreign languages, has bad eyes, and is not athletic. But along the way, she worked in a hospital billing department, as a bookkeeper in a print shop, as a paralegal, and as a security officer.

In semi-retirement, she began to write full-time, at least when not pursuing her other hobbies: reading, cats, cooking, costume projects, and spinning wheel repair. And no, she can't spin. That will have to come after the spinning wheel repair.

~*~

Learn more about Kathleen Buckley at
https://www.facebook.com/anunsuitableduchess/
or email kbuckley87110@gmail.com

Thank you for purchasing
this publication of The Wild Rose Press, Inc.

If you enjoyed the story, we would appreciate your
letting others know by leaving a review.

For other wonderful stories,
please visit our on-line bookstore at
www.thewildrosepress.com.

For questions or more information
contact us at
info@thewildrosepress.com.

The Wild Rose Press, Inc.
www.thewildrosepress.com

Stay current with The Wild Rose Press, Inc.

Like us on Facebook

https://www.facebook.com/TheWildRosePress

And Follow us on Twitter
https://twitter.com/WildRosePress